BIRTHRIGHT

The Crystal Throne - Book 1

KIM FEDYK

TOCARRA

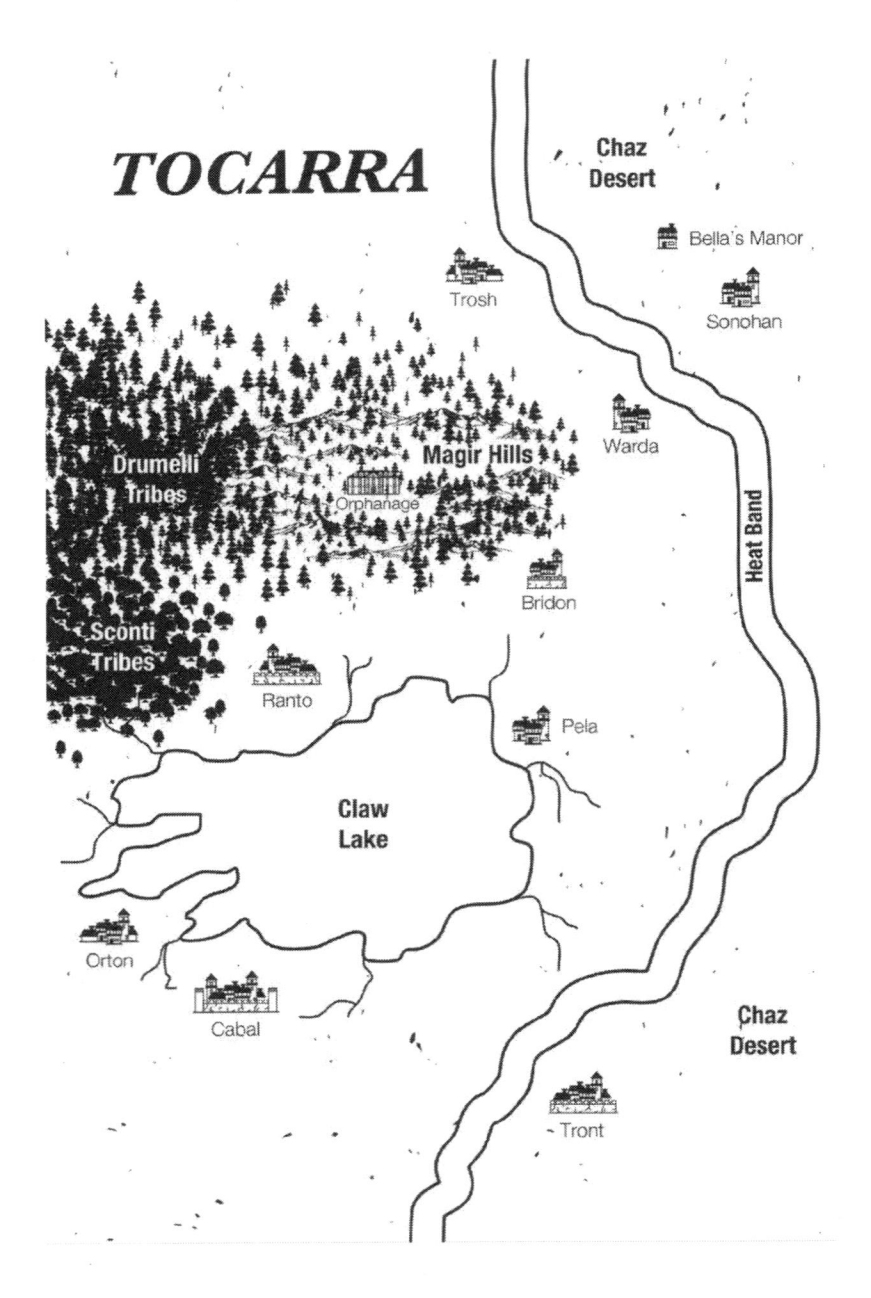

OHERRA

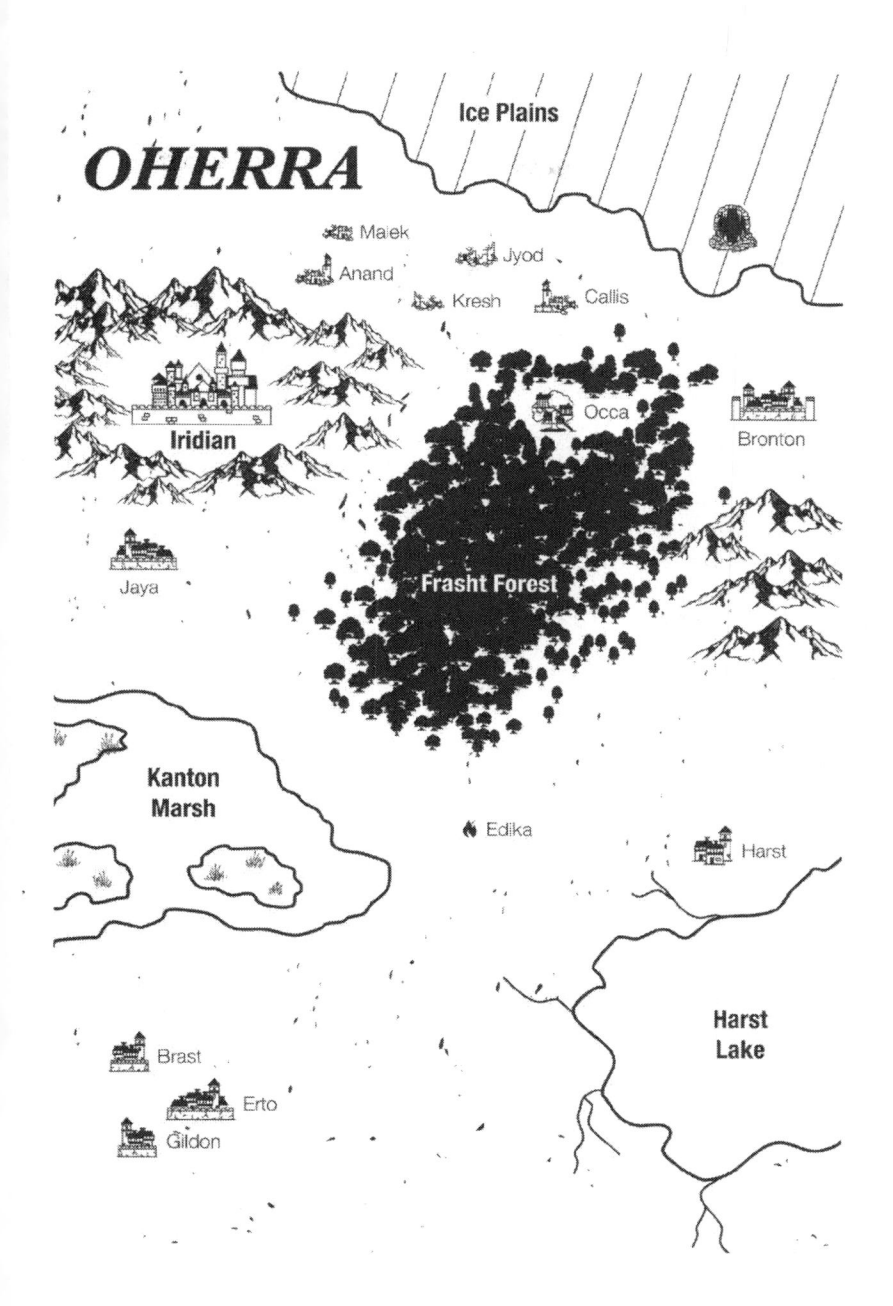

Ice Plains

Malek
Anand Jyod
Kresh Callis

Iridian

Occa

Bronton

Jaya

Frasht Forest

Kanton Marsh

Edika

Harst

Harst Lake

Brast
Erto
Gildon

Chapter 1

The day Arleth first learned that her world was not a safe place had began as inconspicuously as any other.

It had been a bright and sunny late spring day. The kind that makes one forget about the bitter cold of a winter just passed and gives the promise of warmth and rebirth. Arleth was standing with her back pressed up against a towering willow tree in the center of the orphanage courtyard. It was midday so both suns were high in the sky, bathing the courtyard in light. The water flowing through the fountain at the far end was sparkling in the sunlight. Multi-coloured fish were swimming lazily through the pond at its base. But ten year old Arleth didn't care about the beautiful scene laid out all around her. She had been in the orphanage as long as she could remember, and she was well accustomed to the scenery. Besides, she had an important mission to accomplish.

"Ready or not, HERE I COME!" She shouted gleefully at the top of her voice. She gazed anxiously about for any sign of her friends; any feet that were sticking out or a head that was not properly ducked behind cover. There! Behind that bush she could have sworn she saw a flash of yellow. It was hard to tell though through the dense purple leaves but Flora had been wearing a yellow sweater and she was just small enough to squeeze behind the bush if she had her back to the wall. Arleth crept along, edging slowly towards the bush. She could have easily ran and covered the distance in a few strides, but that was no fun. An important part of their game was to make the person hiding think they were still safe. Getting as close to them as possible before they knew they were caught was the mark of a real master, and Arleth secretly prided herself on being the best hide-and-go seek player of all her friends.

KRAAAA KRAAAA

"Sssh!" Arleth whispered bending down to try and silence the Gaiwar that had walked over to her unnoticed. The orphanage kept a few Gaiwars as pets and Arleth as well as the other children loved to play with them. Now however, its loud noises would ruin her game and she did not want to be found out so soon.

KRAAAA KRAAAA, it repeated.

"Sshh!" Arleth bent down and rubbed its furry belly. She looked at it with half annoyance half amusement; Gaiwars really were quite cute creatures. As she thought this she had momentarily stopped rubbing its belly. It was now looking at her mournfully and was jumping up and down on its two short stubby legs.

"Okay okay," she whispered. She resumed stroking its belly. Soon its large ears flopped over onto its face and its large brown eyes started to shut. With a contented smile, the Gaiwar wrapped its tail around its body and lay down on the soft grass. Within seconds it was asleep. Arleth spared one last glance at it and then resumed her search. She hesitated; Flora must have heard the Gaiwar's noises and would know that she was discovered. Maybe she should go and find someone else first so Flora would think she was safe and then being lulled into a false sense of safety, Arleth could descend upon her.

DING DONG DING DONG. Arleth's thoughts were interrupted by the bell signalling that their lunch-time recess was over. Darn! Arleth thought. She had been so close too! The purple bush in front of her rustled and out popped Flora.

"I knew you were there," Arleth exclaimed. "If it wasn't for the Gaiwar I would have got you before the bell."

"That's not surprising," said Flora a bit sadly, "You always find me first." Arleth looked at her face and laughed.

"Oh don't look so sad Flora, it is just a game after all." Arleth slung her arm around Flora and Flora, her momentary sadness forgotten, smiled and put her around Arleth. They were best friends, like sisters really. They had both been in the orphanage for as long as they could remember and had spent practically their entire lives together. Such things then as who won hide-and-go-seek were of little importance to Arleth if it made her friend sad. Besides, although Arleth was more athletic, Flora was always better than her at singing and dancing; two things that made their teacher Mrs. Appolbaum shake her head at Arleth in frustration.

The differences didn't end there though. Arleth was tall for her age with an athletic build and a dark complexion; olive skin, black hair and striking violet eyes. Even at such a young age it was clear to everyone that she would be stunningly beautiful when she grew up. Flora, promising to be no less beautiful was nonetheless completely different with blonde hair and light blue eyes.

Smiling, and arm in arm, Flora and Arleth made their way across the courtyard. All around them their friends' heads popped up or out of their hiding places.

"It's lucky for you the bell rang," Amelia said to Arleth as she popped out from underneath a set of stairs, "You never would have found me in my hiding place."

"I wouldn't be so sure," Arleth said confidently. "And besides you can't use that spot anymore because now I will look their first."

Similar remarks continued for a few minutes as all of Arleth and Flora's friends joined them. All five of them, Arleth, Flora, Amelia, Canille, and Janaya marched arm in arm through the courtyard, heading inside and back to their studies.

Neve met them at the entranceway. The orphanage Mother smiled at them and handed them each a piece of pastry.

"Here. Take this. They were leftover from lunch. But hurry! Don't be late for class, and don't tell anyone!" She winked at them, turned and walked down the hall ahead of them.

"THWANKS" all five of them chimed in together, their mouths full of pastry. Without slowing, Neve waved over her shoulder at them and disappeared into a side-room. Arleth smiled. Neve was by far her favourite of the twelve Mothers at the orphanage. Arleth was only one of ten children assigned into Neve's care, but she had always shown a special fondness for Arleth. As often as she was able, Neve would sneak Arleth and her friends treats and would show them secret passageways and hiding places.

When Arleth had gotten very sick three years ago, Neve had brought a mattress and slept beside Arleth until she had recovered. She had held her hand and sang to her when the horribly painful spasms had racked her small body; wrapped her in blankets when she broke out in cold sweats and sat hugging her for hours when she awoke screaming from the dreadful nightmares that couldn't be recalled upon waking but left an overwhelming sense of dread and terror. Arleth couldn't remember her own mother, but she loved Neve as though she were her real mother.

Trying to discreetly rub crumbs and jelly off her face, Arleth settled into her desk at the back of the classroom and smiled triumphantly at Flora beside her.

"Just in time," she whispered. Flora nodded her assent and was about to say something when the loud shrill voice of Ms. Witrany cut in.

"Arleth! Flora!" She shrieked, "Be quiet! Class is starting. Must I separate you two?"

"No ma'am, we're sorry," said Flora right away.

"We will be quiet," agreed Arleth.

But Ms. Witrany, seemed not to have heard them. She had already started the lesson. She taught history and culture and, although in Arleth's opinion she didn't seem to know that much about anything interesting, Ms. Witrany was deeply passionate about the subject. Once when describing the marriage ceremony of the Drumelli tribe, her long pale face had flushed bright pink with excitement and she had flapped her sticklike arms up and down as though she was going to take off in flight.

Arleth listened briefly to Ms. Witrany.

"Okay class, today we are going to talk about the evolution of the fashions worn by the Drumelli princesses. First..." Arleth had already stopped listening. She didn't care about the history of what had happened on her own world of Tocarra, and especially not about some dusty old clothes. Arleth was interested in magic, adventure and the magnificent creatures that lived on some of the other ten worlds. But Ms. Witrany did not seem to know very much about any of the other worlds, only their own boring one.

As Arleth knew this was because the ten worlds were pretty much shut off from each other. Although everyone on each world knew of the existence of the other worlds, travel between them was quite limited. In each world only a few powerful individuals had access to magical artefacts that opened up a passageway between worlds. Each world contained at least one artefact, but the use of the artefacts was very limited. They only allowed passage to those worlds that were the closest and needed to lie dormant for long periods before their power could be used again. The most powerful of these artefacts Arleth knew, was the Crystal Throne on the faraway world of Oherra. It was the one magical device in the whole universe that allowed passage into all of the worlds.

Unfortunately for Arleth, her own world of Tocarra was a remote backwater. Although the ruling house of Pelona had the ability to travel to a few of the other worlds, they hardly ever did and consequently there was virtually no travel into Tocarra from any other world. Tocarra was essentially shut off from the rest of the universe. Arleth felt certain that the Royal Court must have at least some current knowledge of the other worlds, but the regular Tocarrans and especially a child such as herself would probably never find out very much.

"Three hundred years ago, the Princess Felorine made the dramatic decision to adorn her dress with the delicate buds of the...." Ms. Witrany droned on.

Arleth looked out the window. Two thousand years ago, the worlds had been linked more closely together she knew. More people were able to use magic and travel between worlds was very common. But greed and ambition had led to The Great War, the one hundred years of ruthless combat for domination that consumed the worlds' rulers. The destruction was terrible and many of the worlds were very close to total annihilation. As such, ten of the most powerful sorcerers and sorceresses in the universe pooled their magic to find a solution. They realized they couldn't completely cut off the worlds from each other; the worlds might need each other in the future. Their solution was the artefacts, magical vessels that would restrict the passage through the worlds to only their owners. As an added safeguard in case the vessels fell into the hands of evil in the future, each one was only able to form a passageway with a few of the closest worlds. That way, such wide-scale destruction would not be able to occur again. In the eventuality that such an evil person did manage to come to power in one of the worlds, the Crystal Throne was created. The holder of this artefact would be able to monitor the worlds and ensure that peace would remain. The throne was entrusted to the most virtuous of leaders, the King of Oherra, Falcon Amara. Falcon along with Laken Ayan, the strongest of the ten sorcerers and their ancestors eternally afterwards were entrusted to protect the throne and safeguard the peace of the universe.

Each of the remaining sorcerers and sorceresses went to one of the other nine worlds with a few artefacts in their possession. Practically shut off from each other for the last two thousand years, the ten worlds had developed independently from each other. The artefacts were handed down the generations and in many worlds, the ancestors of the original magicians came to power and now were kings or queens. Peace remained for the last two thousand years and with it, interest in the other worlds all but vanished.

Deep in thought, Arleth gazed at her reflection in the window. The sky had gone black and she could easily see herself scratching her cheek.

Falcon Amara must have been a really mighty person she thought to herself. He had probably been really handsome too and.... *Black!* The sky was black? There was no way the sky should be black she reasoned to herself, it could not be very much past midday. But sure enough, looking out the window, the sky had indeed gone as black as night. Stunned, she realized that Ms. Witrany had stopped talking. Looking around her she found that both her teacher and classmates had noticed the same thing that she had. They were all staring wide-eyed out the window.

"What is that?!" Shrieked Amelia. She was trembling and her face had gone white.

Arleth turned back to the window and looked towards where Amelia was pointing. Arleth felt her jaw drop open in shock at what she saw before her. Through the darkness she saw a line of greenish light. It was moving and seemed to be making a shape, but she wasn't sure what it was making. Arleth was vaguely aware that the room had gone deathly quiet; no one was making a sound. Everyone's attention was fixed on the green light out the window.

But what was it and what was happening?

Beside her she heard a clang, Flora, her hands trembling, had dropped her pencil. She made no effort to pick it up; indeed she didn't even seem to notice. Arleth gazed intently at the green light. It had made a straight horizontal line and was now drawing a vertical line, connecting to the very end of the right side of the horizontal line. With mounting horror, Arleth watched. She thought she knew what it was creating. The vertical line started to curve. Arleth made an audible gasp. She felt a deep pit start to form in her stomach.

It was a door! The green light had outlined an enormous door in the thin air.

What was the door leading from thought Arleth with terror. More importantly, though, what was on the other side of the door? Who or *what* would come out when the door opened? Arleth felt herself shaking, she had never been so terrified in her entire life.

With a burst of green light, the door flew open! In the doorway, just visible, illuminated by the greenish-yellow haze behind, stood a cluster of immense dark shadows.

All around, her classmates screamed. Arleth realized with surprise that she too was screaming. She felt something grab at her arm. She turned and had a split second to gaze into Flora's terrified face before they both crashed to the ground amid their upturned chairs. Flora had involuntarily flung herself backwards in an effort to distance herself from the creatures coming out of the door. In doing so, she had fallen off her chair, grabbed onto Arleth and they had both fallen. Arleth turned towards Flora. They flung their arms around each other and clung on, shaking and crying. All around her, her classmates were screaming, shaking, running, crying and staring with horror out the window. Canille had fainted with fright and Ms. Witrany was unsuccessfully trying to revive her.

"Wwhat i i is happ happening?" Shuddered Flora, her eyes bright with tears.

Arleth and Flora both turned towards the window. The shadows were starting to take form. A recognizable form had started to materialize from the center of the shadows. Arleth's gaze took in its black robes, hooded face and human shape. She gave a cry of alarm; it was a sorcerer!

She could make out two green-tinged and sickly looking hands sticking out from the dark folds of the figure's robes. Behind the deep hood, nothing of its face was visible except for a pair of menacing red eyes that looked about with undisguised blood-lust. Around the sorcerer, dozens of dark, winged creatures had become visible and were starting to take flight. Arleth looked with terror at their huge mouths that were open in otherworldly cries, calling for blood and destruction. Sharp fangs and rows of yellowed teeth were distinctly visible, standing out from the pitch black of the creatures' bodies.

Arleth felt Flora's grip tighten on her shoulder. She tore her eyes away from the terrifying sight and looked at Flora. Behind the girl's tears, Arleth saw a look of horrified understanding that she knew was mirrored in her own face. The figure standing not fifty paces from the window was no ordinary sorcerer. She looked again at the greenish hands and terrifying red eyes. He was a Dread Mage, a sorcerer devoted so completely to evil that his body had started to show the visible signs. The wicked acts he had used his magic for had turned his outward appearance into a mirror of his inner immorality and corruption.

"How... Why?" Screamed Flora.

Arleth shook her head, she was just as surprised as Flora. Dread Mages had last been seen during The Great War two thousand years ago.

"RUN!" Screamed Ms. Witrany, pushing the class out the door, with the still unconscious Canille slung over her shoulder. But the class needed no encouragement. Most of them had already ran screaming out of the classroom, and joined the other children, teachers, and Mothers running through the hall.

Arleth grabbed Flora by the shoulders and together they got off the ground and made a dash for the door.

"Hurry you two," yelled Ms. Witrany grabbing Flora's arm and pulling them in front of her.

Suddenly there was a bright flash of light and a deafening crash. Glass flew everywhere as the creatures burst through the window. The force of the impact sent Flora and Arleth tumbling to the ground. Arleth felt Ms. Witrany's body crash into her back as she too fell. Arleth was so terrified that she was only vaguely aware of her aching knees and bruised shins. She and Flora scrambled to their feet. Arleth noticed that blood was dripping from her cheek, a shard of glass must have grazed her when the window burst open.

Arleth heard a blood-curdling cry terrifyingly close behind her, instantly followed by a sickening crunching noise and an agonizing cry of pain. As Arleth and Flora ran through the door, the bloody bodies of Ms. Witrany and Canille flew past them and crashed into the hall wall. They hit the wall so hard that some of the bricks cracked. Flora and Arleth screamed and ran down the hall as fast as they could.

Arleth was so terrified, she could feel herself trembling and the pounding of her heart. Sparing a brief glance beside her as they ran, she saw that Flora was ghastly white.

"C-Canille, did you see? She..." Flora left the rest of her sentence unfinished. Arleth grabbed Flora's hand and nodded.

"Come on, maybe we can make it to one of our secret hiding places. Maybe they won't find us" Arleth could see the image of Ms. Witrany and Canille's bloody and broken bodies when they had hit the wall and slumped to the ground. She tried not to imagine what would happen if she and Flora were caught. Behind her they could hear the screams and crashes as the Dread Mage and his creatures attacked everyone in their path. She heard a man's voice yell something and suddenly the whole hall erupted with green fire. As they turned at a bend in the hall, Arleth looked back and saw the Dread Mage and four creatures coming through the flames directly at them.

"Faster!" Arleth screamed, "They are following us"

"Arleth! Flora!" yelled Neve, materializing in the hall before them. In a few steps she covered the distance between them

"Get behind me and run! Just ahead is the kitchen, you don't have time to go anywhere else, go hide in the storage room. I'll slow them down here."

Arleth and Flora hesitated, they didn't want to leave Neve. The creatures had just turned into their hall and were making their way directly towards them.

"GO!" Screamed Neve.

Neve turned from them and faced the Dread Mage and his creatures. She held up her hands and a brilliant red light shot from her hands into the nearest winged beast. With a cry of agony, it burst into flames and disintegrated. The Dread Mage roared in fury.

Arleth and Flora turned and ran. Neve was a sorceress? Arleth couldn't believe it. But she had little time for shock. From behind her came otherworldly death cries as Neve killed more of the Dread Mage's creatures. Arleth and Flora reached the kitchen door and ran inside. They heard a female voice cry out and a deep roar of laughter. Neve! Thought Arleth. Please don't die!

"Where's the storage room?" Screamed Flora in blind panic. Arleth hurriedly looked around the room and saw the door, slightly open at the far side of the kitchen.

"There!" Arleth pointed and sprinted to the door with Flora close behind her. Arleth reached the door and pushed it farther open so they could squeeze through. Once inside, Arleth turned around and saw Flora coming in, only seconds behind her. A faint smile was on Flora's tear-streaked face.

"We made it! We will be safe n.." But her sentence was never finished. At that instant a spear of green light flashed through her chest. Arleth had an instant to see the look of horrified shock on

Flora's face and then a pair of green hands grabbed on to Flora and threw her out the door.

"FLORA!" Arleth yelled. Her legs felt numb and she felt herself collapse on the floor. A shadow fell across the door and she looked up into the terrifying face of the Dread Mage. Arleth screamed and tried to back her way further into the room, but her legs were not responding. It was going to end here she thought, she was going to die, just like Canille and Ms. Witrany and Flora. The Dread Mage gleamed at her with his read eyes and she saw a shadow of a smile from inside his hood. He lifted his hand, ready to destroy her with his green fire. Not knowing what else to do, Arleth, with tears streaming down her face, hugged herself and looked down at the ground. She didn't want to see the fire that would kill her. She stared at the ground and braced herself for the attack.

But instead of the searing pain she expected, she heard the Dread Mage make an angry strangled cry. Arleth looked up and saw that the Dread Mage, had been trapped in a pulsating red light that had woven its way around him like a net. With a cry of fury, the Dread Mage was flown across the room. Neve's head poked in the door, briefly checked that Arleth was still alive and closed the door behind her with herself on the outside. Arleth heard screams and red and green lights flashes were visible from the crack under the door.

Arleth sank into the ground, trembling with heart pounding. Flora was dead! She almost couldn't believe it. All she could see was the image of Flora's face, mouth open in a small "O" of shock, with the saber of light thrust from her chest. She didn't think it was possible, but she cried even harder and rocked back and forth.

Arleth heard the door to the storage room open. Was it the Dread Mage, come to finish her off? Arleth held her breath and looked up. With a sigh of relief she saw Neve's face looking at her. Arleth stumbled up and ran into Neve's arms. She felt Neve wince and Arleth pulled away. She looked at Neve and cried out. Neve was covered in blood. The entire right side of her body had been burned and her clothes were hanging in tatters. Her left arm was hanging awkwardly and it looked like her shoulder had been dislocated.

"Oh Neve!" Arleth cried. Neve gave a faint smile.

"Don't worry about me," she said weakly, 'Run Arleth, get away from here as fast as you can. The Dread Mage is not dead yet." As if in response Arleth felt a stirring behind Neve's shoulder and saw the

Dread Mage, slumped on the ground, hood flung back, stirring back into consciousness.

"But what about you?" Cried Arleth.

"It's okay Arleth. He will wake up soon. This might be your only chance to escape. Run Arleth, don't look back." Choking on her tears, Arleth nodded

"I love you Neve" She cried.

"I love you too Arleth. Now run."

And Arleth did, she ran out of the kitchen, through the orphanage, hardly noticing the dozens of dead bodies she passed. Tears streaming down her face she burst out of the orphanage door and with one last glance at the building, she turned and ran as fast and as far as she could until she collapsed, exhausted, miles away.

Chapter 2

Arleth sat on an over-turned bucket with her long legs outstretched before her. The sunlight shone through the open door, casting a band of light across her chest. It was still morning but even in the shade of the stable, the heat was sweltering and Arleth could feel a bead of sweat trickle down her back. She looked down at her dirty, brown bag-like dress that had faded in the sun and harsh climate. Futilely she tried to brush a particularly dirty patch off the bottom of her dress, but she just succeeded in getting the dirt and grime on her fingers and spreading it even farther along her dress. It had been seven years since that horrific day and Arleth thought about how much had changed since then. She was no longer the optimistic, carefree child that had encountered the Dread Mage. She was fully aware of how harsh and unforgiving her world could be and of how utterly alone she was. Arleth felt the tears form at the corner of her eyes. For what must have been the thousandth time she wished that day had not happened and that she could still be playing games with Flora and having Neve sneak pastries to her. The tears rolled down her cheeks, making streaks down her dusty face and neck. Angrily Arleth tried to wipe the tears away. She was ashamed at letting herself cry like a little child.

No matter how many times she had wanted, Arleth had not let herself cry for a long time. Full of self-pity and heartbreak, Arleth had cried non-stop for months after the incident. Countless times she had wished that she could have died too so she wouldn't have to be so alone. Every day had been a struggle. Then one day she realized that all her crying had not brought Flora, Neve or anyone else back to life. With a burst of maturity that only comes to those who lose everything, she decided that she needed to stop feeling sorry for herself. For whatever reason she had lived when everyone else had died. She had to live so the memory of Flora and Neve would continue. Dying would solve nothing. She needed to survive because she carried them in her heart and as long as she was alive, she felt that in some small way, Flora and Neve were also alive.

She quickly tried to brush her tears away.
TWHAP

A wooden rod came crashing down on her head. Arleth, stunned for a split second looked up into the familiar face of her tormentor. Deep in thought she had not heard him approach. She was now even angrier at herself for crying; she definitely did not want *him* to see her cry.

"Hahahahaha, crying are we?" The rotund boy said with malice, clearly loving that he had caught Arleth in her misery. Maybe I should tell my mother that you need more work to do, since you seem to have lots of time to sit here and do nothing."

With a barely repressed sigh, Arleth came to her feet. She had learned long ago that although she could hurl insults better than he, it was not wise to do so. The boy standing in front of her was Kiran Sneel, the teenage son of her owner Bella.

After the attack of the Dread Mage, Arleth had kept running, stopping only when she collapsed. The orphanage had been deep in the Magir Hills. The nearest town was Bridon, 25 miles away, but Arleth had known the general direction. When she had been eight, Arleth, hungry for adventure had begged Neve to be taken with her when the woman went into the town to pick up some supplies. At that time, Arleth had not understood why the orphanage had been so secluded and why they were never allowed to go outside the boundaries. She had found it stiflingly boring. But now she understood; the forests surrounding the Magir hills were home to bands of slave traders who sold their "merchandise" at Bridon. Bridon itself was the center of the slave-trading market and wealthy people from all over Tocarra went there to buy slaves.

By pure luck, Arleth had managed to avoid the slavers in the forests, but she had been snatched up almost as soon as she entered Bridon's city limits. She had been auctioned off in the center market square the next day and bought by Bella Sneel, a wealthy merchant who lived across the Heat Band, deep in the Chaz Desert. It had taken them almost two months to reach Bella's home just outside of Sonahan. They had stopped at every major town on the way so Bella could trade the valuable lynstones that could only be obtained in the Chaz desert. It had been slow going with the horses laden down with silks, spices, wood, barrels of water, and the useless trinkets that Bella or Kiran had coveted. On top of that, Bella insisted that her carriage not be bumped or jolted because she might gasp or frown or even worse, hit the side, and thus ruin her perfect complexion.

Bella was a cruel but frivolous and empty-minded woman. Although Bella was convinced she was the most beautiful woman in Tocarra, Arleth thought she was the ugliest woman she had ever seen. Just like her son, Bella was short and rotund, having the appearance of a ball. She had unnaturally short limbs so her pudgy hands and feet stuck out like they were an afterthought, added by a comic painter to make a sphere into a human. She covered her face in thick white powder, convinced that it made her look like an angel. She had a large mole on her cheek that she liked to describe as a beauty mark. She painted her mole black so that it could be seen under her white powder. Her features were completely disproportionate with a large pointed nose and small eyes that were an unremarkable shade of gray and were set too close together. Her hair was so blonde it was almost white and, although she was only 40, it was starting to thin and in some places she had gone bald. In short, Arleth thought that Bella's complexion should be the last of her worries.

    She had been married 20 years ago and the union had produced Kiran, but it had not lasted long. Apparently her husband had taken a routine trip through the Heat Band to the border towns to trade. The story was that he had been ambushed and killed by thieves. Arleth thought it was much more likely that he couldn't stand to look at his wife any longer and had taken the excuse to run away.

    Looking at Bella's sneering son standing in front of her, she thought of the many suitors that had come to ask for Bella's hand in marriage. The results were always the same; messengers were sent to the far corners of Tocarra with news of Bella's beauty, virtue and wealth. All that came would take one look at her, make some transparent excuse and run away leaving a trail of dust behind them. The last one had come just a few nights ago Arleth recalled. He had been a lord or something from the town of Trosh. Arleth had led him into Bella's sitting room and had taken her place by the door. It had given her the perfect vantage point. Bella came in wearing a ridiculous yellow dress, batting her eyelashes in what she thought was a seductive way, but really just made her look like she had something in her eye. Her suitor had paled, looked around her (a large feat in itself Arleth noted with amusement) hoping that she was hiding a prettier Bella behind her. Realizing that the chalky rhinoceros in front of him was indeed Bella, he emitted some small gagging noises in his throat, made some excuse that the desert heat was too much for him and he couldn't hope to live in such a climate and ran out the door so fast that Arleth barely had time to open it for him.

A smile had involuntarily come to Arleth's face when she thought of this. Realizing that Kiran was watching her, she tried to hold it back and was only partially successful. She succeeded in making her face into a half grimace/sneer. Kiran mistook her expression for pain, thinking he had hurt her with his blow earlier. With a smile of undisguised pleasure, Kiran hit her a few more times with the rod and for good measure, kicked the back of her legs as she walked past him.

Although the blows were far from light, Arleth barely felt them. She was still picturing the suitor's expression when he raced out the door. She smiled again and this time she couldn't suppress it. It didn't matter though, Kiran, almost as large as his mother had given up following her, winded from his exertion. He had satisfied himself by waving his arms up and down and hurling insults at her. Arleth smiled larger and even permitted herself a small chuckle. She needed to take advantage of what small joys there were in her life and Bella's exploits usually provided this pleasure. But, she realized with alarm, she couldn't stay lost in such thoughts for very long. She had been in the stable a long time and she had to hurry back to the mansion.

By this time, Bella would be just finishing off her bath. As one of Bella's personal servants it was her duty to stand outside the chamber to wait for the woman to bathe. No one was allowed to actually be inside the room with Bella because she did not think a lowly servant should have the honour of seeing her perfect, angelic body. Although Arleth was supposed to be waiting outside for the instant Bella would emerge, she knew that the grotesque woman would languish in the bath for hours. This gave Arleth at least an hour to leave and safely be back before Bella noticed her absence.

Today Arleth had gone to the stables near the back of the estate's grounds. But, lost in thought, she had spent too much time there. She knew that Kiran would tell his mother that he had caught Arleth there, and that she would be punished. However, if she could be back before Bella emerged from the bath at least she could avoid being punished twice.

She reached the mansion and saw that Chuck, the head cook had opened the kitchen's back door. He was outside, emptying a pot of scraps into the garbage.

Great! Arleth thought to herself, the bath chamber was located at the back of the house, near the kitchen. If she cut through the kitchen she could reach it in a lot less time than if she was forced to go from the front. She might just make it!

Chuck looked up and smiled at her as she dashed past him and into the kitchen. Luckily there was no one else there. She could trust Chuck not to tell anyone that she had been out, but most of the other servants would jump at the chance to rat her out to Bella. On Bella's orders, any servant who informed on another servant was given half a day off. It led to hostile living conditions and bitter animosity between the servants.

She peeped outside the kitchen door and seeing no one, crept along the hall to the bathing quarters. As she neared the room, she saw that the huge oak door was still closed.

Great! Bella was still in her bath. As quietly as she could, she ran the rest of the way and took her post outside the door. Almost immediately, the door opened and Bella wobbled out. On instinct, Arleth lowered her head in a bow as Bella walked past her. Eyes on the floor, Arleth heard Bella make a small grunt and saw a large shadow coming her way. She quickly looked up and had a split second to grasp what was happening before a pile of Bella's wet towels and dirty clothes landed on Arleth's head.

Disgusting! Arleth thought to herself. It was probably a good thing that the pile of laundry was on her head because Arleth knew that she was making a face. With caution, she backed up a bit until she felt the weight of the wall behind her. Leaning against the wall, she lifted her left knee up and balanced shakily on one foot. Arleth pushed the pile down against her raised knee and shoved her head through the top of the pile. With a small gasp of air, she put her arms under the pile and her chin on the top and hurried down the hall after Bella.

When she caught up to Bella, she was breathing heavily under the weight of the laundry. Bella made an exasperated grunt.

"Shut up! You are so loud, can't you be quiet? You are disrupting my thoughts."

Arleth wanted to say what thoughts? But she held back and instead said "Sorry Ms. Bella it won't happen again."

Arleth struggled to calm her breathing and unleashed a tirade of insults at Bella in her mind. Arleth sighed to herself; Bella had reached the door to her bed chamber and was tapping her foot impatiently.

"Are you going to make me wait all day you lazy swine?"

Arleth hurried in front of Bella and struggling, shifted the laundry to one arm and with effort managed to open the door for Bella to walk through. But the woman was angry from having to wait. As she walked by, she kicked Arleth in the shins. With a gasp of pain, Arleth cried out and dropped the laundry. The kick had been hard and her shins felt like they were on fire. Arleth quickly bent down to retrieve the fallen articles and was hit on the back of the head by Bella's meaty hand. Arleth wobbled a bit, momentarily dazed.

"How can you be so clumsy? You are the most useless girl that ever existed. All you have to do is carry my clothes and you manage to drop them."

Arleth looked up and started to say sorry but she was interrupted by a slap in her face.

"Shut up, your voice is irritating me. And don't you dare look at my face, you don't deserve the privilege. Go get me some honey wine and pick up my clothes!"

Arleth lowered her head and quickly picked up the laundry. She exited the room as quickly as she could. Her shins were burning and she knew that bruises were forming. Her lip had split from a ring on Bella's finger when she had slapped her and there was a thin line of blood running down her chin. As she deposited the laundry down the chute and went to the kitchen to pour Bella's honey wine, Arleth thought about all the things she would like to do to Bella. As she re-entered Bella's bed chamber, carrying the wine, she was picturing pushing Bella out a top-story window to see if she would bounce. With this joyous thought, her shins and cheek almost didn't hurt as much.

* * *

Here it comes, Arleth thought with dismay. It was early evening and Arleth was standing in Bella's private dining chamber waiting for the woman to eat her dinner. In walked Kiran who looked over at Arleth, shot her a smile of pure malice and practically skipped over to his mother. Bella, seeing her son, smiled up at him from her seat.

"Good evening mother, I have had the most wonderful day."

"That's great dear," said Bella gesturing for Kiran to bend over to her so she could kiss him on the cheek. This having been completed, Kiran sat down on a chair beside his mother.

"You will never guess what I caught her doing today when she was supposed to be outside your bath chamber," said Kiran in a delighted voice gesturing in Arleth's direction.

"What was she doing Kir-Kir?" Said Bella glancing over at Arleth with disgust. But Kiran didn't answer right away, he took his time getting comfortable on his seat and stretching. He looked over at Arleth again and smiled. He loved making her suffer and he wanted to drag out this particular pleasure as long as possible.

"What was she doing?" Bella repeated getting impatient.

"Well... I was walking around the back of the house today and a wounded bird caught my eye. I decided to go and step on it but as I got closer I saw that the door to the stable was open. I thought to myself what is the door to the stable doing being open? I knew that all the horses were supposed to be fed earlier in the morning and there should be no one there. So being the clever boy that I am I instantly realized that one of our servants was shirking their responsibilities. When I looked in the stable I saw that girl sitting on a bucket. She had probably been there the whole time you were in the bath and she was crying! Ha! Being a responsible person I hit her with a rod a few times but that is not nearly enough punishment for one such as her who is so negligent in her duties. What if someone had tried to walk in on you on your bath mother? Or what if you had needed something and no one was there to get it for you?"

"Yes you are very right my son. This girl is a useless, lazy twit. She needs to be taught a lesson." Bella's was so angry that her face had started to turn a light pink, a hard feat considering how thick her white powder was. She was literally shaking with rage. Bella stood up, her dinner forgotten for the moment.

"COME HERE!" She yelled at Arleth. This was perhaps the last thing she wanted to do, but she rushed over to Bella anyways.

"You are an ungrateful, selfish brat," Bella shrieked slapping her across the face with such force that Arleth gasped and fell to the ground. Arleth could feel the tears coming and she cupped her hand to her throbbing cheek.

"GET UP!" Arleth scrambled to her feet as she fought back the tears. There was no way Kiran would get the pleasure of seeing her cry for the second time in one day.

"I keep you in this house, I give you food and I let you look at me every day, and this is the service I get? You can't even wait at the door? You disgust me so much I can't even look at you! Kiran do something with her."

"Gladly mother," Kiran replied with a glimmer in his eye. He stepped in front of Arleth so he could see the expression on her face and he punched her hard in the stomach. Arleth grunted but didn't let herself cry out. She kept as straight a face as possible. Kiran was not satisfied, so he punched her again, this time harder. Arleth felt the air knocked out of her and she felt to the ground with a thud. She curled herself up on the ground and grabbed her stomach. Kiran, still not satisfied kicked her a few times. Arleth hugged herself and put her hands over her head to protect it from his foot.

"That's good Kiran, take her outside and let her spend the night in the cold. Inform Chuck that she is to get no dinner tonight and no food at all tomorrow. See if that doesn't teach her a lesson."

Kiran grabbed Arleth's arm and hauled her to her feet. Arleth stumbled along beside him, aching everywhere. Dark bruises had formed on her shins from earlier and every step she took was painful. Her face felt like it was swollen already and she knew her stomach would hurt her for a few days. Kiran dragged her through the halls as violently as he could manage and pushed her down the front stairs. Once outside, Kiran dragged her to a large wire cage in the front of the property he unlocked the door with a key he carried around his neck and pushed her inside.

"Have fun," Kiran said with a sneer. "Let's see what kind of night you will have in nothing but that dress when the sun goes down." I will be thinking of you shivering in the cold with pleasure when I am tucked up in my warm bed tonight."

With that he locked the door and pranced away, greatly pleased with himself. With pain, Arleth sat up and leaned against the side of the cage. Every part of her body was throbbing. Gingerly she put her hand to the side of her face and winced. Her cheek was swollen and as she looked at her hand she noticed that her cut lip had re-opened and was bleeding again. It didn't feel like any of her ribs were broken, but they were tender just the same. She leaned over to look at her shins and the pain lanced up her stomach. Yes she thought, her stomach would be sore for a long time. Her shins were a nasty shade of purple and were covered in sand from where she had been thrown on the cage floor. Carefully she wiped them clean and looked down at her right ankle. That was the reason she couldn't escape. Around her ankle was a metal band about one inch thick: a Grapel, the customary escape-prevention tool that all slaves on Tocarra wore. If she left the estate grounds, or tried to break it, a loud alarm would go off, alerting everyone to her effort. As if that wasn't enough, the Grapel would also emit a beam of red light skyward that would tell everyone where she was.

She had definitely thought of escape. She could probably break the Grapel and leave it on the ground. They would hear the alarm and come running to the beam of light emitted from the device, but she wouldn't be there. But she knew that the device would sound the alarm and light up as soon as she started to break it. She would likely not have the time to break it before someone had already found her. Even if she did manage to get away without being caught, Sonohan was in the middle of the Chaz desert and beyond that was the Heat Band. There were no other towns in the desert and it would take days to reach the Heat Band; that is assuming she even travelled in the right direction. The Heat Band itself was 20 miles wide and impossible to traverse without a guide. Constant sand storms, flowing molten rivers and scorching heat would kill anyone who didn't know the correct path to follow.

She started to shiver, the sun had gone down and it had become cold. Out here in the desert, the temperature could go near freezing at night and dressed in nothing but a thin dress, Arleth knew she was in for a cold night. Her skin broke out in goose bumps. Painfully she slipped her arms inside her dress and pulled up her legs closer to her stomach so she could stretch the dress out to cover them. She wrapped her arms around her knees and hugged herself.

She let her thoughts wander, thinking of Flora, Neve and her lost childhood. Shivering and throbbing with pain, she finally fell asleep.

* * *

In a distant world, far away from Arleth and her suffering, a dark figure backed into the shadowy recesses of the hall. He struggled to control his rapid breathing, and put a hand on his chest to steady his heartbeat. He was excited; excited and anxious. Even though he was cloaked with a concealing spells, he was still terrified of being discovered. The spell he knew, would only protect him from a magician in the castle being able to sense his presence, but it would do nothing if someone were to walk by and see him. Involuntarily, he shuddered. He could only begin to imagine what would be done to him if he were caught, especially if he were to be discovered now, deep in the King's private quarters. There could be no explaining why he was there, no errands he could say he had been running. No one but Rogan was allowed this far into the King's quarters. No, although he had been successfully spying on the King for close to three years, if he were caught now it would be over - *he* would be over. He moved farther into the shadows, pressing his back against the cold stone wall.

Hidden in the shadows, he scanned the hall left and right, there were no signs of movement, no sounds at all. Rogan and the King had left, engaged in business elsewhere, their secret meeting concluded. The man felt his heartbeat slow and quietly let out the breath he didn't know he had been holding. Calming down a little, his anxiety gave way once again to excitement. He almost couldn't believe what he had overheard. His master would be so pleased with this information. It could even change the course of the war he thought, startling himself with this important realization. When he thought about it this way he was quite proud of himself. He had seen the look on Rogan's face when he whispered to the King and saw the King's look of surprise. When the two had instantly hurried off in the direction of the King's private chambers, the man had been instantly intrigued. He had taken the dull green pill containing the concealing spell (he made sure he always had a couple on him for just such important occasions) and had snuck off after them.

Behind the closed door, believing themselves to be alone, Rogan had told the King what he had discovered. The King was going to be leaving Iridian Castle in a week's time and heading to some distant land that the spy hadn't heard of. There was some "official story" as Rogan put it that the reason for the visit was some stones and something about a family history. But the man wasn't interested in the official story and he knew his master wouldn't be either. The real story, the real reason the King was leaving was what was important.

The man thought about his next course of action. He had to tell his master about the news and quickly if anything was going to be done. With a thousand thoughts running through his head, the man crept quickly down the passageways back to his room. The concealing spell would wear off soon and he didn't want to still be here when it did. He was in a good mood, thinking that finally after so many years, things might finally turn out right.

Chapter 3

The messenger came early the next morning. Through the bars of her cage Arleth saw him approach the mansion. He was dressed in black and carried an unfamiliar dark blue standard with a picture of a silver crystal in the middle. He was riding an animal that Arleth had never seen before. The beast was pitch black and looked like a horse except that it had six legs and two tusks. For an instant, the messenger looked in Arleth's direction and this gave Arleth a chance to see his face clearly. The dark features and hard expression told Arleth that he was no ordinary messenger carrying a request from one of Bella's suitors. In fact, she thought, looking again at the animal he was riding, he might not even be from this world! She was instantly intrigued. Arleth watched him approach the front door, be bowed in by a host of servants and disappear into the house. She wished that Kiran would let her out soon so she could find out what the messenger had to say. But she knew that was probably not going to happen.

Arleth was exhausted. She had slept fitfully through the night, waking up several times, shivering from the cold. Her face was still throbbing, her stomach hurt when she breathed in deeply and her shins were a deep shade of purple. With the sun out again, Arleth could feel the heat begin to return to her body. At least for now she thought, being in the cage wasn't so bad. It was already hot, but not unbearably so and with her body injured the way it was, she didn't mind not having to follow Bella around everywhere.

But she did want to find out about the messenger and being stuck in this cage wasn't going to get her any answers. She heaved a deep sigh, felt a shooting pain in her torso and instantly regretted it. Who could the messenger be? Maybe he was from some distant area on Tocarra and his lord wanted to trade for the Chaz Desert's lynstones. Or maybe she thought, getting excited, he *was* from another world.

Arleth yawned. She was deeply intrigued by the messenger but she was also tired. She looked outside her cage and saw no sign of Kiran, or anyone for that matter. She would go to sleep until Kiran came. She wouldn't find out anything about the messenger sitting here anyways and if he carried an important message, she could be sure that all the servants would be talking about it. She leaned against the bars of the cage and fell back asleep.

* * *

Arleth woke a few hours later to a persistent jabbing in her ribs. Sleepily she looked around and saw a dark shadow in front of her. Covering her eyes from the sun she peered up into Kiran's chubby face. He had come into her cage to let her out and was poking her roughly with a stick.

"Wake up you!" He bellowed down at her, rapping her head repeatedly with the stick. His eyes briefly scanned her bruised legs and swollen face and a broad smile came to his face. "How you feeling?" He sneered at her, letting out a deep throated laugh. "I for one had a wonderful night; I had a *hot* bath and then reclined in my *warm and cozy* bed while I had my back massaged and ate candied figs."

What a creep, Arleth thought to herself. Really, his greatest pleasure was making everyone around him suffer, and it wasn't just limited to the servants. Just a few days ago, Arleth had seen Kiran in the yard through Bella's bed chamber window. He had caught a red-backed lizard and Arleth had seen him pull out a pocket knife and slowly cut the lizard's tail off. The sight had made her sick and she had quickly turned away, but she could only imagine what terrors he had inflicted on the poor creature.

Arleth stumbled to her feet and followed Kiran out of the cage. She had taken only a few steps when Kiran abruptly stopped and turned around, a sinister look on his face. He pulled a small pastry out of his pocket and wafted it in front of Arleth's face.

"Hmmmm, smells good don't you think? I almost forgot about this pastry here; I had so much breakfast that I was stuffed. But this looked so good I just had to take it with me." He then proceeded to messily stuff it in his face.

"You're not hungry are you?" He said, his voice thick with insincerity.

Arleth's stomach grumbled, she hadn't eaten since yesterday morning. She shook her head at him though; she could at least pretend that his torments had no effect on her.

"No? Well that's good then, because this pastry is delicious." With that he turned back around and continued leading Arleth to the mansion.

Arleth *was* very hungry, but she didn't pay much attention to Kiran, for her curiosity had taken over. Now out of the cage, she thought it would only be a matter of time before she found out about the messenger. One of the servants would have overheard his conversation or even been in the room when he was delivering his message. If it was important, by now almost all of the household would know. The more she thought about it, the more the six-legged tusked horse-like creature interested her. Thinking back, she was certain that Ms. Witrany had never mentioned any animal like that like living on Tocarra and Arleth had definitely never seen it before. She felt certain that the animal and its rider were from another world.

But what was his message? She thought with a sense of disappointment that it could just be a suitor for Bella, even if he was from a different land. Bella's self-promoting efforts stretched far and wide.

But Arleth just didn't think that was the case. She remembered his face when he had momentarily glanced at her and she brought to mind his dark, hardened features. He looked like a dangerous man, a man not accustomed to delivering messages. No, she definitely didn't think he carried an ordinary message.

As soon as Arleth stepped inside the mansion, she could see that her suspicions were correct; the whole place was a flurry of excited activity. Servants were bustling up and down the main stairs and through the front hall carrying bundles of laundry, saddle-bags filled with food and long lists written on sheets of parchment. Everywhere Arleth looked was hurried, purposeful activity. Who *was* the messenger? What was he doing here in Sonohan? Her thoughts were interrupted by Kiran's harsh voice in her ear.

"Don't just stand there! My mother is waiting for you in her bed chamber. You have already wasted enough of her time being in that cage." Kiran gave her a shove down the hall and then turned and went back outside.

As she walked through the mansion to Bella's bed chamber, Arleth caught snatches of conversation as servants hurried past her.

".....Messengers to all the border towns....Bella wants seven new dresses made of the finest silk....start digging at dawn tomorrow morning....He's coming in a week..."

Someone was coming in a week! And whoever they were they were pretty important to be occasioning all this frenzy. But aside from this, she couldn't piece the few bits she heard into anything coherent. Since Arleth spent most days secluded with Bella in her chamber, she knew that she was unlikely to find out any more while Bella was awake. She made a mental note to talk to Chuck about it tonight after Bella had gone to sleep.

Arleth passed the remainder of the day in restless anticipation. The usually boring tasks of grooming Bella, bringing her food and sitting by her while she rested were made even more excruciating by her curiosity about the messenger. The minutes felt like hours and Arleth constantly looked at the great mahogany clock in the corner of the room, checking the passage of time. It seemed like weeks for both suns to finally set and it took all her effort not to tap her foot impatiently or sigh in frustration. Thus it was with tremendous relief that late at night, Bella finally went to sleep and Arleth was released from her duties.

After silently closing the door behind her, Arleth raced down the hall to the kitchen. She hoped Chuck would still be there; Bella had gone to sleep pretty late tonight and Chuck might have gone to sleep himself by this time. As she rounded the corner, she was delighted to see that there was light coming from the kitchen. Chuck must still be there!

Chuck smiled at her as she walked in, "Hi Arleth. Are you hungry?" He was clearing the dishes from the servants' dinner and was putting the extra meat away in the freezer. Arleth looked longingly at the food,

"I'm being punished and I'm not allowed to have any food until tomorrow. If someone sees you giving me food, you will be in trouble." Chuck looked around and seeing no one, put some meat, a slice of bread and some dried figs on a plate and handed it to Arleth.

"I don't see anyone. It's pretty late, everyone has probably already gone to bed, it's ok. You must be starving, just eat quickly, you don't want to be caught either." Arleth took the food gratefully,

"Thank you so much Chuck!" She wolfed down the food in a matter of minutes and handed the plate back to Chuck.

"So," said Chuck, "I don't think you came here just for food. Let me guess. Since you were in the cage all morning and then shut up in Bella's bed chamber until now, you don't know about the news the messenger brought." Arleth smiled at Chuck and nodded; he knew how curious she was. Chuck walked over to a bench and sat down, motioning for Arleth to sit beside him.

"The messenger came from Absalom Amara, the king of Oherra." Arleth gasped excitedly and jumped up.

"From Oherra? The legendary house of Amara, the holder of the Crystal Throne? What does he want?"

Chuck laughed at Arleth's reaction. "Sit back down Arleth," he said amusedly, "If you let me finish my story I will tell you."

Arleth sat back down a little embarrassed and nodded anxiously at Chuck, "Ok go on!"

"So, King Absalom has heard about the Chaz Desert's lynstones. Apparently hundreds of years ago, his ancestors used to trade for these lynstones with the Sneel family, but trade stopped for some reason... I don't know why. Bella of course inherited her family fortune and business ten years ago with the death of her father. King Absalom wants to re-open lynstone trade with the Sneel's, and therefore with Bella."

"So why is everyone so anxious? Why is everyone so busy and hurried?"

"Ah, that is because the King will be coming here in a week's time. He wants to personally check the mining of the lynstones and make sure that their quality is as good as he has heard."

"He will be coming here?! In a week? No wonder everyone is so busy!"

"Yes, Bella has ordered almost half the servants just to go to the mines to start getting the lynstones so the storage room can be filled with them. Also, all of the messengers left this afternoon to go to the border towns to get silk, flowers, and delicacies that Bella doesn't have in stock. Everyone is going to be very, very busy for the next week. But it is very exciting isn't it Arleth? Getting to see the legendary King of Oherra. I never dreamed I would get to see him in my lifetime."

Arleth couldn't agree more. She was literally bursting with excitement. "How long is he staying for? Who else is coming with him?"

"A couple of days I presume. I'm not exactly sure, but he will be staying at least one night so there can be a banquet and he needs to see the lynstone mines in the daylight. As for who else is coming, I would guess most of his retinue and guards."

Arleth nodded, she wondered what the king would look like. She knew at least that he would be human, she had been taught that much in the orphanage. But other than that simple fact, she didn't have any idea what he would look like. She realized with shock that she didn't even know how old he would be. Maybe he would be a couple of years older than her and would be handsome and would like her and take her away with him and she could be his queen... She laughed at herself, what ridiculous nonsense! What king, let alone the king of Oherra, would even look twice at a servant. But it would be great to see the look on Bella's face...

"What is so funny Arleth?" Chuck asked looking at her with a smile. Arleth blushed; she hadn't realized she had laughed out loud.

"I was... just... picturing some ridiculous creatures that might live on Oherra," Arleth replied slowly.

"Ah, well, an old man like me doesn't have enough imagination for that, but there must be some pretty interesting creatures there. When I was very young, my father told me that the magic in Oherra has remained strong since the time of the Great War. There are probably many magical races in Oherra that you or I couldn't even dream of. But, Arleth it is very late and we are both going to have a very busy week ahead of us." Chuck stood up and offered his hand to Arleth to help her off the bench. "I think we should get some sleep."

"I guess you're right," said Arleth a bit disappointed. She would have loved to hear if he knew anything else about Oherra. She yawned, she *was* tired though. "Well then, good night and thanks again for the food."

"No problem, good night."

With a small wave she turned around and walked out of the kitchen and back down the hall to Bella's chamber. She laid down on the floor in front of the door and despite her excitement, she was so exhausted that she immediately fell asleep. She dreamt of Oherra and the most fantastical creatures her mind could think of.

Chapter 4

The week passed by in a flurry of frenzied activity. Just like Chuck had said, half of the servants had gone to start digging in the lynstone mines. This meant that the remaining servants had twice the work to do on top of preparing for the king's arrival. Furthermore, on the fourth day there was a particularly strong sandstorm which delayed the return of the messengers who had travelled to the silk districts of Warda and Trosh. When they finally returned, the seamstress had to work overnight to prepare Bella's seven dresses and Arleth had spent the whole next day into the early hours of the night with Bella while the woman tried them on and complained non-stop.

But despite the obstacles, when the afternoon of the King's arrival approached, everything was ready. Bella's dresses were made and met her approval; all the food for the night's banquet was being prepared; the lynstone storage room had been filled; and the mansion had been cleaned top to bottom and filled with vases of fresh flowers. Arleth took a deep breath, it had been a hectic week, filled with sleepless nights, but in her mind it was all worth it. The day had come; today she was actually going to see King Absalom, the king of Oherra! He should be arriving shortly and she, with Bella and Kiran beside her were lined-up outside the mansion with the rest of the household waiting for him to come. She scanned the horizon anxiously, but didn't see any signs of movement.

Arleth felt pressure on her bare foot and looked down to see a large black beetle crawling across her toes. Normally she would have been disgusted, but now its appearance was an annoying distraction. She absentmindedly shook her foot and sent the beetle flying. When she did she noticed that the bruises on her shins had faded to a light yellow and were barely visible against her tanned skin. She mentally appraised the rest of her body; her cheek too she knew was no longer swollen and her stomach was just barely tender. Furthermore, Bella and Kiran had been so busy preparing for the king's arrival that there were no fresh injuries to take their place. Bella had made all the servants wash their clothes, so Arleth's brown dress was no longer streaked with dirt and grime. Arleth had even stolen Bella's comb this morning when the woman was going to the bathroom and had worked out most of the tangles in her long black hair. All things considered Arleth decided, she was quite pleased with her appearance.

Arleth scanned the horizon again and was disappointed to see that there was still no sign of the king. She could see that some of the other servants had gotten restless and were shifting their weight back and forth on their feet or wringing their hands in anticipation. Kiran, sweat dripping from his pudgy face, complained loudly to his mother about having to wait, and for once Arleth agreed with him. The minutes crawled by. It seemed to Arleth that these moments spent in anxious anticipation lasted longer than the whole previous week. All the hard work of the past week now seemed like a blessing – it has kept her mind occupied and made the time pass faster. But now there was nothing to do but wait for the King and this waiting was unbearable. Even Kiran's complaining ceased to hold her attention for long. Within a few minutes, he had run out of anything new to say and had therefore resorted to making low grumbling noises.

Arleth dug her bare feet into the sand and wiggled her toes. She felt like crying out or jumping up and down. She needed to do something, *anything*, to relieve her anxiety. Her toe wiggling became more violent and she began swinging her foot back and forth, kicking the sand around her. She realized suddenly that she was creating a small dust cloud around her and she abruptly looked over at Bella and Kiran. She expected them to start yelling at her at any moment but they were so anxious themselves that they didn't pay her any attention.

Bella was biting her lower lip and clasping her hands in front of her. Her gaze was riveted on the horizon, not daring to look away for even a second. Kiran had stopped his grumbling and in the resulting silence, the nervous tension was palpable. A loud cry pierced the silence.

"Over there!" Yelled a female servant named Jenny, pointing at the horizon. Arleth looked in the direction she was indicating and gasped. A door was being drawn in the thin air. It was just what had happened seven years ago. With this realization, Arleth was hit with a flood of terrible images and heartbreaking memories of Neve and Flora. In her mind, in striking clarity she saw the door as it had appeared seven years ago at the orphanage. She saw the flash of green light and the door open and the dark terrible monstrous shapes illuminated in front... But no! She thought to herself. This was different, the sky was not black, there was no Dread Mage coming from the door. It was just an ordinary portal between the worlds. And this time, the King of Oherra himself was coming. Yes, this time things were very different.

The door, now fully outlined, opened and a burst of golden light poured out. Although the light was so bright it made it seem like the afternoon sun was dark in comparison, it was not blinding. Arleth realized with surprise that she did not need to shield her eyes, if anything it caused her to relax and sent a deep wave of calm through her.

Is this what a magical world is like she thought? What kind of world is Oherra if the light coming from just its portal has this kind of effect? The light even sounds wonderful, she thought absentmindedly - a deep booming melody. It sounded like nothing she had ever heard before, both delightful and exotic... the light was making noise? Isn't that impossible? She looked closer at the open portal and realized that indeed it was. Emerging from the door in rows of three she saw the source of the music. But what the creatures were she had no idea. In most regards they looked like normal men and women, dressed in simple white garments. They were light-skinned and all had shortly cropped hair that was shockingly red. But what made Arleth so dumbstruck by them was that they each had four arms, two were long and gangly and looked like they would reach down almost to the ground if they were extended. In contrast the other two were short, probably even shorter than a human's arms. The pair of shorter arms was holding a long tube-like musical instrument and the longer arms were racing up and down it, causing the wondrous music.

Arleth was still staring dumbstruck at these miraculous creatures when they abruptly halted. Four rows of three had marched out of the portal in total. In unison they grabbed their instrument with their right longer arm and raised it above their heads. With their instruments held in such a way, which really would have looked ridiculous if the onlookers weren't so awestruck by the spectacle, they quickly marched up and down on the spot creating a drum-roll effect. This continued for a few seconds until the creatures had reached a feverous pace and then instantly ended. A tall male creature in the center of the first row took one pace forward, turned toward Bella and Kiran and bowed slightly.

"Mrs Sneel and young Mr Sneel, King Absalom of Oherra." The man had a booming voice, but it was surprisingly normal, almost human. Arleth was a bit disappointed, but this faded as soon as she looked past them at what was emerging from the doorway. Two massive creatures were slowly coming into view. Arleth let out a cry of fright, behind her she heard a scream and an elderly servant fainted.

Kiran's face had gone white with terror and involuntarily he took a few steps backwards. Emerging from the portal were two giant serpent-like forms. From the waist down, they looked humanoid, despite being about twice the size of a normal human and having skin that was tinged greyish-green. They each had two massive legs that were so thick and muscled Arleth thought that she could easily hide behind one and not be seen. From the waist up however, all comparison ended. Branching out of each creature's torso was a long, snake head. Two bright yellow eyes gleamed murderously behind scaled lids. The creatures moved to the side of the portal and stopped, standing with their feet spread apart. A pair of clawed arms held a 6 foot moon-shaped axe in front of their bodies menacingly. A cluster of green tentacles emerged from some spot on their backs and spread out around them in an array, withering back and forth as if they had a life of their own.

Now that the creatures had come into full view, the servants started screaming. Some had gone deathly white and were riveted, frozen in place. Others were backing slowly away, their mouths opened in cries of terror. Still others were beginning to run away.

"Be calm everyone!" The voice came from the lead musician who had spoken before. "Do not be alarmed by these creatures. They look hideous but be assured that they are the king's personal guards. As long as he is not in danger, they will not strike. You have nothing to fear." No one looked very certain of this, but those who had began to run, turned and crept cautiously back. Slowly the screams died out as the musician's words registered and people gradually began to calm down. As the moments passed and the creatures still stood rooted to their spot on either side of the portal, everyone relaxed a bit. Although still wary of the creatures, some even started to smile at their mistake.

Arleth, for her part, felt a bit ashamed that she had cried out, but she quickly got over it. The king still hadn't come out yet and this was the man she had been waiting to see. She tore her eyes away from the terrifying guards and looked into the portal once again. Another shadow was emerging, a single one this time. One that looked like a human's size. Arleth felt her heart race. This must be King Absalom! Arleth thought to herself. This was the moment she had been waiting for, the event she had never expected to witness in her entire lifetime.

The shadow materialized into a man, and what a man he was! Arleth felt her jaw drop open in shock and could do nothing to stop it. She no longer cared about the serpent guards, and as she looked around her Arleth noticed that no one else was paying them much attention either. Now that the king had appeared, their former terror was forgotten. The presence of this man consumed their full attention. He was by far the most handsome man she had ever seen. In reality, she had never even dreamed that a man could be so perfect looking. He was clearly much older than her, probably early 40s, but that did not take away from his appearance in the slightest. He had dark green eyes, the kind that could either pierce through you to your soul or lighten up in laughter at a moment's notice. He had chiselled features and dark, tanned skin. A gleaming silver circlet sat upon his head, resting on his dark curly black hair. Physically he was tall, muscular and powerful looking. He was wearing a tight-fitting black shirt and pants, with high silver boots. Around his waist was a silver belt with a crystal buckle and across his shoulders was a dark blue cape that was bordered with silver thread that gleamed in the sunlight and had a large crystal stitched in the middle.

Arleth watched admiringly as he strode over to Bella and Kiran. Through his shirt she could see the outlines of his chest and abdomen muscles. Arleth felt her heart racing and beads of sweat begin to form on her brow and it wasn't just from the heat. This man was gorgeous!

In a few moments the King had made his way over to Bella. Arleth had been paying such close attention to this stunning man that she hadn't even glanced in Bella's direction and now she almost wished that she had. The ridiculous round woman was fluttering around like a deranged butterfly. She was batting her eyelashes and baring her ugly mouth at the King in what she could only have thought was an endearing smile. Bella, Kiran and Arleth bowed their heads to the king when he approached them. Looking over at him with bowed head, Arleth saw him smile. He took Bella's enormous hand and kissed it.

"Raise your head Bella, a beautiful woman like you does not need to bow to me." Bella positively floundered with joy and gave a disgustingly awkward curtsy. Arleth and Kiran also raised their heads.

This man was amazing, Arleth thought. He must have learned to be diplomatic as a ruler. Arleth thought it was a small miracle that Absalom could manage to put the words "Bella" and "beautiful" into the same sentence and not throw up. But he had managed to do so and had even made it sound believable. With awe, Arleth listened to the rest of his exchange with Bella.

"I am oh so very glad you came. I just know that you will love the lynstones. They are my family treasure you know, considered to be the most beautiful and precious gems in all of Tocarra. Just like me, I may add, but of course you have already noticed that. Yes, you are a very wise man, I think you will find the beauty of the lynstones does *almost* match my own."

"Yes, I have heard many rumours of both your beauty and the lynstones. I have seen with my own eyes that your beauty hardly does justice to your considerable reputation, and I imagine that the lynstones will please me just as much."

Oh this man is good thought Arleth to herself. Arleth could only imagine what Bella's reputation was, but she was certain it was not the positive image that Bella envisioned. Far from being known as the most beautiful woman in the universe as Bella certainly thought she was, she was more likely known as a self-obsessed, pompous, ugly and frivolous woman. All the disgusted and seriously misguided suitors must have spread that reputation far and wide. For her reputation to have travelled as far as Oherra was unlikely, but it was probably part of royal diplomatic protocol to learn about the other worlds and people you were visiting. Thus, Arleth imagined, King Absalom would have been fully informed about Bella and was probably laughing inside right now at his wit and the grotesque woman's total ignorance. Bella had clearly taken what King Absalom had just said as a compliment as she was flopping around (that was really the only word for it) in glee.

With a few more pleasantries, King Absalom disengaged himself from Bella and turned his attention to her son.

"And you Kiran, I can see that your mother's good looks were passed on to you. You are a fine and handsome young man, you must have to beat the girls off with a stick."

Psht! Arleth thought, the only girls he beat off with a stick were her and the other female servants that he loved to torment. Kiran was staring at the king with a blank look; he was too dumb to even understand what he was saying.

"Hehe yes, sticks," muttered Kiran stupidly.

King Absalom looked dumfounded for a moment at Kiran's utter incomprehension, but quickly recovered.

"Yes, well I guess you needn't worry about that anymore since you have such a beautiful fiancée," King Absalom said turning to Arleth.

Fiancée Arleth thought. Ha! What sort of bad luck must you have to end up with an idiot like him.... her thoughts broke off in mid sentence...Why was the King staring and smiling at her? She looked around and noticed that Bella and Kiran were also staring at her. Kiran with that all too familiar blank expression and Bella with anger and horror just beginning to register. The other servants had also turned their attention to her. In fact, as she looked around, she saw that she was the center of attention. What had she missed?

The king had now turned towards her and reached for her hand. *The King of Oherra was holding her hand!*

"I am afraid I don't know who you are my dear; my foreign ambassador did not tell me about you." He looked behind him with a slightly frustrated look, then shook his head, smiled, and returned to look at Arleth. "Well no matter, it is clear that you must be Kiran's fiancée. Your beauty casts a shadow on the other young women here. I must admit, I am enchanted. If I wasn't twice your age I'm afraid I would have to fight Kiran for you."

Arleth felt her cheeks redden in embarrassment and she had to admit, with pleasure. The king of Oherra thought she was beautiful! She was probably smiling stupidly she realized, perhaps she even looked as funny as Bella. She gave a quick look over at Bella who was literally blowing smoke from her ears in anger. No, she didn't think it was possible to look that bad, at least she hoped so anyways.

All of a sudden she felt herself being propelled violently forward. It was lucky that the king had let go of her hand and stepped back a few paces, otherwise she would have fallen into him. As it was, she was shoved so hard that by the time she had regained her balance, she was practically standing on his toes.

"You can take her! She is not my fiancée," Kiran said with disdain. "She is just a stupid servant girl. I wouldn't marry some*thing* like that!" He spat on the sand by her feet, spraying the back of her calves with his saliva. Arleth could feel the spittle dripping down her legs. But as disgusted as she was, she was more pre-occupied with the gravity of the situation. She stepped back a few steps so that she was standing a bit behind Kiran, but far enough away that he couldn't strike out at her.

Arleth glanced furtively around her. Everyone had gone deathly silent and were staring at the scene in front of them, alternating their glances between her, the king and Kiran. They were all wondering the same thing, what would king Absalom do? It was embarrassing enough that he had made the mistake of thinking a servant was Kiran's fiancée and that he had given her such high compliments. Indeed he had even said he would want to marry her if he were younger. This in itself was bad enough, but Kiran, in his idiocy had made the whole situation that much worse. Instead of humbly correcting the king's error, Kiran had been condescending and disdainful. In not so many words, he had implied that the king was an idiot for complimenting Arleth. Diplomacy between the Sneels and the king could be broken because of this, in fact, it could even cause diplomacy between the two worlds to suffer. Did Kiran not realize that the king of Oherra was the most powerful person in the universe and he had just insulted him?

King Absalom's face clouded over in anger and he took a menacing step towards Kiran. Arleth held her breath, not daring to exhale. What would happen? From the look on Kiran's chubby face he still didn't know what he had done and was completely oblivious to the angry king in front of him. Should she say something? Should she apologize to the king for allowing him to think she was Kiran's fiancée? Maybe, but she didn't want to make the situation worse or make Bella any more angry at her. She already knew she would pay for this mistake later; Bella was too jealous for her not to retaliate. Arleth was still mulling this over in her head when Bella, with surprising astuteness, stepped between Kiran and the smouldering King. With a meaty hand she pushed Kiran behind her and turned to face the king.

"I apologize on my son's behalf," she began. "It was the fault of this stupid servant, she is always causing trouble. Very stubborn you see. She is always playing at being better than she is. Your Excellency would have course thought she was Kiran's fiancée because she was standing right beside him, when her place is behind and out of *sight*." Bella said the last word with added emphasis and turned to glare at Arleth with undisguised hatred. "I will make sure that she is suitably punished for causing this incident."

Surprisingly, the king had stopped walking towards Kiran when Bella had began her speech. His face now seemed to be lightening. He didn't seem to be angry anymore, just annoyed. "Your son should learn his place in the universe," he growled at Bella. "But I accept your apology, there is no need to upset diplomacy because of such a small matter." Arleth let out her breath in relief. "And you don't need to punish this servant, what sort of king would I be if I let others suffer for my mistakes?" He smiled again at Arleth.

"That is wonderful," said Bella in a tight tone. She was angry that the king had stood up for Arleth, but she wasn't as stupid as her son to let it show. "Let's continue to the mansion, there is a banquet being prepared in your honour."

"Splendid," said the King, gesturing to his retinue to follow him. As he turned to do so, Bella glared at Arleth. Despite the king's admonition, she knew she was going to be punished. But at the moment, Arleth didn't really care. She was in shock at how charitable and kind the king had been. With such a great man as king, Oherra must be a wondrous place she thought to herself. King Absalom had turned out to be everything she had dreamed him to be and much more. Deep in her thoughts, she followed behind Bella, Kiran and the king as they made their way back to the mansion. Among other things, she was imagining what Flora would have said if she were here to witness this. At times like this, despite all the time that had passed, she missed her friend even more. Engrossed in such thoughts, and with her back to the portal, she didn't notice the rest of the king's retinue emerge. She was unaware that eight more serpent guards had now joined the original two, or that dozens of beautiful scantily-clad women and a handful of other normal looking persons had also appeared from out of the portal.

And she certainly didn't notice the hooded figure that emerged after everyone else, just as the portal was closing. The man whose face was barely visible but whose eyes gleamed all too brightly with murderous venom. The man who stared fixedly in their direction and stroked his long wicked-looking dagger affectionately.

Chapter 5

Val Odane watched the king as he walked away, striding confidently; the crystal on his robe swaying back and forth with each step. He felt nothing but hatred for this man, wanted nothing more than to see him dead. Almost two decades of warfare had solidified this feeling, a feeling he knew could never go away. He grasped his dagger even tighter, his powerful forearms flexing from the effort. His father had given him this blade when he was just a child. The stern man had taught him how to use it, drilling him tirelessly in the caves around Iridian Castle. Now, at age 28 fighting was second nature to him, this dagger a normal attachment to his arm.

Val looked once again at the retreating figure of the king. How easy it would be to throw his dagger at the man's unprotected back. To kill him here, on this distant planet. But he knew it was not that simple. His ability was not in question; he had no doubt that he could aim his weapon effectively for a kill even at this distance. The problem were the Grekens, the king's personal guards. They had a magical bond to the king which required them to protect him to their very last breath. Any weapon aimed at the king, be it arrow, dagger or magical spell would divert off course, hitting one of the Grekens instead of the king. Thus it was not even possible for an assassin to get close to the king until all of the Grekens were dead. And even if someone managed to kill all the creatures, the king himself was a formidable opponent. No, it was not possible to kill King Absalom without an army.

Val shook his head to clear his thoughts, killing the king wasn't why he was here. He needed to stay focused. He had an important mission to accomplish, one that if he failed could mean the loss of the war. But if he succeeded, he looked again at the retreating form of the king, could finally spell the end for that man. For the time being he put thoughts of murder out of his head; he needed to make a plan.

He reviewed what he knew and realized it wasn't very much. Their spy in the castle had only been able to tell them what Absalom had discovered was hiding on Tocarra. They had all been shocked at the news. Most of them had been too young to remember. How King Absalom had found out was unclear, but the how was unimportant. Val's mission was to get to the target before the king did. The fact that

Absalom likely already knew exactly what he was looking for, and might even have found them, only made matters even worse. For what must have been the thousandth time, Val cursed that all the artefacts were locked up in Iridian Castle. If he had access to one, he could have beaten the king here and already be back on Oherra. Involuntarily his hand closed on a circular object in his pocket.

A concealing spell.

The first one he had used had worked perfectly allowing him to sneak undetected through the portal behind the king's retinue. This next one.. well.... to call it a long shot would be putting too much of a positive spin on it. All he had to do was hope the king would led him to the target or at least give him a clue to who it was. Then beat him there, grab them undetected, convince them to follow a complete stranger *AND* somehow sneak them and himself back into the portal behind Absalom's retinue quietly so they would be undetected when they returned to Oherra. That is assuming Absalom even opened up the portal to go back home if had failed and didn't wait on Tocarra as long as it took until he succeeded.

Easy Right?

Val huffed to himself. "Well it's not like you have much choice." He knew quite well this was the best (*only*) plan they had and he had to try everything in his power to make it work.

Ok so what is my plan? Val gathered his thoughts.

Tonight, he knew, there was going to be a banquet in the king's honour. Thus the king would be tied up and wouldn't be leading him anywhere. Val's stomach grumbled, he looked past the mansion where the king had disappeared to the nearby town of Sonohan. He would spend the night in a tavern, get a hot meal and try to gather some information. If anyone knew anything, nothing opened lips and "refreshed" memories better than a few pints of ale and some tavern air. Tomorrow morning, rested and hopefully more informed, he would be in a better position to snatch up the target and bring her back to Oherra. With a small smile he turned and walked toward the town. He would worry about getting back to Oherra later.

* * *

Arleth looked at the designs she had drawn in the sand and made a face. She was trying to draw a picture of the Greken that was standing several paces in front of her. But no matter how hard she tried she could not make her drawing anything more than disconnected squiggles. With frustration she wiped her hand across her drawing, covering it in a layer of sand; she was certainly no artist.

At the banquet last night, she had learned that the snake-like creatures that served as the king's personal guards were called Grekens. After learning about the special bond between them and the king, she was no longer afraid that one would spontaneously hurt her. But she was even more curious than before. She was amazed that a creature could be magically bonded to a human. She wondered if other Oherran creatures were bonded in this way as well, or if it was just something the king was able to do. She looked up at the Greken again, it was standing perfectly still, feet slightly apart, its wicked-looking axe resting in the sand. It was paying her no attention, constantly moving its eyes back and forth scanning its surroundings for danger. Arleth certainly didn't envy anything that got in its way. She bent her head down and attempted to draw the creature again.

She was sitting on the sand, at the back of the mansion's grounds just outside the lynstone mines. Bella had indeed been jealous of the attention that the king had shown to her. After the banquet had ended, she had brought Arleth into her room, yelled at her for a while and punched her a few times in the stomach. The beating wasn't very bad, Arleth assumed so as not show any visible signs; the king *had* expressly advocated against punishing her after all. But that wasn't the end of Bella's revenge. While she, the king, many of the other servants, most of the king's retinue and all but one of his Grekens went into the mines, Bella had ordered Arleth to stay here. So here Arleth was, sitting on the sand in the scorching heat, trying to make the best of her situation. She guessed that they would probably be at the mines for the better part of the day, and she was terribly disappointed that she wouldn't get to see the king for that whole time. Her only consolation was that Kiran had been told to wait with her. Bella had not trusted Arleth to stay where she was and wanted to prevent her from escaping while everyone else was down in the mines. Kiran's company was far from enjoyable, but at least he was stuck out here as well. King Absalom had suggested leaving one of his Grekens for added security in case Arleth managed to slip away from Kiran.

She looked over at Kiran now. He, like the Greken was utterly ignoring her. He was engrossed in tormenting the worms that lived under the sand. He would dig into the sand, pull them out and then throw them as far away as he could. It would have been quite easy to run away if it was only Kiran watching her. She could have easily outrun the chubby boy. Her grapel would have gone off as soon as she reached the outskirts of Bella's property. But it would have been a gamble whether or not Kiran could have gone down into the mines, gotten Bella and come back to find her before she had reached the relative safety of Sonohan. She might have made it. If she could have gotten the grapel off in the town she might have been able to hide for a couple of days until some traders left to go to one of the border towns across the heat band. She might have been able to sneak aboard one of their wagons, and once across she would have been free. It would have been extremely risky and she would have had a slim chance of succeeding. But she knew she would have risked it.

But the Greken stopped all of that. There was no way she could escape with the Greken there. The king had specifically ordered the Greken to make sure Arleth stayed where she was, and Grekens obeyed their king to their last breath. Even though it wasn't paying attention to her she knew that it would be alerted the moment she made an escape attempt. She would much rather stay a slave than have that creature after her. So she sat in the sand, legs curled up under her, drawing pictures like a little girl to pass the time.

She tried drawing the Greken again. Maybe if she looked more closely at the beast she would be able to make a better drawing. She concentrated on its head, squinting her eyes to see every detail. Doing so she noticed for the first time the oblong shape of the scales and the way they slightly overlapped with the ones beside. Ha! She had missed that the first time. She might just get the hang of this after all! Painstakingly she drew the creature's head in the sand with her forefinger, outlining each individual scale. She was determined to draw the Greken well and besides, she had all day.

Arleth, her head bent down in concentration, didn't notice that Kiran was silently approaching her. He had lost interest in his game and had come to see if tormenting her could ease his boredom for a time. He was standing practically over top of her and she still hadn't noticed him. He leaned over to see what she was doing and seeing that she was in the middle of drawing he grinned maliciously. With a surprisingly swift motion he kicked a pile of sand over her artwork and laughed at the anger in her face.

What a creep! Arleth thought. What a terrible, good-for-nothing, fat bozo. Still on her knees in the sand, she looked up at Kiran's chubby, gloating face with loathing.

Kiran snickered. "What a little girl, drawing pictures in the sand. What kind of a... baby...." He trailed off in mid-sentence, his eyes fixated on something behind Arleth's head. From the look in Kiran's eyes, he was clearly frightened of whatever it was that he saw there. Arleth slowly turned around.

Immediately she saw what had caught Kiran's attention. Not fifty paces from where she sat, a large hooded man was running directly at them. In his hand he was holding a long dagger. Behind her, Kiran let out a strangled sort of scream and ran off in the opposite direction. Arleth cursed him under her breath; she hadn't expected any bravery from the chubby boy, but at least he might have served as a diversion so she could run away. *You don't have to outrun the bear, just outrun the person you are with.* For an instant she regretted thinking such a cruel thought, but it went away when she realized that Kiran had done the same thing without a moment's hesitation.

As quickly as she could on shaking legs, Arleth got to her feet. The man was coming at her fast, dagger held in front of him. Trembling, Arleth appraised her situation as rationally as she could. Kiran had ran off in the direction of the lynstone mines, but the man would be upon her before Kiran could even *reach* Bella and the king let alone them coming back for her. She could expect no help from there. She herself wouldn't be able to run away, she had already waited too long and the man was running at her too fast: he would overtake her in moments. So what was she going to do? She felt the bile rise in her throat. She was terrified. She had no way to defend herself, nothing she could do to avoid what was coming.

She stood frozen in place hands slightly raised in front of her. The man was so close now she could see the outlines of his face beneath the hood. What would happen when he reached her? Would he take her prisoner? Would he kill her? Would it be painful? An image came to mind of a 10 year old little girl running through an orphanage with the bodies of her friends and teachers broken, bleeding and mangled lying all around her. She shuddered, she had seen death, had heard their screams. She knew what someone's face looked like when they knew they were dying. She didn't want to experience that, she didn't want to die here, alone in the middle of the desert. She felt tears come to her eyes and she quickly shut them. If she was going to die, she didn't want to see it.

Suddenly, she felt a fierce gust of wind. She opened her eyes and saw something gray and massive shoot past her and crash into the man.

Of course! Arleth thought with relief, the Greken! In her terror she had completely forgotten about the creature. The creature that was now her life-line. Another realization dawned on her; the hooded man was not after her, he was after the king! She was just in the assassin's way, but that didn't mean he still wouldn't kill her. A hardened killer wouldn't care about the life of a teenage girl, especially one who got in his way. But, Arleth began to relax a bit anyways. With the Greken fighting the man she felt a bit safer. As dangerous as this man looked Arleth didn't think he could fight that beast with only a dagger. At least she hoped so anyways. Arleth stared at the fight unfolding in front of her.

The fight that would probably decide whether she lived or died.

The force of the Greken colliding into the man had caused his hood to fall off and Arleth could now see the man's face clearly. He was ordinary enough looking except for a long scar running diagonally down his right cheek almost from the inside of his right eye to his right ear lobe. She watched as the man ducked and narrowly avoided a powerful swing from the Greken's axe. Deftly, the man sprung up to the Greken's side and plunged his dagger into the beast's thigh. The dagger was thrust three quarters of the way in, but the Greken hardly seemed to notice. Arleth watched in amazement as a few of the creature's tentacles grabbed onto the ones beside it with teeth-like pincers and formed into a thick arm the size of a small tree trunk. It flung itself at the man's head, cracking into his skull with a sickening crash. The man stuttered backwards from the force of the impact. His hand was still grasping the dagger, which had been ripped out of the creature's leg by the powerful blow. A thin line of blood dripped down his head and ran down his cheek. The Greken roared, swinging its serpentine head in the direction of the man and glaring at him with its yellow eyes. The creature took a step forward and lifted his axe above his head. With a hiss of anticipation, the creature brought the axe flying down, aiming for the top of the man's head.

Arleth closed her eyes, she didn't want to see the axe connect. The Greken was too powerful for the man; he would be split in two. With her eyes tightly shut, Arleth winced expecting to hear the man's scream at any second. But the moments passed and the scream didn't come. Hesitantly she opened her eyes and stared at the combatants in surprise. Somehow the man was not dead. Instead he had met the axe blow with his dagger and was holding it off above his head. The Greken was much more powerful though and it didn't look like the man could keep it up for much longer. His face was strained from the effort and he was slowly bending under the Greken's force. With a hiss of fury the Greken took one of its hands off the axe and swiped at the man with its claws. The man, not being able to move out of the way, was hit square in the chest. The claws ripped through his shirt and exposed his bare chest. The Greken raised his arm once more and again struck at the man's chest. Ribbons of red appeared as the claws shredded through his skin. The man grunted in pain and clenched his teeth together. The Greken smiled and raised his arm to his mouth. With a long forked tongue, the creature licked the man's blood off of his outstretched claw. It hissed in satisfaction and glared at the man in triumph.

The man yelled at the creature and with a burst of strength he shifted to one side, narrowly missing the Greken's axe as it came crashing down beside him. For a moment the creature's axe was stuck in the sand and in that instant the man launched himself lightening fast at the creature. He raised his dagger and with a fierce, two-handed blow sliced through the Greken's wrist. There was a spray of blood and the axe crashed to the ground with the Greken's severed hand falling on top of it. Arleth grimaced in disgust and put a hand to her mouth. The Greken screeched in pain and rammed its head into the man, pushing him backwards a few steps. But the man quickly regained the advantage, rushing at the Greken and ducking to avoid the tentacles lashing out at him. With a fluid motion he raced behind the Greken, slashing through any tentacles he couldn't avoid. The man rammed his dagger into the base of the creature's back and watched as the Greken's legs collapsed under him and he fell to the ground. With astounding agility, the man climbed up the creature's back and dug his dagger into its neck. The Greken's yellow eyes opened momentarily in surprise. Its body convulsed a few times and then went still, head hunched over, dagger still protruding from its neck.

But Arleth missed the Greken's last breaths. As soon as the man had plunged his dagger into the beast's back and the creature had collapsed Arleth had started to back away. She was now full-out running as fast as she could away from the man and toward Sonohan. She had realized then, as unexpected as it was, that the man was going to defeat the Greken. The way she saw it, she could either stay where she was and wait for the man to do the same to her, or she could run and try to gain enough distance that the man either wouldn't be able to, or wouldn't be interested in trying to catch her. Also, she thought with excitement, if she managed to out-run the man, with the Greken dead, she might be able to escape! This thought spurred her to run faster.

With the excitement of the dead Greken and the assassin outside the mine, it was perhaps possible Bella wouldn't notice right away when she reached the mansion's outskirts and her grapel went off. Or she might notice but be too preoccupied with the dangerous hooded man.

She smiled, she must have ran a long way already. The man wouldn't be able to catch up to her; she had left when they were still fighting and it looked like the man had sustained some serious injuries. As far away as she was now, it wouldn't be worth his time to come after her. After all, she was just a slave girl and of no interest to whatever goal this man had.

Her smile grew larger; she was going to escape! This strange man had unintentionally given her the best chance she was ever going to get. Her bare feet pounded against the sand as she ran and she breathed in the humid air deeply. This was how her freedom was going to begin!

She cast a look backwards at the mansion and years of servitude she was leaving behind and let out a gasp of horror.

The man was running after her.

Chapter 6

She tried not to panic but it was no use. When she had turned back for that split second, she had also seen the lifeless, bloody body of the dead Greken. If this man could do *that* to a Greken, she could imagine all too vividly how easy it would be for him to do the same to her. She felt like screaming, crying and throwing up all at the same time. She could hear the blood pounding in her ears and her breathing became more ragged as she struggled to control her mounting terror. Ahead of her, less than a mile away, the town of Sonohan beckoned. If she could reach the town, she would be much safer than out here in the open desert. She still didn't stand much of a chance if the man found her, but in town at least, it would be harder for him to do so. In a city there were buildings she could hide behind and crowds she could blend in with.

She was a fairly fast runner and she estimated that it would take her about ten minutes to reach the town. But did she have that much time? She risked another quick glance backwards, half expecting him to be right behind her, ready to grab her at any moment. The man was still following her, his steely gaze fixated on his prey. But Arleth noted, with a small sense of relief, that the man was still about 200 paces from her. She allowed her gaze to stay on him for a few more moments and satisfied herself that he wasn't gaining any distance on her. Blood was soaking through his shirt from where the Greken's claws had slashed him and he appeared to be stumbling ahead more than running. She looked forward again and permitted herself a small burst of hope. In the man's weakened state, she would be able to reach Sonohan ahead of him and she had a chance to lose him in the bustle of the crowd. But how long would he keep looking for her? She didn't think that he would give up so easily, not with the look she saw in his eyes. And once she reached the town, how long could she really expect to stay hidden from this man?

What so soon before had seemed like an opportunity for escape had quickly turned into a deadly cat and mouse game. And she didn't really like her chances, not by herself anyways.

She did have one hope though. One she could barely stand to think about. But as much as she hated it, the fact remained that her best chance of survival was Kiran. He had ran off as soon as the man had appeared – that was over 15 minutes ago. The chubby boy was by all definitions a mamma's boy and Arleth hoped that his irritating instinct to run to his mommy at every turn would hold true here. Although Bella and Kiran would be utterly useless, a strange man attacking one of the King's personal guards would surely be a cause for concern. She felt certain that King Absalom would go to the spot where the fight had been and however unwillingly, Bella and Kiran would have no choice but to follow. Upon seeing her gone, they would assume that she had run away and their cruel natures would spur them into finding her. Although driven by hate and revenge, the two of them would provide some measure of protection if they found her before the man did. She couldn't believe that she was actually looking forward to them finding her, but she realized with dismay that she really didn't have much of a choice.

But something kept nagging at her, *why* was this man following her? She thought about what she knew. He had not looked surprised to see the Greken and he clearly knew how to kill it. That could only mean that he had also come from Oherra. But why would such a person come here anyways? Maybe he was after the king, trying to assassinate him when he was relatively unprotected and away from home? Posesson of the Crystal Throne was certainly something worth the risk. Perhaps he just wanted to kill her to clean up loose ends. Maybe he didn't want anyone to be alerted to his presence.

But she didn't really think that made sense. If so, why didn't he run after Kiran, and why did he run at *them* in the first place? Why not go directly to the king? Arleth wasn't an expert in assassination but she didn't think that running straight at a Greken in the open desert wasn't a good technique for someone trying to maintain secrecy.   BEEEP BEEEP BEEEP BEEEP BEEEP ......

Her thoughts were abruptly cut off by the loud alarm. A beam of red light flared up from her foot into the sky where it hovered for a few moments before forming into the word,

RUNAWAY

in huge accusing letters. A female voice sharply cried, "Runaway slave, number 012, property of Bella Sneel."

Arleth swore to herself, she had forgotten about the grapel she was wearing. Even though she was still at least a quarter of a mile from Sonohan, she must have reached the border of Bella's property.

Now she had a beam of red light flaring up from her foot into the sky and the word runaway floating above it, following her as she ran.

This is just great, Arleth thought to herself. As if things weren't bad enough, now the man had a beacon flaring in the sky leading directly to her. Now she certainly wouldn't be able to hide for very long in the city. She really had to rely on Bella and Kiran finding her first. Her only consolation was that at least *they* would be able to find her easily as well. How desperate her situation had become! Arleth put her head down and continued running as fast as she could towards Sonohan.

* * *

Huffing and puffing, Kiran gasped his way to the opening of the mines. There were two Grekens standing guard by the entrance, but for the moment Kiran didn't notice them. The Grekens for their part had quickly appraised the freckly boy as not threatening and were instead looking at him curiously. They watched as he stopped a few feet ahead of them and bent over at the waist; hand on his heart, chest heaving up and down.

The entrance to the mines was a man-made cave which shielded the caverns below the ground from the frequent sandstorms. Not only did the cave block the sand from filling up the underground passageways, but at its inception it had also served an equally important function – defence. The cave dated from the time of The Great War and during the hundred years of conflict, the lynstone mines were one of the few targets on Tocarra of any interest to the warring factions. The cave had served to protect those defending the mines from being surrounded in a battle. Attackers would only be able to get into the mines from the one entrance which could be heavily defended. The magical charms and defensive barricades were long gone, but the cave remained as a testament to the bitter struggles of previous generations.

Of current importance, the way the cave was positioned, with the entrance facing the Sneel mansion meant that the Grekens weren't able to see the fight between the strange man and one of their comrades happening a distance behind them. It also meant that Kiran, having just rounded the corner of the cave wall hadn't yet seen the Grekens watching him. He was still bent over, struggling for breath.

Finally his breathing became slower and Kiran, with his head still down started to focus on his surroundings. It was then that he noticed there were two huge shadows in the sand. With a start he jerked upwards and saw the Grekens standing a few feet in front of him.

"EEEEEEPPP!" Screamed Kiran, stumbling backwards onto his ample behind. With his bottom in the sand, he scuttled backwards like a crab in an effort to distance himself from the creatures. In this effort he failed as within a few moments his ran up against the cave wall. This was just too much for the boy to take. He pressed his back up against the cave, curled his knees to his chest and with eyes glistening with tears yelled, "MWWWAHHHMMMY."

The Grekens stared impassively at the scene in front of them. Unable to feel amusement, and long since losing their curiosity in him, they viewed him as an inconsequential distraction.

"MWWAAHMMMY," Kiran shouted again through his sniffles, "HEEELLLP!"

"Kir-Kir?" Came Bella's voice from somewhere in the back of the cave. "What is it?" She materialized out of the darkness and upon seeing her snivelling son, wide-eyed and pale, huddled against the cave wall she rushed over to him. Squatting down beside him she put her arms around him and held him to her chest. "What is it? What happened?"

"Ma a an c a m me, ran atttt mee," Kiran said between sobs. "Sc c carry, he had a a a dagger."

"Shh, there, there Kir-Kir," said Bella patting her son's back. "Calm down, I can hardly understand you. Try to stop crying."

Kiran nodded and sniffed into his mother's chest. He rubbed the tears from his eyes and started his story again, "I was s i i itting when I saw a man. He was ru u u nning at me and he had a dagger."

"What did he look like exactly?" Said King Absalom. He had followed Bella up out of the mines but until now Bella and Kiran had not noticed him.

Kiran looked up at the king, "I d d don't really know. He was wearing a hood. I couldn't see his face. He was tall and he was carrying a long dagger."

"And he was running at you?" Demanded the king.

"Ye e ess," Stammered Kiran, "Right at me!"

A look of alarm passed over Absalom's face. "Well it's a miracle that you weren't harmed." Absalom paused for a second as if the thought had only just come to him, "Weren't you with that servant girl? Did she not run away with you?"

For a moment, Bella and Kiran stared blankly at the King; both had forgotten about Arleth. But slowly realization dawned on the pair; anger appeared on Bella's face and sheepishness replaced the dull stare on Kiran's.

"Kiran!" Roared Bella, pushing her son away from her so that she could glare at him. "Where is Arleth?"

"I don't know," said Kiran looking down at his feet, "I left her there when I ran."

"You left her there?!" Raged Bella. "Do you know how much money I paid for her? Do you have any idea how annoying she will be to replace? I bought her in Bridon, do you remember?! Bridon! The capital of slave traders, where there is the best selection in all of Toccara. And you couldn't be bothered to at least take her with you when you ran away?!? She is probably already dead, and utterly useless to me....."

Kiran squirmed in his mother's grasp, desperate to look away from her accusing stare. He racked his small brain for something that he could say to stop her yelling. In doing so, his eyes fell upon the Grekens standing directly behind her. The creatures were now more intent, axes held firmly in their claws, waiting for direction from their King. Of course! Kiran thought to himself; there had been a Greken with him and Arleth. The Greken would definitely kill the man, Arleth would still be alive and his mother wouldn't be mad at him anymore. And, he thought feeling especially clever, he could tell his mother that he had known the Greken was there and that was why he had run. He didn't think his mother would realize that he had just thought about the Greken now. He silently congratulated himself on being so brilliant.

"..... and I just can't believe that you would do this to me," Bella continued with her angry tirade.

"Mommy," Kiran interrupted hesitantly at first, and then more confidently "Mommy!"

"What is it? What do you have to say for yourself?"

"Well, there was a Greken with us mommy. That is why I ran away. I knew that the Greken would kill the man. I didn't want to get in the middle by mistake and get hurt." Kiran was quite proud with his lie, and he was so confident that he decided to add for good measure,

"I thought that you would be glad that I ran away. I thought that you would be happy I didn't get hurt."

Instantly the anger drained from Bella's face, to be replaced by a smile. She pulled her son to her once more, her anger evaporated, "Oh you are so smart my Kir-Kir. I should have known such a brilliant boy like you would have known what he was doing."

Kiran smiled into his mother's chest. He had done it! She had believed him!

"And of course I'm glad that you aren't hurt. It was very smart of you to run away so that you wouldn't accidently get injured."

Meanwhile, King Absalom had been thinking to himself. He had listened to the foolish pair just long enough to discover that Arleth had been left behind. Unlike Bella and Kiran, though Absalom had immediately remembered that he had left a Greken behind to guard Kiran and Arleth. But for the king this wasn't a relief. From the description that Kiran had given him, as limited as it was, the king had a pretty good idea of who the assailant with the dagger was. If his suspicions were correct he knew that a single Greken would be no match for *that* man. And if that was the case.....he felt an accustomed surge of panic.... He had to go to where he had left them, and he had to go fast.

"I am finished looking at the lynstones for now," said King Absalom as calmly as he could. "I would like to find out who this man was that tried to attack your son, Bella. I am going to go back to where we left them."

Bella thought that this was a completely stupid thing to do. Why did it matter who the man was when her Kiran was safe and the Greken would have already killed him? But she wasn't about to argue with the King of Oherra.

"Go back into the mine and get the rest of my servants and take them back to your mansion. I will get my answers and bring your servant girl back with me."

"Of course King..." she broke off in mid-sentence. At that moment, over a mile away from where they stood, Arleth's grapel had gone off and Bella had just seen the red flare. She stared at it in disbelief, unable to comprehend how Arleth was escaping.

King Absalom looked in the direction Bella was staring, "What is that?"

"It's my slave's grapel; since it went off it means that she has reached the edge of my property and she is escaping." Anger came to Bella's face, turning it a nasty shade of purple. "We are coming with you. I can't let that stupid girl escape!"

King Absalom didn't have time to argue; his servants would find their way back to the mansion. He wasn't too worried about them. Besides, if the grapel went off it meant that his Greken was dead and he was running out of time. "Alright," he replied. "Hop on to a Greken, we have to hurry!" Without further instruction, he turned to the nearest Greken who had bowed down to allow the King to scramble on his back. The tentacles on the beast's back formed a sort of chair, into which Absalom climbed. A few remaining tentacles wove themselves across the king's lap, strapping him in. Absalom muttered something to the Greken, and without a glance backwards, rode off into the distance.

Bella and Kiran stared in horror at Absalom riding off into the distance and then beside them at the Greken who was bowing down waiting for them to climb on. They were both terrified to be anywhere near the beast, let alone to be riding on it. Bella looked once more at the retreating figure of the king and then at the red flare. Her anger at Arleth outweighed her fear. "Come on!" She growled at Kiran, "Let's go! She is not going to get away with this." Clumsily they climbed onto the Greken's back and clung on for dear life. The Greken sped away after his king. Awkwardly they bounced up and down on the Greken's back like two very ugly very loud sacks of potatoes, screaming in terror the whole way.

Chapter 7

Absalom dismounted and rushed over to the bloody and very dead body of his Greken. He felt no sadness for the creature; Grekens were magically created. They had no life except what was given to them, no purpose beyond protecting their king. They had no hopes, no ambitions, no thoughts of their own. His sorcerer Rogan could easily make more. No, what was troubling to the king was who had managed to kill the creature. And, if his suspicion was correct, how he had followed him here, indeed how he had even known to come here.

Absalom inspected the Greken's body. He noted the severed hand and the sliced tentacles. He walked over to the creature's head and saw where the death blow had struck. He saw the gaping hole at the base of the beast's neck and the river of blood that was still oozing from it. It was Val Odane. He was certain. None of the others killed that way, none except for maybe Val's father. But that man was short and broad; he didn't fit the description given by Kiran. Besides, Val was practically Aedan's brother, it made sense that he would have been sent.

A speck of blue in the sand caught Absalom's attention. Curious, he bent down to get a closer look. Partly buried in the sand was a small blue object. That looks just like a ... Absalom thought, as he brushed the sand away ... yes it was! A concealing spell. Val must have dropped it during the fight. With a look of disgust, Absalom threw it back on the ground and stepped on it, crushing it under his boot. How he hated these irritating pills. Aedan never seemed to have a shortage of them. Rogan was right, Aedan's sorceress Selene must have figured out how to make them. This time though, seeing such a pill was satisfying for Absalom. It meant that Aedan had not been able to find an artefact that could open a portal to Tocarra. Val must have snuck through his own portal by using a concealing spell. This was good news because it meant that this was the only way Val could go back to Oherra. Even if Val found the girl before him, he couldn't bring her back to Oherra by himself. Absalom chuckled to himself, there was no way that he could lose. Even if Val managed to find Arleth first, they would have to wait for him to open the portal and he would be waiting for them. He still wanted to find her first though, who knows what Val would say to her in the meantime.

Absalom was surprised, Aedan was usually better prepared than this. The king guessed that Aedan must have been in a rush. Absalom mulled this over in his head. If Aedan had independently discovered that the girl was here on Tocarra, he would have made every effort to create a better plan. Indeed Aedan wouldn't have even known that he had learned the same thing. Aedan must have planted another spy in Iridian castle. Nothing else made sense. There was no other way that Aedan could have found out that he knew Arleth was on Tocarra and the exact time when he would be opening the portal so Val could sneak through. Absalom silently cursed himself he should have been more careful when he and Rogan had discussed the discovery. He should have taken more precautions while planning his trip. He had grown cocky and if Aedan had happened to have a Toccaran artefact, the consequences would have been disastrous. But the king wasn't a man to be made a fool of twice. In the future he would take the necessary safeguards and as soon as he got back to his castle he would root out each and every one of Aedan's spies. Now though, he had to concentrate on finding the girl.

He looked over at Bella and Kiran. The ridiculous pair were still strapped to the Greken's back, still clinging on as if they would fall down at any moment. They had arrived a few minutes after he did and had not stopped bickering ever since. Bella was yelling at Kiran for allowing Arleth to escape and Kiran was yelling back at his mother for not caring about him and for making him ride a Greken. Although Absalom found their snivelling drivel tiring, he smiled. It was quite fortunate that Arleth had ended up here. The two had never once questioned why a man had run at Kiran and Arleth, how he had beaten the Greken or where he was now. They were too preoccupied in their own petty interests. Once he found Arleth it would be a simple matter to take her back to Oherra with him. He could tell these two almost anything and he could be sure they would believe him. Thinking about it, these two were so dumb that he probably hadn't even needed such an elaborate cover story involving the lynstones. Oh well, he thought, it was better to be prepared. He took a deep breath; he would need to yell loudly to be heard over their incessant racket.

* * *

While King Absalom was yelling at mother and son to be quiet, a mile away in the town of Sonohan, Arleth crouched behind a fruit stand. The owner of which was a small balding man who was staring at her in surprise. His gaze travelled from the girl crouched down behind his merchandise up to the red flare and the words "Runaway" written in the sky. Arleth followed his glance and pleadingly put her fingers to her lips in an effort to keep him silent.

"RUNAWAY!" The man screamed at the top of his lungs. "I found her, she is right here!" He waved his arms in the air and pointed at where Arleth was hiding.

Jerk! Arleth thought. This was the third time in as many hiding spots that this had happened. Did no one in this town have any empathy towards escaped slaves? She got up and looked around her. Instantly she noticed her assailant at the other end of the alley. He had been alerted by the balding man's cries and was now running directly at her. Cursing she bolted through the street in the other direction. The last time he had found her, she had thought she had heard him yell something. She wasn't sure what - it sounded like her name, but she knew that was impossible. She had ignored him and kept on running. It was probably someone else's yelling she had heard. As though to confirm her conclusion, this time the man remained silent in his pursuit.

She raced down the street, weaving in and out of the crowd. Most of the townspeople just stared in interest at the slave girl and the man chasing her. However, some of the people she passed reached out to grab her. Undoubtedly they thought that the man chasing her was her owner and if they helped him, they would be given a reward. Luckily, she managed to avoid them all and turning a corner, found herself in a deserted side street. How long was it going to take Bella and Kiran to find her? She didn't know how long she could keep this up for.

Running down the street she noticed with horror that the street she had turned into was a dead end. She stopped and turned around, maybe she would have time to run back out before the man reached her. She took a few steps forward before she saw the man turn the corner into the alley. Heart hammering, she turned back around and ran deeper into the alley. She looked desperately for a way out. A small alley she had missed, a ladder, an open window into a home. But there was nothing. The man was only a few paces away from her; she could hear his footsteps on the ground behind her getting ever closer. She could feel the tears start to form in her eyes. She had run all the way to Sonohan, she had evaded the man for this long all to die here, alone, in a deserted alley. She didn't want it to end like this, but she was running out of options.

Suddenly, at the very end of the alley lying in the corner she noticed a long log. She had no idea what it was doing there but it gave her an idea. She had no delusions that she could beat this man in a fight, but she might be able to at least stun him long enough so that she could run around him and back out of the alley. She knew it was a long shot, but it was the best and really only option she had. With a deep breath to steady her heartbeat, she went over to the log and bent down to pick it up. It was then that she noticed that there was a small gap. The last house on the right side of the alley did not match up completely with the back of the house at the end of alley. It left a small crevice that wasn't visible from the street. Arleth thought that she was probably small enough to fit inside. If she wedged herself in far enough, the man wouldn't be able to reach her. With no further thought, she thrust herself inside and squeezed in as far as she could. It was a very tight fit and she could feel the bricks grazing against her skin. The bricks were uneven and she could feel her shins and cheek get cut by some of the bricks that stuck out. Although it hurt, she gave her pain very little thought. She could put up with it if it kept her alive.

Suddenly a hand reached for her and narrowly missed her dress. The man was right outside! She wedged herself a bit farther in. He grabbed for her again, but he couldn't reach her. She could hear the man cursing outside. Slowly, Arleth's breathing slowed; for the moment she was safe. But her problem was hardly solved. She couldn't stay here forever and she certainly couldn't go back out the way she had come. The man would be waiting for her. That left her one option: to keep squeezing her way forward and hope that it would have another exit. To that aim, she continued to push forward. The bricks continued to graze against her body and she was certain now that some had cut into her skin. But she realized that the passageway wasn't getting any narrower which meant that she could still go forward. She didn't hear the man's curses anymore. He must have given up yelling and had decided to wait silently for her to come out.

The crevice was still too narrow for her to turn her head around. And so she had to feel her way forward with her right hand. After a few minutes she realized that the bricks were no longer grazing her cheek; the passageway was getting wider! She cautiously turned her head to face forward. With delight she discovered that she now had room to do this and also that there was light ahead of her. If she kept going, within a few minutes she would be out of here and with any luck the man would still be waiting for her on the other side. Spurred on by hope, she pushed her way faster through the tunnel.

All of a sudden the light ahead disappeared and she felt a heavy hand grab her arm. With a scream, Arleth tried to free herself from the grasp, but wedged in as she was, she had no leverage with which to do so. The hand started pulling her towards its owner. The man must have realized that she could get through the crevice and had gone to find where she would end up. Desperately, ignoring the pain against her face, she pushed her face towards her right hand and with all her might bit down on the hand that was grabbing her. A woman's voice cried out in pain and the hand quickly retreated.

A woman's voice? Arleth thought to herself. Was it Bella? It could be, but it could also be a townsperson. The man, upon seeing her enter the gap could have easily enlisted the help of some of the town's people. They would undoubtedly know where she would exit from. Children especially might use this crevice as a hiding place and they with their parents encouraging them would be more than happy to help the man they thought was a slave owner. Arleth stopped moving forward. She didn't know which direction she should go. The man could be behind her waiting for her or he could be ahead of her. She didn't know any longer. She froze where she was and put her hands at her sides. At least it would be harder to grab her now.

At least that was what she thought, and continued to think as she was roughly pulled out of the crevice and deposited on the ground outside.

Chapter 8

Arleth closed her eyes against the onslaught of sunlight that met her as she was pulled out. She could feel strong hands holding on to her as she fought, kicking and screaming against her captor.

"Calm down Arleth," a deep voice said, "You are safe now." Surprised, Arleth went silent and stopped kicking. Slowly she opened her eyes, bracing against the sun and looked into the handsome face of King Absalom. He was staring at her bemusedly, his hands still clasped tightly around her wrists. They remained frozen like this for a few more seconds and then the king, satisfied that he was indeed holding a girl rather than a wild animal, released her. A smile came to his lips as he put his arms back at his sides and he backed away from her a few paces.

Arleth, was now able to see her surroundings and when she looked around she immediately noticed two things. First, she was standing in the middle of a large open area that might have been the central marketplace of the town. It was crammed with people who had all stopped what they were doing and were staring at her with interest. And second, the purplish blotchy colour of Bella's face indicated that Bella was very far from pleased with the whole situation. In fact, the woman was positively fuming with anger. If it was possible for steam to actually blow out of a person's ears, Arleth felt certain that now would be the time for it to happen. But since it wasn't, Bella's anger had instead decided to display itself in a disgustingly contorted face, and a bulging vein at the side of her head. She was trying to say something, but as angry as she was, she couldn't get the words out. She could only manage to open and close her mouth violently like a fish gasping for air. Arleth also noticed that Bella was cradling her right hand which was starting to turn the colour of her face. So it *was* Bella that she had bitten! It was comforting to know that she had least managed to inflict some small injury on her.

Arleth felt her lips begin to curl up into a smile. She tried to control it, but the distortions and soundless mouth opening of the violet-coloured beach ball in front of her proved too much for her to handle. She smiled broadly and then not able to control herself burst out laughing. What the heck, she thought. Bella was already furious at her and despite the unpleasant situation Arleth knew she was in, she couldn't help feeling a bit elated. A few minutes ago in the alley she had felt certain she was going to die. And now, even though she knew that punishment was imminent and no end to her slavery was in sight, at least she would be alive to talk about it. But what *was* "it?" She still had no idea why the man had been running after her or who he was. Ever curious, she wanted to find out, but Bella, even more infuriated by Arleth's laughing had regained her voice and interrupted Arleth's musings with a loud shriek.

"ARLETH!" She yelled coming towards her menacingly. "How dare you try and run away from me! You stupid, good-for-nothing brat! I paid good money for you and on top of that I am generous enough to give you a roof over your head and food every day. I shouldn't have been so kind to you. You are nothing! Worse than the sand I kick under my feet and yet I keep you in my house. And you dare to try and run away from?!?" During this tirade, Bella had crossed the distance between them and was now standing toe to toe with her. Bella raised her meaty hand to slap Arleth in the face. Arleth closed her eyes and braced herself for the impact.

But it never came.

"There is no need for that," King Absalom said grabbing Bella's arm in mid-swing. "I think it is pretty obvious that this girl was running away from the man who killed the Greken." Absalom had grown tired of diplomacy and stopped caring about choosing his words so carefully. He had just about enough of these two stupid, irritating buffoons. He had come as close as he wanted to losing Arleth to Val and he didn't want to waste anymore time being diplomatic with these idiots. "Your son ran away when he saw the man running at him. This girl, Arleth, was left behind. She must have been terrified and when she saw the man kill the Greken and continue coming after her, she did the only logical thing, run away in the opposite direction. It just so happened that the opposite direction was away from your property and into the town, which set off her grapel."

Bella had turned to face the king when he had grabbed her arm and was now staring at him in undisguised loathing. She jerked her arm free from his grasp with an angry grunt and clasped her hands in front of her. She wasn't stupid enough to try and hit Arleth again, but with the way her hands were clenched together with her knuckles going white, it was clear that she was using all of her effort to restrain herself. "I don't really think it is any of your business to interfere in the punishment of my slave," said Bella in as restrained a voice as she could manage.

"In that you are quite wrong," said Absalom. "By the terms of the Settlement of Edika laid out after The Great War, the King of Oherra has a duty to keep peace in all of the worlds. If it is my responsibility to maintain diplomatic relations for the entire universe, I think it is safe to presume that stopping a slave from being persecuted wrongfully is quite within my right." Although Absalom kept his voice calm and even, Arleth thought she saw a hint of a smile. She couldn't be sure though, if it was there, it was gone almost as soon as it had appeared.

Bella looked ready to explode. Although she knew that the King of Oherra was more important than her, she didn't enjoy being reminded of it. She especially didn't like that the King had chosen to remind her by standing up for her disobedient slave. And to make matters even worse, she had been utterly embarrassed not only in front of Arleth but in front of the dozens of townspeople who had been curiously watching the whole spectacle. Most of whom were now talking animatedly to their neighbours in hushed tones, but the snatches of conversation that drifted out were enough to set Bella's blood to boil.

".... hahahaha you're right she *does* look just like a purple bubble with arms...."

"..... Actually to me she looks more like a mouldy juka berry, see how her face isn't solid purple, but splotchy...."

".... Ah yes, that is true, but bubbles are larger. Ok how about a very oversized mouldy, juka berry?"

"Well that serves her right for being so snobby. I always said she was too proud for her own good....."

".....Oh certainly, but really how embarrassing, to be told off in front of her own slave."

Arleth listened to these exchanges with amusement. It certainly felt good to have Bella told off in front of her. After all these years of being bullied and tormented by Bella, it was satisfying that the woman was finally being put in her place. It was even better that all these people had been here to witness it. And *even* better that she had been the cause of it. It was sweet revenge at its finest.

But why had the king interfered for her? He certainly didn't have to. What would he care if a slave was being mistreated?

Bella for her part didn't seem to understand it either. She was still standing with her hands clasped tightly in front of her, anger etched on every feature of her face. But she hadn't yet responded to Absalom, mostly because she really had nothing to say. Bella knew he was right; his authority was far superior to hers. Although her pride had been sorely wounded, she could think of nothing that would repair it. So, uncharacteristically, she had made a quite intelligent decision: she would remain silent until she had something to say.

"I'm glad you agree," said Absalom, continuing on as though he hadn't stopped. He pretended not to notice the way Bella was glaring at him with pure hatred. Instead he looked over at Arleth, his gaze drifting down to her ankle and the grapel that was still emitting a bright red flare. "Well since we have satisfied ourselves that she is not running away, I think it is past time that blasted thing was turned off." With that he pulled out a small blade that had been tucked into his belt and walked over to Arleth.

"Put out your leg for me please," said Absalom bending down in front of her. "I won't hurt you. If I can just break this thing...." He trailed off, intent on what he was doing. He grabbed her foot and put it on his outstretched leg. Then, shoving his fingers between the grapel and her skin so as not to cut her, he started sawing at it with his knife.

Arleth didn't think it was going to work, she thought the grapel would prove too strong for the king's blade. But to her surprise she saw that it was indeed starting to cut through. The blade must be a lot sharper than it looked she thought. But she supposed that only made sense: the creatures were certainly different on Oherra, of course their weapons would be too. No matter how strong the king's blade was though, she knew that the grapel would not shut off once it was off of her leg.

Bella knew that too and it made her smile through her anger. She couldn't take away her past embarrassment, or make the townspeople stop their gossip, but she could take satisfaction from the fact that Absalom would look foolish when he realized he didn't know how to turn off the grapel. She looked on with anticipation.

"There almost done," said Absalom, cutting through the last bit of the grapel. The device broke apart in his hand but it was still emitting a bright red beam. To Bella's horror the king didn't even seem fazed. He put both pieces in his hand, stood up and dumped them into Bella's arms. "I'm sure you have a way to turn this off. Otherwise Toccarra would be filled with red beaming lights."

Bella spluttered something incomprehensible in reply and looked sadly down at her broken grapel. She pressed a small blue button on the inside of one of the pieces and said, "Bella Sneel. Runaway has been captured." Instantly the red light turned off and the words "Runaway" disappeared from the sky.

"Much better. Now," said Absalom, turning to face Arleth again "I have more important matters to attend to." Arleth stared at the man in disbelief. In the past five minutes he had embarrassed Bella, stopped the woman from hitting her *and* taken off her grapel. Why he would do any one of these things for her she had no idea. And he had done all three as if they were nothing. She felt like whatever he was going to say next would be just as surprising.

"The man that killed my greken and then chased after you, did you see his face?"

"Yes I did. He was wearing a dark hood but during the fight with the greken it fell off and I could see his face clearly."

"What did he look like?"

"Well," said Arleth thinking back, "He was pretty ordinary except for a long scar across his face; brown hair, brown eyes."

Absalom nodded to himself. Now, not only did he know for certain that it was Val, but the man had unwittingly given him a plausible reason to take Arleth back with him to Oherra.

"I believe that the man was following you because you saw his face. Back on Oherra, I have been plagued by a group of secretive assassins called the Black Thorn. They wear all black, cover their faces with hoods and carry long daggers. Am I correct in assuming that the man had these characteristics?"

"Yes he did," said Arleth

"As I thought, they must have gotten wind that I was travelling to Tocarra and one of their number must have followed me here. I am of course less protected here than on my own planet. Unfortunately, we have never been able to catch one of them alive. The fact that you saw his face meant that you could identify him. And that is very dangerous information for their group. He had to kill you so that you couldn't lead me to him and then through him to the rest of his associates. However, he failed and that works out wonderfully for me. I would like you to come back to Oherra with me. You would be very useful in identifying this man, and to be honest you aren't safe here anyways. Knowing how persistent these particular assassins are, he won't stop trying to kill you until he has succeeded. I have my own servants of course in my castle, but I daresay I treat them better than I have witnessed them get treated here. I believe you will have a better home with me in Oherra than you had here. What do you say? Will you come and help me?"

Arleth was speechless. She was being invited to go and live in Oherra, in Iridian Castle itself! Of course she wanted to go. She couldn't remember wanting anything more in her entire life. She wouldn't have to endure Kiran's taunts and Bella's cruelty and she would get to travel to a whole other world. A magical world, the *most important magical world*, the one that she had dreamed about for her entire life. Arelth was about to open her mouth to give her enthusiastic approval, when Bella loudly interjected.

"Don't be ridiculous. You can't just go around stealing other people's slaves. I paid good money for her."

"I can actually," Absalom interjected "But don't worry, I will compensate you. And I believe you will find my offer more than fair. Let me see, you probably paid about 200 shintins for her. Your money is worth less than Oherran money, but since I am taking away your property and you have arranged comfortable accommodations for myself and my servants in your mansion, I will give you the same in Oherran coins. 200 renes. I believe you will find the exchange rate greatly in your favour and Oherran money can be used anywhere in the universe.

Bella's eyes literally popped out of her head. "200 renes? For her?" Bella was far from cultured but she knew money and she was well aware that 200 renes was almost double what she paid for Arleth.

"Mother, that is a lot of money isn't it? Why would he pay so much for such a useless id.." Bella quickly quieted her son with a hand over his mouth. She looked at king Absalom and smiled as sweetly as she could. "That sounds like a deal."

"And what about you Arleth?" Said Absalom turning to face her. "Is that ok? Would you like to come to Oherra with me?"

Arleth was so surprised and so happy by her sudden turn of luck that all she could mutter was a "Hmmm" followed by a vigorous nod.

"Good that is settled then," said Absalom. "We will leave this afternoon. I don't want to stay here for another night when there is an assassin running loose. I'll gather my servants and then we will be leaving. I will discuss the lynstones with my advisors when I return to Oherra and in a few weeks I will send an envoy with my decision."

"Sure that is fine," Bella replied. She was more than happy to see the king leave early. She had made a huge profit on her slave and if she didn't have to spend another night hosting a banquet it was even better. As far as she was concerned, the sooner he left the better.

Absalom turned and started walking back to the city's gates. Arleth followed him in a daze. She barely noticed the crowd part for them to pass, her walk to the edge of town or the Greken she rode back to Bella's mansion on. Her mind wasn't on Tocarra, but deep in her imagination, busy thinking about what Oherra would be like.

* * *

"And he put her in her place in front of all those people? I would have liked to see that!"

Arleth was sitting in the kitchen with Chuck, back at Bella's mansion. Word had travelled fast once they had returned; it had only been a matter of minutes before the whole household knew that Arleth was leaving for Oherra with the king. But they weren't leaving immediately: Absalom needed to organize his servants and arrange his departure. So Arleth had been given a few hours to pack her belongings and say goodbye to her friends before they had to leave. Since she had no belongings and no one she could call a friend aside from Chuck, she had decided to sit with him for her remaining hours in Tocarra. She was in the process of telling him what had happened.

"Yes he did! Bella was so angry her face was actually purple."

Chuck started laughing and Arleth laughed along with him. "Well that is something, isn't it? But Arleth, enough about that, you are going to Oherra! You must be so excited."

"Oh Chuck I am! I am so excited I can barely contain myself. I want to jump up and down, laugh uncontrollably, scream for joy and run around the mansion all at the same time. I can't believe that I am actually going to go to Oherra. I always dreamt about seeing a magical world and Oherra is by far the most magical world there is. And now I get to actually live there."

Chuck smiled at her, "I am so happy for you Arleth."

Arleth thought for only about the hundredth time in the past couple of hours about how lucky she was. Only this morning she had been desperately running for her life. Her only thought was how she was going to survive to the next moment. As a measure of her plight, she had even been looking forward to seeing Bella and Kiran. She had been faced with slavery or death, none of which were attractive and she had chosen accordingly. But now, not only had she managed to run away from the assassin, but by the sheer fact that she had seen his face, the king had invited her to come to Oherra with him. She would never have to see Bella and Kiran again.

That fact by itself was worth celebrating.

She had to admit that it was a bit strange that he had given Bella so much money for her. But she guessed that he must be very intent on catching the assassins. No matter how accurate a description she could give, it would certainly be better to have her with him in Oherra so she could actually spot the man. Besides, what seemed like a lot of money to her or to Bella was probably nothing for the King of Oherra. And who was she to question the actions of a king? She had been given some good luck and just because she wasn't used to things going her way didn't mean that she should question them. She pushed any further questions of this nature out of her mind.

At that moment, the kitchen door opened and in popped a sandy blonde head. It was Sally, one of Bella's bath slaves. "The king is leaving now. He is waiting for *you* to join him." She punctuated "you" with as much venom as she could muster. She was jealous of Arleth and didn't try to hide it. Arleth pretended not to have noticed Sally's tone,

"Thank you Sally, I will be there in one minute," she said, smiling innocently at the blonde girl. Sally just glared at Arleth with pure malice. Arleth couldn't say that she blamed her really. There was no difference between the two of them; they were both roughly the same age, both had been Bella's slaves since they were young children, but now Arleth was going to leave Bella forever, while Sally was stuck here indefinitely. If their situations were reversed, Arleth would have liked to think that she would have acted differently but she really wasn't sure. That thought only made her feel slightly bad for the girl though; Sally had never been nice to her. In fact she was one of the worst tattle-tales among all of Bella's slaves. She had gotten Arleth into trouble more times than she could count. Arleth hated to admit it, but she was enjoying Sally's jealousy quite a bit.

She looked into Chuck's kind, wrinkled face. He was smiling at her warmly. She did feel bad for him though. He had never partaken in the gossip and backstabbing of the other slaves. He had always been nice to her, giving her treats here and there. Since Flora died, he had been the closest thing to a friend she had. Sadly Arleth turned to face him, grabbing both of his hands with hers.

"I will miss you Chuck," said Arleth. She almost wished she could bring him with her to Oherra. She felt guilty leaving him behind when she was leaving to another, more exciting world.

"I will miss you too," said Chuck. And then as if he were reading her mind, "Don't worry about me Arleth. An old man like me gets used to things, doesn't like to change. But you are a young, curious woman. Go and have your adventures."

"Oh but if only you could come too."

"No Arleth, I have lived my whole life on Tocarra, who knows if I would even like Oherra? Besides, the desert heat is good for my old bones. Here, take this." He gently removed his hands from within hers and walked over to the other side of the kitchen. He returned carrying a small package. "It's not much, just some bread and dried fruit, but I don't know how long your journey is and you might get hungry."

Arleth took the bundle from him gratefully and gave him a big hug. "Thank you Chuck. Good bye."

"Bye Arleth. Have many great adventures for me, ok?"

"I will."

Arleth turned and walked out of the kitchen behind Sally. She cast one last look back at Chuck and waved before she disappeared around the corner and into the hall. She walked down the hall and through the mansion, ignoring the glares and whispers of the other slaves she passed. At the main entrance, she was met by one of Absalom's servants who led her outside. Absalom was standing in a circle with Kiran and Bella, his servants and Grekens arranged behind him. Undoubtedly the three of them were saying their diplomatic goodbyes. But the tension was evident. Bella hadn't forgiven Absalom for embarrassing her in front of all those people, but she also didn't want to lose the 200 renes for Arleth or a trade agreement for the lynstones. So she was being as diplomatic as possible, but still making a statement by not having any of her slaves coming to see the king off. Absalom saw Arleth almost immediately,

"Ahh there you are," he called to her. "Come now, we should be leaving soon."

Arleth hurried over to where they were standing.

"I look forward to hearing from you soon," said Bella, finishing off their conversation.

"Yes, I will send word in a few weeks. In the meantime, I hope that both you and your son stay well. Hopefully we can usher in a new era of trade between the Sneels and the Amaras." He turned towards Arleth, smiled and gestured her to follow him. Arleth looked at Bella and Kiran, she desperately wanted to say something to them. To tell Bella that she was an oversized buffoon or to laugh in Kiran's face. But Absalom had already started walking away, and she realized, disappointedly that doing either of those things was very childish. She didn't want to appear like a little child in front of Absalom. Besides, she had already had her victory over them; they could never bother her again. Proud at herself for taking the high road, she turned and walked after Absalom.

She had only taken a few steps when she stopped. Oh but it was so tempting. She looked at the king a few paces ahead of her, he still hadn't looked back at her. Well, she thought, maybe just a... she turned and looked back at Kiran. She gave him the ugliest face she could make and stuck out her tongue. Kiran looked at her in shock. She smiled as she turned back around. That had been well worth it; there was time to be mature later.

Absalom hadn't noticed Arleth making faces at Kiran. In fact he probably wouldn't have noticed if she *had* started yelling insults at the pair of them. For he was deep in his own thoughts. He had lied to them all. He had no interest in Bella's lynstones, not even in the slightest. True there had been a trade agreement between the Sneels and the Amaras generations ago, but at the moment he had more important things to worry about than trade. He had also lied to Arleth about why he wanted her to come to Oherra. Val wasn't an assassin, there was no group of assassins after him, and if there were he certainly didn't need her help to find them. But his lie had served him well. She had believed him and it had allowed him to take her off of Tocarra with him. He couldn't tell her the truth, not here and certainly not now. If she knew the real reason why he wanted her, why she was so important to him, she would be overwhelmed. No, he had done the right thing; he would tell her when the time was right.

He called one of his grekens over to him and muttered something in its ear. He knew that Val would be following behind in the portal, he had to; he had no other way back to Oherra. And Absalom wanted to make very sure that Val did make it back. He wanted Aedan to hear of Val's failure first hand. It would spur him to do something rash. Something like coming after her alone. She was too valuable to Aedan for him to just accept defeat. He would have to do something. And Absalom would be waiting when he did. If Arleth could allow him to finally capture Aedan after all these years, she would be very useful indeed. Absalom looked back at Arleth and smiled. She smiled back unaware of the thoughts going through the king's head. That girl had the power to break the years of stalemate between him and Aedan. But she was blissfully unaware of her importance. Absalom hoped he could keep it that way for a little while longer.

Chapter 9

Arleth hadn't known what to expect when she walked through the portal, but she had certainly never imagined what she now saw. First of all, she hadn't really walked *through* the portal at all, more like *into* it. She was standing at the entrance of a wide, dark tunnel. Even though the portal was still open behind her, with more of Absalom's servants filing through, it was so dark that she could barely make out the shape of the king who was standing only a few feet in front of her. It was as if the tunnel was sucking in the light. She felt something brush against her shoulder and she flinched involuntarily. Someone was passing beside her. She heard soft voices ahead and a few more shadowy forms materialized out of the gloom, joining the dark figure of the king. A slow eerie melody drifted out of the shadows. It began softly, barely audible and then grew steadily louder until it reached a constant pitch. A woman's voice started singing,

> Through the dark I call to thee,
> From every corner, crevice or crack
> Wake from sleep and fly to me.
>
> Be mindful of your ancient pact,
> Hidden in shadow for evils past,
> Bound to serve those seeking way.
>
> Hear this song I sing to you,
> Light our way and guide us through.

Arleth began to hear a faint rustling far in the distance. As she listened, it grew louder and became more defined. It sounded like thousands of wings beating together. Along with the sound, a faint circle of light began to form on the right side of the tunnel. At first it was just barely visible, a faint glow in the darkness, but it steadily grew larger and larger until a significant area of the tunnel had been illuminated. It was bright enough now that Arleth could see that the tunnel wasn't straight, but turned sharply to the left about 400 paces in front of her. It was from around this bend that the source of the light and the fluttering noise was coming from. Whatever the woman had called in her song was approaching from there. Arleth had no idea what would emerge around the corner but she was pretty sure that whatever it was, there were a lot of them. She could feel her heart pounding in excitement. She had only just stepped out of Tocarra and she was already going to witness something remarkable.

The light continued to grow larger and larger, reflected onto the tunnel wall. The fluttering noise, accompanying the increasing light, had grown almost deafening and Arleth found herself covering her ears with her hands. A sharp gust of air blew into her, knocking her back a few paces into the person standing behind her. But Arleth hardly noticed the gentle push that helped her regain her balance, for at that moment, the creatures had finally emerged from around the corner. Arleth stared at them in delight; completely transfixed.

They were magnificent!

Hovering in the air above them were thousands of tiny winged creatures. They had stopped flapping and were instead soundlessly floating with their wings outstretched. Arleth stared at the creatures wordlessly. She racked her brain for all the creatures she knew, had seen, or had heard about, but none of them even came close to describing what she now saw. Each creature appeared to be slightly different than the one beside it. The only thing they seemed to all have in common were their wings, which glowed so brightly that they bathed the whole tunnel in light. Aside from that, Arleth didn't even know where to begin to draw similarities. They were all different colours; some were gold, some blue, some green; and some were colours that Arleth didn't even have a name for. Some appeared to have two legs, some had four or six, while others didn't appear to have any legs at all. The more she looked at the creatures, the more varieties she found. Arleth felt certain that if she had spent days just looking at each one closely, she wouldn't be able to find two that looked quite the same.

One of the creatures detached itself from the mass and floated down to hover around Arleth's nose. She gave a delighted laugh and held out her hand. It flew down and softly landed in her palm. Slowly, Arleth brought her hand to her face and stared at the creature curiously. The creature stared right back at her, just as curious as she was. Its skin was the colour of magenta and looked shiny and smooth. It had four arms that were spaced equal distances from each other in a row across the front of the creature's body. On top of its head there were three black antennae that were all leaning in Arleth's direction. Below its wings at the back of its body was a long curled tail that ended in a triangle shaped tip. Despite how strange it looked, Arleth thought it was adorable.

"Hello little one," she said softly. "What are you?"

"They are garrupi," said Absalom with a smile on his face coming to stand beside Arleth. The creature flew away, startled by the newcomer and both Arleth and Absalom watched as it floated back up to join its friends.

"Garrupi?"

"Yes. They are a very ancient race. A long time ago, before the Great War, they lived all over Oherra. They were nomads, living wherever the fancy took them."

"Why do they all look so different?"

"They have the remarkable ability to change their features and skin colour at will. The only feature they are stuck with are their wings. As a result, you will find no two garrupi that are exactly the same. Quite fascinating really."

"So what happened to them," said Arleth, anticipating the story. "Why are they here in the portal?"

"Well," said Absalom, looking vaguely annoyed that he had been interrupted again, "They committed a grievous sin."

"What did they do?"

"If you let me finish..." Absalom said a bit angrily, the annoyance showing more clearly on his face. He was a man who wasn't used to being interrupted, especially not by one of his servants. When the King of Oherra spoke, everyone around him listened.

Arleth nodded hurriedly, "Sorry."

Absalom stared at her for a couple more seconds as if to make sure she wasn't going to say anything further and then continued. "As I was saying, the garrupi committed a despicable crime.

At that time, the Garrupi desperately wanted to live in a southern Oherran city called Whinton. Situated on the coast and surrounded by lush forests, it was said to have been a very beautiful city. It was prosperous, cultured, and vibrant. It is no surprise then, that the garrupi were drawn to it. At first, the town's leaders had no problem with the garrupi living there. Whinton was home to many different races and the garrupi were just one of many. However, their nomadic, free-spirited way of life started to cause problems. They refused to pay taxes. They set up their homes wherever they pleased even if it was in the middle of a street or on someone else's property. Such things as private property and belongings meant nothing to them. But probably worst of all, they would impersonate prominent city officials and leaders. Since they could change their size, features, and colour at will they could perfectly copy anyone they chose. On one particular instance, a group of young garrupi thought it would be fun to kidnap the city's leaders and impersonate them. A group of delegates from the neighbouring world of Sancronea were due to meet with these city officials. They met with the garrupi youth instead, not knowing that they were imposters. The garrupi insulted the delegates so thoroughly and caused so much trouble that a war was almost started. After this incident, when the confusion was sorted out and the real officials were back in power, a council met to discuss the problem of the garrupi. It was decided that the garrupi as a whole were too dangerous and too troublesome to be within the city and the entire population was banished from Whinton.

The garrupi thought this was a terrible injustice and so they banded together and attacked the city. In the battle that ensued, the city was burned to the ground and thousands of people were killed. After the fires were finally put out and the dead accounted for and buried, it was concluded that something drastic had to be done with the garrupi.

The most powerful sorcerers on Oherra decided to curse them. Their entire population was dispersed and sent to live in the darkest places on Oherra; in caves, mountain passes, underground caverns. Anywhere that the sun never touched, and they were forced to live in these places generation after generation for eternity. As a nomadic race, this was a terrible punishment to bestow upon them. Their freedom to live where they wanted had been taken away forever. This wasn't enough for the sorcerers though. They didn't just want to punish the garrupi, they wanted to humiliate them. And so they enchanted their wings to glow with inner light and bound them through the song that you just heard to aid any and all travellers who happened to be entering one of these shadowy places. The sorcerers also cast a restriction spell on the garrupi, which limited their ability to change size. Before, size was one of the features they were able to alter at will. They could become much larger than a man or smaller than a mouse or anything in between whenever they wanted. But the restriction spell ensured that they could not grow larger than ten inches. This was of course a further method of humiliation, but it was also pragmatic as it limited their ability to cause harm in the future.."

Arleth had remained silent through the entire story, but now she had some questions. What the garrupi had done was indeed terrible, but she didn't think it was fair to punish a whole race for the crimes of a small minority. Also, they had committed these crimes thousands of years ago. Why should the current generations of garrupi still be so severely punished for crimes they never committed? She wanted to voice these thoughts but she knew better than to tell them to Absalom. He seemed quite satisfied with the garrupi's punishment. Instead, when she was certain that he had finished his story, she said, "Oh, I see. That *was* a very terrible thing that the garrupi did." She hoped she sounded convincing.

"Yes it was. But as it turns out their punishment has been quite useful to me. I would be hard-pressed to light up the portal so well if it wasn't for them."

Arleth nodded and looked up at the garrupi hovering in the air above her. Throughout the conversation she and Absalom had been walking down the tunnel and they had just reached the bend. The two of them were at the head of the procession and as she looked back she could see that Absalom's servants were still entering the portal. The garrupi had dispersed and were hovering above the whole line of people. They glowed so brightly that Arleth could clearly see down to the opening of the portal where she had come from and ahead of her around the bend. Absalom was right; the garrupi served a very valuable purpose here in the portal.

Arleth and Absalom rounded the bend and the portal opening disappeared from sight. They walked side by side for a few minutes in silence. Arleth had a hundred questions she wanted to ask, but she restrained herself. Absalom didn't seem like a man who had a lot of patience and he had already been kind enough to tell her the story of the garrupi. And she reminded herself, she had already managed to annoy him by constantly interrupting him with questions. She looked over at him striding confidently along beside her. He was still walking beside her though. If he was annoyed with her wouldn't he have left her side by now? She wasn't sure and she certainly didn't want to overstep her bounds, although she wasn't really sure what her role was. She had noticed that with the exception of a few words with his Grekens, Absalom didn't talk to any of the other servants except for a few perfunctory commands. Certainly he hadn't spoken to them the way he had just conversed with her. Well, she concluded, there was only one way to find out exactly how he viewed his relationship with her. She would ask one more question. A simple one, one that wouldn't require a lot of explanation, but one that she was quite curious about.

"How long until we arrive in Oherra?" Arleth asked.

Absalom looked over at her in surprise. He appeared to have been lost in thought, but surprisingly he didn't seem annoyed that his thoughts had been interrupted. "Sorry I didn't catch that."

"How long until we get to Oherra?" Arleth repeated.

"Oh, about 3 hours."

"3 *hours* !?!" Arleth couldn't help but interrupt.

"Oherra and Toccara are on opposite sides of the universe so it is a longer journey than it would be to travel to closer worlds" the king said briskly.

Absalom looked like he was about to add something else, an admonishment perhaps, but at that moment one of his Grekens came up beside him. Absalom looked at him and walked quickly ahead of Arleth, distancing himself from her. She saw the Greken gesture behind him and then Absalom smiled. They continued talking together for a few moments and then the Greken fell back in line somewhere behind Arleth. Absalom remained by himself at the head of the procession. Arleth wondered what the Greken had said, Absalom certainly looked interested. But she was curious, not stupid and she knew better than to ask *that*.

At the head of the procession Absalom smiled to himself. Val had entered the portal just as it was closing. He had known he would, but hearing it from his Greken had been very reassuring. His plan was working perfectly, actually, if he was honest with himself it was working out better than he had planned. He hadn't counted on Aedan finding out about Arleth being on Tocarra, but now that he had and Val had failed to reach her in time, it was just all the much better for him. Absalom couldn't wait to reach Oherra; the real fun was about to start. He looked briefly behind him at Arleth walking a few metres behind him. She was looking up at the garrupi and didn't notice the look he cast her way. Talking to her had dampened his spirits a bit. He hadn't thought it would be hard to win over a teenager. Especially a girl, he had certainly been more than successful in previous such endeavours. But she was different, she was much too curious and, if the rest of her family was any indication, she was probably quite clever too. He had already lost his patience with her; he would have to be more careful in the future. He needed her on his side; he couldn't afford to slip up again. She had to trust him.

Chapter 10

By the time they had finally reached the end of the tunnel and Absalom was preparing to open the way into Oherra, Arleth felt like she had been walking for days. Absalom had stayed by himself, a little ahead of the procession for the remainder of the journey. He hadn't spoken to anyone for the whole time; not to Arleth, any other servants nor his grekens. For that matter, none of the servants or Grekens talked to each other. Arleth thought this was a bit strange, but she didn't know what sort of rules Absalom had. She supposed it was quite possible that the king preferred to travel in silence. Since she really didn't know, Arleth remained silent too and didn't try and talk to any of the servants near her. Watching the garrupi occupied her attention in the beginning, but she lost interest in them after a while.

Left alone with only her own thoughts, she began to realize how exhausted she was and how much her feet hurt. The mile-long sprint across the desert and the chase through Sonohan, would have been enough to hurt anyone's feet. But Bella had never believed in giving her slaves shoes and so Arleth had ran all that way barefoot and was now walking barefoot through the tunnel. The floor of which was uneven and at frequent intervals a jagged stone would cut into one of her bare and already tired feet. Every step she took was painful.

But none of this dulled her excitement about going to Oherra. In fact, if anything, she grew more and more excited with each painful step she took down the tunnel. She hadn't had a clear picture in her head of what it would be like to go through a portal into Oherra. But having to walk through a tunnel for three hours had never crossed her mind. Although the details had always been fuzzy in her mind, the one thing she had assumed was that it would be faster. That one minute she would be in Tocarra and the next she would be in Oherra. The fact that this hadn't happened and she had nothing to occupy her attention, had made the wait unbearable.

As such, it was with great relief that almost three hours after they had entered the tunnel, they finally reached the end and Absalom halted the procession. Without looking back, he held his hand up above his shoulder to signal everyone to stay where they were. Arleth and the rest of the servants stopped where they were and waited for Absalom to open the portal. The servants were indifferent, they had seen this many times, but Arleth was practically jumping up and down with excitement. She desperately wanted to run up beside the king to watch what he was doing and get a closer look at how he opened the portal. It took all of her restraint to stay where she was, about 5 paces behind the king. She shuffled a bit to the side, practically standing on the person beside her in order to look around the king to what he was doing in front of him. The servant beside her looked at Arleth a bit curiously and moved over a few steps to give her room.

Even with the new vantage point, Arleth was disappointed to discover that she still couldn't see very much of what Absalom was doing. The way he was standing, with his feet firmly planted, shoulder-width apart, his body was effectively shielding what he was doing. She sighed sadly. Maybe if she craned her neck enough she could see around him. She took one more step to her right, and pivoted on her foot, craning her neck as far as it would go. It was at this moment, when she was outstretched most ungracefully and her face wore what could only be described as a constipated grimace, that she realized she was being watched. Her clumsy attempts to see what the king was doing had caught the attention of those servants standing nearest to her. They had all turned in her direction and were now staring at her.

Arleth looked slowly around her at all the faces staring back at her and blushed.

She silently chastised herself; what a great first impression she was making. Just wonderful! She was going to start off her new life in a new world with everyone thinking she was a lunatic. She smiled as endearingly as she could and fished around for something that she could say to redeem herself.

"Kandahanana cruente tosk," shattered the silence and saved Arleth from her embarrassed suffering.

These certainly weren't the words that Arleth had in mind, in fact she didn't know what they meant or even what language they were in, but they probably worked better than anything she could have said. Absalom had begun to open the portal and with these strange words, a light had begun to appear in front of him. Although Arleth couldn't be sure, the light looked to be originating from a small point directly in front of the king. Absalom turned and motioned to the Greken on his right and as he did so, Arleth was given a momentary glimpse of the king's left arm. She saw that tattooed on his wrist, no bigger than a fingernail was a silver crystal. It was from this symbol that the light was emanating from. It started as a small beam of concentrated light coming from his wrist and as she watched, the beam moved of its own accord to outline a door in the wall of the tunnel.

So this was how the Crystal Throne worked! Arleth was fascinated. The king's own body served as the means to open the portal! Arleth had never imagined that the legendary Crystal Throne artefact would be the king himself. But if she thought about it, she guessed that it did make sense.

Arleth was roughly jolted out of her reverie by a strong shove from behind. A greken had rushed up from behind her, not even noticing anything in its way as it hurried to stand at the king's side. The force of the impact caused Arleth to lose her balance and she stumbled a couple of steps to the left, waving her arms wildly in an effort to stay on her feet. This she managed to do, but for a few seconds she remained disoriented. As it was, her eyes saw while her mind gradually comprehended, the portal opening in front of her, the light slowly outlining the shape of the door and finally the door now completely illuminated, burst open to reveal the Oherran landscape.

Arleth, let out a gasp of excitement, which was quickly replaced by a small sigh of disappointment. She only had a brief glimpse of what was though the portal before it was quickly blocked by the burly bodies of the grekens who huddled together in front of the king. They formed a solid grey wall protecting the king from whatever possible danger could be awaiting him in Oherra.

Although she had spent the day being chased by an Oherran assassin, this was the first time that Arleth had thought about how dangerous this new world could be. She had realized this of course, it would have been hard not to after the day she had, but before now her excitement had been so great as to drown any other feeling out. She had also realized although she tried not to think about it, that just because the assassin had failed to kill her the first time did not mean he wouldn't try again. She was still very much in danger. If the man had chased her across the desert and through a whole city just to protect his identity he was not likely to give up so easily. She realized also that human assassins were most likely one of the least dangerous enemies on Oherra. There were bound to be hundreds of creatures on Oherra that Arleth had never even imagined existed, and Arleth was not naive enough to presume that they would all be friendly.

For the moment though, Arleth felt relatively safe surrounded by all the other servants, the Grekens and the king. She felt herself begin to relax and it wasn't long before her excitement had once again taken over and she was again anxiously awaiting when the Grekens would move out of the way and she could have her first real glimpse of Oherra.

Unfortunately, the procession moved slowly and Arleth had somehow shifted farther back in line. This time, she resisted the urge to sway to the left or right to see around them, remembering what had happened last time. As patiently as she could, she slowly walked behind the servants in front of her, feeling quite proud of her restraint. After a few minutes, she reached the door of the portal and as the servants directly in front of her stepped through, Arleth gasped at the beautiful scene laid before her.

The portal had opened on a small rise and so as the servants stepped out, they had stepped downwards, giving Arleth an unobstructed view. She was standing in a large circular valley about five miles in diameter. Surrounding the valley on all sides, enclosing it protectively was a wall of towering mountains. The tops of many were so tall that they were lost in the clouds. Arleth had never seen mountains so tall before, in fact she had never seen mountains before at all and she stared at them for a few seconds in amazement. She wondered how far the tallest of the mountains extended to, and what it would feel like to walk through the clouds.

Returning her attention to the valley, she saw that directly in the middle, equidistant from the surrounding mountains stood Iridian Castle. As a young girl learning about the histories of the worlds, Arleth had imagined plenty of castles, her mind giving plausibility to the most impossible creations of her imagination. But Iridian Castle was unlike any castle that she had ever imagined. The castle itself was entirely white, a kind of material (Arleth had no idea what) that seemed to glow with an internal luminescence. The sun was high in the sky and was glittering brightly off of its surface. Surprisingly though, the effect was not blinding; the castle appeared almost to absorb the sun's rays and cast them back out in a gentle ray of light. This gave the castle an ethereal quality that Arleth thought was wonderful; she thought it made the castle itself appear magical.

Arleth looked closer at the castle, her eyes running over the details of the structure. The castle appeared to be composed of eight separate sections of all different shapes and sizes that were each connected at ground level to the ones beside them by tall clear tunnels. Dozens of towers came up from the castle, some emerging from on top of one of the sections, while others were built to rest against the main bulk of the castle. Connecting all the towers to each other and to the main buildings were layers of twisting pathways. They were clear, and appeared to be built of the same material as the tunnels. But what was so fascinating to Arleth was that they connected the towers and buildings outside! The pathways ran at all different levels, some close to the ground, while others were hundreds of feet in the air. The ones higher up appeared to be completely enclosed while those nearer to the ground looked to be open, almost like a normal road back home on Tocarra.

Even more remarkable was a waterfall right in the middle of the castle. It appeared to have its base in a central courtyard but how it was standing there with no supporting mountain or water reserve Arleth had no idea. It appeared to just be hanging in the sky. Arleth was certain that this was created from magic, there was no way such a thing could exist otherwise. There was a brilliant rainbow gleaming in front of the waterfall. Her eyes followed it downwards to the base of the waterfall which was hidden by the walls of the courtyard. But she could see four openings in the wall through which four rivers of water burst forth. Once outside the courtyard, they each turned sharply from their central joining at the base of waterfall to cut across the valley, one flowing in each direction; east, west, south and north, dividing the valley into four sections. Arleth could not see where the rivers ended but she thought that they would probably end at the mountains, and she imagined, they would likely end as surreptitiously as they had began.

Arleth heard some mutterings behind her and she turned to look at a row of angry servants who were gesturing to each other and glaring at her. Arleth had been standing still while she was looking around her and now she was holding up the procession. She smiled embarrassedly and hurried down the slope after those in front that had continued walking and had left her behind.

For the next hour or so she walked, following those in front of her and although she didn't stop again, she couldn't keep from glancing constantly around her to take in as much of the scenery as she could. Unfortunately though, crammed as she was between rows of servants and now on flat land, she couldn't see very much of the valley around her. What she did notice though were the thousands of soldiers and Grekens strewn around the valley. Some were stationed near the mountains as if standing on guard from something beyond them. Others were sitting in small circles eating, resting or sharpening weapons. While yet others were in squadrons running through drills and daily exercises. It seemed clear to Arleth that Oherra was at war. There was a tense air among the soldiers, made even more palpable as the King strode through. Every soldier, be it Greken or man was alert. Even those who were resting or eating had their weapons close at hand and seemed ready to spring into action at a moment's notice.

Arleth realized now even more than before that she had gotten herself into something very dangerous. This was not child's play, it was not a joke. Going into Oherra was not all fun and games and excitement. Not that realizing this made her regret her decision in the least. She would have taken almost anything over having to spend the rest of her life as a slave to Bella. But more than that, she had yearned for adventure and magical worlds ever since she was a little girl learning about them from her teachers in the orphanage. It was childish to assume that such adventure would come without danger and Arleth realized that deep down she had already known and accepted this risk when she had first stepped out of Toccara and entered the portal.

When they reached the doors to the castle, the procession halted. Absalom called one of his servants over to him; a slight girl no older than Arleth with long auburn hair and a freckly face. The girl nodded, and with a small bow, turned away from him and made her way over to Arleth.

"The king wants me to show you to your quarters and give you a tour of the castle. Please come with me."

"Ok," Arleth nodded. Absalom had gone off to the side a few feet and was conversing in muted tones with two of his Grekens and with a towering giant of a man who had appeared out of nowhere. The rest of the servants, having reached their home had all dispersed. Most had gone into the castle, but some had remained outside, hurrying to whatever task they had yet to do.

With no further words, the girl turned and walked into the castle and Arleth hurried after her.

* * *

It had taken Arleth all but five minutes to realize that her tour guide had next to no personality. Her first hint had come a few seconds after their meeting when Arleth, striding beside the girl, introduced herself and asked the girl what her name was. The girl had looked at her curiously for a few moments and then said, as if Arleth had asked the most ridiculous question in the world, "I don't know. I haven't really thought about it." Arleth had been taken aback by this answer, but assumed that maybe the girl just had a quirky sense of humour. Arleth had tried again. But after two further minutes in which Arleth's friendly conversation had been met with nothing but silence, Arleth had come to the conclusion that the girl had the personality of a floor mat. Arleth had not tried to initiate conversation a third time and instead had walked beside the girl in silence.

They were now standing in a long narrow room, lined on both sides by rows of single beds. The girl was standing at the door waiting for Arleth to look around. She seemed utterly uninterested in what Arleth was doing and was instead looking out the nearest window sleepily. Arleth walked down the rows of beds until she came to one that looked untouched. There were no clothes laid out on it and it did not appear to have been slept in. Although the girl hadn't said anything beyond, "You can find a bed here," Arleth presumed that since there was nothing on this bed that she could take it. Arleth sat down on it for a few moments, bouncing up and down. She hadn't slept in a bed in seven years; not since she had been in the orphanage. Bella had had her sleep on the hall floor outside her bedchamber. Beside each bed was a small table with a lamp and two drawers. Arleth was a bit disappointed that she didn't have anything to put in them as she had been forced to leave everything behind when she fled the orphanage and Bella had certainly given her nothing to keep. What would she use then to mark this bed as her own? She looked at her clothes to see if there was something she could take off to put on the bed. But all she was wearing was the ugly brown dress that had served as her only clothes for the last seven years. She looked over at the girl and decided to ask her a question.

"Are there clothes for me to wear? Like a uniform or something. I noticed that all the servants wear the same clothes." The girl turned from the window to stare at her. She stayed like this, just looking at

Arleth for a few seconds and then replied, "In the drawer." The girl returned to looking out the window.

What a ridiculously odd girl Arleth thought to herself. She bent down and opened the top drawer and saw that there was indeed a pair of clean, neatly folded clothes. She supposed that this bed had been meant for her then. It would have been nice of the girl to tell her this! Arleth picked up the clothes and held them up, admiring them. They weren't much, just a light blue dress with a white sash that tied at the waist. But to Arleth they were the first new clothes she had seen in seven years and she thought they were marvellous. She contemplated asking the girl to leave the room when she changed, but she realized that the girl was paying her absolutely no attention so it really didn't matter. Happily, Arleth slipped out of the filthy brown bag-like dress and into her new clothes. Compared to her old attire, the dress was soft against her skin. She tied the sash around her waist and did a small turn, watching as the bottom of the dress twirled around her knees as she moved. Arleth smiled to herself contentedly. She left the brown dress on the bed and looked again at the girl staring out the window. She noticed that the girl was wearing leather sandals on her feet. How nice it would be to have shoes again! Arleth thought to herself. Rather than ask the taciturn girl any more questions, Arleth opened the bottom drawer and found to her delight a pair of sandals resting inside. She slipped them on and tied up the leather laces. They fit quite nicely. Smiling, Arleth took a few moments to bounce up and down on the bed a couple more times and to stare admiringly at her shoes before walking over to join the girl by the door.

The rest of her tour continued very much like the first part had. Aside from a few perfunctory comments to point out the rooms they were passing the girl walked beside Arleth in silence. Although Arleth wished the girl was friendlier as she had a million and one questions to ask, Arleth was also happy to just look around and absorb what she saw.

What struck Arleth almost at once, was how large the castle really was. From the outside it had looked enormous, but walking around its mazelike corridors from the inside made it seem like just crossing from one end to the other was an endless journey. And that was just the parts that Arleth was shown. The girl had stopped outside a massive oak door that screened off an entire wing of the castle explaining, in one of her more chatty moments that "This is the chamber of the king. No one is allowed in there. Only when we are invited do we go there."

Furthermore, Arleth, much to her dismay had not been taken to any of the towers and so she had not had the chance to travel on any of the twisting outdoor pathways she had seen from the valley. When she had inquired about this she had a received a flat, "No, off bounds." This off course had made Arleth even more curious and she had secretly sworn to herself that before the week was up she would try and sneak into one of the towers. She not only wanted to walk on one of the pathways swirling through the clouds, but now that it was off limits, she wanted to know what secrets, if any, were hidden there.

Another part that Arleth had been particularly fascinated by was the courtyard, where the enormous waterfall had its base. Arleth had vaguely seen it from the valley, but at such a distance she couldn't make out very much. But now up close, she had clearly seen all the details and they had taken her breath away. The waterfall formed a giant pool in the centre of the courtyard, and as she had seen from the valley, it exited the courtyard from four separate archways in the wall. The pool was clear and sparkling and there were a few women swimming lazily through it. The girl had explained that this was the courtyard for the king's harem and only they were allowed to swim in the pool. Arleth had no idea what a harem was and she didn't bother to ask. The girl had looked a bit angry when she said this and Arleth guessed that whatever a harem was, this girl was not part of it. Arleth hadn't given it much attention anyways she didn't really care, as she didn't like swimming. Her attention had already turned to the luscious garden spread all around the pool. To Arleth, this was much more interesting.

Directly surrounding the pool were large dark green trees with huge leaves about half the size of Arleth's body. They draped down on all sides, the leaves on some of the lower branches stretched into the pool and floated at the edge of the water. Farther back from the pool were all sizes, shapes and colours of flowers. One massive yellow flower in particular had caught Arleth's attention. It was off to the side near the far wall of the courtyard, separated a little distance from any flowers around it. It had a thin green stalk that shot upwards from the ground and about four feet above the ground it divided into five separate branches. On each branch hung one long cone shaped yellow flower. Intrigued, Arleth had walked over to it and gently touched one of the yellow cones. When she did, a small pink vine had appeared from the top of the cone, almost like a tongue and had rubbed against her hand. Arleth had laughed delightedly and had stroked the flower as she would a favourite pet.

Arleth had wanted to spend hours in the garden looking and touching all the flowers, plants and trees. But the girl had grabbed her arm and pulled her urgently away, "Time for dinner," she exclaimed as if this was the most exciting announcement she had ever made. Arleth had reluctantly followed her out of the courtyard but had made a mental note to return as soon as she could to explore on her own.

* * *

A few hours later after she had eaten dinner and helped the other servants clean up she lay awake in bed listening to the even breathing and occasional snores of the other servants sleeping next to her. Tomorrow morning she would be shown her duties and would begin her work as one of Absalom servants. She hadn't seen Absalom since they had parted outside of the castle, but she assumed that either tomorrow or soon after he would call for her so she could describe in detail what the assassin looked like. She hoped it was soon; she didn't want to forget any of the details. Arleth yawned and turned over on her side. What a marvellous, wondrous, exciting, surprising day she had had. This morning she had woken up in Tocarra as one of Bella's slaves and tonight she was going to sleep in Oherra clear on the other side of the universe, about to start her new life as a servant to the handsome king Absalom. Contentedly, she nuzzled her head into the pillow, and closed her eyes. Within a few moments, exhausted as she was from the day's adventures, she had drifted off into a deep sleep.

* * *

As Arleth slept peacefully, King Absalom was wide awake on the other side of the castle. Since returning to Oherra, he had been busy conversing with his chief military commander, Tom Buckrow. The giant had nothing new to report; in a stalemate of a war that had been going on for years a few days wouldn't change things very much. But what had taken so long were the new strategies Absalom was going over with Tom. The commander had just informed

Absalom that while he had been in Tocarra, Rogan had finally managed to create the first successful Imari. An Imari was the result of the combined minds of Rogan, Absalom and Tom; a ruthless, bloodthirsty and cunning fighting creature fashioned from dark magic. Upon hearing this today, Absalom had gone to see the creature for himself and had been more than pleased with the result. He had spent the rest of the day with Tom planning strategies and battle routes. Of course many more Imari had to be made, but Rogan was more than up to the task. He relished in this kind of work and would likely have hundreds made within a month's time. It was Rogan that Absalom was now going to see.

He strode through the dimly lit private hall leading from his bed chambers to those of his sorcerer and knocked on the huge stone door. Gingerly Absalom placed the knocker back against the door. It was shaped like a human skull and Absalom suspected that it probably *was* a human skull. This was a new addition and Absalom thought it was a bit much, but right now he only noted it absentmindedly near the bottom of an ever growing mental list of things he needed to look at. There was a familiar grating sound and the door opened slowly inwards. Absalom found himself standing toe to toe with his sorcerer who stepped out of the way and beckoned Absalom to enter.

"Have you seen my Imari?" Rogan said immediately in his raspy voice by way of greeting.

"Yes it is quite pleasing, I believe it will give us a firm advantage over Aedan."

"I quite agree. I aim to have three hundred created by month's end. As you have seen, a straight combination works quite well, but I believe that I can also make enhancements to key features. Once I have tested the original models in battle, I will test out this theory."

"What kind of features?"

"Longer talons, sharper eyesight, perhaps wings to scout out the mountains better. We will wait and see how the first models fare in battle. But I imagine that any of these adjustments will be a good improvement."

"Of course of course." Absalom was interested in the Imari but right now he had more important things to discuss. "I was successful in bringing her back with me."

"I imagined so," said Rogan, "I wouldn't imagine that you would have returned without her."

"Yes but the ... acquisition ... was not smooth."

Rogan raised an eyebrow questioningly, "How so."

"There was a complication. Val Odane followed me through the portal. He must have used one of those blasted concealing spells. He found Arleth and chased her halfway across the desert and through a city. It was lucky that I got to her first."

"Aedan couldn't have found out about her on his own. Only we were able to obtain that information, only we have the means, and I don't believe in coincidence. Even if he had somehow managed to find out about her, it is hardly possible to have happened at the exact same time that we did."

"Exactly," said Absalom, glad that Rogan understood what he was getting at. "Aedan must have planted another spy in the castle, it is the only explanation."

Rogan nodded thoughtfully, "I will cast some spells, lay a trap. Rest assured we will have them captured within a few days." Rogan hesitated, something else had just come to his mind, "With such a complication how did you get her to come with you?"

Absalom smiled, glad that Rogan had asked this question. He never tired of showing off how clever he was, "It was quite easy actually, I fed her some nonsense about how Val was a member of a secret assassin group, I believe I used the name the Black Thorn..."

Rogan grunted in disgust. "Yes I know," continued Absalom, "It was not the best name I could have come up with but it did the trick. I told her that she was the only one that had ever seen the face of one of these assassins and that was why he had chased her. I explained that I needed her to come with me so she could identify the assassin and through his confession I would be able to catch the rest of his group."

"Not a bad story," Rogan said approvingly, "I still think it would have been easier to just enchant her, with free will it can get... messy."

"We have been through this," said Absalom testily, "We cannot enchant her except as a last resort. Her abilities work better if her mind is her own, you said so yourself. It will be much easier to do what we need her to do if she does it by her own volition."

"I don't have to fully enchant her Absalom, I can leave her mind mostly intact. Just sway her will to our desires." They were entering into the same argument they had repeated several times in the last couple of weeks. Ever since Rogan had realized that Arleth's life was still being written into the Erum; when they had discovered she was still alive.

"That is too much of a risk," Absalom responded. "As we both know, Arleth's ability will make it harder to enchant her. If you only partly control her mind it is likely that it won't work anyways... or worse. We have now read the Erum, remember how much trouble the last one, Jeneane had with her ability. She struggled because she wasn't 100% confident in what she was doing. Her ability was shaky at best because she never fully believed in what she was using it for. If we partly enchant Arleth and it goes wrong, or if she is able to warp even a small fraction of the enchantment spell, think about what would happen? She wouldn't trust us, and so obviously she wouldn't trust in what we were getting her to do. Even if you were able to force her to use her abilities the way we want her to, she herself wouldn't be confident and it would be Jeneane all over again. You would have to fully enchant her to erase any chance of that and then you Rogan would have to control her *and* her ability. No it is much smarter to concentrate our efforts on getting her to trust us."

"And what if she doesn't trust us after all of our *efforts*"

"If that happens then we will have no choice. Even enchanted, we will still be able to use some of her power. It will be better than nothing."

"And, enchanted or not, after she has done what we want?"

"We will kill her. Once she knows her power, she will be too dangerous to keep alive."

This effectively ended the argument, killing her was something they both agreed on.

Rogan stayed quiet for a few moments as if thinking, "You let Val back in the portal with you right?"

"Of course!"

"Then Aedan will be knocking on our door soon enough..."

Absalom smiled, "I'm counting on it. And I have a few surprises in store for him when he does."

Rogan looked into Absalom's eyes and smiled, "Humans are so sentimental. I'm sure Aedan won't come here without a plan, even as tied to his human emotions as he is, he wouldn't be that stupid. But it won't matter though, once he comes he won't escape."

"No he most certainly will not." And then I will have both of them, Absalom thought to himself. With Aedan captured, the rebellion would certainly lose force, but with Arleth on his side as well, there would be no way for his enemies to win. He almost regretted having the Imari now, it seemed like overkill ... *almost*.

Victory was sweet, but crushing, annihilating victory was much, *much* sweeter. Absalom smiled broadly and thought of how Aedan's head would look sticking from a spike.

Chapter 11

Val slowly crept his way through the mountains. After losing Arleth through the crevice in the corridor in that Tocarran town he had heard Absalom's voice and knew that he had lost. He had crept to the edge of the crowd and observed the exchanges between Bella, Absalom and Arleth. He knew in his injured state he was no match for the king as well as the two Grekens that had been standing with him. As much as he hated to give up, he had decided that it was better to admit temporary defeat and live to tell Aedan what had happened than to throw his life away meaninglessly. With that decision made, he had separated himself from the crowd and hidden himself in a small alley.

There he had tended to his injuries.

He had ripped two lengths of cloth from the bottom of his shirt, tying one around his head and the other one, wider than the first around his chest. From his hiding place he had watched Arleth and Absalom walk by. He had waited a few minutes and then he had slowly crept out of the alley and followed them back to Bella's mansion. He had hidden at the edge of her property, out of view but close enough that he could see when the portal was opened. He had managed to go through the portal without being detected and now, on the other side, he was making his way through the mountains to join up with Aedan and the rest of his friends. He was just at the edge of the inner ring of mountains and although he was safely hidden from view by Absalom's patrolling soldiers, he could see down into the valley. The procession had just reached the castle gates and even though it was too far to see clearly, he knew that within a few moments Arleth would go inside the castle and it would become infinitely more difficult to reach her.

For the hundredth time since this morning he sighed to himself. If only he hadn't failed. Now in his failure he was putting more people at risk. He knew that Aedan wouldn't be upset; in fact he was likely not even to show his disappointment. Although younger than Val by two years, Aedan was the kind of man that Val felt honoured not only to know but to serve and call his best friend. That only made his failure even more upsetting though. He hated to let Aedan down. Especially in this case when the cost was so great, when so much was at stake. He knew Aedan well enough to realize that he would now take things into his own hands. He would go personally to the castle. He would feel responsible for Val's injuries and would insist that he alone go.

They had all known that Val was likely to fail. Tobin had done a remarkable job in finding out about Arleth and in getting the information to them in time, but with no artefacts they had to rely on the Crystal Throne. And they had all known how faulty that plan was. There was slim to no chance that had Val been able to actually retrieve Arleth that he could have crept through the portal with the king and not been seen. But they had to try. At the very least, through trying they knew what she looked like and they knew for certain that she had been taken to the castle. Still, if only he had been able to get her....

With difficultly and with an annoyed shake of his head, he put his failure out of his mind for the present and concentrated on his path through the mountains. He walked a few more paces just along the inner ridge and then with practiced movements, turned sharply to the right and cut through a small crevice, travelling deeper into the mountains. Val knew these mountains well; he had been travelling their paths since he was a small child. He didn't need to concentrate to navigate his way through, he knew their twists, turns and dangers as well as he knew his own body. But what he did need to be alert to were Absalom's soldiers. The king always had them stationed near the mountains on the lookout for one of Aedan's followers. They weren't stupid enough, *anymore*, to actually venture into the mountains; they were Aedan's home now and he knew how to defend them and lay an ambush. But that didn't mean that a well-positioned guard wouldn't see Val walking along the paths and report back to his master the route that Val had taken.

Their stronghold was safe; a large natural cavern in the mountains that had one small, easily defendable entrance and a narrow crevice in the back for a secret escape if need be. Their sorceress, Selene, had cast secrecy spells all along the passes closest to the entrance. If any of Absalom's soldiers happened to pass by, they wouldn't see the entrance.

If they were human, they would instead find themselves wanting to stare in the other direction or have a suddenly strong urge to return home.

If it was a Greken or another one of Rogan's creatures incapable of human emotions, Selene's secrecy spell made it so the creature would simply not see what was right in front of them.

In addition, Selene had cast powerful protective magic at the entrance itself as an added safeguard in case a lucky soldier did manage to somehow circumvent her secrecy spells. So far no one had and their stronghold was so well protected naturally, that very few soldiers had even ventured close enough to come within range of Selene's web of secrecy spells. But that didn't mean that Val could be careless and he continued to pick his way carefully through the passes. As he did, he thought about the hard years that had brought him here.

It had been 10 years since Val, his father, Aedan, Selene and a few hundred terrified Oherrans had first entered the mountains. It had been just after Absalom's northern annihilation campaign. In three weeks time, Absalom's armies had wiped out all five of the North's thriving cities. Anand and Kresh had fallen first, within days of each other. Being taken by surprise, they had hardly even put up a fight. Next came Callis and Jyod. Jyod had been famed for its strong military and it had put up a good fight, holding Absalom's forces off for almost a week. But it too fell and was utterly destroyed. The final northern city, Malek surrendered and opened its gates to Absalom's armies. Absalom had been so enraged by this display of cowardice that he had singlehandedly butchered every member of its royal family and nailed their heads to the city's walls. From all five cities, every man, woman and child that was not killed in the fighting had been captured and made into Absalom's servants. Val shuddered to think about what had been done to these people; he well knew the nature of Rogan's "experiments."

Only a few thousand Northern citizens had managed to escape the slaughter. Many of them travelled south, to the fortified cities there or to neighbouring villages to warn family and friends. But hundreds had joined with Aedan.

More had joined later; most notably Winn Firwood the young lord of Jaya, a mid-sized city that lay about three miles outside of the mountains. Winn's father had been a close friend and ally of Aedan's and resultantly Winn and Aedan were childhood friends. After the destruction of the north, Winn made the rational decision to abandon his city, taking into the mountains with him every single citizen.

Aedan had been overjoyed to have Winn and his formidable army, numbering in the few thousands.

Now, ten years later, Aedan was hiding near to fifteen thousand people from all over Oherra in his mountain stronghold. Seven thousand of these were his fighting force. Not nearly enough to lead a full out attack on Absalom, but enough that the war had been in a dead-locked bitter stalemate for the past six years. Aedan couldn't defeat all of Absalom's forces and Rogan was constantly making more anyways. But this didn't stop Aedan from coming down from the mountains at dark, and with a handful of soldiers steal from Absalom's men or kill them while they slept. Whenever Absalom's armies ventured into the mountains or tried to cross them, Aedan would attack. The mountains were now his home and he knew them better than Absalom. Aedan always defeated Absalom in these mountain skirmishes. However, Absalom couldn't kill or, much to his annoyance even find where Aedan's stronghold was and so the two were locked in a stalemate, neither able to get the upper hand on the other.

The southern cities would have greatly helped Aedan's cause. But nine years ago they had decided to barter with Absalom rather than to end up with the same fate as the north. They gave Absalom hundreds of men, woman and children each year to act as subjects for Rogan's experiments and in exchange they were left alone. Aedan knew that they would gladly join him if they could be assured the safety of their citizens and the continuation of their cities. But Aedan couldn't guarantee this and so the present situation ensued.

Val stopped walking and looked around. He had reached the boundary of Selene's secrecy spell. Carefully he raised his right arm and thrust it forward, crossing the invisible frontier. He didn't want to put more than his arm through, and risk activating the magic, in his weakened state even an arm might be too much. A sorceress was linked to the magic they cast and Val knew that Selene would sense his presence the minute his arm touched the invisible threads. He only hoped that he hadn't put too much of his body into it and had activated it on himself. But a few minutes later when he heard soft footsteps and saw the familiar face of Selene smiling at him, he realized that he had not. She was a beautiful young woman with light, almost white blond hair and pale, milky skin. The three of them, her, him and Aedan had been close friends since childhood and Val loved her as he would a sister.

When she got closer to Val, the smile left her fair face and was replaced by a look of concern.

"Val you are hurt," she said, reaching for his arm and drawing him through the invisible border. If she retained contact with Val, the spell would not work on him. She turned him around so that he faced her and with her hands on each of his arms she looked him up and down, taking in his bruised face, bleeding head and the blood-splattered bandages wrapped around his chest. She noticed also, of course, that Arleth wasn't with him, but she didn't say anything about it. She knew that Val would be berating himself for his failure, and especially in his injured state she didn't want to add to his pain. Instead she put her hand to his chest and asked "Greken?"

Val nodded. "Bastard of a creature got me good, but I killed it in the end. A dagger right through the neck."

Selene smiled. There were two things she could always count on with Val; his eagerness and pride in battle and his foul language. She looked mockingly at his bruised face, "Maybe you could have killed it a little sooner?" A white light emanated from her hand and flowed into Val's chest. "That will stop the bleeding; it should heal by itself in a few days."

"Thanks," Val said in a mock affronted tone, "You know killing a Greken is not easy; they *are* specially designed for the sole purpose of causing death. Slimy Bastards."

"No I suppose not." Then with a sly smile, "I guess it's a good thing I am so skilled at healing you then... even though I am not specially designed for such a task. Where *would* you be without me?"

"Quite happy I presume," said Val laughing. He gave her a playful shove and she smiled.

"I am glad you are alright Val, even though I had no need to be I was still worried about you."

* * *

"No! Absolutely not! That is madness!" The outburst shot through the cavern, causing a slight echo. Some nearby children looked up from their game at the group of adults sitting off to the side.

They looked at each other and hurried off, a few paces away, continuing their game farther from their conversing leaders.

"Wait a minute Graydon," Said Winn calmly to his hot-headed younger brother. "I'm sure that Aedan has a plan."

But Graydon was not about to be pacified so easily, "I'm not saying she isn't important, but is she really important enough to risk Aedan's life? Having Val go all the way to Tocarra was bad enough, but I saw the logic in that at least. But now? What good would it be if Aedan goes in to get Arleth and dies? We would be in almost the same position we are in now, except worse. Arleth will not be able to command armies and formulate battle strategies like Aedan. She won't even be able to use her abilities for a while, not until she is taught the basics at the very least. Heck, we don't even know for sure if she will want to help us even after we tell her who she is. She is a teenage girl; in all likelihood she will be terrified just to be on Oherra not to mention being in battle and having people try to kill her."

"You are right in a lot of respects Graydon," Said Selene. "But you are forgetting something very important. Now that Absalom has Arleth, we can be certain he *will* use her abilities. It might be a stalemate now, but as soon as Arleth's power is realized Absalom will have the distinct advantage. Under his control, she would turn into a monster. At the very least, regardless of who she is, we cannot let that happen. Trust me. I do not like the thought of Aedan putting himself in danger any more than you do, but we really don't have any other option."

"Fine," said Graydon, seeing the reason in Selene's words, "But it is absolutely necessary that *Aedan* goes. If we are just simply going in and bringing her back with us, do we really need to risk our leader? Anyone could go. I would go."

"No," said Aedan. "Although I value your courage and loyalty towards me I cannot risk anyone else. It was hard enough for me to send Val to Tocarra, knowing, as we did, what a fool's errand it was. I will not make that mistake again. I will go myself."

"But.." interjected Graydon. Winn shot his brother a hard look, quickly silencing him.

Aedan continued, "Besides, Absalom has a clever tongue and a persuasive personality, especially with women. He won't hesitate to use all of his tricks, everything in his power to convince Arleth that he is in the right. We don't know what he has already told her or what she thinks of him. But we have to assume the worst. We have to plan for the eventuality that he already has her deeply in his thrall. Therefore, I would be the most logical choice to go. Who would be better to convince her of who she is, of who I am, than me?"

For the first time Bain, Val's father spoke, "I agree Aedan, this does make the most sense. But please tell me you have a good plan. We all know that you will be spotted and likely captured the moment you come within reach of the castle."

To this Aedan smiled and looked beside him into Selene's beautiful face. "Yes we have come up with something quite clever."

The rest of the group edged closer to him and listened in rapt attention as he, with the occasional explanation from Selene, outlined their plan. A half an hour later, after a few minor tweaks from Val and Winn, their strategy had been outlined and perfected. Even Graydon was now in agreement with the rest of the group. "That is quite a plan," he admitted admiringly. Although he was a hot-headed young man of twenty, he wasn't too full of pride to admit when he had been wrong. Of course he would never exactly say the words "I was wrong," but admitting the plan was a good one was practically the same thing.

"How long will you take to prepare what you need Selene?" Asked Bain.

"Three days. I will gather what I need tomorrow and create the spells and Alondrane right after. Three days from today, Aedan will be able to leave."

"Excellent," said Winn "The faster we can proceed the better. Time is definitely not on our side."

They all nodded their agreement.

* * *

Later that night, while Arleth was sound asleep in her bed and Absalom was plotting with Rogan, Aedan lay awake staring at the roof of his tent. In the ten years Aedan had been living in the cavern, they had made many improvements to their living conditions. But one of the first things they had done was to build small tents for each family as it had been readily apparent that privacy was one of the greatest concerns. The result was a sort of make-shift town within the cavern.

Aedan felt rustling beside him and looked into Selene's sleepy face. "Can you not sleep?" She asked him groggily.

He didn't answer right away but instead looked away from her, staring at the far end of his tent. "Our plan will work won't it?" He asked her after a few moments. "Val is entirely against it; he took me aside after our meeting and voiced all of his concerns."

She turned completely towards him and propped herself up on her elbow so she could see his face more clearly in the darkness. "You know how Val is." She responded "He is going to object to any plan that puts us in danger."

"I know, but doesn't he have a point this time?"

Selene stared at him the darkness, not sure how to answer.

Aedan saved her from a response by repeating his question, "Our plan will work won't it?"

"I think it will," Selene said slowly. "But Aedan..."

"... We don't really have much of a choice?" he asked, finishing her sentence.

She wasn't going to use those words exactly, but that was generally what she was going to say. She cupped his cheek in her hand and gently turned his face so he was looking at her. "Absalom has her now. If we *don't* do anything, he will win. Even with a worse plan we would have to go for it." Aedan knew this as well, but it comforted him to hear her voice her agreement again. He wasn't afraid of going to Iridian castle and confronting Absalom, but he *was* afraid of throwing his life away meaninglessly. If he died for nothing, what would become of Oherra?

Aedan wrapped his arms around Selene and held her close to him. He rested his cheek on the top of her head.

"Don't worry," she said "I won't let that traitor kill you before I've had a chance to marry you. Absalom has another thing coming if he thinks I have wasted all this time with you just to see you killed before we can grow old and have grandchildren together."

Aedan laughed, "I almost feel bad for Absalom now. There is no dealing with Selene Ayan when she has her mind made up."

Selene smiled into his chest, "You wouldn't know Aedan, I always give in to you."

Aedan laughed even more. "In what world?" he joked.

"I don't know," she replied sullenly. "I thought it sounded romantic."

He squeezed her against him even tighter, laughing the whole time. After a few seconds he could hear Selene's muffled laughter join his own.

They laughed together for a time before, both relaxed now; they fell asleep with smiles still on their faces.

Chapter 12

Arleth sat at the long dining table in the servants' hall, slurping her soup. It was a delicious, thick, hearty broth filled with chunks of meat, noodles and vegetables.

It was lunch time on her third full day on Oherra and she had spent the whole morning cleaning a glass tunnel by hand. Right after breakfast, her tour guide from the first night had grabbed her and led her to a storage closet off of the dining hall. With no further ado she had turned to Arleth, "It is Wednesday, every Wednesday the glass tunnels are cleaned." The girl had then grabbed a handful of towels, a bucket of water and a bottle filled with some kind of soap and thrust them at Arleth. For the remainder of the morning the girl and Arleth cleaned the floor of the glass tunnel which connected the building containing the kitchen and servants' quarters to the main hall. Arleth had found this task utterly boring and couldn't believe that in a magical world, there wasn't an easier, *magical* way to clean the halls. But it seemed, that there wasn't or at least not one that anyone cared to use. So Arleth had silently scrubbed, polished and dried all morning.

It had been a very boring morning and, much to Arleth's disappointment, the previous two mornings (and days) had been quite similar. When she had woken up on her first morning, refreshed and excited she had expected that she would be called on by Absalom at any minute. But the next two days both came and went and Absalom hadn't made any attempt to question her about the assassin. In fact, she hadn't even seen Absalom since they had exited the portal together three days ago. She didn't give it much concern though, as she assumed that the king of Oherra would have to be a very busy man, but she *was* disappointed. It would have been a welcome break from the monotony of her chores.

It wouldn't have been so bad she realized if the other servants were the slight bit interesting. She was used to hard work, having been a servant for close to half of her life. Also, she had been pleased to note that the chores she was doing here were much easier and less labour intensive (and disgusting) than the ones she had done as Bella's personal servant. But at least there she had Chuck to talk to every once in a while. And while the other servants were hardly pleasant, they had at least seemed human. She could count on them to be talking, bragging or laughing at any moment of the day. But here.... all of the servants monotonously completed their chores. Arleth had tried to talk to several of them on numerous occasions, but aside from answering her questions they had made no further effort at conversation. And what was most strange to Arleth, none of them offered her their names.

The screech of a chair being rubbed against the wood floor to her left distracted her from her thoughts. She looked beside her. Her tour guide from the first night was getting up from her meal. It was only half eaten but the girl didn't seem to notice. She turned to Arleth,

"I have to go outside. I have been assigned to bring the soldiers their daily meal. After you eat, finish cleaning the halls like I explained."

With that she grabbed her soup bowl, pushed in her chair and walked purposively down the dining hall to the kitchen.

Arleth was elated! The woman had been her shadow every moment of the day. With her hovering around her 24 hours a day, she had no chance to go back and explore the courtyard she had seen in her tour. But now.... it seemed like she would have at least a couple of hours to herself!

Excited, she quickly gobbled up the rest of her soup. She had no intention of continuing to clean the hall. As far as she could see it was already sparkling clean. But this of course, wasn't her reason; she was going to take this opportunity when she was alone to go back and visit the courtyard. And, if she had more time perhaps she would also climb up a tower and travel on one of the outdoor pathways!

She quickly strode down the aisle between the two long tables and, depositing her dishes in the empty kitchen, exited into the hall. Leaning her back against the wall, she looked right and left to see if anyone was coming. But the hall in both directions was deserted. Relieved, Arleth let out the breath she hadn't realized she had been holding and started to make her way down the hall.

The courtyard was in the centre of the castle, and if she remembered correctly from her tour the other night, it was fairly close to where she was now. If she walked down this hall, through the glass tunnel, across the main hall, through the next glass tunnel and turned left she believed she would find herself in the courtyard. It was at times like this that Arleth was very glad that she had been born with a great sense of direction. Not too many people would have been able to find their way so easily. Especially considering that she had only been shown once and that night she had been coming in the opposite direction. But Arleth navigated her way with ease, as if she had been travelling these halls her whole life.

She couldn't afford to be complacent just yet though. She still might encounter someone in the halls who would be curious about where she was going and disrupt her plans. Arleth went over again in her head what she would say. She would adopt a confused expression, which should be quite believable considering she was a new servant, and say that she had been looking for the storage closet but that she must have gotten lost. Arleth figured that in such an eventuality, she would be shown to the storage closet and then when the person left, she could just turn around and go back again. She knew her way from the storage closet after all, and it would just delay her trip by a few moments.

But even as she was going over her excuse in her head, she didn't really expect to have to use it. The atmosphere in Iridian castle was much different, Arleth had noticed, than it had been in Bella's mansion. At the mansion, Arleth would have been hard-pressed to walk down a hall at practically any time of day or night and not see at least one other person. There was constant hustle and bustle, due in large part to Bella's incessant and petty desires. Here, the halls were practically deserted; except for an occasional servant, Arleth hardly saw anyone during the day. For example, Arleth had passed only one other servant during her whole tour the first evening and this morning the only people that had passed her while she was cleaning the tunnel were a couple of messengers. She supposed that since the castle was so enormous, people would not encounter each other as much, having much more space in which to live. Also, the fact that there was clearly a war going on and there were thousands of soldiers camped outside, also added to the lack of activity inside.

However, the attitudes of the servants themselves did seem... *different*. Her thoughts returned to where they had left off in the dining hall when she had been interrupted. The servants were definitey different. Where Bella's servants had been constantly concerned with the goings on of everyone else, and their favourite pass-time was to spy on their neighbours, the servants here seemed utterly unconcerned with each other. They hardly ever spoke to one another, and when they did, Arleth had noticed that it was always about something practical and related to their work.

She couldn't quite put her finger on why, but these servants seemed different somehow than the ones at Bella's mansion. More boring certainly. She hadn't liked the constant gossip and frivolity of the servants at the mansion, but she didn't know if she would like the practicality and seriousness of these servants any better. That would be a problem for another time though. For the moment, she was quite glad that the servants were like this; it meant that even if she did come across someone they would be very unlikely to even care what she was doing, let alone stop and question her.

Arleth kept walking until a few minutes later, she reached the huge mahogany doors that led to the courtyard. She paused in front of the doors breathing excitedly; just as she had expected she hadn't come across anyone and she didn't see or hear anyone nearby. She smiled, she had made it! She just had to push open the door and step inside and she would be safe and sound in the courtyard once again. Slowly Arleth pushed one of the huge doors open. It was heavy and it took both of her hands and her full strength to open it just wide enough to squeeze through. With effort, she managed to press her way through the opening she had created, and with a last burst of energy, tumbled onto the soft grass on the other side.

Picking herself up, and straightening her dress, Arleth glanced around at her surroundings. Leading from the door was a stone path that branched into three separate trails a little ahead of where Arleth was standing. She had taken the middle path with the girl the first time, and that one had led almost directly to the waterfall in the centre. She didn't really care that much about seeing the waterfall again, so she decided to take one of the other two paths. She looked to the right and the left, contemplating. To the right, the path led through what seemed to be a garden of flowers. But Arleth could tell instantly that this wasn't like any sort of garden she would have found on Tocarra. Here, the flowers were all different, none were the same as their neighbours, and none appeared to be anything similar to any flower that Arleth had ever seen before. Each was a different shape or size or colour than the plant standing beside it.

Looking to the left, the scene was drastically different. Where the right path had been visible far into the distance, winding through the flowers, the path to the left disappeared into darkness a few metres ahead. It led into a dense cluster of trees that formed a tunnel around the path blocking out any light - the path literally disappeared from sight. Feeling rather adventurous at the moment, Arleth wanted to find out where the tunnel of trees led. The right path seemed boring now by comparison; the left was much more mysterious. Her mind made up, she started walking down the left path.

She had only gone a few feet down the path when she reached the cluster of trees. Arleth paused for a moment at the entrance, taking in the tunnel of trees spreading out before her. At first glance, the trees themselves were pretty ordinary – just like the ones she had seen every day on Tocarra. But when she looked closer, she noticed something strange. The roots of each tree were not underground, but instead hung suspended a few inches off the ground. Even more fascinating, the roots grew outwards to the right and left, connecting each tree to the one beside it. To Arleth, it seemed almost like the roots were the trees' arms and they were reaching out to hold hands with their neighbours. The top of each tree was bent to extend over the path, its branches touching those of the tree on the opposite side. The resulting canopy blocked any light from reaching the ground and created the dark tunnel that had so attracted her. With a smile, Arleth took a step forward.

She was surprised at how soon the darkness engulfed her. In only a few feet, it had already become so dark that she could no longer see the path ahead of her clearly. And in a couple more steps she was in total darkness; she couldn't even see her own hand outstretched in front of her. Arleth didn't really think this made logical sense; shouldn't she still be close enough to the entrance for at least a little light to filter through? She hadn't made any turns either; the entrance should be *right* behind her. Sure enough, when she turned around to check behind her, the entrance was there a few feet away, its brightness mocking her. But what she noticed was that although the entrance was fully illuminated, none of the rays of light shone through. It was as if there was an invisible wall where the first set of trees stood, which prevented any light from penetrating further. The light literally stopped at the tree-line. This was no natural way for light to behave and Arleth felt certain that magic was involved. For about the twentieth time since she had crossed over into Oherra, she realized just how different life was here. It wasn't just that Oherra had sorcerers and sorceresses or magical creatures, but that the world itself was infused with magic. Even the laws of nature that she knew did not seem to apply here.

Arleth felt certain that she would be continuing to discover new things in Oherra for years to come. It was hard to believe, after seven years of tedious drudgery, how much her life had changed in a few short days. Others might have been terrified by this realization or at least felt a bit out of place, but not Arleth.

Being in the orphanage and then a servant to Bella, Arleth had never really had anything to call her own; and with the death of Flora and Neve, nothing to hold on to. She had never felt like she belonged on Bella's estate, and any remembrance of the feeling of belonging had died with everyone she had ever known that terrible day at the orphanage. Thus, although she was on a completely new world and everything here was different than what she was used to, she didn't feel any more alienated than usual. What was left was just her burning excitement.

She turned back away from the entrance and started walking slowly down the path, deeper into the tunnel of trees. Although it was pitch black, Arleth felt perfectly safe. She had long since outgrown her childish fear of the dark, and besides, she didn't presume that there would be anything dangerous in the courtyard of Iridian Castle. That being said, she still had to walk carefully so she wouldn't poke an eye out on a tree branch or fall into the trees on either side of the path. She walked slowly, holding out her arms. She couldn't see the path to know if it turned, but with her arms outstretched, she would feel if she came close to the trees on either side and she would be able to stay reasonably in the middle of the path.

She continued like this for a while, aware that she probably looked ridiculous. She knew it was foolish to be thinking this though, as there was no one around to see her. Even if there were, they couldn't possibly see her in the darkness. Besides, they would probably look just as ridiculous navigating in the dark as she did. She smiled embarrassedly at her vanity and when she did, her mind turned involuntarily to thoughts of Bella. It was impossible for Arleth to think of vanity and *not* conjure of an image of that woman. She smiled again, this time remembering the look on Bella's face when King Absalom had put her in her place in Sonohan's town square. She pictured the woman's fish-like gaping and incredulous stare and sighed contentedly. It was perfect justice for such a narcissistic and proud woman.

Arleth, lost in such pleasant thoughts, didn't notice right away when a greenish light appeared on the path ahead of her. It wasn't until the light was bright enough that she could see the trees on either side of the path that she noticed that something had changed.

The tunnel had opened up into a small clearing. It was a square grassy enclosure, surrounded on all sides by a thick row of trees. The trees were a bit shorter here and their branches didn't quite meet each other. This meant that a bit of light came through from the top, and when reflected on the trees, cast a faintly greenish light over the clearing.

In the middle there was a life-size statue of King Absalom carved from a dark gray stone. One arm was holding a sword drawn and raised, pointing directly ahead and in the other hand the statue was holding ... Arleth gasped in shock. No, she shook her head, she must be wrong. What kind of a man would have a statue made of himself holding *that?* She took a few steps closer and found to her horror, that she had been right.

The statue's left hand had been carved holding a severed male head by the hair.

This statue was clearly meant to depict some great victory that Absalom had won. The king's face had been carved looking regal and confident, as the hero. But Arleth couldn't tear her eyes away from the face carved on the severed head; a look of unmistakable agony. Even carved into stone, the emotion on that face touched Arleth's heart.

Why would Absalom have a statue like this? What kind of a person would want future generations to remember him as the man holding the severed head? Arleth couldn't help feeling a bit repulsed. But almost immediately, her repulsion faded; King Absalom was the king of Oherra, the peacekeeper of the Universe. He wouldn't have a statue like this of himself just for fun. The man with the severed head must have been horrendous, a brutal monster; and King Absalom would have surely been a hero for defeating him. Arleth still thought it was a bit gross, but she supposed that such a terrible man could almost deserve to have had his head cut off.

A rustling to Arleth's right caught her attention. She immediately froze; she shouldn't be here and if she was caught... well she didn't really know... but she could imagine it wouldn't be pleasant. The noise grew louder, whatever or whoever it was, was coming closer. Arleth started breathing faster, she had to move! She couldn't be found here. Her best bet was to try and run back into the tunnel of trees and hope that she wouldn't be seen. But she didn't know if she had enough time for that; the noise had sounded pretty close. She had to try though – she didn't want to get in trouble in her very first week here. For all she knew, if she was too much of a hassle, Absalom might send her back to Tocarra once she gave him the information he needed about the assassin. And the last thing Arleth *ever* wanted to do was to go back to Bella and Kiran.

That terrifying thought gave Arleth the added adrenaline she needed. With a burst of speed, she turned around and rushed into the tunnel of trees. Breathing heavily, she looked at the clearing but it was still empty. Arleth edged backwards a few feet, deeper into the darkness and crouched down to make herself less visible. As soon as she had done so, a bush to the right of the clearing gave a violent shake and a dark form sped out.

It was a small ginger-coloured cat.

Arleth took one look at it and burst out laughing. How ridiculous, she thought; almost having a heart-attack over a cat. Feeling rather foolish, Arleth stood up and walked back into the clearing. The cat, now aware that it was not alone, perked up its ears and looked at the stranger curiously. Arleth smiled reassuringly and held out her hand.

"Come here," she cooed. "I won't hurt you."

The cat stared at her for a while as if hesitating and then slowly it padded its way over to Arleth. It stopped just out of arm's reach, staring shyly up at her. Carefully, so as not to alarm it, Arleth lowered herself to her knees, her hand still outstretched, beckoning the animal to come closer. But the cat didn't move - it stayed just where it was staring at Arleth. On her knees, Arleth edged herself slowly forward. The cat still stayed where it was. If she could move just a little bit closer she would be able to pick it up. She shuffled forward until she was in reach and to her delight the cat still hadn't moved.

"I'm just going to pick you up now ok?" She cooed to it gently, reaching out her arms.

The cat looked at the hands coming closer to it and scampered away into the bushes on the far side of the clearing.

"No!" Arleth gasped. "Come back!" She hurried after the cat, crawling into the bush where it had disappeared. There it was, with its back to her, licking its paw. It hadn't noticed her yet. Perfect! Arleth reached out again to pick it up. But she had moved her hand no more than a few inches toward the animal when she froze dead in her tracks.

A human hand had appeared. It reached for the cat and effortlessly picked it up, pulling it up and out of Arleth's sight. Arleth held her breath and waited where she was a few seconds to see if the hand would come back. But it didn't and Arleth exhaled quietly. Who was there? The quick glimpse that Arleth had gotten of the hand had told her that it belonged to a female. It was too slender not to. This relaxed Arleth a little bit; it meant it wasn't Absalom.

As carefully as she could, she parted the branches in front of her to see if the owner of the hand was still nearby. Sure enough, on the other side of the bush in which Arleth now sat was another clearing and in it sat a woman. The cat was curled peacefully in her lap and she was stroking it gently. But that wasn't what Arleth had noticed first. The first thing that Arleth *had* noticed was that the woman was completely naked. She had long blonde hair that was pulled forward over each shoulder. Arleth was glad, for the sake of her modesty, that the woman's hair was long enough that it covered her breasts.

What was this woman doing here Arleth thought? She didn't appear to be a servant. Then she remembered her tour and the naked women who had been swimming in the pond at the base of waterfall. This woman was probably one of them. The bushes directly behind the blonde woman parted and another woman came into view. She was also completely naked and Arleth felt embarrassed to be watching them. She was about to turn around to leave, when the newcomer looked down at the blonde woman and said something that Arleth found quite strange.

"You are splitting, have you not been swimming in the pool lately?"

"No I suppose I haven't been, maybe not for a couple of days."

"Why not?" The second woman said a bit harshly, disturbing the cat so that it ran away.

"I'm not really sure," the blonde woman said sounding a bit confused. "I know that yesterday I was going to go swim like we normally do, but I saw this cat and I got distracted and so I followed it. I guess I never went back to swim again..." she trailed off. She seemed to not know how to finish her sentence. Suddenly her head jerked up staring in fear at the second woman. "You won't tell Rogan will you?"

"I don't know. I think I should, he always tells us to let him know if something out of the ordinary happens. And you splitting is certainly something quite strange."

"Oh please don't," the blonde woman begged. "I don't think I could bear another one of his remedies." Tears began to form in the corners of her eyes. "Please don't, last time it hurt so much."

The other woman looked down at her and Arleth saw something change in the woman's blank expression. A hint of compassion maybe? "Ok..." the woman said slowly. "But please go in the pool now."

"Thank you!" The blonde woman wept, a smile starting to form on her face. She wiped the tears from her eyes. "I will definitely go to the pool right now."

The second woman reached down and held out her hand to the blonde woman. She still seemed to be unsure about the decision she had made. The blonde woman seemed not to notice and grabbed the woman's hand and pulled herself to her feet.

It was at this moment, when the blonde woman turned to walk back out of the clearing that Arleth saw what splitting was. She put her hand up to her mouth to stop herself from gagging. What was going on? All down the back of the blonde woman, right next to her spine was a thick red incision. It ran all the way from the base of her neck to her tailbone and had to be at least one inch wide. It looked like the woman's skin was literally peeling away from her body all along this line. The tatters of it hung unevenly on either side of the split. Strangely enough though, Arleth didn't see any blood; inside the cut was an angry red colour, but it didn't appear to be bleeding at all.

Arleth's head started spinning and she felt like throwing up. She was glad she was sitting down otherwise she probably would have fainted.

How could the woman have not been in terrible pain? How could someone have an injury that size and not at least know it was there? Who were these woman that needed to swim in a pool so as to not have their bodies fall apart? How did they get to be like that? And who was Rogan? The woman had been clearly terrified of him. Even the second, stony-faced woman had changed her mind when his name had been mentioned.

Involuntarily, Arleth shivered; suddenly she didn't feel so safe anymore. For the first time in a long while, she felt acutely aware of how alone she really was. She wanted to talk to someone about what she had just seen, she wanted to ask questions, find out about what was going on. But she had no one.

She didn't feel like exploring anymore today, all her enthusiasm had left her body just as that woman's skin was somehow leaving hers. All Arleth wanted to do now was go back to the glass tunnel and continue cleaning like she was supposed to have been doing. She wanted to find out what was going on, but right now she just felt drained.

She crawled out of the bushes and back into the clearing. She ran through it, passing the statue which didn't seem nearly as heroic anymore, and into the tunnel of trees. She continued running down the path until she saw the reassuring light from the courtyard up ahead of her. Hurriedly she ran across the courtyard back to the huge doors that would lead her out into the hall. With all her effort she pulled one of the doors open slightly and squeezed her way through. Back out in the hall, the door swung silently shut behind her. Suddenly exhausted, she slumped down on the floor with her back leaning against the closed door. She steadied her breathing as much as she could and with a determined effort tried not to think about what she had just seen. After a few seconds, Arleth knew this would be almost impossible and so she stood back up on shaking legs and started walking back to her cleaning duties.

She had only taken a couple of steps when a strong, muscular hand clasped onto her arm and spun her roughly around.

Chapter 13

As she was spun around, Arleth looked up into the face of her assailant. With a growing feeling of dread, her eyes travelled along the handsome contours of his face, taking in the dark curly hair, stunning green eyes and tanned skin.

She was looking into the face of King Absalom.

His expression was unreadable, yet Arleth was sure that he had seen her leave the courtyard. The room she was in was completely open and either of the two halls that led to it had a perfect, unobstructed view of the courtyard door. For him to have reached her so quickly after she left the courtyard, he must have been coming down one of the halls when she had run out. Her thoughts had been so preoccupied with what she had seen that she hadn't even bothered to check if there was anyone else around her. She silently cursed her lack of observation and thought frantically for some reason she could have for being in the courtyard. But Absalom seemed oblivious to Arleth's distress and when he spoke, it was in a neutral voice, without any trace of anger.

"Arleth," he said, letting go of her arm "I need you to come with me for a while. I need you tell me every detail about the assassin now, when you can still remember him. We will go to my chambers, follow me."

With that, the King turned and walked away, leaving Arleth staring after him. She looked at his retreating figure, momentarily taken aback. That was it? He wasn't going to ask her why she was in the courtyard? She thought that was strange, but then again, why *would* he question why she had been there? Just because Arleth knew she shouldn't be there, didn't mean that the king would know. The castle was too big and there were too many servants for him to know, or even care, where each of them was supposed to be at every moment. Arleth felt a bit foolish for worrying; Absalom probably had no idea she wasn't supposed to have been there. Breathing a sigh of relief, she hurried after him.

Arleth followed Absalom through the castle in silence until they turned down a hall that ended in a massive double door. There were two Grekens standing imposingly, one on either side of the door. Upon seeing the king, they lowered their raised weapons and pulled the doors open for Absalom and Arleth to enter. Arleth followed the king through the entrance, into a dimly lit circular room. She looked around hungrily, trying to absorb as much of her surroundings as she could. She was distinctly aware that she was one of the few people in the entire universe that had been or would ever get to step foot in the king of Oherra's private chambers. That being said, she wanted to remember as much detail as possible.

The walls were panelled in a dark cherry-coloured wood and the floors were covered in a deep red carpeting. There were no windows and the only light was coming from a chandelier which hung from the ceiling in the middle of the room. The room itself was massive although it seemed to have no purpose other than to act as a main hall; aside from a small table, there was no other furniture. Instead, there were four doors, all of which were closed, leading off of this room. Also, to Arleth's immediate right was a winding staircase leading up to what she imagined were the king's bed chambers.

Absalom led her across the room to the second door on the left. He opened the door effortlessly and motioned for Arleth to go through ahead of him. She obeyed and found herself standing in a small sitting room. It was a cozy little room with a stone fireplace in the corner and a bookshelf across the far wall. Arleth noticed immediately that there was no wood in or near the fireplace and so she guessed that unless it was heated through magic, it was just for show. The bookshelf on the other hand, was jam-packed with books of all shapes and sizes. It looked like the original attempt was to keep a neat organized system, but over time as more and more books were added, Absalom had clearly just fit in books wherever there was space. In some shelves the books were in two rows or they were just crammed in haphazardly ontop of the existing row. At some point, he seemed to have given up on the shelves all together and just put them in disordered piles on the floor. The glass doors which covered the front of the bookshelves were all wide open. Arleth smiled in spite of herself, so the legendary King of Oherra, wasn't perfect after all. He was messy and disorganized just like everyone else. Then again, he most likely was a lot busier and definitely had a lot more responsibility than everyone else so he had a good excuse for being messy, but regardless, Arleth was still amused.

While Arleth had been looking around the room, the king had closed the door behind them and had deposited himself in one of the huge red armchairs in the centre of the room. Arleth now turned her attention to him and noted that even seated comfortably in his untidy sitting room, he somehow still managed to look regal. But he also looked quite impatient she realized with alarm and so she quickly hurried over to him and with an apologetic smile, sat down in one of the chairs beside him.

Absalom turned to face her and with a smile said, "I hope you are beginning to adjust to life here." He was used to wooing women to meet his own needs, and even though some had been very powerful, it didn't matter; they had succumbed to him all the same. Arleth was just a child alone in a foreign world; she should be no problem at all.

"Yes, I suppose I am," Arleth replied. "Everything is very different here than on Tocarra, but I find it exciting. I will get used to most of the differences soon I imagine."

"Very good," Absalom replied nodding. "And I trust that you find the food and your clothing satisfactory?"

"Yes, thank you. They are both wonderful."

"Good, good," Absalom said quietly, almost to himself. "And you were given a tour right? I believe I instructed someone to give you one?"

"Yes, one of your other servants showed me around the castle."

"And what did she show you?"

"Um," Arleth said, thinking back, "She showed me all the rooms; the kitchen, the dining hall, the servants' bedchambers..." She trailed off, not wanting to list everything that she had seen. "Basically she showed me the whole castle except for your chambers and the towers. Oh and she also showed me the courtyard."

"And did you like any of the rooms in particular? Anything catch your interest?" He had seen Arleth leaving the courtyard, and he had seen the terrified look on her face. She had definitely seen something in there that had scared her. He had a couple of ideas what it could have been, but he wanted to see if she would tell him of her own accord. It would be a good test of how much she trusted him

"I think the whole castle is amazing!" Arleth started excitedly. "I love the glass tunnels in between the rooms. I saw the pathways from outside and I think they are fascinating. How do they hang like that? There was nothing like that on Tocarra."

"Yes, Iridian Castle is an architectural marvel," Absalom said dryly. "Anything else that you liked?"

"Oh yes," Arleth continued. "The courtyard!" She stopped abruptly with a sinking feeling. He had seen her leave the courtyard and he was trying to get her to tell him why she was there again today. He must have known that she shouldn't have been there after all. She really didn't want to lie to the King of Oherra, but she had no other choice. She just had to make her lie sound as plausible as she could. "Yes I found the courtyard particularly interesting," she said slowly. "Practically everything in it was new to me; the plants on Oherra seem to be entirely different than the ones I am used to from Tocarra. I was so captivated the night I had the tour that I dropped my bracelet there. I went back just now to try and find it. Unfortunately I couldn't, but I wanted to get back to my duties and so I left the courtyard anyways."

She looked at Absalom's face carefully. She hadn't been wearing a bracelet, in fact she had never even owned one in her entire life. But it was the first thing that had come to her mind. She hoped Absalom would not have paid much attention to what she was wearing. If he hadn't, her story was perfectly believable. His face looked impassive, there was no sign that he thought she was lying. He was just nodding at her encouragingly. Just in case, she decided to change the topic, "The girl that gave me the tour, what was her name? I asked her but she wouldn't tell me. She was kind of weird, she didn't talk at all and she said she didn't know what her name was."

Absalom's face had a neutral mask, but beneath his calm disposition he was seething. She clearly didn't trust him yet; he was not fooled by her story. He knew for a fact that she had not been wearing a bracelet. And on top of it all, he now had to answer another one of this girl's stupid questions. "Her name is Sara," He lied, giving the first name that popped into his head. "Some of the servants are very private; they don't like to talk about themselves with newcomers. Don't worry, she should open up within a couple of weeks." He hoped that would put her off for a while. He was tired of this pointless drivel. "Anyways," Absalom said in a serious voice, "We must now turn to more serious matters. I need to find out about the assassin."

Arleth nodded, "Of course."

Absalom smiled. It didn't matter if Arleth told him what she had seen or not, Rogan's memory extraction spell would find out what she was hiding. Of course he would have preferred Arleth to tell him herself, but no matter, he could be patient. She would trust him eventually.

Arleth smiled back at Absalom, unaware of what he was thinking. She hoped she would be able to remember everything about the assassin, she desperately wanted to help him.

"So Arleth, I am not going to be asking you questions or have you give a description of the man who chased you. Such methods are only as good as the memory of the person questioned and inevitably, humans are forgetful creatures. This is too important to leave room for error, therefore, we will be using a memory spell."

Arleth was a bit frightened but she didn't want Absalom to know so she said "Ok," as bravely as she could.

"It is a completely harmless spell. It does not affect or alter your memory in any way. It just uses magic to probe into your memory and extract the truth from what you have experienced."

"What do I have to do?"

"It is quite simple. I will guide your thoughts by giving you questions that I want you to think about. You need to hold the answer to that question in your mind and the memory spell will take the answer that you are holding and probe through your past experiences and extract everything that is related to that thought that you are holding. For example, if I ask you to think about what the man looked like, an image would form in your mind of his face, his stature, his clothing. Am I correct?"

Arleth nodded, a clear image of the man had already appeared in her mind.

"So the memory spell would latch on to that image and sort through all your past experiences that have to do with it. So in this case, every instance you had seen that face, even if you didn't consciously remember it, would be extracted."

A thought had come to Arleth's mind, "Would you be the one doing the memory extraction?"

"No, my sorceror Rogan would be doing it. But I would be here, asking you the questions." Absalom was going to say more but Arleth had given a curious reaction when he had said Rogan's name and it had given him pause.

Absalom watched Arleth carefully, he was sure that it was Rogan's name that had caught her attention. There were hundreds of reasons why Arleth should be afraid of the man, but she shouldn't be afraid of him yet. He felt certain that something had happened in the courtyard and whatever it was, it had to do directly or indirectly with his sorceror.

"Is something troubling you?"

Arleth hesitated. She didn't how much she should tell him. The fact that Rogan was the king's sorcerer gave her pause. Maybe she had misinterpreted what she had seen. She laughed a bit, "I guess I am just a bit nervous about having magic used on me. But that is silly isn't it?"

Absalom smiled, "It's natural to be afraid, but don't worry, it is perfectly safe." He knew she was lying, she had too much of a reaction when he had mentioned Rogan's name. He wished she trusted him more easily, but regardless, Rogan's memory extraction would tell him what she wouldn't anyways. "There is one more thing about the spell though."

"Yes," said Arleth cautiously.

"You will need to keep your eyes closed so that there will be no outside influences to distract you from your thoughts. Unfortunately, due to the seriousness of the situation, I will need to put a blindfold on you to make sure that you do not open your eyes."

"That is fine," said Arleth. "I understand how important this is." She was still afraid, not really about Rogan anymore, but just about the magic being used on her. But she realized her fears were probably misguided and she didn't want Absalom to think she was a baby.

Good, Absalom thought. It didn't matter at all to the efficacy of the spell if her eyes were open or closed. But he couldn't let her see Rogan. He reached into his pocket and pulled out a long length of cloth and smiling reassuringly tied it around Arleth's head, covering her eyes. If she saw Rogan, she would definitely remember him. A 10 year old child does not go through the kind of trauma she went through at the orphanage and not remember who it was that attacked her.

There was a soft knocking on the door.

"Rogan is here now," Absalom said to Arleth, "I am just going to let him in, and then we will begin the memory spell shortly."

Arleth nodded her assent and waited for the king to return. She could hear his footsteps walking towards the door, the sound of the door opening and whispered conversation between two male voices. Then the door closed and two sets of footsteps walked back towards her. She felt someone come to stand behind her and a pair of hands rested themselves on her shoulders. Arleth jumped a little in spite of herself.

"Rogan needs to have physical contact with you in order for him to use the memory spell," Absalom explained. "He will have his hands on your shoulders for the duration of the questioning, but that should be all you feel. The magic itself does not produce any sensations or side effects. Are you ready to begin?"

Arleth nodded again.

"Very well, here we go."

For the next half an hour, Absalom asked Arleth a bunch of questions about the assassin. He didn't care one iota what she answered, but it had to look like he did. After all, this was the pretence he had given for having her come to Oherra with him. So he asked her all the questions he could think of; what the assassin had looked like; what weapon he had been holding; if he had said anything to her. Arleth answered all of them as best she could, and Rogan extracted as much as *he* could. Absalom was just wrapping up with his questions about the assassin, but he still needed to ask the only question he cared about. He looked up at Rogan to signal that he was ready. Rogan returned the king's glance with a knowing stare; he was ready too.

"Rogan," Absalom called to his sorcerer, emphasizing the man's name "I think we are done here." He was speaking slowly, trying to give Rogan as much time as possible. "I have asked all the questions that I needed to. Thank you very much for your help." He looked at Rogan inquiringly, had it worked? Rogan smiled and nodded – he had got the information he needed. Arleth had been deep under Rogan's memory spell and so when Absalom had said Rogan's name, her thoughts had unconsciously drifted to where she had last heard his name. Rogan had then been able to extract the entire event, without Arleth even realizing that she had been thinking about it.

"Ok," Absalom said. "You can leave now, thanks again for your help." Rogan withdrew his hands from Arleth's shoulders and walked out of the sitting room. He didn't want to be seen by Arleth, but he knew that Absalom would still want to talk to him so he entered into Absalom's study, to the right of the sitting room and closed the door behind him.

Once Rogan had left, Absalom removed Arleth's blindfold. She blinked a couple of times adjusting to the change of light, and rubbed her eyes.

"So, what did you think about the magic. It was painless just like I said wasn't it?"

"Yes, it was. I didn't feel a thing," Arleth said feeling quite foolish at her previous worry. She had felt absolutely nothing out of the ordinary. "I feel kind of silly for being afraid now," she confessed.

"That's ok, you don't need to feel silly," Absalom said soothingly. "Magic *can* be harmful and it can be scary, especially to someone who has never experienced it before. But just remember that no one here in the castle will harm you with magic, or without. The only thing you could be worried about are the assassins, but you should be quite safe here in the castle. The castle itself is guarded by magical charms and you have the added protection of both Rogan and myself. You can think of both of us as your protectors if you like. I know Rogan views himself that way – he uses his magic to defend Iridian castle and protect everyone inside it."

"Thank you," Arleth said feeling reassured.

"No, thank you my dear," Absalom said. "You have given us valuable information about the assassins. We will be a lot closer to catching them thanks to your help. But I am quite busy right now, so I must show you out." With that, he took Arleth's arm and led her out of the sitting room, through the main entrance and out of his chambers. He walked with her a little bit down the hall until it split into two paths. Here he stopped, "I must leave you now Arleth, take the right hall until you see three doors, then take the middle door and keep going straight down the hall. It will lead you back to the courtyard. It is a different route than how we came here, but it is faster."

"Thanks," Arleth smiled and turned towards the hall on the right. Absalom watched her walk down the hall for a few moments to make sure that she was going to follow his directions and then turned and walked back to his chambers.

Rogan had emerged from Absalom's study and was waiting in the main entrance hall when Absalom returned.

"So," Absalom demanded, "What did you find out?"

Rogan didn't answer right away, but instead motioned his head in the direction of the sitting room. Absalom nodded impatiently and followed his sorcerer back into the room.

"Well, she went into the courtyard this afternoon to explore," Rogan began, lowering himself into one of the armchairs. "She came across two members of your harem and one of them was splitting."

Absalom groaned, "And she saw the splitting?"

"Yes," said Rogan, "And she overheard their conversation in which my name was mentioned." He reiterated it for the king. "You know, it would just be easier to enchant her. Clearly she doesn't trust you yet or she wouldn't have lied to you about why she was in the courtyard, or why she was alarmed when she heard my name."

Absalom looked at Rogan angrily, "You were standing at the door listening." It was more an accusation than a question.

"Yes," said Rogan shamelessly. "But that part is not important, don't you think enchantment looks more attractive now?"

"No, not yet," said Absalom stubbornly. "I am still trying to make her trust me, she is just a child, it shouldn't be that hard. She will trust me eventually"

"But she is *his* child." Rogan interjected.

"Besides," Absalom continued as though Rogan hadn't spoken, "I gave her some sentimental nonsense about how we are here to protect her and how you use your magic to defend those in the castle. I'm pretty sure she bought it."

Rogan still looked sceptical.

"Don't worry," Absalom said, "I am not going to leave something this important up to chance. If it is clear that she is being swayed against us, or that I will not be able to make her trust me completely, I will not hesitate to have you enchant her."

"Alright," said Rogan. He turned to leave.

"And Rogan," Absalom called after him, forcing him to turn back around. "Do something about those two in my harem; their amount of free-will is troubling."

"Just the two of them?"

Absalom thought for a moment, "Good point. Recombine all of them. If some are starting to disenchant, others might be as well. Besides, I am getting bored with them; some new combinations would be nice. You haven't made me a red-head in a while."

Rogan smiled with a cold glint in his eye. "I will see what I can do."

* * *

Just as Absalom had said, Arleth came to a series of three doors. Following, his directions she opened the door in the middle and made her way down the hall it opened into. She was thinking about the memory spell and about Absalom's sorcerer. She was so lost in her thoughts that she didn't notice that the door didn't shut behind her. It was stopped by a foot, inserted just as the door was closing. As Arleth walked obliviously down the hall, the owner of the foot crept his way through the door and closing it silently behind him, melted into the shadows.

Absalom had been right, the spell was completely painless. She had felt nothing out of the ordinary. In fact, if he hadn't told her that there was magic being used on her, she would not have even known. She was glad that Absalom had been honest with her though, explaining the magic to her and reassuring her that everything would be fine. Absalom really was a great man. She didn't know anything about kings, but she didn't think that many of them would have taken the time that he had to make her feel comfortable.

Then why hadn't she told him about the women in the courtyard? She had already confessed that she had been there and it wouldn't have been hard for her to have seen them in the search for her bracelet. Absalom would have been able to answer her questions about Rogan. Arleth didn't know why she hadn't asked. Although she trusted Absalom and because of him, his sorcerer, something had held her back from confiding in him. She couldn't quite put her finger on it. It was possible that since she hadn't had anyone to call a friend, except for maybe Chuck since Flora had died seven years ago, maybe she couldn't trust anymore. That fateful day had certainly taken away her childhood innocence and made her more wary and suspicious, but for some reason she didn't think that explained her reluctance.

The sound of footsteps behind her interrupted her thoughts. She turned around to see who was behind her, expecting to see another servant or perhaps a messenger or soldier; the footsteps had been too light to belong to a greken. But when she turned around, there was no one there, just an empty hall.

That was weird she thought. She must have imagined it. She turned back around and started walking down the hall again. She had gone a few steps when she heard the footsteps again, this time they sounded closer. Arleth spun around immediately and this time, she saw a dark form melt into the shadows to her right.

There was definitely someone there, and whoever it was, was clearly following her and didn't want her to see them. Maybe it was the assassin that had chased her on Tocarra! Or one of his accomplices. Absalom said that he would protect her, but she couldn't go back to him now; the assailant was blocking that path. Her only hope was to out run whoever it was. She needed to reach a communal area like the kitchen or dining hall before the shadowy figure caught up to her. Arleth felt a surge of terror and started running down the hall.

She had gone no more than a couple of steps when a firm hand covered her mouth and another grabbed her waist and pulled her into the shadows at the side of the hall. She felt some fumbling around behind her and momentarily the hand that had clasped around her waist was removed. Arleth, already struggling against her attacker, took the opportunity to give them a strong elbow to the stomach. A male voice gave a grunt of pain, and then the hand grabbed her around the waist again, this time tighter. She fought in vain as she was pulled into a dark room off of the hall. Her captor kicked the door shut behind them and just like that, she was engulfed in total darkness, the prisoner of a man she felt pretty sure didn't have good intentions.

Chapter 14

Arleth tried to scream, but all that came out was a faint muffled noise; the man's hand was clasped too tightly around her mouth. But that didn't stop her from struggling. She twisted and squirmed in his grasp, trying to get free. The man was too strong though; she was struggling with all her force, but his grip never loosened on her. Beginning to get frantic, Arleth started thrusting elbows behind her into what she presumed was the man's stomach. She didn't know if it was hurting him, but she had to do something. She couldn't just let herself be submissively captured. The man's grip still didn't loosen and so she took her right foot and kicked backwards at him with all her might. The man cried out in pain and staggered backwards a bit.

"Wait! Arleth, stop. I'm not going to hurt you."

Hardly listening to what he was saying, she kicked him again. This time, the blow hit him in the knee and he collapsed onto the ground. But his grip never loosened on her mouth and waist and so he brought her down with him. With a grunt, Arleth landed on the man's lap as he crashed into the ground. Winded, Arleth stopped struggling for a few seconds. The man took the opportunity to speak again.

"Arleth, wait!"

Her raised elbow paused in mid-air; how did he know her name?

Encouraged by her response, he spoke again, "Arleth, I am not going to hurt you, I am a friend."

"mmh dh mnn knmh mh mnhm?" Arleth asked, her voice completely muffled by the man's hand. She had stopped struggling, but her elbow remained in mid-air ready to strike.

"I am going to remove my hand from your mouth ok? But you have to promise me you won't scream. Can you promise me?"

"mm hmm," Arleth nodded.

"Ok," said the man. He slowly removed his hand from her mouth, ready to put it back if she started to scream. His other arm remained around her waist.

Arleth didn't scream though, instead she repeated her question, "How do you know my name?"

"I saw you a long time ago. You wouldn't remember me."

He removed his grip from her waist and Arleth climbed off of his lap and sat down facing him. She didn't understand what he was saying, but she didn't think he was a threat to her.

"You know my sister Arleth. Or I guess I should say *knew* her, I suppose she must be dead now or this situation would never have happened."

"Your sister? I really don't think I do.."

"Neve."

"Neve was your sister?" Arleth said incredulously. "But how come you never came to visit her, how come she never mentioned you? How come you are here on Oherra and she was on Tocarra?"

"Things were quite," he fished around for the right word, "*complicated* here. I was not sure she was even alive, and I can imagine that she wouldn't have known if I was alive either. I am sorry, I can't explain more, it is not my place to do so. I can see how this would make me seem dishonest to you. I can assure you I am telling the truth ... but I suppose that won't be enough for you." He hesitated, thinking, "I know, ask me any questions you like about Neve, and I will answer them for you."

"Alright," Arleth said. "What was Neve's favourite colour?"

"Blue," the man answered immediately.

"Yes, that is correct, just like her eyes."

"No," the man corrected, "Her eyes were green. A pale green with flecks of gold."

"Did Neve like singing?"

"Yes, she did. She was older than me by five years and one night I remember when I was a child, there was a terrible storm and I was afraid. She held me and sang to me for hours until I fell asleep. She had the most beautiful singing voice..." His voice broke off. He was trying to hold back tears.

Arleth for her part could feel the tears begin in the corner of her eyes. "I miss her so much," Arleth cried.

"So she is dead then," said the man sadly.

Arleth burst into tears, "I believe you," she sobbed at the man. "I loved Neve so much." The man reached for her blindly in the dark and, finding her shoulders, pulled her to him. He held her against his chest for a couple of minutes, until Arleth had stopped crying and he had regained his composure.

"Can you please tell me how my sister died," the man asked quietly.

Arleth nodded and told him what had happened that day seven years ago. "Thank you," the man said in a choked voice when she had finished. "I never knew what had happened to her; it helps to at least get some kind of closure." They sat in silence for a few moments and then abruptly the man said, "I'm sorry Arleth, I have been selfish. I don't have much time and there are some very important things that I need to tell you. I shouldn't have been wasting it asking you about my sister."

"What do you have to tell me?" Arleth asked, intrigued.

"Absalom is not who you think he is. He is not the rightful ruler of Oherra. He is a very bad man, his sorcerer, Rogan, is even worse."

"But," Arleth started in protest.

"Please let me finish," the man cut her off. "I don't expect you to believe me just yet, but please let me say what I have to say." Arleth stayed silent, and the man continued, "You have probably noticed that there is a war going on. This war has lasted just over a decade, and for all that time neither side has managed to defeat the other. It is a struggle for the claim to the throne of Oherra. The rightful heir; Aedan Amara leads the struggle against Absalom. For the last three years I have been here in Iridian Castle spying on Absalom and reporting back to Aedan."

Arleth wasn't sure what to believe, "Are you a member of the Black Thorn?"

"The what?"

"The Black Thorn, the assassin group that has been attacking Absalom and who chased me in Tocarra?"

The man sighed, "I don't know what lies Absalom has told you but there is no such thing as the Black Thorn and no assassin group. I don't know who chased you on Tocarra, but I can assure you it wasn't a member of an assassin group. Listen," the man said growing anxious, "I have stayed here too long as it is, it is not safe for either one of us." Arleth heard a shuffling and a small ball of light appeared in the air between them. The man was holding it up, and fumbling in his pockets for something. In the dim light Arleth could just make out his face: pale, freckled skin, red hair, green eyes and a short, scruffy beard. Well, Arleth thought, at least she knew he was definitely telling the truth about being Neve's brother. He was perfectly the male version of her.

"Here," the man said holding out a small blue object in the palm of his hand. "I don't expect you to believe me right away," he repeated, "The position of the King of Oherra has a legacy of greatness and unfortunately for me right now, that legacy has been misplaced onto a very evil man. But you are a clever girl, you must have noticed some of the strange things that happen in this castle. Have you wondered yet why none of the servants smile, talk, or even know their own names? Why there are no towns in the valley? No communities, no animals, no people? Please take this," he said, extending his hand towards Arleth. "It is a concealing spell. It won't make you invisible, you will still have to hide, but it will ensure that no one can sense your presence using magic. Don't worry, I use them all the time, it is how I sneak around the castle undetected." With that he, grabbed another one from his pocket, showed it to her to prove that he was taking the same pill he had offered to her and popped it in his mouth. Hesitantly, Arleth picked up the pill from his hand and examined it. It was a small cylindrical tablet. There was absolutely nothing remarkable about it. She shrugged her shoulders, there was no harm in keeping it; she didn't have to actually take it.

"Take this too," the spy said handing her a small key. "There is a tower right next to the main hall. If you go up the stairs in the main hall and across the corridor, you will see the entrance to the tower. If you go down the stairs there to the very bottom you will find yourself in the dungeons. Close to the entrance there will be a huge black door. It will have strange green markings on it and a red hand. This key will open the door. Inside, you will find the answers to your questions."

Arleth took the key from the man and loosened the belt from her dress. She shoved both the pill and the key behind the belt, against the fabric of her dress, and pulled the belt tight, hiding both from sight.

"Please be careful Arleth, it is not safe for you here. I wish I could take you with me, but that would put you in even more danger. I fear you will not see me alive again. Goodbye Arleth, it was nice to meet you." With that, he extinguished the light, turned and exited the room, leaving Arleth alone in the darkness.

Arleth didn't know what to do, she was shaken and confused. She didn't know what to think, who to believe, so she just stayed where she was, sitting in the dark room, contemplating her options.

On the one hand, the man was definitely Neve's brother. He looked too much like her and knew too much about her, to have been making that up. He had been clearly upset when he learned that she had died and how she had been killed. Arleth couldn't imagine that anyone who loved Neve as much as she did, Neve's own brother, could have wicked intentions. But she also couldn't believe that Absalom was evil - he seemed too genuine, too sincere. He had shown her nothing but kindness since she had come to Oherra, in fact, he had gone out of his way to make her feel comfortable.

But then again, what the spy had said about strange things going on in the castle was true. Arleth *had* wondered why the servants never talked and she *had* thought it was strange that the girl who had given her the tour said she didn't know her own name. But Absalom had explained this to her; the servants were just private, they didn't want to open up to her just yet because she was a newcomer. That had made sense to Arleth at the time, but now she wasn't so sure. *Was* there something else going on?

And the girl in the courtyard; her injury had been horrendous. Both her and the second woman had been terrified at the mention of Rogan's name. Upon hearing that Rogan was the king's sorcerer and in his presence, she had dismissed the incident – the girls must be prisoners or something and Rogan was in charge of them. But if she took what the spy said as the truth, that Rogan and Absalom were not the kind, moral people she thought they were, then the whole event made a lot more sense. Remembering the innocent faces on the two girls and the way the cat trusted the blonde one, it made much more sense if Rogan and Absalom were the malevolent ones. But, she didn't know who those girls really were, she reminded herself and she didn't want to judge something so important just based on appearances. Also, if the spy had been telling the truth about them, then he was also telling the truth about there being no assassin group, nothing called the Black Thorn. And *that* confused Arleth even more. If there were no assassins after the king, than whom had that scar-faced man been and why had he been chasing her? And stranger still, if there were no assassins, why had Absalom made up that lie and taken her to Oherra with him?

Arleth sighed, she had gone over everything that she knew, and it had gotten her nowhere. She was still just as confused as when she had started. There was also something gnawing at her, something that didn't quite make sense with what the spy had told her. It had to do with Absalom not being the rightful king of Oherra. She couldn't quite put her finger on it, but she knew there was something, some fact she had learned that didn't make sense if he wasn't the real king. Whatever it was though, stayed infuriatingly just out of her grasp.

Well, Arleth thought, I am not going to get the answers I need sitting here. She put her right hand down on her belt, feeling the key and the blue pill beneath. I guess I have no other choice she thought. It also didn't hurt that she was insanely curious about what was behind the door, especially since it was in one of the towers that was off-bounds. She wouldn't be rash though, for once in her life she would not run on her emotion. She would remain calm, and if she still had the same frame of mind tomorrow morning as she did now, she would check out what was in the dungeons first thing after breakfast. With her mind made up, she fumbled around in the dark for the door knob and pushed the door gently open. She poked her head out and looked down the hall in both directions. Not seeing anyone, she exited the room, closed the door behind her and made her way down the hall. She would go back to the tunnel she was supposed to have been in this whole time, and clean it in blissful boredom until it was time for dinner.

Chapter 15

It was late at night and Selene was exhausted, she had spent all day (and the two before it) perfecting the Alondrane. But as tired as she was, she couldn't sleep. She was sitting outside her and Aedan's tent with her back against the cold stone of the cave wall. Except for a couple of soldiers on guard a fair distance away from her, everyone else was asleep. She held the Alondrane in her hand, studying it, checking once again if there was anything wrong with it. She had made them before, but none quite like this one and certainly not one for such an important purpose. Her life had always been in danger by using them, that was just the nature of how an Alondrane worked, but this time she was also endangering Aedan. If it didn't work properly, he would die. It was that simple, if she had miscalculated, Absalom would capture Aedan and he would die a slow and tortured death. That was why she was awake now, checking and re-checking her Alondrane. Running all sorts of magical tests on it to make sure they all responded properly. So far they all had. She just had one more left to try.

She rolled up one of her pant legs and placed the Alondrane against her bare skin. It stuck perfectly, as though it belonged there. She knew it would, that was one of the first tests she had run. That wasn't what she was testing this time. She rolled down her pant leg to cover the Alondrane and stood up.

"Onantra" she said firmly. Instantly, the Alondrane detached itself from her skin, slid down her leg and rolled along the floor of the cave until it stopped some five meters away from her.

"Good," Selene said quietly to herself. She walked over to retrieve the Alondrane and rolling up her pant leg again, placed it against her skin one more time. This time, she sat down.

"Onantra," she said. The Alondrane responded the same way it had before, but Selene wasn't quite satisfied. She tried one more time, this time lying down flat on her stomach, with the Alondrane on her chest.

"Onantra," she repeated. Once again, the Alondrane responded the same way. Smiling, Selene bent over to retrieve her Alondrane. It seemed perfect. She picked up the shimmering object and finally satisfied, put it in her pocket.

* * *

Deep in the dungeons of Iridian castle, a spear of green light flashed across a cold stone room. It was thrown expertly and it soared soundlessly through the air until it reached its target. With a sizzle of burning flesh, it lodged itself neatly into the sinews of the prisoner's arm, just below the elbow. Neve's brother cried out in terrible pain and clenched his teeth together in a futile effort to reduce his suffering.

He had spent the remainder of the day after meeting with Arleth hiding from Absalom and Rogan. He had known it was a pointless venture though. The night before, he had overheard the two of them talking; something had happened on Tocarra that made them sure they were being spied upon. Even so, he hadn't been about to give up his mission, and so he had known it was only a matter of time before one of them was able to catch him. That was why he had risked everything to give his message to Arleth. If he had more time, he would have been more delicate, explained things more fully, perhaps even tried to smuggle her out of the castle.

"AAAHHH!" he cried out again, this time louder. But it was too late for all of that now.

"So Tobin, how does it make you feel, that I am going to kill you with the same magic that I killed your sister?" Said Rogan tauntingly, firing a thin spear of green light through his left thigh.

"You're an ugly bastard," the spy said through gritted teeth.

Rogan started to laugh, a hollow, joyless laugh, "That is hardly the point now is it?" He bent down in front of the tortured man and stroked his chin with one of his long fingers. Rogan had long nails and a thin line of blood appeared along Tobin's chin. "But insults are not very nice are they? What would your poor sister think?" Abruptly Rogan stood up and fired two more spears of green light, this time one into each of Tobin's feet. Rogan left them there for a few moments, watching the blood pool around the edges of the spears. Then with a hiss of satisfaction, he ripped out the spears with a wave of his hand and watched in delight as the pooled blood started to drip down the man's legs in delicious, red rivulets.

Tobin was starting to feel dizzy, both from the pain and the blood rushing to his head. After catching him, Absalom had dragged him down to the dungeons and had hung him upside down by his ankles from a low ceiling beam. For the next half an hour, the king had questioned him as he hung suspended from the beam. Occasionally, as he asked questions, he had pushed Tobin so that he swung back and forth, or had casually twisted him around and around until the ropes holding him up were tight and then let him unwind, spinning him in fast, dizzy circles. This was done not so much to torture Tobin, as to ease Absalom's boredom and give him something to occupy his attention. Both captor and captive had known that the questioning was a farce. There was nothing that Tobin knew that Absalom didn't. He had learned long ago that Aedan didn't give his spies any information so they couldn't betray him later in just such a situation. The spy wouldn't know any of Aedan's plans. The only information that the spy had that Absalom wanted was where Aedan's stronghold was. But retrieving this information was impossible. It would require either having him draw a map, which would inevitably be purposefully inaccurate and impossible to follow anyways due to Selene's magic, or keeping him alive and forcing him to show them. But once again, even if the spy was somehow coerced into showing them the true path, either through magic or threats, they couldn't get anywhere near the entrance anyways if Selene didn't want them to.

So Absalom had just gone through the motions for fun. He enjoyed this man being at his mercy, loved that the man knew that every second, every minute he was drawing closer to his death. Absalom relished this kind of power over human life, this kind of control. But, Rogan was so much more *creative* than he was at actually ending life. Besides, his sorcerer enjoyed it so much that Absalom almost felt bad not letting him. And tonight, Absalom was in a particularly generous mood. Perhaps it was because his Imari were finally ready, or because he had Arleth and even though she didn't trust him yet, he was confident she would. Whatever the reason, he had decided to let Rogan do *all* of the torturing this time. And now, looking at the state the man was in, Absalom was very glad he had – Rogan was quite gifted.

Tobin groaned softly and stared at the stone floor beneath him. There was a huge pool of blood underneath him. He realized it was his own, and groggily marvelled at just how much blood a human body had. He was in so much pain – every part of his body burned. He had known how cruel both Absalom and Rogan were. He had known they would torture him and that he wouldn't die quickly, But the pain was becoming too much to bear. He hoped that Arleth would use the key, that she would find what was behind that door and that she would somehow escape from the castle. If that happened, then his three years of spying would have been put to good use, and he could almost bear his suffering now. Thankfully, he felt the pain begin to lessen as his mind became hazy; he was drifting off into blissful unconsciousness.

Rogan had looked down at Tobin when he heard him groaning and could tell that he was about to lose consciousness. That would be no fun, he still wanted to play. He bent down beside Tobin and put his hands on his back. A pale green light pulsed from his fingertips; that should ensure he stays conscious, Rogan thought. But just as he was about to remove his hands, he sensed something in Tobin. He changed his magic slightly, shifting some threads slightly into a different pattern. Using the new spell, he probed deeper and smiled, stepping back from his prisoner.

"So Tobin," Rogan said, "I am so glad that you didn't drift off on me. You see, now you can feel all the pain, the way I want you too, and you have the added bonus of being able to listen to a very funny story I have just discovered."

Tobin groaned again, all his pain returning in a rush. He didn't know what Rogan was talking about, but he could imagine that he wouldn't find the story funny at all.

"Now Tobin, I know you don't understand anything about magic, so let me explain a little something to you. You see, there are some spells that are so similar to each other that by weaving one, you can still sense the faint presence of the other. When such similar spells are woven, even when the sorcerer is actively casting one of them, anything that is a trigger for the related spell will still be felt. Let's use for example, a memory extraction spell and the spell that I just cast on you to prevent you from going unconscious. Now as it just so happens, these spells are about as similar as two spells can be. They both require the user to go into the mind of their target and cast threads between their conscious and unconscious sensations. For memory extraction, it is important to extract both conscious and unconscious memories, and for the revival spell that I just used on you, it is imperative to separate the conscious from the unconscious. Really it comes down to a few differences in the threads woven for each spell. In one, unconscious and conscious are joined, in the other; the thread is broken and moved, so that the two are disjoined. Oh I can see that you are starting to see what I am getting at." Rogan smiled at the expression starting to form on Tobin's face.

Tobin, did know what Rogan was hinting at. He felt a terrible, gut-wrenching guilt, why had he thought about Arleth?

Rogan continued, "At the moment that my hands touched you in order to cast my revival spell, you thought about Arleth." Rogan gleamed with pleasure, enjoying every second of his explanation. "As I just mentioned, I sensed her name, it was pulsating on the corner of the spell I cast, so I rearranged some threads to let her name in, and low and behold I had cast a memory extraction spell. And what a naughty boy you were hmm? Telling her that Absalom was not the rightful ruler? Giving her a concealing spell? Giving her a key to my private experimental chamber?"

"You won't win. Even if you stop her from finding out about your experiments, she will question other things. You can't stop her from finding out the truth. You need her alive or she will be useless to you."

Rogan smiled, "There you are only partly right Tobin, we surely won't kill her, at least not until she does what we want. But she certainly doesn't have to have her own free-will does she? And thanks to your little escapade, she will lose that forever."

They are going to enchant her! Tobin thought with horror.

"Isn't it nice that you will die knowing that you singlehandedly ended Arleth's life as a free-thinking human? Oh and also how you just cost Aedan the war? How delightful!"

With that, Rogan shot another spear of green light from his fingers. This time, he held on to it, directing it to Tobin's neck. "Goodbye Tobin," he said, smiling down at the man's face. Slowly, enjoying every moment, Rogan slid the spear of light sideways across his neck.

Tobin screamed. He screamed in agony at Rogan ending his life and he screamed knowing what would happen to Arleth. This last torture ended quickly though, and soon his screams abruptly stopped. There was a soft thud on the floor and Rogan extinguished his green light. He turned and faced Absalom.

"So, we are going to enchant her *now* right?"

"Yes," said Absalom, conceding to his sorcerer. He knew that Arleth was curious and if left alone, she would definitely go and check out the room that Tobin had given her the key for. It was a simple enough matter to stop her from doing this, or even to let her, but have Rogan cast a shade over the room so that she didn't see what was really there. But the spy had been right, even if they did that, there wouldn't be a shortage of other things she would question and now, having her suspicions piqued, she would be hyper vigilant for anything out of the ordinary. He hated to admit it, but Rogan was right. The safest thing to do now was to enchant her and worry about the details later. "Yes," he said again. "We will enchant her first thing in the morning."

* * *

Arleth sat bolt upright in bed, shaking. She thought she heard screaming, but as soon as she concentrated on it, it was gone. She had probably imagined it, a remnant of her nightmare. She couldn't remember the details, but she was sure of three things. There had been a lot of screaming, a lot of blood, and now she had a terrible sense of foreboding. Her skin was cold and clammy, the sheets soaked through with her sweat. The lamp on her night-table had been knocked over – she must have been kicking in her sleep. What exactly had she been dreaming of? She wished she could remember. But then again, taking measure of her rapid heart-beat, and sweat-soaked sheets, maybe she was lucky she couldn't remember.

Arleth looked around her in the darkness; everything was quiet, the only noise being the even breathing and occasional snores from the other servants sleeping in the room with her. No one else was awake. Still, Arleth couldn't shake the sense that she was in danger. Quietly, she climbed out of bed and crept her way down the rows of beds to the door. She opened it a crack and peered out, looking both ways down the hall. It was dark, but she didn't see anyone or anything out of the ordinary. She closed the door again and walked over to the window. Except for a few campfires lit by the guards on night-watch, the valley was dark. She watched the guards for a few minutes just to be certain; everything seemed normal.

Still afraid, but not knowing what else to do, Arleth got back into bed. She propped up her pillow against the wall and leaning against it, pulled the sheets up over her raised knees to rest under her chin. Her eyes darted this way and that around the room, looking for any moving shadows. She felt a jabbing in her side – she had left her belt on when she went to bed, not wanting to risk having the things the spy had given her found or stolen. It felt like it was the key that was now poking into her. She shifted her position slightly and it went away. Having been reminded of her encounter with the spy, Arleth realized that she had just made up her mind. She was definitely going to go and check out the room tomorrow morning. Something was going on in this castle and Arleth wanted to find out what it was.

Propped up against the wall the way she was, with her hands tightly clasping the sheets beneath her chin, it was a long time before she finally drifted off to sleep.

Chapter 16

Aedan looked at the gates ahead of him, squinting to protect his eyes from the sunlight. It was mid-morning and he was standing just outside Iridian Castle. There was a horrifyingly familiar form stuck to one of the doors. He squinted harder trying to make out what it was. The sun was reflecting directly in his eyes, making it impossible to make out anything beyond a vague outline. Still, he had a pretty good idea what he was looking at. He desperately hoped he was wrong.

He kept walking towards the entrance, keeping his eyes fixed on the object. As he drew closer, the gates became larger and larger, until they blocked out his view of the sun and he was at last able to see the form clearly. He drew his breath in sharply and stopped dead in his tracks.

Nailed to the door was the head of his spy, Tobin.

"Bastard," Aedan muttered under his breath. He knew that Tobin's death had not been quick and had certainly been anything but painless. Even though both Absalom and Rogan would have known they would gain nothing from interrogating him, they would have tortured him just for fun.

"I'm so sorry Tobin," Aedan said softly. There was nothing he could have done to protect his spy. Even if he had found out that the man had been discovered, he knew that Tobin wouldn't have left Iridian Castle, especially now that Arleth was there. Knowing this didn't ease Aedan's guilt though. He felt personally responsible for Tobin's death. He looked up at the dead man's head again and felt a tear begin to form in the corner of his eye.

The thick nail had been driven through Tobin's skull so hard that his entire forehead was caved in against the door. Even still, the look of pain in his face was unmistakable. His eyes were still open wide and his mouth was frozen in a scream.

'I *will* kill you Absalom Drae', Aedan vowed, for not the first time. 'Before this war is over, I will kill you. I will kill you for everyone that you have butchered so mercilessly.'

There was an angry hissing from his left and a strong serpentine hand yanked him violently forward. Aedan stumbled a few steps, but managed to regain his balance without falling down. Once he was steady on his feet again, he looked up in loathing at the Greken who had his arm in a vice-like grip.

'And I will kill you too', Aedan thought. 'You and the rest of you nasty beasts', he turned his head and his eyes travelled to the other eight Grekens who had him surrounded in a tight circle.

As if hearing his thoughts, the Greken yanked him again. This time Aedan was unprepared and he fell face first into the dirt. As he pulled himself out of the dirt, he thought about how he had gotten here.

He hadn't tried to sneak into Iridian castle undetected. He had known there was no point; it had been built specifically to prevent an ambush. Aedan remembered his father explaining this to him when he was a young boy. He and his father had stood on one of the higher, enclosed pathways overlooking the valley. Aedan had listened in admiration as his father had explained how their ancestors had specifically chosen to build Iridian castle in this valley as it provided the best defence. A young Aedan had felt safe and secure listening to his father describe how difficult it was to attack the castle. He had never imagined then that twenty years later he would be on the other side, trying desperately to attack such an impenetrable fortress, wishing that his forefathers had been a little less clever.

The castle was located in the exact centre of the valley, meaning there were two and a half miles of flat, open land in any direction between the mountains and the castle. Not only would Aedan have been easily seen from the battlements as he made his way across, the valley was strewn with soldiers, guards and Grekens. Even a concealing spell wouldn't have helped him; it would only have made his presence undetected by magic. If anyone had looked in his direction, he would have been seen and in the open valley, he would have had no place to hide. Coming at night he would have had more of a chance, at least the shadows would have hidden him better. In the darkness, with the help of a concealing spell, he might have been able to sneak his way past all the guards, even the Grekens, but there were still the magical charms and defensive spells placed all over the valley and around the castle itself.

No, Aedan had known it was futile to try to sneak in, so he hadn't bothered. He had left his stronghold at dawn and when he had reached the valley, he had calmly walked out into the open. It had only taken a few seconds for the guards to notice him and within minutes he had his escort of Grekens. He knew that Absalom would have sent out orders not to kill him; Absalolm would want that honour for himself. So, as contradictory as it sounded, Aedan knew the best way for him to get into the castle was to be captured. Once inside, Selene's alondrane would do the rest – hopefully.

Their plan was far from perfect, but it was the best one they had and now that he had been captured, Aedan just had to hope that it would work.

While Aedan had been reminiscing about his childhood, the gates to the castle had been opened. He was now being forcibly led through into the inner yard – the space between the castle proper and the battlements. Yet another defensive measure Aedan wished his ancestors had not been scrupulous enough to create.

In peaceful times, this inner yard had served as a market-place. On Sundays, the townspeople living in the surrounding valley would all bring their goods and set up stalls. Each market was a bustling, joyous occasion and lasted from dawn to late into the night. When the sun went down, the vendors would pack up their stalls, torches would be lit, the court musicians would start to play and the whole town would sing and dance the night away. Aedan and Val had loved these nights. As young children it was the only time they were allowed to stay up late, and many of Aedan's fondest childhood memories were of these nights.

All of that had changed when Absalom came. Now there were no more marketplaces, no more dancing or singing, no more joyous occasions – no more townspeople. Aedan looked around sadly. Where there once was grass and flowers, there was now scorched earth. The carefree townspeople had been replaced with miserable, malnourished soldiers huddled around campfires. They looked up as Aedan was led by; they all knew he was the enemy leader. It didn't matter that, thanks to Rogan's enchantments, they didn't remember he was really the rightful heir to the throne; they were surprised that their enemy's leader had been captured and they watched open-mouthed as he was led by.

With a breaking heart, Aedan looked back at these wretched men. He never ceased to be disgusted by the level of decay that his father's society had undergone at the hands of Absalom. It was hard to believe, even having witnessed it, that one man could have destroyed so much so fast. Even if Aedan was able to rescue Arleth and win the seat of Oherra back from Absalom, he would still face a steep uphill battle to rebuild everything that Absalom had destroyed. A tear of frustration formed at the corner of his eye and he wiped it quickly away with his free hand.

His movement was instantly mistaken for some kind of escape attempt. The Greken who had been dragging him along by the arm, abruptly let go and pushed Aedan to the ground. He emitted a loud hissing noise and thrust the blade of his axe towards Aedan's face. The other seven Grekens hissed angrily in response and also thrust their axes at him. Aedan froze in place where he had been pushed to the ground. He was afraid to move with the blades of eight axes, wielded by eight very angry Grekens, just inches from his head.

His situation had suddenly become quite precarious. Aedan's whole plan rested on the fact that the Grekens would bring him in one piece to Absalom. If they killed him now, he would never be able to save Arleth. He knew that Absalom would want him captured alive and had been sure that Rogan's enchantments would not provide the Grekens with enough free-will to kill him. He had been one hundred percent certain last night, sitting beside Selene and Val from the safety of his stronghold. But now, surrounded by a ring of angry Grekens who looked like they would like nothing better than to chop him into little pieces, he wasn't so sure. They had been specifically created to protect Absalom, and although Aedan didn't intend to attack Absalom now, the Grekens wouldn't know that. Aedan was their main enemy after all, and now that they were nearing the castle, would their drive to protect Absalom prove to be stronger than their commands not to kill Aedan. He didn't know the answer and this terrified him - would this careless dismissal of the Grekens cost him his life, Arleth's life and his country? Why had he wiped the tear from his face? He should have known what would happen – these creatures were ruthless killers.

"Stand down!" A man's voice commanded angrily.

Instantly the Grekens lowered their weapons and turned to face the man who had issued the order.

"Bring him here." The Greken who had been dragging him before, grabbed on to his arm again and pulled him forwards, through the castle doors into the main entrance hall. The Grekens in-front of him moved off to the sides giving the commanding man a clear view of the captive. It was too dark for Aedan to see who was in front of him, but he didn't need to wait for his eyes to adjust, he knew the sound of that voice as well as he knew his own.

"Aedan Amara," said Absalom mockingly, "How nice of you to drop by."

* * *

"Aedan Amara?" breathed Arleth. So Neve's brother had been telling the truth! Absalom was not the rightful heir to the throne – this man was. She looked at him closely, appraising him. Physically, he was a young man, probably only about 10 years older than her, but he had the hardened expression of someone much older. He was dressed in simple, mud-covered clothes and surrounded by menacing captors, but somehow he still managed to look confident and proud. His very presence made Arleth know with certainty that this man was a born ruler.

Aedan suddenly looked up in her direction and Arleth quickly ducked down to hide behind the railing. She crouched motionless for a couple of seconds not wanting to risk being seen. She counted to 10 slowly in her head and then cautiously raised her head a fraction above the railing, just far enough that she could see over. No one seemed to be looking up in her direction. Still, she didn't want to be caught and so she didn't go back to standing, but instead rested on her knees. This way her eyes were just barely above the level of the railing and she could easily duck down if someone looked up again.

Arleth was on the second floor landing overlooking the main entrance hall. After her horrible feeling of dread the night before, Arleth had woken up determined to find what was behind the door with the green markings and the red hand. And so after a hurried breakfast, she had taken the concealing spell pill and snuck off to follow the directions Neve's brother had given her. She had just reached the second floor landing when she heard a commotion and had looked down. That was how she had seen Aedan Amara brought in by the Grekens and the initial exchange between him and Absalom. They were saying something further right now.

"So," said Absalom, "I knew you would come here and try to pull off a valiant escape attempt. But I never thought it would be so easy to thwart you. All those years in the mountains are making you soft in the head I suppose."

Aedan smiled at him, a thin, humourless smile. "Oh but Absalom you misunderstand me. I came only to see you. You are such a wonderful host after all."

Absalom laughed dryly and motioned with a flick of his hand. Instantly a Greken raised the tentacles on his back and whipped Aedan across his face with them. Arleth let out a small gasp and covered her mouth with her hand to avoid making a noise. Aedan, although there was a red cut across his cheek, hardly seemed to notice, indeed he didn't even flinch.

They continued talking but Arleth didn't follow what they were saying – something about an Alondrane and so her mind drifted back to what Neve's brother had said.

If Aedan was indeed the rightful heir of Oherra, than that meant that Neve's brother was likely right about everything else - and he had said that Absalom was evil. She was smart enough to realize that in a war, each side always classified the other side as evil, Ms Witrany had explained it in one of her classes on the history of the Great War. As a result, Arleth was not instantly inclined to take Neve's brother's opinion that Absalom was evil. But if he wasn't an Amara, why *would* he be king if not through devious means. Also, listening to the way he was acting with Aedan, his whole demeanour had indeed seemed to change. Since she had first met Absalom outside Bella's manor on Tocarra, he had acted noble and gracious. Arleth had assumed that was his normal disposition, but now listening to him interact with Aedan, this new personality seemed more natural. It was as if he had been putting on a show the whole time and now when he thought there was no one around he was acting his true self.

Also, Neve's brother had said that there was nothing called the Black Thorn. She was inclined to believe that he had been telling the truth about this as well. But then, if there was no Black Thorn who was it that had been chasing her and why had Absalom brought her with him to Oherra? And why, if he was truly evil and clearly at least not the rightful heir, had he been so nice to her? She still didn't begin to understand the answers to these questions and this troubled her. More troubling, was that Neve's brother had said she was in danger and the goose bumps forming on her arms told her she believed him. She needed to find out what was behind that door. Neve's brother had seemed to think what she found there would at least answer some of her questions. She would go there first and then decide what to do next later.

She looked back down at the scene below her. Absalom was starting to strip Aedan of his clothes. Arleth closed her eyes and quickly turned her head, embarrassed. She wasn't sure how far Absalom would strip him but she didn't want to be there to find out. She crouched back down and crawled her way down the hall to the tower entrance at the far end. She rushed down the stairs leading to the dungeon, intent on finding her answers.

* * *

"Now, now," said Absalom. "I know that bitch Selene wouldn't let her precious Aedan go into Iridian castle unprotected now would she? She would have crafted a special amulet just for you, something to keep you ever so safe."

Aedan's face distorted in anger, he hated Absalom and he would not allow him to talk about Selene that way. He lunged forward, but the Greken held him firm.

Absalom laughed, "So I see that I was right," he said mistaking, Aedan's anger for an admission of guilt. "So what would she make for you? I'm willing to bet she made an Alondrane. She wouldn't want you to be all alone, she would insist on helping you. How sickening, but quite useful for me isn't it? Now she would want it hidden somewhere on you, under your clothes...."

Absalom started ripping off Aedan's clothes. It was at this point that Arleth had started crawling down the hall, and before she had even reached the tower, Absalom had already stripped Aedan naked. He ran his hands along Aedan's body, searching for a hidden Alondrane. He started at his head and worked his way down.

Aedan started laughing. "Absalom you are enjoying this aren't you? This must just make your day, no I suppose it would make your whole month. I guess all those rumours were true?" Aedan was trying to anger him so he wouldn't keep searching. If he found the Alondrane both him and Selene would be as good as dead.

Absalom grit his teeth together and slapped Aedan across the face with the back of his hand.

"Your pathetic tactics are not going to work. Do you really think I am that stupid?"

"I know you are that stupid."

Absalom reached under Aedan's armpit and smiled, "Well I'm smart enough to find the Alondrane am I not?" He grabbed it and held it up to the light. It was small, circular and skin coloured. Against the skin, it would be invisible to the eye, only by touch could Absalom have found it. He looked into Aedan's eyes and with a swift motion threw it on the ground shattering it. For extra effect he dug his heel into the pieces, grinding them into the floor.

Aedan wasn't bothered by this; Selene had been smart enough to make a decoy. The real Alondrane was still hidden on Aedan's body. But he certainly didn't want Absalom to know that and so he acted as though there had only been the one. His mouth opened in shock and he stared down at the pieces in fake horror and sadness.

"Oh Aedan come now, you don't have to act so surprised. I know that was a decoy. You wouldn't have come here with no other discernable plan and had only one Alondrane on you."

Absalom shook his head side to side and smiled maliciously. He continued searching Aedan's body for the real Alondrane. After a few seconds of searching, his hand stopped behind Aedan's right knee.

Aedan's whole body involuntarily flinched. He had found it! Just like he had with the decoy, Absalom held the Alondrane up to Aedan's face, thoroughly enjoying the pain and misery he saw there.

"Well now, it seems you are not nearly as clever as you think you are Amara. Any last words to your precious Selene? Any touching, heartfelt remarks? No?"

And without even pausing for a second to give Aedan time to say anything he smashed the Alondrane on the ground. This time, as Aedan looked down at the broken pieces, he didn't have to fake his horror and sadness, they were quite real.

"Take him to the dungeons," Absalom ordered one of his Grekens. And then looking at Aedan, "I will keep you alive just long enough so you can see Arleth give in to my desires. That way you can die knowing that you failed utterly and completely. Knowing that you will NEVER get Oherra back."

Aedan had one last second to stare heartbroken at the Alondrane pieces on the ground before he was knocked unconscious by a swift blow to the back of his head and roughly dragged down to his dungeon cell.

Chapter 17

Rogan roared in frustration and violently shook the servant girl by the shoulders. Just like him and Absalom had decided last night, Rogan had set off first thing in the morning to go and get Arleth and take her back with him to his chambers so he could enchant her. That had been his plan anyways. Things hadn't turned out so neatly.

First, just after an early breakfast, Rogan had sensed Aedan just on the outskirts of the valley. He had set up sensory spells all around the edge of the mountains; it was his first line of defence for knowing whenever anyone unexpected was nearing the castle. Of course, using a concealing spell would make the user invisible to his enchantments, but they were still useful in some circumstances. Such as now, when Aedan had no need to use a concealing spell and so Rogan had advance notice of his approach. He had rushed up the stairs to Absalom's bed chambers and knocked violently on the closed door. Within a few minutes Absalom had appeared and Rogan had hurriedly told him of Aedan's approach. Absalom had gotten out his binoculars, looked through one of the windows in his bedroom and upon confirming it was indeed Aedan, rushed out of his room closely followed by Rogan. Absalom had given orders to eight of his Grekens to meet Aedan and escort him to the castle unharmed. He then rushed off to prepare for Aedan's arrival, giving Rogan a number of tasks to see to as well.

Absalom wanted Aedan to know instantly that his spy was dead and so Rogan had gone down to the dungeon and retrieved Tobin's head that was still lying in a pool of blood, now dried, on the floor. He had cast a few threads of magic to ensure that Tobin's face retained all the horror and pain of his death and then he had gone to the front gates of the castle and violently nailed the head to it.

Rogan had then spent the better part of an hour ensuring that all of his enchantments around the castle were in proper working order. He had also set up a few surprises that Aedan would be sure to encounter unknowingly. His personal favourite was a Ranin Bud, a devious piece of magic that Rogan had just finished creating and was especially proud of. He had placed it invisible, in the dungeon cell set to go off when Aedan was thrown in. It would attach itself without a trace to Aedan and would stay there unnoticed until it was time for it to detach and grow to maturity. Rogan would never admit it to Absalom, but he almost hoped that Aedan *would* escape so that his Ranin Bud would not just be a precaution – he wanted to see it in action and witness its delicious destructive power.

It was after these tasks that Rogan was finally able to turn his attention to Arleth. He hadn't thought the delay would have had any impact at all. The servants followed a strict schedule and they had just started breakfast by the time Rogan entered the dining hall. But much to his anger he had found Arleth already gone. No one knew where she had gone; but Rogan had a pretty good idea. The only reason she would have skipped breakfast, or at least rushed it so much was if she wanted to investigate what was behind the door that was unlocked by the key Tobin had given her.

It didn't matter too much to Rogan if she found out the truth about his experimental chambers. He was going to enchant her anyways so regardless of her prior feelings she would have none after and would do as they ordered. However, it was true that Arleth's special talent, why they needed her worked so much better by free will, Rogan had to admit that Absalom was right in that. So the less she knew, the less she questioned, the more free will Rogan could leave with her after enchanting her. But once she entered his experimental chamber, the likelihood that she could have any free will left to her at all was very slim. Rogan had to find her fast, or their job would become a lot harder.

Rogan's thoughts were interrupted by the realization that he was holding something heavy in his hands. He looked down at the limp form of the servant girl he was still shaking by the shoulders. While he had been thinking he had been rocking her so violently that he had broken her neck and she now lay lifeless. Rogan's hands on her shoulders were the only thing keeping her upright – it was this unexpected weight that had knocked Rogan out of his reverie.

He pushed the girl disgustedly to the ground so she fell in a tangled heap, her head sticking awkwardly out to the side.

"Clean up this mess," he barked at the servants sitting nearby eating their breakfast. He turned decisively on his heel and with a flap of his robe; he stormed out of the dining hall.

* * *

Arleth, her heart-racing, stared at the door in front of her. It was exactly what Neve's brother had described; black painted wood, strange dark green markings and a huge red hand that covered the better part of the door. Part of the hand had been painted on top of the markings, but whether this had been on purpose or as an afterthought it was impossible to tell.

Arleth loosened her belt slightly and reached behind it into the folds of her dress to where she had hidden the key. She pulled it out and slid it into the lock. The moment the key touched the inside of the lock, there was a loud hiss. Arleth jumped back in shock and quickly looked around her – had someone followed her here? But as she turned from side to side, she could see no one there with her. Confused, Arleth stepped closer to the door and put her ear right up against it. Was someone on the other side? A creature, perhaps a Greken, put in place to guard the room from intruders? She stayed listening at the door for a dozen heartbeats, but she heard nothing, no shuffling, footsteps or breathing other than her own. She relaxed a bit, there didn't seem to be anyone or anything on the other side of the door. Besides, she reasoned, she was pretty sure that Neve's brother wouldn't have forgotten to mention something as important as the fact that the room he had given her the key for was guarded by a violent, hissing creature. She thought momentarily of the possibility that Neve's brother wanted to cause her harm. But she dismissed that idea almost the instant she thought of it; if he *had* wanted to hurt her, he had certainly had the chance.

Satisfied in her logic and more interested in finding out what was behind the door than in wasting time thinking about what the hiss *had* been, she turned the key in the lock. The key turned, but only slightly; Arleth felt a lot of resistance, as if something was pushing against her efforts. She raised her left hand and putting it on top of her right, she tried turning the key again. This time, with the added force of her second hand, she felt the key turning farther. She heard a series of clicks and the sound of metal grating against metal. With a final grunt, using all of her remaining effort, she forced the key as far as it would go to the left. There was a final click and the door swung slightly inward. Arleth plucked the key from the lock and with a deep, anxious breath, she pushed the door open and stepped inside.

The smell hit her like a punch in the face.

She staggered backwards a few steps, unable to stop her body from recoiling in disgust.

"What.... is in.... this room?" Arleth coughed, putting her hand up to cover her nose and mouth. It smelled like a nauseating cocktail of mould, rotten meat and the whole host of human bodily functions – from both ends. Even with her hand over her nose, Arleth's eyes started to water and she felt the bile begin to rise in her throat. She felt herself getting a bit light-headed from the stench and she had to steady herself by placing her hand on the door frame.

She certainly didn't want to turn back, but at the moment, she didn't know how she would be able to continue. As dark as it was, it was impossible to see very far. But even still, Arleth had the sense that the room stretched quite far into the distance. And she had to find *something* in all this gloom. Something that Neve's brother had thought was vital for Arleth to see. But she had no idea what she was looking for or even if she would know if she found it. Normally, this would not have bothered Arleth in the slightest. It was an adventure. But she didn't enjoy the thought of spending potentially hours immersed in this disgustedly smelly room – and worse, not even knowing what was causing the odour.

Maybe she could just go back and try and find Neve's brother again. Get him to tell her what he had wanted her to find. Yes, that would work... She was just about to turn around when an image of his face flashed into her mind. As clearly as if he was standing once more before her, she saw the fierce intensity and ray of hope in his eyes as he had handed her the key in the dark storage room. Instantly Arleth felt guilty. That man had risked everything to meet her and tell her about this room and she was going to turn away just because it smelled bad? What was wrong with her?

Unbidden, the face of Neve and then Flora came to her mind. She saw their faces glowing as though angels, laughing and talking to her, seeing memories from her childhood. Then instantly the happy images turned to the picture, forever burned in Arleth's mind of Flora's face her mouth opened in an "o" and her eyes wide in shock as the spear of light stabbed through her chest. Arleth squinted in pain and shook her head to clear it.

She felt like a terrible person. There were a lot worse things than a bad smell.

Feeling quite ashamed, she walked decisively through the door and pushed it shut behind her.

As she was shutting the door, she noticed that the back of it was covered in metal gears and cogs of all sizes. No wonder the door had been so hard to open she thought to herself. Turning the key in the lock only activated the nearest gear. That gear then turned the one next to it which turned the one next to it in sequence. It was only when all of the gears and cogs were turning that the door would open.

It was so dark that she couldn't make out more than a few feet in front of her and she had nothing to light her way. So Arleth made her way cautiously, walking in what she guessed was the centre of the room. She walked with one hand out in front of her protectively, one hand covering her nose and her eyes darting back and forth into the darkness on either side of her. Although she didn't want to admit it to herself, she was afraid that something would jump out at her from the darkness. Something that she wouldn't be able to see until it was too late. She scanned the darkness more closely as she walked. But, she didn't see any movement in the shadows and the only noise was the soft patter of her feet as she walked.

Reassured for the time being, Arleth's thoughts turned to what *was* in this room. And how was she supposed to find it when it was so dark?

She had been walking down the middle of the room for a while and she hadn't come across anything but open space. Arleth thought about the instructions Neve's brother had given her. He really hadn't given any clues about what she was going to find here or where she should look. Just that this room would answer all of her questions. For all she knew then, this whole room could just be a long hall and what she really wanted was in an adjoining room. She would walk through the whole room and find nothing but the back wall. Even if there weren't side rooms, she had still found nothing going the way she had. Perhaps it was time to try something new.

Arleth turned to her right and with her hand still held out in front of her, she searched for the side wall. She had taken no more than five steps to her right when her outstretched hand knocked into something.

Something cold and slippery.

Reflexively Arleth jerked her hand back and stopped dead in her tracks.

What had she just touched?

Arleth took a small, cautious step forward and squinted into the darkness. She could make out a large cylindrical shape in front of her. It was twice as wide as she was and stretched up farther than she could make out, which given the darkness might not have been more than a few feet. Arleth stepped closer to it and put both hands out to touch its surface. As she had noticed before, it was acutely cold and so smooth as to be almost slippery.

Something about this object seemed vaguely familiar to Arleth but she couldn't quite place what it was. She ran her hand farther along its surface – as far up as she could reach, down to the ground and as far left and right as her arms would stretch. Everywhere she touched had the same feel and texture. The same cold, smooth surface with no imperfections or divisions of any kind. As she was examining the object in this way, it came to her what had seemed so familiar. It seemed like a gigantic bottle or jar.

But if she was right, what was inside it?

Instinctively she pressed her face to its surface to see if she could see into it. At first she couldn't make out much of anything. But after a few moments shapes started to take form and she could see what was inside. Although what she *was* seeing she had no idea.

There appeared to be some kind of fluid flowing inside the cylinder. It was hard to tell for sure in the dark, but it looked clear with a faint blue tinge. Inside the fluid were hundreds of string-like shapes. They were all roughly the same size - about the length of Arleth's hand and were a drab gray colour. As she looked closer at the shapes, they appeared to be swimming through the fluid.

Were they alive?

As some of the shapes passed near the edge of the cylinder where she was standing Arleth observed them more carefully. They didn't appear to have eyes or even faces and they looked to be moving completely at random with no goal to their motion. She didn't think they were living, thinking creatures but based on what she had seen so far in just a few short days on Oherra, Arleth wasn't ready to rule anything out.

Something reddish about a foot downwards in the fluid caught Arleth's attention and she ignored the string-like 'things' for a few moments. She bent down slightly to get a closer look at where the colour was coming from. There appeared to be a platform suspended in the fluid separating the swimming strings and the fluid on top from those on the bottom. Arleth couldn't see any visible difference in the stringy forms or the fluid on either side. She wondered why they were separated.

Looking down into the fluid she could see that there was yet another platform. It was a bit less than a foot lower down than the first one she had seen. How many different levels were there?

She lowered herself down to the ground slowly, counting the levels as she went. In total there were four levels below the one that she had first seen. In each one, there appeared to be no difference between the inhabitants of it and the ones above and below it. She stood back up again and looked up into the fluid. Sure enough there was another platform in the fluid above her head. She was willing to guess that the whole cylinder was divided into these equal sections.

But why?

As she was contemplating the answer to this question, one of the stringy shapes detached itself from the pack and swam straight at Arleth. Deep in thought, she didn't notice it until it was right in front of her eyes. It rammed into the side of the cylinder with such force that it made an audible "TWACK." The force of the impact caused the stringy form to fall down into the liquid where it stayed motionless for a few seconds as if startled before resuming its prior unsystematic swimming as if nothing had happened.

Arleth on the other hand, let out a startled yelp and staggered back a couple of steps to her right. Her right foot tripped on something furry lying on the floor and with her arms flailing in front of her she fell to the ground with a crash. She landed on her back with such force she was momentarily winded.

It was at that instant, when she had no breath to scream that a pair of large, bright green eyes appeared directly in front of her.

Arleth stared up at the disembodied eyes in horror. She opened her mouth to scream but no sound came out. Her body was sluggish from her fall and it was with great effort that she managed to scuttle slowly back away from the eyes. Her escape attempt didn't last long as within a few paces she felt a familiar smooth, cold surface at her back. She had backed up into another one of the gigantic jars. Arleth brought herself up into a sitting position and pressed her body as much as she could into the cylinder. She was literally trying to melt into the surface and become invisible to whatever was in the shadows in front of her.

Her heart was beating rapidly and Arleth could hear the thumping of her chest. She put her arms up in front of her in an attempt to protect herself from whatever was about to come at her through the darkness. She turned her head rapidly from side to side scanning the shadows for any sign of movement. She didn't see or hear anything – even the eyes had disappeared. But instead of calming her, this worried Arleth even more. She knew that something was there, right in front of her, but she had no way to know where it was, or even if it *was* in front of her still. She continued scanning rapidly her head and eyes jerking back and forth.

Was the creature watching her, waiting for the right moment to attack? She pictured a blood-thirsty creature, standing right beside her, with its head hanging above her ready at any moment to snap her up in its jaws and swallow her whole. Her breath was coming in ragged gasps – she was too terrified to even try and control it.

Precious seconds passed, but there was still no movement in the shadows and nothing had snatched her up. A glimmer of hope shone in her mind – perhaps the creature couldn't see in the dark! She remembered the concealing spell she had taken just as she had entered the room. Neve's brother had told her that it would hide her presence magically (whatever that meant) but it wouldn't make her invisible. But hopefully the darkness would.

If she just sat here maybe the creature wouldn't be able to find her and it would get frustrated and leave her alone.

That thought lasted all of two seconds.

The green eyes reappeared in front of her and a tired, male voice said, "Who are you?"

The return of the eyes startled Arleth and she involuntarily jerked her head back, slamming it into the wall of the jar-cylinder behind her. It made a faint 'thud' and would probably give Arleth a bump later. But she was so preoccupied that she didn't even realize she had hit anything.

It took Arleth a few seconds to get over her initial surprise of having the creature talk to her, before she could respond. Even still her voice was far from calm.

"Whhhoo aaree you?" Asked Arleth nervously.

"Ahh what rude manners you have, I asked you first," responded the creature with a touch of laughter in its voice.

This creature, whatever it was, didn't seem to be dangerous, so Arleth relaxed a bit. Enough at least that her voice had returned to normal.

"My name is Arleth."

"Arleth?..." Said the creature curiously. "Do you have a last name Arleth?"

"No," she responded a bit sadly.

"Ahh," there was a pause and then "I see."

"But you never told me who you are."

"You are very right Arleth, I suppose it is I who has bad manners then. My name is Zeeshan. I am a Talywag from Occa.

"What is a Talywag?"

"Oh my you must not be from around here hmm? Talywags are quite popular creatures on Oherra if I do say so myself. Well, hmm how do I explain... Us Talywags are rather small in stature, not remarkable in physique or bravery, I'm sorry to say. But our intelligence is legendary. Not to brag, but we have double the brainpower of a human such as yourself. Occa is our capital city, it lies on the outskirts of Frasht Forest to the east of Iridian Castle."

"How did you get here then?"

"My mom wanted to make a pie for my father's birthday dessert. So, my best friend and I, Thom, had gone into the forest to collect berries. We were playing and joking with each other and we didn't see the Grekens approach. I had just enough time to see the Greken fully in front of me before I was knocked unconscious. I woke up here, naked in this room fastened to the wall with this apparatus strapped to my head."

Although Arleth had a dozen questions she wanted to ask, she decided to ask the least important one first.

"How old are you?" What he had said made Arleth think that he was a child, perhaps younger than her. But his voice and demeanour were of a much older man.

"I am seven."

"So where is your friend now?"

"He is.. gone." The way Zeeshan said 'gone' gave Arleth pause. There was a tremor in the boy's voice as if he were about to cry.

"What do you mean gone?"

"This is a horrible place. The king here is not good, not if he allows things like *that* to happen here."

Arleth was even more intrigued. Perhaps this child would be the answer to her questions about Absalom.

"What do you mean," she said gently.

"Some green sorcerer came down here with another evil-faced man. They were leading a couple of growling snow bears from the north. The sorcerer strapped them to the wall beside us. Then he uttered some words in a language I did not know, some kind of spell. And then... then..." His voice broke into a sob.

Arleth gave him a few seconds to collect himself and then she prodded gently again. "And then..."

"And then Thom and one of the bears started to scream, the most horrible sounds you could ever imagine. It sounded like he was being ripped in two. It was terrible. Slowly Thom's body began to change. He grew in size and stature, his hands and feet spread into talons, white fur grew all over his body, his head expanded to twice its size and his eyes bulged into two huge green orbs. The bear slumped against its chains, there was nothing left but bones. Hovering above Thom's head were hundreds of strange stringy things. The sorcerer said some more words and those things flew into the jar that you are now leaning against."

Arleth was speechless, she stared in open-mouthed horror at what Zeeshan was telling her.

"After they had finished with Thom, they turned to me. It was the most excruciating pain I have ever felt. I can't even describe it. My body was ripped from me and replaced with something hairy, huge and foreign. The sorcerer and the man soon left and I fainted into a painful haze. I don't know how long I lay there, perhaps days, drifting in and out of consciousness. I don't know what happened to me during that time. The only things I remember were the pain and the groans of Thom beside me to tell me that he was alive and still there.

The sorcerer, the man and a third dark-haired man came in at last. They talked for a bit and seemed pleased with Thom but they had agreed that I was a 'failure.' They took Thom with them when they left. He didn't seem the same. I mean of course he wasn't the same, we both weren't. But his mind seemed different. He obeyed every command of theirs instantly with a 'yes master' and didn't even look back at me when he left with them. That was perhaps a day ago, it is impossible to tell here, and I haven't seen them since."

Arleth didn't know what to make of this. To say she was horrified and shocked would have been a tremendous understatement. She had a hundred more questions. But she didn't think that Zeeshan would have the answers. Why had they captured this boy and his friend? What had they done to them? And why? She didn't have a doubt in her mind now that Absalom was bad. No one could do something like this to another living creature and be good. But this revelation of course brought with it a flood of new questions.

She decided it didn't hurt to see how many of her questions Zeeshan could answer. She talked with him for close to twenty minutes. But, as she had thought, he didn't know many answers. He had no idea why they had been captured. He was also clueless as to what had been done to them or why. She asked him what Neve's brother had told her – if Absalom was the rightful king. Once again the Talywag, being a child, didn't know for sure.

Zeeshan also told Arleth a bit about his friend Thom. And Arleth listened with sympathy. She knew what it was like to lose a best friend. Although Thom wasn't dead, the way Zeeshan had described him after the 'incident,' he might as well have been.

The young Talywag was in the middle of telling a particularly funny story of him and Thom and how they had outsmarted a good-for-nothing bandit when Zeeshan abruptly stopped.

"Did you hear that?" He asked tensely.

Arleth perked up her ears but she couldn't hear anything. "No, I don't hear anything," she said slowly.

But Zeeshan wasn't convinced. He continued listening intently. Arleth still didn't hear anything but she remained silent and strained her ears for any sounds of movement.

All of a sudden she heard a very faint clicking noise. She listened harder. It sounded like footsteps, and they were getting louder.

"Someone is coming! Quick hide behind me," whispered Zeeshan urgently.

Arleth had moved closer to the creature when they had been talking and now she was sitting practically in his lap. She felt two huge furry hands pick her up and move her backwards.

"My waist is chained to the wall," Zeeshan explained quietly. "You will have to climb up and wedge yourself between my back and the wall."

As quickly as she could in the darkness, she felt for the wall with her right hand and Zeeshan's back with her left. She carefully climbed off the platform provided by his hand and felt herself fall down a bit into the crevice left by his back. Her back got scraped a bit on the way down but she hardly noticed.

No sooner had she reached the relative safety of her hiding place, then the door to the room burst open, with a fury of green light and two figures stood illuminated in the doorway.

"Rogan, did you really have to break down the door," said the familiar but angry voice of Absalom.

"It's no matter," said a second, raspy voice. "I can easily fix it."

There was a "hmph" in reply and the raspy voice said a few inaudible words into the darkness. The room immediately lit up and Arleth, her head peaking out slightly from behind Zeeshan's back saw the owner of the second voice for a split second before she tucked her head back behind him for cover.

She would recognize the green skin, blood-curdling red eyes and pitch-black robes anywhere. Standing not twenty feet from where she hid was the creature whose image had been burned in her mind for the last seven years. The creature that had killed everyone she had ever known. The Dread Mage that had reduced the orphanage to a wasteland of death and scorched rubble. Arleth covered her mouth with her hands to stop herself from screaming.

Chapter 18

Aedan slowly opened his eyes and looked around disoriented at his surroundings. He didn't immediately realize where he was as he looked through the gloom. Then slowly he saw the metal bars on three sides boxing him in and felt the cold, damp wall at his back. With a sinking feeling, Aedan realized where he was – a dungeon cell deep under Iridian castle. As he sat huddled and naked on the floor, the events of a less than an hour ago flooded back to him in a rush. How he had been taken captive by the Grekens, been brought to Absalom... and then how the man had smashed the two Alondranes and had him knocked out and thrown in here.

But as Aedan continued looking around at the cell he was in, he started to smile. He was cold, naked, and had a pounding headache, but the first part of their plan had worked! The cell he was in only had one solid wall, the rest were open bars and although he was chained to the wall, the cell was so small that he could almost touch the bar in front of him with his foot. *This* was the part that had worried both him and Selene so much – what kind of cell would Absalom put him into. They had known that Absalom would search him for Alondranes – it was one of Selene's trademarks after all. The usurping bastard was smart enough to realize Aedan wouldn't have come here without a plan. But Aedan and Selene had planned on that and had tailored their actions accordingly, and had hidden a third – real – Alondrane on Aedan's inner thigh. The real stumbling block was the cell – if he had been put in a solid cell with no bars or in a cell much larger than this one, their plan wouldn't have worked. Val had been particular angry about this part – he didn't like putting his friends at risk. Val liked simple, failsafe plans that guaranteed success.

But both Aedan and Selene had agreed that Absalom would most likely put him in a cell such as this one. First, they knew that most of the cells were like this one, as they had been when Aedan's father was still king. Second, Absalom knew how an Alondrane worked and he was just cocky enough to put Aedan in a cell such as this so he would forever regret that he *could have* escaped had he been smarter. Absalom would assume he had out-witted Aedan and would not even think of the possibility that it could have been the other way around.

Aedan started laughing, how predictable Absalom was! His laughter brought over a Greken who had been standing guard outside the cell. The creature hissed and slammed its huge arm into the bars of the cage.

Good! Aedan thought, there only appeared to be one Greken, and one by itself would cause no problem for Selene. Aedan waited a few moments for the Greken to lose interest in its captive. It turned away and walked back to where it had been standing before; a few feet in front of the cage. Aedan turned as far to the right as he could, which wasn't very far at all being chained as he was to the wall. But even a little bit would be enough to get Selene behind the Greken so she could have the element of surprise.

"Onantra," he whispered.

Aedan felt the Alondrane detach itself from his inner thigh and roll down his leg. It fell to the floor at his feet and rolled silently across the cell, through the bars and out into the room beyond. It stopped five feet from where Aedan sat – exactly the distance Selene had tested it for.

Aedan whispered again, "Selene!"

It shimmered faintly in the dim light of the dungeon and started to expand. Aedan looked ahead nervously but the Greken hadn't moved. So far, the creature didn't seem to notice what was happening a few feet behind it. Aedan bit his lip in anxiety and looked back at the shimmering Alondrane. If only she could appear before the Greken noticed her. It had already expanded to the general size of Selene, but so far it had no discernable shape. In a couple more seconds, a violet light twisted violently upwards and then sideways as if stretching into shape. There was a small "crack" and the light flickered briefly and then went out. In its place stood the very beautiful, very comforting figure of Selene.

Aedan sighed in relief but it was premature – the "crack" had finally alerted the Greken and it turned around and immediately saw Selene standing in front of it. With a hiss it ran at the slim woman in front of it. But Selene hadn't yet seen the Greken, she was looking into the cell at him.

Aedan eyes went wide with fear, "Selene! Greken!" He yelled, turning to look to the left at the creature that was already in mid-lunge.

Luckily Selene was quick to respond and within a heartbeat she had turned to face her oncoming attacker. She ducked just in time to avoid a vicious claw to her torso and then swung her head down out of reach of its extended tentacles. The Greken wheeled around quickly to face Selene again, but she was ready for it. Crouched cat-like on the ground she extended her arms and a bolt of red light flashed from her palms. Four of the creature's tentacles (two on either side of its head) immediately rose up and wrapped itself around the Greken's neck. The creature made a strangled hiss and clawed at them in vain. Selene sent another bolt of red light at the creature, this one hitting it square in the chest. The force of the impact wasn't great but it was enough to startle the creature for a few seconds. It was all she needed. With a swift 'X' motion of her hands she tightened the razor sharp tentacles around its neck. They tore into the tough scales of its neck without mercy. The Greken's eyes bulged out in fear and it made a last desperate effort to loosen his own tentacles from around his neck. But it was too late. With a grunt, Selene made a final swift motion with her hand and the tentacles sliced through the creature's neck. Its serpentine head fell to the ground in front of it with a thud. Its body twitched violently once and then went still. It remained standing in place for a few impossible seconds and then slumped to the ground to join the head that it had been attached to a few seconds before.

Still crouching on the ground, a strand of blonde hair fell across Selene's face and she calmly tucked it back behind her ear. She stood up and walked over to the dead Greken. She plucked up the Greken's ring of keys from the ground where they had fallen and came over to Aedan's cell. The third key she tried was the right one and she opened the door and walked the one step over to Aedan. She bent down in front of him. With a long finger she tapped him gently on the nose,

"We will have to shove this in Val's face when we get back."

Aedan laughed, "I think he will be glad to have this shoved in his face."

Selene gave him a look of disbelief.

"Ya you are right, although he will be happy to see us, he will likely be mad that our, what did he call it? 'Haphazard bird-something?'

"Bird brained"

"Yes that our haphazard bird-brained plan worked."

They both smiled picturing Val's face.

Selene, using the keys she had taken from the guard, unlocked Aedan's chains and they both stood up. Aedan stretched and looked at Selene. She was looking at him with concern.

"What is it?"

"You are naked!"

"Yes? Please tell me you brought me clothes."

"But I didn't," Selene said apologetically, "I thought that they would put your clothes back in the cell with you."

Aedan thought she was joking. "So what is in the bag you are wearing," he asked, looking at a small brown travelling bag she had slung across her shoulder.

"Oh that?" She said twisting to see it more clearly. "That just has some food, concealing spells and some other supplies we might need."

"Oh," Aedan said sadly. He was already quite cold and he didn't much like the idea of walking around Iridian castle completely naked. But what other choice did he have? He looked at Selene again, she was wearing a cloak. "Give me you cloak Selene and then I can at least cover myself from my waist down."

"Good idea!" She unfastened her cloak and handed it to Aedan. He took it and bent his head down to concentrate on tying in around his waist.

He didn't see the smile on Selene's face.

"Aedan," She said innocently after he had just finished securing the cloak. "Here."

She tossed him his clothes.

Aedan took one look at his clothes and lunged at Selene. She easily avoided his playful swipe and laughingly caught him as he stumbled into her, caught off balance by her evasion. She pushed him gently away, "Put on your clothes Aedan. We want to rescue this girl not scare her away."

Despite himself, Aedan could feel a smile forming on his lips. He didn't want Selene to see it, so he quickly turned his back to her in what he hoped she would interpret as an act of modesty and started putting on his clothes. Selene, smiling and shaking her head slightly at Aedan's back, put her cloak back on.

Five minutes later, Aedan finished dressing and they walked out of the cell together. The laughter was gone from both of them. Selene handed Aedan a concealing spell. They looked at each other through the gloom in understanding and crept out into the dungeon. They had their jokes but the truth was they both realized that the next part of their plan was the hardest. They had to find Arleth before someone realized Aedan had escaped; searching through a castle swarming with enemies; knowing they had to avoid Absalom and Rogan but not having the slightest clue where they were; find Arleth when they also had no idea where she was; convince her to come with them; and then after doing so, have all three safely sneak back out of the castle to their hideout in the mountains. Thinking about it like this, it certainly seemed like what they had done so far – getting into the castle and escaping the dungeon was the easy part.

* * *

Wedged between the wall and Zeeshan's back, Arleth fought to control her mounting horror. She was so shocked that she couldn't even scream, her mouth opened instead in a silent "o." Arleth's eyes were opened just as wide, but she was not staring at Zeeshan's furry back directly in front of her. Her eyes were a million miles away, across the universe, seven years in the past witnessing again that day in the orphanage when she had last seen the Dread Mage.

She realized then that she had never expected to see it again. For no logical reason she had somehow assumed that after she had ran out of the orphanage, Neve and the Dread Mage had killed each other. It had never occurred to her that the Dread Mage would have survived. But here it was, standing not twenty feet in front of her. The murderer who had destroyed everything and everyone she had ever loved.

But *why*?

Why *was* it here on Oherra in Iridian Castle. Her mind flashed to the snatches of conversation she had heard in the dark when the door had been opened. It had been talking with Absalom, they had seemed almost....partners? But that was impossible.... *wasn't it*? Absalom had called it a name hadn't he? He had called it, something with an S... no it was an R. She strained her memory, 'Richard? No...

Ronan? No that wasn't quite right.... Rogan! Yes he had called the creature Rogan.' The name seemed more familiar to her though.

With a sudden shock of realization, it hit her. The remaining colour drained from her already pale face.

Rogan was the name of Absalom's sorcerer. The king of Oherra's sorcerer was a Dread Mage?!? *The* Dread Mage that had killed Neve, and Flora, and Janaya and... everyone, everyone at the orphanage but her.

She felt Zeeshan squirm slightly in front of her. The sudden movement interrupted her thoughts for a few seconds and she looked up to see why the Talywag had moved. Right away she noticed that she was the reason. In her horror she had dug her nails into his back so hard that thin rivulets of blood were dripping onto her fingers. Quickly she removed her nails. She wanted to say "sorry" but was afraid of being heard. Instead she rubbed his back gently over the wound in an attempt to apologize. Zeeshan stopped squirming and he seemed to relax (relatively speaking) once more.

Arleth was only vaguely aware however that her soothing gesture was having this effect – as another, equally terrifying thought had just come to her.

Arleth had let Absalom's sorcerer perform magic on her – he had probed her mind! The Dread Mage that she had seen brutally stab Flora before her very eyes had, had his hands on her shoulders just yesterday, performing a spell on her to extract her memories. It felt like an icy cold hand had clenched over her heart. Her breathing came in ragged gasps and she felt like she was going to be sick. Absalom had said the spell was harmless, but she no longer believed what he had told her.

What had he done to her?

Was she going to turn into something like Zeeshan? Had he done the same kind of thing to her? Would she also transform? Obviously it hadn't happened right away like it did with Zeeshan, but would she start changing today, tomorrow, five days from now? Or was she even now changing into something different than herself. Her mind involuntarily flashed to the beautiful woman she had seen in the courtyard. The woman with the horrendous gash on her back. Would she end up like *that?* The thought that she had absolutely no idea what he had done to her terrified her to her core.

"Arleth?"

The sound of her name jolted her thoughts back to the present.

"Well I don't see her do you," Absalom said derisively to his Dread Mage.

"No," Rogan admitted.

"Really," Absalom responded angrily, "I don't understand how this could have happened. All you had to do was keep an eye on her, and then collect her for me this morning. I was busy with Aedan as you know. But *I* successfully managed to capture *him*. But you, what *were* you doing? We *knew* that Tobin told her to come here. We *know* how curious she is. It doesn't take a genius to figure out that here should have been the first place to look. Now she is gone and could be anywhere. Aedan is down in the dungeons too, in case you have forgotten. Think for a second what could happen if she runs into him?"

Rogan was practically shaking he was so angry with Absalom's arrogant words. He managed to hold in his angry retorts but he glared at Absalom with hatred.

"I was busy with a few things." He said it with such venom that it gave Absalom pause for a few seconds. But he quickly recovered and continued on his tirade. This time though, he was a bit gentler.

"I mean Rogan, you *were* the one that was so anxious to enchant Arleth. You would think that she would have been your top priority this morning."

Rogan remained silent but the hatred was still in his eyes.

"She is not here anyways so we had better look elsewhere. It's not like she can leave the castle. Aedan is locked up, Tobin is dead, and the servants are mere puppets. No one will help her. We will find her today and by nightfall she will be enchanted. Just you see."

With that he took a final glance around the room, turned on his heal and strode out of the room. Absalom followed silently after him. He slightly regretted getting so angry with Rogan. Not for sentimental reasons, but for practicality. Their partnership was based on mere convenience – neither could rule Oherra by themselves. There was no emotion or good will involved, simply a cold calculated rationality. This ensured that no matter how angry they became, neither of them would backstab the other. But it still didn't hurt for

Absalom to be on the safe side anyways. He shivered ever so slightly as he passed through the open door and into the hall.

Unaware of such evil politics, Arleth climbed slowly out from behind Zeeshan, desperately trying to make sense of what she had just overheard.

She no longer had any doubts as to the truth of what Neve's brother had told her. Absalom was clearly not the virtuous leader he pretended to be. The eerie lack of personality among all the servants; the woman in the courtyard with the gaping wound; and of course the information that Neve's brother had given her, had all made her wary. Wary enough to come down here and find out for herself. But until the events of this morning, she wasn't sure if her suspicions, if they were even warranted, should lie with Absalom, or elsewhere.

Now though, she was certain.

Neve's brother had told her that a person named Aedan was the rightful heir to the throne. And this morning she had seen this person and heard Absalom call him "Aedan Amara." But that was nothing compared with what Zeeshan had told her and what she herself had witnessed in this room. There was no way that a man whose personal sorcerer was the Dread Mage who had massacred everyone in the orphanage was a good person.

And now, both Absalom and the Dread Mage were looking for her. *And they wanted to enchant her.*

Arleth didn't know what "enchanting" was, but she didn't have to, to be terrified. Just the way they had talked about having to find her brought chills to her spine.

"All you had to do was keep an eye on her, and then collect her for me this morning." Collect her, like she was a personal possession with no free will of her own.

But why *were* they looking for her? She was just one of Absalom's many servants. Why would they invest so much effort into finding her? Why was she so important to them? And even more puzzling, she had been in Absalom's private chamber yesterday. Rogan had her in his thrall, he could have done anything to her at that moment; he could have "enchanted" her. She wouldn't have had any idea. But they obviously hadn't done this yesterday and they had made no effort to stop her from leaving. What had changed?

She didn't even begin to have an answer to any of these questions.

But she had no intention of waiting around to find out. She had seen firsthand what happened to people when that Dread Mage was hunting for them. The death and destruction that followed in the creature's wake. She only had one choice.

She had to escape from the castle.

But how?

Absalom and Rogan were probably the two most powerful men in the universe. She had to somehow elude them, in their own castle, a castle that was probably covered in magical protections designed to prevent exactly what she was trying to do right now. On top of that, the castle and the grounds were crawling with Grekens. Even, by a miracle, if she somehow managed to get outside of the castle walls, there was still a huge open valley that she had to cross until she got to the mountains.

And what then? She might be relatively safer from Absalom and Rogan there but she couldn't stay their indefinitely. What would she eat?

Or *what would eat her.* She realized she had virtually no idea what creatures were in this world, what plants were safe to eat, how far away or in which direction any other towns were, and even if any such towns she might come across would be friendly towards her.

She sat down dejectedly on the floor. Tears began flowing freely down her face and she wiped at them with trembling fingers.

What was she going to do?

There was a rattling as Zeeshan attempted to move closer to her in a gesture of comfort. But his restraints barred his movements.

"Don't cry Arleth," Zeeshan said as soothingly as possible. "You can still escape. Hide here maybe until dark. They have already looked here I doubt they will do so again. Perhaps when it is dark you will have a better chance of escaping."

Zeeshan! In her terrified stupor, she had momentarily forgotten about him. As scared as she was, she felt ashamed that she had not thought about the Talywag. How could she have thought about her escape plan and not remembered he was trapped here as well?

His suggestion made sense, but only if she alone escaped and she couldn't just leave him here. He was still just a child. Not only that, but he was the only friend she had on Oherra. She also knew that he would die or at the very least lead a horrible life if he stayed here and she couldn't do that to him.

Somehow, as impossible as it seemed, they would have to find a way to escape together.

That brought her back to the question that she was still no closer to answering: *But how to escape?*

With a bolt of excitement, Arleth suddenly remembered something. This was Zeeshan's home world! He would know what creatures to look out for and what they could eat to survive! He would know where to go after they reached the mountains. Perhaps she could even live in Occa with him and the rest of the Talywags.

"Zeeshan! I will get us both out of here!"

Hope momentarily flashed in the young Talywag's face but was gone a moment later.

"How can you do that Arleth? I am restrained to the wall by this thick band around my waist. Not only that, but I am huge now. It would be much easier for someone your size to sneak out alone than to have me with you."

"Don't be silly Zeeshan. I am not going to leave you. Besides you had a good plan. If I can get you out of your restraints, we can both hide here until it gets dark and then find a way to sneak out. We can make for the safety of the mountains together. When it is dark there will be less chance of being seen when we cross the open valley. Perhaps someone might even mistake you for a Greken in the dark? And as for me, I should blend in with the rest of the servants. Once in the mountains I think we should be safer, at least from Absalom and Rogan. Then hopefully you will be able to lead us back to Occa."

Zeeshan thought about it for a while, "I would like to hope that I really can escape with you Arleth, but how will you get me out of this?" He looked down at the heavy metal band across his waist.

"Maybe it can be broken somewhere," Arleth offered, walking over to him.

She put her hands out to touch the metal. As soon as her fingers touched its surface, she jerked them back reflexively. It was cold! But not a cold that Arleth had ever experienced before. Just from the brief contact, the skin on her fingers had turned red, as though she had been out in the cold for hours. She balled up her hands in fists to warm up her fingers and looked up at Zeeshan curiously. This band was against his bare skin! How was he not shivering from the cold? Even with all the fur on his body, she found it hard to believe that he wouldn't feel the cold even a little bit. But he didn't seem to notice in the slightest. Instead he was just staring at her, hoping that she would find a way to release him.

Shaking her head in wonder, and bracing for the cold, Arleth put her hands back on the metal and felt along its length as fast as possible while looking for any gaps or hinges that might allow her to open or even break the band. When she reached the spot where the band connected to the wall on the left side of Zeeshan's body, she felt a rough indent. She removed her frozen hands and when she warmed them up in her armpits, she looked closely at the spot she had felt. She had originally thought that the band attached directly to the wall. But she now realized that there was small ring that connected the wall to the metal band. The ring didn't look as sturdy as the rest of the band. If she could somehow break that ring, that side of the band would break free from the wall and Zeeshan would be released.

Excitedly, she explained what she had found to Zeehsan. "Maybe if you pull your body as hard as you can away from the wall and if I also pull on the band at the same time, it will come free?"

The Talywag was doubtful, but he wasn't about to argue.

"Ok, on the count of 3. 1....2.....3...." Arleth and Zeeshan both pulled as hard as they could, the Talywag grunting with the effort and Arleth clenching her teeth and putting her foot against the wall for leverage.

After 10 seconds, both of them were exhausted from the effort. Arleth collapsed on the ground and let out a deep breath. Zeeshan slouched back against the wall breathing heavily.

The band hadn't budged.

They rested for a minute or so until they had regained their breath and then they tried again. This time though, their energy had been reduced and so they pulled less strongly and gave up quicker.

The ring attached to the band still remained firmly embedded in the wall.

They both slumped against the wall in disappointed silence. The best plan Arleth had thought of, had failed horribly. She had no intention of giving up, but her desperate brain wasn't helping her to find a new strategy.

"Hey Arleth," Zeeshan said suddenly. A plan had begun to form in his mind, it was a long shot but it was worth a try and they had no other plans. "Do you think that if you had a knife you could chip away enough of the wall around the ring that it would weaken enough that we could pull it out?"

Arleth thought about it for a moment, "Ya!" She said sitting up straighter against the wall. "It would probably take a number of hours. But we can't really sneak out of the castle safely until it is dark anyways. So I will try it!"

Although neither of them would admit it to the other one, both Arleth and the Talywag realized their plan probably wouldn't work. It was doubtful that Arleth could break away enough of the wall in weeks let alone a couple of hours to get the ring free. But they had thought of no other options and it was certainly better than just sitting there doing nothing.

What would happen if nightfall came and Zeeshan was still trapped? *Would she just leave him there?* Arleth couldn't bear to contemplate that thought. So she pushed it to the back of her mind and put on a brave face for the sake of the young Talywag.

"I will sneak back up to the kitchen and get a couple of knives. It shouldn't take me too long." She smiled at him as reassuringly as she could.

Zeeshan smiled back. "Be careful!"

Arleth nodded, took one last look at the Talywag and hurried out of the room.

Zeeshan watched her go, wondering how he would be able to convince her to leave him there when nightfall came and he was still trapped.

Arleth poked her head of the room cautiously and looked in both directions down the hall. Seeing nothing, she tip-toed out the door and turning right, crept along the wall hiding herself in the shadows. For the third time today, she was glad that Neve's brother had given her the concealing spell and that she had remembered to take it. She knew, as he had explained, that she wasn't invisible and that if Rogan or Absalom spotted her she was done for. But she hoped that the shadows would hide her enough so that if she did pass them, they wouldn't see her. She continued down the hall walking as softly as she could.

All of a sudden she heard two sets of footsteps almost directly behind her.

Arleth froze, her left foot extended in mid-step. As soundlessly as she could, she pivoted her body and pressed her back against the wall, wishing that she could melt into the bricks and disappear.

The footsteps continued, getting a bit louder it sounded like the owners were only a few feet away. Cautiously, so as not to make any large movements that would give her away, Arleth moved her eyes left to see who it was. She had expected to see Absalom and Rogan just metres from her. But instead the hall was deserted. Surprised, Arleth turned her whole head to look at the hall behind her, but still she didn't see anyone.

Had she just imagined that she had heard footsteps? She supposed it was possible that her imagination and fear were playing tricks on her. Arleth smiled in the darkness, how foolish she was. She started to turn back around and continue down the hall when she heard the footsteps again. They were unmistakable this time.

But why couldn't she see anyone?

Arleth heard a man's whispered voice right beside her. It was so close that she could feel the breath on her neck.

It was because whoever they were, they were creeping in the shadows like her.

And they were practically on top of her.

Her realization came too late. Before she had time to move even an inch, a heavy form bumped into her. She heard a man's voice utter a curse, and then both of them went tumbling to the ground. Arleth, with the man's weight pushing down on her, fell hard against the floor and rolled into the centre of the hall. The man in mid-fall had pushed himself off of her and had consequently fallen not on top of Arleth, but a bit off to the side. She had a second to see the man as he came into the light of the hall before a second body crashed on top of him. The man let out a deep grunt as the second form landed on him. And then almost quicker than Arleth would have thought possible had she not seen it with her own eyes, the second person flipped off the first man and spun around crouching in a defensive position right in front of Arleth.

Arleth, still lying where she had fallen, looked up at the figure and saw that she was looking into the face of a beautiful blonde woman. She could tell by the woman's clothes that she was not a servant; she was wearing light coloured pants, high boots, and a long cloak. But that didn't mean that she wasn't dangerous. Arleth raised up her arms to shield herself from the mysterious woman. But before she had raised them fully, she looked at the woman's face, and then slowly, unsure if she was doing the right thing lowered them back down again. The woman was smiling at her.

The woman hadn't said anything to her, but looking into her calm face, Arleth felt soothed. She didn't think this woman was a threat. Arleth sat up and crossed her legs in front of her, facing the woman. The woman opened her mouth to say something but at that instant the man who had fallen into Arleth reached out his hand to her. The woman turned, grabbed it and pulled the man up to sit beside her.

The man was looking at the woman and as of yet still hadn't looked at Arleth. The woman smiled at the man, and nodded her head in Arleth's direction. The man followed her gaze and for the first time saw Arleth. He looked at her for a few seconds, blinked, and then stared at her in disbelief. He continued staring at her, as if taking in each feature and then a broad smile appeared on his face.

He turned to the blonde woman again, "Talk about great luck."

"I know! This was supposed to be the hardest part of the plan."

Both of them turned back to face Arleth.

"Is your name Arleth by any chance?" Said the man.

"Yes," responded Arleth absentmindedly, not really paying attention to what he was asking her. Her thoughts were busy elsewhere; she had just realized that she recognized this man! "I know who you are. I saw you earlier today, when Absalom captured you. He called you Aedan Amara. I was watching from....." Arleth broke off in mid-sentence. She had just become conscious of what he had asked her.

He had asked her if her name was Arleth. How would he know that?

"Why.... How do you know my name?"

Aedan looked at her for less than two seconds and then burst out "You are my younger sister Arleth."

Beside him Selene put the palm of her hand up to her forehead in amused disgust.

Chapter 19

"Really?" Selene said in disbelief, "Really? That is how you tell her?"

"Well she already knew that I was Aedan Amara so I didn't have to give her that whole background bit...... And well I was just excited." Aedan smiled at her sheepishly

Despite herself, Selene smiled back. Aedan Amara was the love of her life, and she respected him more than anyone else in the world. As a leader, he was brave, honourable, determined, and fair. One hundred percent devoted to the Oherran people. The fate of this whole world rested on his capable shoulders, where it had rested for most of his life. It was a heavy burden to carry, and she knew it took its toll on him, but as she looked at the expression on his face now, he seemed like an excited child with no cares in the world. She perhaps loved this quality most about him – despite everything and everyone that depended on him; despite all the hardships he had endured, he was still young at heart. Selene also knew how much he had wanted to find his sister and how happy he was to be able to see her in front of him right now. He had always regretted not knowing his sister, thinking, as they all had, that she had died all those years ago with their parents. Neither of them had imagined it would be this easy to find Arleth. But Selene was glad that she had been; she loved seeing the pure, overjoyed expression on Aedan's face.

But, she noticed, one person who did not seem to be as overjoyed as they were was Arleth. She looked shocked, shocked and a bit nauseous.

"I am your si... you are my br... *I am an Ama*..." Arleth trailed off. The shock of everything she had witnessed today and now this proved too much for her to handle. Her head started to spin and the corners of her vision blurred. She vaguely saw Aedan's concerned face wavering dizzyingly in front of her and then all became dark.

Arleth woke up a few minutes later. She had been moved to the side of the hall and was propped upright against the wall. Aedan and Selene were crouched in front of her. Selene was gently tapping Arleth's cheek in an effort to bring her back to consciousness.

"Ah," Said Selene, when she saw that Arleth's eyes had opened. "Welcome back."

"What...happened?" Said Arleth slowly, still disoriented.

"You fainted."

"I fainted?..." Arleth knew that she was acting very stupid, but her mind wasn't working the way it should. It seemed sluggish – she must be still struggling to return to normal consciousness.

"Yes," said Aedan, cutting in. "I am sorry Arleth, Selene is right, I shouldn't have burst something like that on you so suddenly. It is no wonder that you reacted the way you did."

What is he talking about? Thought Arleth confused. What did he burst on me? Then all of a sudden it all rushed back to her.

He had said that she was his sister. Arleth couldn't believe it, she must have heard wrong.

"But it is true Arleth," continued Aedan, "You are my sister. You wouldn't remember of course but both of us were born right here in this castle." Aedan had a faraway look in his eye. "Mother was so happy when she found out she was having another baby and I was excited too. I was only ten when you were born, but I remember all the celebrations well." Aedan's expression all of a sudden turned dark and there was look of hatred in his eyes. "And then before you were even a couple of months old, there was the attack. I never saw you again... I assumed until recently that you had died."

This was unbelievable news, but for some reason, maybe it was the sincere look in Aedan's eyes, she believed that he was telling her the truth. Arleth looked closely at the man sitting in front of her. He *did* look a lot like her she had to admit. They both had the same dark hair, olive skin and violet eyes. She had never before seen anyone else who had the same violet eyes that she had. When a young Arleth had questioned this, Neve had always told her that her violet eyes were unique. Only a few people in the universe Neve said, would have violet eyes like she had. Arleth had smiled at this and had felt very special.

It wasn't just Aedan's physical features that resembled her own though. It was his whole persona. She couldn't explain it but she felt drawn to this man, connected to him in some way. Looking at him crouching in front of her, smiling gently at her when she caught his eye, she *knew* that he was her brother.

But if Aedan Amara was her brother that meant that *she was an Amara too?*

"So my real name is Arleth *Amara*?" She said it carefully, feeling out how it sounded.

"Yes," said Aedan smiling. "You are Arleth Amara. You come from a long line of kings and queens who have ruled Oherra going back many generations."

Arleth had a million and one questions she wanted to ask, but she wasn't given a chance to ask even one more.

"I hate to interrupt," Selene said with sincerity "But don't you think we should get out of the hall. I mean you just escaped from the dungeons Aedan and both of us are not exactly welcome guests here."

"Right," said Aedan. Thankfully, Arleth seemed to believe him and Selene was right, they couldn't risk being in such an open place for long. He would answer the many questions he was sure Arleth had, and tell her more about their past when they had reached a safer place.

"Are you ok to stand?" Selene asked, reaching out her hand to Arleth.

Arleth wasn't sure, so she grabbed on to the woman's hand for extra support. "Thank you.... *Selene?*" That was the name she thought Aedan had called her.

Selene nodded at her, "Yes, I'm Selene Ayan. Come on we have to get going." Selene turned and started to walk away down the hall, Aedan was right behind her.

"Wait!" Arleth called as loudly as she dared and ran after them a few steps. They stopped walking and turned back around to face her. "I have to get my friend. He is a prisoner in that room right there." She gestured in a general backwards motion. "I can't leave him behind."

"Your friend...?" Selene said slowly.

"Yes, Zeeshan. He's a Talywag from Occa....or at least he was..."Arleth paused for a moment thinking. "Now though, I don't know if he would still be considered a Talywag... But anyway he is chained up in that room right back there. If we don't save him he will die here."

When Arleth mentioned that her friend was a Talywag, both Aedan and Selene stared at each other in worry. *What was a Talywag doing locked up in Iridian Castle?* Absalom and Rogan had never had an interest in them before, what did they want with them now?

"Ok let's go rescue him." Selene said as she started walking back towards Arleth, "Take us to where he is."

"Wait, the chains are very strong. With both of our strengths pulling on them, we couldn't get him free. We will need something to break them with. I was going to get a knife from the kitchen..." Arleth trailed off – Selene had just walked right past her with a complete disregard for Arleth's warning.

Aedan put a hand on Arleth's shoulder and smiling, turned her around. "Don't worry, chains won't stop Selene."

"No but they are really strong." Arleth protested.

Aedan smiled even wider, "Just wait and see." With his hand still on her shoulder, he pushed her gently down the hall.

Up ahead, Selene stopped walking, waiting for them to catch up.

"How far is the room?" Selene asked, when they had caught up to her.

"It's only a few more feet, just around that bend," Arleth said, still doubtful that this slender woman would be able to free Zeeshan without a weapon of some kind.

Selene nodded and continued down the hall at a steady, but cautious pace. After a few seconds, she abruptly stopped. With a small gasp, she put her hand up to cover her nose and mouth. She had just reached the door to the room, which Arleth in her haste to find something to free Zeeshan with, had left slightly open. The horrid stench of the room had been allowed to drift out into the hall, catching Selene off guard.

Arleth, coming up beside her quickly realized that the smell did not lessen with familiarity. She too let out a small gasp and covered her nose with her hands. *How did I spend so long in that room?* Arleth thought to herself.

Looking up into Selene's face, Arleth was surprised to see that her expression was not one of complete disgust. Instead, it was mingled with a profound sadness.

"Aedan..." Selene said gently, turning her face to look at him. Her eyes were shiny with unshed tears.

"I know," Aedan replied coming over to stand by Selene's side. He grabbed one of her slender hands and held it in both of his. "I remember."

Arleth was confused. How could they have such a reaction to the *smell* of a room they hadn't even gone inside yet?

"What's going on?" She asked.

Selene and Aedan both turned at the same time to look at her. But it was Aedan who spoke first.

"10 years ago, Selene, I and a small group of our companions travelled north. We were about your age then and we had heard chilling tales that the armies of Rogan and Absalom had wiped out the five northern cities in less than 3 weeks time. It is referred to now as the Northern Annihilation. It was an unprecedented, horrific attack and our mentor, Bain, insisted that we go to see the destruction. Among other things, he wanted us to witness first-hand the monsters we were fighting against. What we saw will forever be burned in each of our minds.... Every last city was burned to the ground, not a single person left alive. Hundreds of bodies lay littered on the ground, lying where they had been slaughtered. No one had survived to bury their fallen comrades, the sun beating down on them. And the crows..." Aedan trailed off, lost for a moment in his horrendous memories. "But what really struck us was the smell, *this* smell. And when we realized what it came from..."

"We went to each of the five cities, and at each one the destruction, the smell, everything was the same." Selene continued the story where Aedan left off. "When we had reached the last city, we could no longer ignore the feeling that we were being followed. I cast out a few spells and within minutes we had located a small band of about one hundred ragged, men, women and children. They were the few, and *only*, survivors that had managed to escape the slaughter. Although the survivors were from all five of the cities, their stories were identical. Rogan hadn't killed all of the citizens after all, but what he did to them... might even be worse." Selene paused for a second and wiped a single tear from her cheek. She swallowed audibly and then continued in a steady voice. "Rogan rounded up all the men, women and children still alive, and taking them outside the cities' limits, enchanted them all."

There was that word again, Arleth thought – *enchant*. But what did it mean? Rogan had wanted to cast some sort of enchantment on her.

"What does that mean, 'enchanted them all,'" Arleth asked.

"It's a spell, a very evil dark magic that corrupts the user. It is something that I would never try. I am afraid it has become somewhat of Rogan's speciality, his trademark so to say. It takes the very soul out of a person and makes it something *different.* It decays or rots the soul, causing the horrific but characteristic stench we now smell."

Selene paused for a moment, thinking. She cast around for a way to explain the spell in a simple way so that Arleth, someone who had no experience with magic, could understand. Having found something she continued slowly. "The outward appearance of the person is left, so they look completely normal. But inside they are nothing of what they were before. An enchanted person is just an empty shell filled with the instructions put into them at the time of enchantment. For all intents and purposes they are no longer alive."

Arleth shivered involuntarily. So this was what Rogan was planning to do to her! She suddenly felt very lucky that she had run into Neve's brother when she had. If she hadn't, she would have had no clue about this room, wouldn't have been down here in the first place, and she would have been all too easy for Rogan to find and enchant.

"Rogan enchanted the men to be his soldiers and the women and children to be his servants." Aedan explained. "Absalom has an army of men who would never fight for him if they were themselves, and a house of servants 'designed' to follow his every whim. We don't know if there is anything left in them of the person they used to be. If they know somewhere deep in their mind what they are doing, but they can't control their actions."

Arleth gasped in horror and suddenly she remembered the servant girl who had given her the tour when she had first arrived in Oherra. "The servants are all enchanted you said?"

"Yes," Selene and Aedan said together.

Arleth nodded sadly. "I thought they were just weird, not knowing their own names, not talking to me or each other. But they weren't... they were.... I feel terrible for thinking such mean things about them. I had no idea."

Selene smiled at her gently and put her arm around Arleth's shoulders. "Don't feel bad my dear. You had no idea, how could you know what they were?"

Selene drew away from her suddenly and held her at arm's length. "Arleth, you said that the Talywag in this room is your friend?"

"Yes," Arleth said slowly.

"So you were talking to him then."

Arleth nodded again, what was Selene getting at?

Selene turned and looked at Aedan, but when she spoke it was more to herself. "This means that her friend is not enchanted. At least not fully. But Rogan has perfected his enchantment spells; he would never get them wrong, not now. And that smell, it *is* the rotting of a soul destruction, I am sure of it"

"Greken," Aedan said suddenly.

Arleth looked around, expecting to see a Greken rushing towards them, but she didn't see any movement in either direction down the hall. What was Aedan saying?

But Selene seemed to know exactly, "Oh my god," she breathed, her eyes opened wide in horror. "You're right."

What was he right about? Arleth thought confusedly. There was no Greken around them.

"He is doing experimental combinations again. That must be it." Selene turned to look at Arleth.

"Arleth, your friend... did he mention anything about an experiment or magic being done to him? Or maybe that he was different now in some way than he was before?"

"Yes," Arleth replied immediately, remembering all too clearly, what Zeeshan had told her. She recounted the story that Zeeshan had told her of his transformation. When she was finished, Aedan and Selene looked at each other in worry.

"So he *is* doing the experiments again." Selene said in affirmation. "But the last time he did those was when he made the Grekens and that was almost five years ago. Remember what our spy Jine had overheard then? The combinations had proven a lot more demanding on Rogan's power than the straight enchantments. He hadn't created much more than 50 of them, but he had been severely weakened for almost a full year afterwards. He wasn't even able to perform simple spells for months. After causing such a heavy toll on his abilities, and no news of any new attempts, we always just assumed Rogan had given up."

"Tobin was right to be so worried about this chamber." Aedan replied. "He thought something was happening here that was different. And he was right." He felt somewhat responsible. Thinking Rogan had given up had seemed like such an obvious assumption at the time. But now, he wondered, would this oversight prove deadly?

If they hadn't assumed Rogan had given up, could they have prevented this new wave of experiments?

As if reading his mind, Selene put her hand on his left shoulder and squeezed gently. "We can't know everything Aedan. And even if we did, we wouldn't have been able to prevent Rogan from becoming stronger." And then in a louder voice, "But he has become stronger, so we need to hurry."

With that, she quickly pushed open the door and walked into the entrance. She cupped her hands together and muttered something. A tiny ball of white light appeared in between her hands. Carefully she removed her top hand, so that the ball of light rested in the palm of her bottom hand. She raised her now free left hand so that it was hovering in mid-air about an inch above the ball of light. In quick, fluid motions, she stroked the air above the light. As Arleth watched, the ball of light grew steadily larger until it was roughly the size of her head. This seemed to be the size that Selene wanted, for she paused her stroking and looked thoughtfully at the ball of light she had created. She bounced the ball of light gently on her bottom hand so that it hovered in the air in front of her face. Selene then put both hands under the ball of light, her palms facing up and blew on it as though she were blowing a kiss. The ball of light glided gently on invisible air currents up and forward to the ceiling at the centre of the room. Upon reaching its destination, it stopped moving and hung inches from the ceiling, suspended in the air.

Hanging from the centre of the room, the ball of light bathed the room in a gentle golden glow. It was now possible to see to all four corners of the room and Arleth was surprised to see that it stretched a lot farther back than she had originally thought. Something else she noticed with quiet alarm was that the arrangement of Zeeshan being chained to the wall in between two of those huge cylindrical jars was not unique. This pattern repeated itself all the way down the room on both the right and left side. Of course, right now the only prisoner was Zeeshan, but Arleth was alarmed at how many "places" there were. There was room for at least two dozen or more prisoners to be held here at the same time! Arleth shivered at the horrible destruction this room was designed for.

"Didn't anyone ever tell you that it's rude to stare?" Zeeshan's deep voice cut through Arleth's thoughts. She turned to the sound of his voice and saw Selene and Aedan stepping quickly back from the chained creature, their faces red with embarrassment.

"Sorry!" Selene spurted out. "It's just, well,... we haven't seen,.. I mean we don't... ah.. hmmm." Not able to find a nice way to say that they had never seen such a bizarre-looking creature before, she turned to Aedan in the hopes of being rescued. Taking the hint, Aedan started to open his mouth, but Zeeshan beat him to it.

"Yes I know," Zeeshan said angrily. "You haven't seen any creature like me before. I am a ridiculous mix of a talywag and a snow bear. And although I haven't yet seen what I look like, don't you think I know full well that my whole body is in ridiculous proportions. I know I still have my huge eyes and my flapping ears, but I can tell that my face is a lot bigger and hairy so I probably look like an oversized dinner plate. I have furry paws with talons, no hands anymore, what I am supposed to do with these?" He raised up his arms a bit in a futile gesture as the chains forced his arms to fall back down to his sides in a rattle of metal. But he continued on "I have a huge fuzzy body and this ridiculously deep growly voice. Don't you think I know all of this! I don't need two perfectly normal humans examining me like some freak show. Thanks but no thanks!"

No one said anything for a few moments. Arleth was too stunned by Zeeshan's until now unseen anger and Selene and Aedan were struggling for the right words to say to sooth the situation. The air was crackling with tension.

Once again though, it was Zeeshan who broke the silence. "Please forgive me," he said a lot quieter, "I don't know where that came from; I didn't mean to be so angry."

Selene walked up to him and put her hand on one of his huge furry paws. "How old are you my dear?"

"Seven..." *Seven, still just a child!* Selene thought sadly.

"And your name."

"Zeeshan."

"Well Zeeshan I am more sorry that I can tell you at what has happened to you." The tears in her eyes gave proof to her claim. "I am a sorceress so when I saw you I was staring not out of shock or horror but because I was deeply saddened by what had been done to you. I can tell what horrible magic was done to you and I know the pain that it would have caused you."

Zeeshan let out a choked cry at this and Selene nodded sadly and rubbed his paw in a soothing gesture.

"Unfortunately the magic used on you crossed more than just your physical appearance. It didn't work all the way, luckily or you wouldn't be here talking to me. But what it does mean is that your natural calm nature is now mixed with the disposition of a snow bear. I am sorry to say but your calm and serene personality will always be at war with the fiery temper of a snow bear. Outbursts like what just occurred won't be unique."

Selene looked up at the child when she said this. Zeeshan stared back at her for a second and then burst into tears. It was just too much for him to handle. Looking like a horrible monster was terrible enough, but also having his personality change, to become violent and aggressive, everything that Talywags were against, that was just too much to bear.

Still stroking his paw, Selene let him cry for a moment and then calmed him down. "There, there it's ok. Your personality isn't set in stone, you will now always have an aggressive tendency inside you; I can't control that. But I can help you so that it remains *deep* inside. You can learn how to control that aspect so that for all intents and purposes you are still the same."

Zeeshan stopped crying. "Really, you would do that for me?"

"Of course."

"Even though I yelled at you."

Selene smiled and nodded.

"Thank you so much," Zeeshan burst into tears again.

Selene laughed gently, "But first things first, let me get you out of these chains."

Selene climbed up on Zeeshan's arm and put both of her hands on the iron bar around his waist. She concentrated for a few seconds and the metal glowed blue, steadily getting darker and darker. Then all of a sudden the bar disappeared completed in a shower of water.

Arleth gasped despite herself. The woman had changed the iron bar into water! Aedan, who was standing beside her, turned towards her, "See I told you Selene wouldn't have a problem freeing him," he beamed proudly. Arleth grunted in response, *well if they had told me she was a sorceress....* Aedan looked over at her and let out a short laugh, smiling in amusement at the look on her face. Arleth tried to be disgruntled but, looking at the smile on Aedan face, made it impossible. She couldn't help smiling back at him. She wasn't really upset anyways; she was relieved that Zeeshan was free. She hadn't wanted to contemplate what she would have done had she been alone and none of her efforts had freed him. But now thankfully she didn't have to worry.

By the time Arleth and Aedan turned back to look at the scene in front of them, Zeeshan was free and he was alternatively stretching and testing out his new limbs. Selene had turned from him and was looking into the nearest jar and nodding silently to herself.

"Come here please," She said turning to beckon Aedan to see what she was looking at.

Aedan walked over to her and Arleth followed him, curious about what Selene had found.

When they had reached the jar, Selene pointed to one of the black string-like fibers floating around in the fluid, "See that?" She said addressing both Aedan and Arleth.

"What is it?" Arleth asked

"It's an essence."

"A what?"

"An essence. How do I explain it? Let's see. The world and everything in it is made of billions and billions of fibers. These are invisible to the naked eye and to people without magic, but sorceresses and sorcerers are able to see and manipulate them. Therefore, most magic is really just weaving the fibers into different combinations to create new forms. It sounds simple, but of course the reality is a lot more complicated. Some forms are not easily created, the bigger or more intricate an object is, the more fibers it has, and the harder it is to alter. And of course it is possible to create entirely new forms by taking fibers from different objects, creatures, wind patterns etc and weaving them into a new pattern. Each sorcerer or sorceress has their own characteristic spells that they create. For example, Rogan has his enchantments, I have my concealing spells or Alondranes. When a magic is created over and over again enough times, the fibers will naturally flow into that pattern when all the necessary components are present. It only takes a gentle push in that direction to create the item. That is when it becomes someone's speciality.

Aedan coughed

"Right," Selene said, "I am getting off topic."

Arleth hardly cared, she found it all fascinating.

"So," Selene continued, "When fibers are woven together they become essences. So for example someone's personality is made up of hundreds of essences and each essence is made up of hundreds of fibers. It is possible to take out an essence out of its host for a short time to study it; to see how the fibers are woven in it. I have done this myself many times to study how to create a new item. But the essence always is returned to its owner. However, the way that Rogan has been doing it is not natural. He has figured out how to harness the essences and trap them here in this fluid so they stay and do not return to the owner. Then he changes the owner so much that the essence no longer recognizes its owner and so it can be put into anyone. This is how he is doing the experimental combinations. He took certain essences out of Zeeshan and held them here. And he took essences out of the snow bear and put them in that jar over there." She pointed to the jar on the other side of where Zeeshan had been held prisoner. "Rogan then exchanged them, replacing Zeeshan's essences with the corresponding ones from the snow bear. These ones here must be what are left over. What no longer would fit together into one host." And then almost to herself, "What horrible magic." Selene turned to look at Arleth.

"See Arleth, almost any combination of fibers can be woven, making the spells that magical beings can do almost limitless. But the universe exacts its price. All magic is symbiotic, meaning a sorcerer doesn't just create the magic, but each spell cast feeds back onto the person who created it. The more evil a spell is, the more people it hurts, the more corrupt you become on the inside, the more the magic will change your outward appearance. That is why all Dread Mages are green and terribly disfigured. That is the outward appearance of the inner corruption that rests in their soul. A mirror of the destruction they have created with their magic."

Arleth gasped, "So Rogan..."

"Yes, Rogan, Absalom's Dread Mage. Each evil spell that he casts makes him more and more disfigured. You can see just by looking at him how much suffering he has caused." Selene practically spat out the last few words, her disgust with her magical adversary quite evident in her voice.

Arleth was thinking of something else, "Even 7 years ago?...." She breathed. *Rogan was that disfigured even 7 years ago? What kind of a horrible monster is he?"*

Aedan's head turned sharply in her direction and he opened his mouth to ask her what she meant. But at that moment Zeeshan had finished experimenting with his new limbs.

"So thank you very much for freeing me, but Arleth who are these two?"

Arleth looked over at Zeeshan, realizing then that she had never introduced them. She opened her mouth to answer, and then stopped. *How was she going to tell someone that the man standing in front of him was the rightful heir to the throne? And that everything he thought he knew was wrong?* She decided to just go for it.

"Well Zeeshan, this is Aedan Amara and Selene. He is the true heir of the throne and Absalom is not. Oh and I am his sister." Arleth looked at him carefully, there was no way he was going to believe her, she was still getting her head around it herself.

"Huh?" Zeeshan stared at her in confusion.

Arleth smiled and tried again. This time she recounted what Selene and Aedan had told her, with the two of them filling in the gaps.

"Oh," Zeeshan said. He was surprised to say the least, but he still had the intelligence of a Talywag and he was smart enough to realize that in this war, he didn't want to be on the side that had enslaved and disfigured him. He thought he believed Aedan, but it didn't matter who was the rightful heir to him right now anyways, he was on the side of his rescuer. Besides, another question had just come to his mind.

"So," he said, directing his question at Arleth, "What were Selene and Aedan doing in the basement of Iridian castle?"

"Oh well that is simple, they were...." Arleth paused. She realized that she had absolutely no idea. "What *were* they doing here?"

Aedan piped in, "We were looking for her."

"Yes that's right," Arleth chimed in. "They were looking for her. Uh who's 'her'"

There was no response so Arleth turned to look at Selene and Aedan. They were both staring at her and smiling.

She didn't understand for a second, and then she realized.

"Me?!"
They both nodded.

Chapter 20

"Where is this blasted girl?" Absalom raged for the fifth time in as many minutes. He and Rogan were in the courtyard; it was close to the last place they had left to look. Absalom, quickly losing his patience, stomped through the grass as though intent on crushing every blade into a thin green paste.

After leaving Rogan's basement laboratory, he and his sorcerer had searched the entire castle for Arleth and had yet to find her. They had searched the dining hall, the servant's quarters, even waited outside the servant's bathrooms for a while, but all in vain. Questioning the servants was a futile attempt, as Absalom had quickly re-affirmed. It was ironic how making perfect, docile workers could prove so infuriating when you wanted something useful from them. They were incapable of lying so he knew what they were telling him was the truth. But the fact that no one had seen her since breakfast wouldn't help them narrow down where she was now. With no free-will the servants were incapable of thinking past the specific tasks they were enchanted for. They swept or cooked or folded; that was what they were programmed for, not questioning the whereabouts of a fellow servant. Absalom cursed,

"Why did we not think to enchant a servant to follow her? What the hell were we thinking?"

Rogan didn't answer; he was lost in his own thoughts. It didn't matter though, Absalom wasn't expecting an answer. He continued on in an unbroken stream,

"Where is this damn girl?" Angrily, he broke off a low-hanging branch from a nearby tree and threw it as forcefully as he could. It hit the trunk of a tree a few meters off, breaking in two with a loud crack.

The sound jolted Rogan out of his thoughts. He turned towards the direction of the sound and saw the King of Oherra pacing around in an angry circle, muttering to himself. Rogan, himself a model of calm composure, stared at Absalom for a moment in disgust. Then shaking his head, he remembered what he had realized right before the tree-branch had startled him.

"Absalom," Rogan said dryly. The king paused in his pacing and looked at Rogan impatiently. "I think Arleth was still in my laboratory when we were there."

"WHAT?" Absalom yelled. And then calming down a bit he rationalized, "Wouldn't you have sensed her presence?"

"That was what I had assumed too. But remember? Tobin gave her a concealing spell; he let that slip at the end. If she had taken it, I wouldn't have sensed her."

"But we looked in the room, she wasn't there."

"But we didn't look everywhere."

Absalom stared at him angrily, "Well where didn't we look then?"

"Behind the failed Imari."

Absalom thought about it. It certainly made sense. She could have easily hidden behind the creature without being seen, it was big enough.

"Shit!" Absalom cursed. "We were there!" He turned towards the door. "We will go back, I doubt she is still there, but we might get lucky."

Rogan turned as well, "And if she is not, I can find out all I need to know from that creature. It would have seen everything and it still has its free-will after all. And I haven't tortured anyone yet today." Rogan smiled at that thought and side by side, he and Absalom raced out the courtyard door.

Five minutes later, they had reached their destination and neither of them was smiling. Absalom's eyes were opened wide in shock, hands over his mouth, and Rogan's face if possible, looked even greener than usual.

Where just over an hour before, there had been a neatly ordered laboratory, there was now complete chaos. The first thing both men noticed was that the Imari was nowhere to be seen. Second was the level of destruction in the room. All of the 7-foot vials that Rogan had so carefully crafted in order to hold the essences at the proper conditions had been knocked to the ground. Some had huge jagged circular holes as though they had been punched by a massive hand. Still others had been sliced clean in half, the dismembered sections still smoking from the heat of the burn spell used. And some had hit the floor with such force that they had cracked by themselves. The fluid inside was still leaking out of the broken vials. It spread across the floor, some disappearing into cracks, but most was accumulating into pools around the vials. The only vial left untouched was the one that contained the essences of the failed Imari.

There was no doubt that Selene had been here. The still smoking vial sections were testament enough to that. But that meant that Aedan was also free; Selene wouldn't have wasted her time here before saving him. Third, they had freed the failed Imari and he was likely with them. The only question still in Rogan's mind was whether or not Arleth had been with them. He was willing to bet the answer was yes. It was too much of a coincidence that the one place Arleth had been told to go, was also the place that Selene and Aedan had visited, while trying to sneak *out* of the castle without being seen. Selene and Aedan would be looking for her; that was why he had risked being caught. And it seemed like they had all met up right in the middle of his, now ruined, experimental chamber.

Rogan spat on the ground in fury. He turned to Absalom who still hadn't said anything and glared at him with pure hatred. *If that stupid ass hadn't missed an Alondrane, none of this would have happened.* Rogan didn't care as much about Absalom's intense desire to control Arleth and punish the Amara family as he pretended to. Absalom's revenge was not a top priority for Rogan. No, what he was so upset about was the destruction of his work. This room was one of Rogan's greatest passions, the summation of his dark intellect, and aside from his torture chambers, the best and most interesting way to quench his bloodlust. But now, it would take weeks to fix everything that had been destroyed due to Absalom's negligence. Rogan breathed in deeply trying to calm himself.

He would take all the servants that had been working in the kitchen today and torture them. If he spread it out long enough it might just last until he had fixed his chamber. It would also have the added bonus of making Absalom believe he was doing this as punishment for them not noticing Arleth leaving. He wasn't of course, but Absalom wouldn't know.

This thought cheered him a bit. Carefully he lifted up his robe and waded into the pool of fluid. He wanted to get a look at the still intact jar. He didn't know why they had left it alone. Perhaps it was meant as a statement of his failure with the Imari, or maybe Selene didn't understand the magic and simply didn't know if destroying the vial would harm the creature. Whatever the reason, Rogan was just glad it was still intact. It would be much easier to rebuild his laboratory if he had one vial still intact. It also meant he could still continue building Imaris one at a time with this vial until the rest of his chamber was rebuilt. It was slow and cumbersome, but at least it was something.

"Rogan," Absalom began, now aware of what his sorcerer had seen almost as soon as he had entered the room. "The way the vials have been destroyed, clearly indicates that Selene and Aedan were both here with the failed Imari. But how can we be certain that Arleth was with them?"

"We can't be," Rogan said slowly. "I can't sense that she was here. But that doesn't mean much. She almost certainly took the concealing spell that Aedan's spy gave her. With such, as you know, she would be untraceable."

Absalom nodded disdainfully. He was well-accustomed to Selene's concealing spells. Over the years, not only had they made it possible for Aedan to be successful in hundreds of ambushes, skirmishes and raids; they had also allowed dozens of spies to enter and nose about the castle. The fact that he had caught, tortured, and killed each and every one of these spies in the end didn't do much to ease Absalom's displeasure. No, the king knew just what a pain in his ass Selene's spells were for him.

What made it even worse, was that try as he might, Rogan had not yet been able to find a way to counter them. Absalom, not one to tolerate any sort of failure, took this particular one especially badly. If only his sorcerer spent as much time on finding a way to stop Selene's blasted spells as he did on torturing and experimenting with his subjects... But bringing up such old disagreements wasn't going to help them now. And although the king wasn't quite as smart as he thought he was, he was still far from foolish. So he forcibly reined in his re-surfacing anger and when he spoke he did so with a calm voice.

"Well, it makes logical sense that Arleth was with them. This chamber was her destination. It seems unlikely that Selene and Aedan would have just happened to stop here after they escaped the dungeon, especially since it is in the opposite direction from their way out, unless they had met Arleth somewhere on route and she had brought them here."

Rogan agreed with Absalom; he too was almost one hundred percent certain that Arleth had been with them. However, unlike the king, he wasn't hell-bent on capturing the girl. If she hadn't been with Aedan and Selene when they caused this destruction, he could count on the fact that she would be soon or might be already. Aedan had come to the castle specifically to free his sister after all, and when Selene broke him out of the dungeon, finding her would have been his first priority. Even still, Rogan knew the danger in letting all three escape together, especially when they had all been right here, under their noses, in the castle.

But he had planned ahead, he had assumed Absalom would miss an Alondrane and Aedan would escape. In fact he had secretly been hoping for just such an outcome. He had planted his own magic, a failsafe so to say in case of such an eventuality. Now it looked like he was going to get to test it. He was particularly fond of his creation; he had never made something like this before and was eager to see it in action. The anticipation of it as well as the torture of the kitchen servants might just get him through until his laboratory was rebuilt.

All he had to do was buy some time.

"I agree with you," Rogan told the king. "Arleth is and was most likely with Aedan and Selene. However, I think we need to be certain."

Absalom nodded his assent.

"If we go to the dungeon I will be able to tell what time Selene used her Alondrane, which will tell us when she and Aedan left the dungeon. With such information, we can better predict if time-wise, they would have met up with Arleth. Also, I have set up traps all over these halls. They are easy enough to disarm, but it is possible that Selene missed one or two; and even if she didn't I can tell the route they took just by the ones that are dismantled and the one that are still intact. They only go up into the entrance of the main hall, just beyond the stairs. I couldn't have the servants tripping them every five minutes; it would have been a constant and daily chore to keep rebuilding them. So out of necessity I couldn't continue much beyond the dungeons. As a result, once they reach the main hall, I can't track them. But we can at least know if they were all together, if they are still down here somewhere, where they went while they were down here, and roughly which direction they went in if they have left."

Absalom agreed. He didn't have a better idea and he generally, although grudgingly gave in to what Rogan suggested when magic was involved. He could see the logic anyways in making sure their prey was at least not still down here in the bowels of the castle, while they went off prancing around upstairs trying to find them. They needed to be certain where they *weren't*, if they had any chance of finding where they *were*.

He told as much to Rogan. Then added, "We need to hurry, we can't afford to waste any more time."

Rogan nodded, looked appropriately concerned and then turned to leave the chamber.

Perfect, he thought. *Like taking candy from a baby.* Rogan's cold eyes glinted with excitement.

* * *

While Absalom was busy in his garden, angrily stamping the grass into green paste; Arleth, Selene, Aedan and Zeeshan were safely hidden halfway across the castle.

As a boy, one of Aedan's favourite pastimes had been playing hide and seek in the winding corridors and halls of Iridian Castle. He and Val had spirited away hours, sometimes even whole days discovering new hiding spots, hidden passages and secret tunnels all throughout the castle. They had fancied themselves true adventurers, heroes out of their old story books. Little did they know then, that their discoveries on such innocent pursuits would turn out to be even more important to them as adults. It was precisely this secret network that had allowed Aedan to have spies in the castle. Early on, he and Val had recognized the importance of such knowledge and together had drawn detailed maps from memory. These were taught to each and every spy that entered the castle. When a spy was caught, the assumption was made that one or all of the secret hideaways they had used had been compromised. These were therefore crossed off the maps and the next spies were told not to use them. Unfortunately over the years, dozens of hideouts had been crossed off. But Aedan and Val had been zealous in their boyhood game and there were still a fair number of available passages.

It was in one of these that the four of them now hid.

Aedan had led them to one of the larger hideouts he could recall, but even still the four of them were cramped. A lot of this had to do with Zeeshan's massive size; he had been forced to hunch over just to fit inside the room. Once inside it had become quickly apparent that in order for him to be even remotely comfortable, he would take up pretty much the entire space by himself. The end result was that

Zeeshan was as spread out as much as he could be in the small room, with Arleth, Selene and Aedan sitting in a row on top of his legs.

Arleth shifted her weight carefully on top of Zeeshan and attempted to stretch her legs out. Her stretch was only partially successful, but she did manage to prevent her right leg from falling asleep, a fate it had been slowly edging towards. She repositioned her legs as best she could even though she knew it was useless. Their plan was to hide out here until nightfall and then sneak out of the castle under cover of darkness. In that time, her legs were going to fall asleep about a dozen times, careful repositioning or not.

Lucky for her, she had about a million questions to ask to pass the time.

First things first, she wanted to know how she had come to be separated from her family and been raised on a different planet with no knowledge of who she really was.

At this question, Selene raised her eyebrows and looked over at Aedan. The room was dark, lit only by a small ball of light Selene had conjured, but even so Aedan saw the glance, smiled sheepishly and nodded, "Yes Selene I get the hint, I will no longer attack my sister with information."

Selene smiled, her white teeth flashing in the gloom, "Just making sure."

"So Arleth," Aedan began, turning his attention from Selene to focus on his sister, "In order to answer your questions, I will start from the beginning."

Arleth nodded eagerly, excited to learn about the history she didn't even know she had until a few hours ago.

"As a child, Absalom lived in the castle with his mother and father. His father, Aban, was in charge of the Royal Guard, the personal army of the king and the highest ranked professional fighting force in Oherra. For a number of years, Aban held this title and was highly regarded and well-respected. Then his wife became pregnant and gave birth to a baby girl. It was said that he took one look at the child and lost his mind. He flew into a rage, took his sword and ran it through both his newborn daughter and his wife.

"Why would he do such a thing?" Arleth asked in shock

Aedan hesitated, "Well..."

"Holding the post of Royal Guard would have been very stressful," Selene cut in, carefully avoiding the glance Aedan was giving her. "It's hard to know why someone would snap."

Arleth nodded, she supposed that was true. "What happened next?"

"Our father decided to exile both Aban and his 13 year old son Absalom. For a while, our father kept tabs on where they went. By the terms of the exile, none of the cities were supposed to let them in. But Aban had been highly respected as the leader of the Royal Guard and our father wanted to make sure none of them decided to make an exception. He knew they had gone to each of the five northern cities in turn and been rejected by each. The last word was that they had travelled north into the ice plains. Then I guess our father either lost track of them or stopped caring. He met our mother, and then 5 years later I was born.

When I was 7 Absalom came back. He was 25 years old then, slightly younger than I am now. He started off as a kitchen servant, but was soon trained into the army. The only person he ever associated with was Rogan – he was only an apprentice sorcerer at that time. I guess that period was where their partnership started, although no one really knows if they had been friends as children or not. Aside from a constant group of different women that would all but follow him around, everyone else avoided him.

Then one day, about two years after he arrived, he disappeared. Rogan was questioned; a number of heartbroken women were questioned, but either no one knew where he went or no one would talk. My father tried looking for him, but when there were no traces of him, he along with everyone else just assumed that after years of exile, living in the castle had proven too much for him and he had left for a more quiet life.

This was very likely the worst assumption of my father's life.

A year later, almost to the day, Absalom came back again. This time though, things were different. For one Arleth, you had been born and were a few months old at the time. Secondly, when Absalom came, he came with an army. An army of mercenary soldiers – the Dursk from deep in the ice plains.

He attacked at night.

I was awoken in my bed by my mother urgently shaking me awake. She told me the castle was under attack and to go hide. As I was racing through the castle I ran into Selene and Val and the three of us, along with Val's father Bain found a hidden passage to hide in. Bain left us there to go fight the intruders and the three of us hid there, waiting for him to return for what seemed like an eternity. We were terrified, shaking, hearing the screams of dying people just outside the door.

Bain finally came back and when I questioned him, he reluctantly told me that you had been killed."

"Wait, what?" Arleth interrupted.

"When Bain went to your crib, he saw a lot of blood." Selene explained. "There was no body, but there were dozens of dead bodies scattered around the room. You could have been easily hidden among them, too small to notice. At that moment Bain made a hard decision. He chose to go back and save the 3 children he knew were alive, rather than risk their lives as well as his own for a baby he was almost certain was already dead."

That sounded very harsh to Arleth. But as cold as it was, she had to admit it did make a certain amount of logical sense. She still didn't appreciate that she had been left to die though. "So clearly I am not dead, what did happen to me then?"

Selene and Aedan shared a look.

"We aren't entirely sure Arleth. We only recently found out that Neve had survived the attack and had taken you with her to Tocarra. And that is all we really know. Somehow Neve was able to sneak you out of the castle and take you across the universe with no one seeing her do it. Exactly how she did it is a mystery."

"But Absalom *did* know I was taken and he knew I was on Tocarra."

Both of them looked at her in surprise. "What do you mean?" Selene asked.

"Rogan came for me when I was 10."

"What?!?" Both Selene and Aedan exclaimed incredulously. Neither of them had any idea that this was the second time Absalom had tried to reach her.

Arleth spent the next 15 minutes telling them about the attack on the orphanage. Aedan was insistent on details and by the end Arleth was almost in tears when she described the death of Flora and how she had left Neve.

Selene shuffled her way over to Arleth and put her arms around her to comfort her. "I'm so sorry Arleth, we know how terrible it is to lose those closest to you."

Arleth hadn't let herself cry over this in years, but now, for some reason she couldn't contain her tears. Perhaps it was Selene's gentle tone and understanding or just the fact that this was the first time she had spoken out loud what had happened to her that day, but Arleth dissolved into incontrollable sobs. Selene just held her, patting her back and stroking her hair. She didn't say anything; she just patiently let her cry herself out.

After about 10 minutes, Arleth's tears had just about dried up. "Thanks," she muttered, wiping the tears from her eyes. "I didn't think it would still affect me so much."

"When you go through a traumatic event, especially when you are so young I don't think you can every really forget about it. And this was probably the first time you had to talk about it isn't it?"

Arleth nodded.

Selene smiled and moved back away from Arleth, but still held onto her hand. "Well I think that it is only natural for you to react this way. I know Aedan, Val and I are still affected by the deaths we witnessed as children and we have had a lot of experience with death since then. And we have each other; you were left with no one. You are one brave girl Arleth."

Arleth certainly didn't feel brave at that moment, but she appreciated what Selene was trying to do.

"And besides," Selene said winking at Arleth, "Sometimes a good cry makes you feel better."

They sat in silence for a few minutes, each lost in their own private thoughts.

"Why do you think that Absalom waited 10 years to try and kill Arleth?" Aedan breathed into the darkness.

"I was wondering that too," Selene said. "I think he probably knew all along that Neve had taken her. But at that time he just didn't care. In the beginning, he was interested in consolidating his power and eradicating any traitors. Then he had the northern annihilation, the subjugation of the southern cities and all his experimental creatures. Think about it, he thought he was invincible, why would he care about a child across the universe?"

"And then we grew up, became more powerful, formed an actual resistance and that child suddenly became more important." Aedan continued. "But he still thought he was strong enough to beat us. So instead of wanting her alive, on his side, he just wanted to kill her, finish the job he didn't do 10 years before."

"Right, but he failed." And in the intervening seven years, we grew even stronger, doubled our numbers and beat him into a stalemate."

"And then he wanted Arleth for her powers, to break the stalemate," Aedan finished.

"But if he had failed in killing her 10 years ago, why would he all of a sudden give up and forget about her for 7 years?"

"Arleth," Aedan said turning to her, "You said that when you left Neve, Rogan was unconscious right?"

"Yes, he was lying on the floor."

"Neve must have cast a spell on him when he was sleeping; made him think he had killed Arleth, something like that. It's the only explanation that makes sense."

"But how would he have known she was alive now?"

"The Erum!" They both exclaimed together.

"Of course," Selene said. "One of them must have found a way to read it. They must have decoded it to track you, but soon realized that it was tracking not one, but two Amaras. And then realized that Arleth was still alive. Aedan, we need to get that book. Now."

"Selene it's too dangerous...."

"If one of them can now read it, it is too dangerous not to. Up until this point it didn't matter as much that we didn't have it. But he can track every single move that you and Arleth make. It won't be a war anymore Aedan it will be a slaughter."

Aedan sighed, he knew she was right. He started to stand up, but Selene immediately pushed him back down.

"Don't even think about it. You know it has to be me. Magic will be needed to get to it."

Aedan looked pained, but he nodded. "Please be careful Selene."

"I always am! Be back in a flash" She winked at him and with a smile at all three of them in turn, she handed her ball of light to Aedan and left the room.

When she had left, Aedan sighed and shook his head sadly. He knew she had to be the one to go, but he didn't like it one bit.

"Aedan, what is an Erum?" Arleth asked.

"*The* Erum. There is only one. The Erum is a book"

"A book?!?" Arleth didn't see what the fuss was over a mere book.

Aedan laughed, "It's not just any book. This one is imbued with tracking magic. It tracks the lives of each Amara currently alive and writes an ongoing account of their daily activities. In essence, it is a self-writing journal."

"Are you saying this book has my entire life history in it?"

"Yes, and mine too. What we have experienced, our feelings, emotions, it tells everything."

"And Absalom has this book right now? And has been reading about our lives?"

"Yes that is why it is so important to get it back. Its real purpose is so that Amaras can look up past relatives and see how they handled a situation. So no knowledge is lost through the generations and so that the mistakes of the past aren't repeated. But it is a dangerous thing in the wrong hands. As a protection, it is written so that only a person from the Amaran bloodline can read it. But it is possible to learn how to read it given enough time, and Absalom and Rogan have been given decades."

"Wow," Arleth said. She sat in silence thinking of all the things that Absalom would have read about her and her skin crawled. She felt very violated. Then, she thought of something else,

"But this is *Iridian* castle. It guards the crystal throne for the rest of the universe. How could it just be taken and the rest of the universe have no idea. Life is going on peacefully on Tocarra with no knowledge that the King of Oherra is not an Amara.

Zeeshan, silent up until this point also chirped in, "And how come my people, the Talywags have no idea that Absalom is not the real king? Occa supports him, throws banquets for him when he comes through."

"Well," Aedan said, "In answer to your first question Arleth, there has been peace in the universe for so long that it has gotten complacent. As you probably know, the worlds aren't as connected as they once were and many of the artefacts have been lost or reside in museums in the royal cities. Not only that, but Absalom spent the first couple of years of his reign playing the perfect diplomat with those worlds that were the most closely connected to Oherra; Senan, Rizod and Lothe. I don't know how exactly he did it, but somehow he managed to convince their ruling families that he had ended a brutal regime and had brought peace to Oherra. I want to believe that he had Rogan conjure up something for him. I want to believe that their kings and queens are not that dumb and gullible. But I really have no idea.... And Zeeshan, about your question. The Talywags do know the truth about Absalom."

"They do?!?"

"Yes, they have been helping us from the beginning."

"But how come I didn't know?"

"The Talywags do not have the strength to stand up to Absalom and, as you know they are a timid race; they don't have the courage to join our army and live in the mountains. So they help us by providing us with food, clothing and other supplies. To protect their people, on the outside they are loyal to Absalom, but they have been leaving us valuable supplies at specific drop off points in the Frasht Forest for years. It is quite a testament to the intelligence and loyalty of your people that they have managed to successfully fool Absalom for over a decade... It's funny actually," Aedan continued after a brief pause, "The Talywags are known as a timid race and they are few in number but they are risking everything to help us. While the heavily fortified cities of the south have a large fighting force and submitted to Absalom almost right away."

Zeeshan smiled, he was quite proud of his people. "Well good! I am glad us Talywags are on your side."

"So am I Zeeshan, so am I." Aedan turned away from Zeeshan to stare into the darkness, thinking about just how true that was. Without the Talywags, Aedan didn't even want to think about how he would get the food and supplies needed to sustain his army as well as the civilians in the stronghold. Not to mention the raw materials they needed to make and repair their weapons and armour. For such a timid race, they were a vital component in the resistance against Absalom.

"Aedan," Arleth said, breaking his train of thought, "What did you mean when you and Selene were talking earlier and you said that Absalom wanted me for my powers?"

"Hmmm?" Aedan said, his mind still a bit distracted, "Oh your powers." He paused briefly, "With your powers, if you were fighting on Absalom's side he would have the advantage in the war."

Arleth just stared at him, her confusion etched on her face.

"Um what powers? I don't have any powers!"

Now it was Aedan's turn to look confused. "Of course you do. It's your birthright."

"It's my what?"

"Your birthright. You know, as a female in the Amaran bloodline? The power every Amaran woman has been born with since the Great War?"

Arleth continued to stare at him.

"You really don't know? How were you never taught this? I mean I know you were on Tocarra, but this is important. It is part of the history that affects the entire universe. I'm surprised Neve never told you anything about it." He paused, "Well I guess maybe she would have if she had been given more time." He paused again, thinking. "Were you taught anything of any other worlds? Please tell me you know the importance of Oherra. About the Crystal Throne, the other artefacts, the Great War, Dread Mages? You were taught at least *that* much right?"

Arleth nodded. "Yes I was taught all of that in the orphanage. We learned the basic history of all the worlds."

"Ok well that is good at least," Aedan said, "I would hate to think that the worlds had become so isolated from each other that children would grow up not learning at least a bit about the others. And I always assumed, that like here, all the worlds would teach their children about the Great War; what caused it, and the solution held by Oherra through the Crystal Throne. I mean that didn't just affect us, the war involved the entire universe."

"I don't know about in other places, but at the orphanage we learned about that early on when we started going to school." Arleth said a bit defensively. "But I still never learned about any female Amaran birthright." She paused for a moment as the reality sunk in, "About my birthright," she amended quietly.

"Well about your magic itself, I can't help you very much – Selene would be much better at it that me. But I *can* tell you about the origin of your powers."

Arleth nodded eagerly.

"After the Great War," Aedan began "The remaining sorcerers and sorceresses put a lot of safeguards in place in order to prevent that scale of destruction from ever happening again. As you know, *I think*, that was when the artefacts were made and the crystal throne, being the strongest was entrusted to the house of Amara."

"Yes," Arleth said, remembering her childhood lessons, "The artefacts were created because cutting off the worlds completely from each other seemed too drastic a measure. The worlds might need each other in the future. But at the same time, it was too dangerous to continue to allow the unhindered travel between them, as it had caused people to get too greedy and ambitious. Many sorcerers and sorceresses had seen the benefit in controlling the entire universe and in the destruction and death they had created in their quest for such power, they had turned into Dread Mages. They had come close to annihilating some of the worlds completely during the century of power struggles.

In order to stop the bloodshed and prevent this from ever being able to happen again, the 10 most powerful sorcerers and sorceresses who were still good, combined their magic to create the artefacts so that travel between the worlds could still occur but it would be limited to a handful of people in each world."

Arleth paused for a second as she couldn't help but smile at the look of proud surprise on her brother's face. She looked over at Zeeshan and could see that he was struggling not to smile as well. She had gone into a lot of detail on purpose, telling him everything that she knew. She knew she was shamelessly showing off, but she was a bit upset at Aedan's attitude when he assumed that just because she didn't know about some power she was supposed to have, she wouldn't know *anything* at all. Well she intended to show him!

"The artefacts worked by creating a passageway between the worlds, but only the person in possession of one could use it. Also, each artefact was only able to form a passageway with a few of the closest worlds and there was a lag period so the weaker ones could only be used every couple of months for example. So it not only restricted travel to a few individuals on each world but also the frequency as well. A few artefacts were dispersed with the sorcerers and sorceresses to each of the 10 worlds. But on Oherra, the Crystal Throne artefact was made. It was the strongest of the artefacts and allowed passage to all of the worlds and only had a lag period of one hour. It was entrusted to the King of Oherra at the time, Falcon Amara and to all Amarans afterwards. It was created as an additional safeguard so Oherra could monitor the other worlds." Arleth finished, rather proud of herself.

Aedan for his part, looked a bit dumbfounded, "I still don't understand how if you know so much about the other safeguards put in place after the Great War – the artefacts and the crystal throne – you were never taught about the last protection – the power inherited by all female descendants of the Amaran line."

In the darkness Arleth sighed.

Zeeshan put of a large paw to his mouth in an attempt to stifle his laughter. He was partially successful, creating a muffled growling noise.

Aedan looked over at the sound Zeeshan made, but was completely oblivious to its cause.

"Oh well, I guess it doesn't matter. It's just rather odd." Aedan continued. "Anyways, another precaution the 10 sorcerers and sorceresses created was to enchant the Amaran bloodline. This took an incredible amount of power and was very difficult for them, but they felt that it was necessary. They had witnessed too much death and suffering to not put everything they had into making sure it would never happen again. So they cast a spell on Falcon Amara to ensure that every female descendent of his would be born with magic capable of defending the crystal throne and Oherra itself if necessary. They called it the power of empathy."

"The power of what?!?" Arleth sputtered, "*Empathy?* How can *empathy* protect anything, much less an entire world?"

"It's not empathy like you are thinking Arleth. It's *empathic* power. It works through your connection with other people and the things around you. It is very powerful, trust me. If you have it under your control, you can get people, objects, animals, nature, *anything* to bend to your will."

"I can control other people?!" Arleth asked incredulously

"Not so much control as influence, there are some limits."

"If this power is so strong how was my mother not able to defend against Absalom's attack?"

"Our mother wasn't an Amara; she didn't have the power that you do. She only became an Amara when she married our father. Only those women *born* into the house of Amara inherit the power."

"But how do you know the power didn't skip me? Are you sure I have it, maybe it skipped a generation or something." Arleth thought back through her life, the brutal attack on the orphanage, then her seven years as a slave to Bella. She certainly hadn't been able to influence anything then. Someone with the kind of powers Aedan described should have been able to control her own life. At least not have ended up as a slave, bending to the whims of such a frivolous and empty-headed woman as Bella.

"No Arleth, it doesn't skip any generations, it doesn't work like that. You have the power. Selene's mother could sense it in you when you were born."

"But I don't have any powers. I can't do magic! I have been a slave almost half of my life – I can't control, sorry, *influence* things!"

"You can't do those things *yet*. And that is understandable; you have had no one to teach you how to use your magic. Selene wasn't born knowing how to use her magic either, she had to learn. But trust me, you have the power in you. You just need to be taught how to draw it out and use it."

"But how do I do that?" Arleth asked, daunted.

"I don't know Arleth," Aedan replied "I don't have any magic myself. I have told you everything I know about your powers, it isn't very much, I know. You would have to ask Selene."

As if on cue, there was a gentle knocking on the door and Selene's voice softly called "Aedan?"

Aedan carefully climbed over Zeeshan and opened the door for her. She scrambled in, closing the door quietly behind her, in her arms she was carrying a small black book that Arleth assumed was the Erum. "Ah Selene," Aedan said, helping her to sit down beside him, "I was just telling Arleth about her powers. She has a lot of questions for you."

"I would love to answer them Arleth," Selene said, taking the ball of light back from Aedan and floating it into the centre of the small room. "But it is night already and we need to be heading back to the mountains. I will answer all your questions when we are back in the stronghold. Every minute we spend in the castle puts us in more danger, especially now that I have the Erum. Absalom will likely know it is missing very soon."

"Did you have any trouble getting it?" Aedan asked.

"No, it was in the library, right where I expected it to be. There were some servants there, but I managed to avoid them without being seen. And the spells that had been put on the book were easy to break.

They were more spells to hide it from sight, rather than to defend it against someone taking it. It is clear that neither Absalom nor Rogan expected the book to be taken. I guess that makes sense though, their servants wouldn't touch it, and the spells that were cast would be enough to prevent any spy that we send in from finding it."

Aedan smiled at Selene, "Well I am glad there were no problems."

Selene nodded her agreement. "Ok we should be going." She fished around in her pocket and pulled out a small blue pill. Arleth recognized it immediately, it was a concealing spell, just like the one Neve's brother had given her. Selene popped it in her mouth, and turned around to crouch in front of the group, her face looked grave.

"We have a few miles of open land to pass through before we get to the safety of the mountains. It is a huge stretch of territory that will be visible from the castle and is patrolled by Grekens and Absalom's soldiers. It will be dangerous and the way we are now, we will stand out like a fox in a chicken coop. To make matters worse, Aedan is known on sight to every member of Absalom's army."

Arleth reached over to Zeeshan and squeezed his furry paw.

Aedan, seeing the fearful look on his sister's face cut in, "But Selene has a plan." He gave the blonde woman a pointed look. "*Right?*"

Selene, startled for a second by Aedan's interuption, saw Arleth's face and hurriedly said "Oh yes, sorry I have a plan."

Arleth and Zeeshan let out a breath almost in unison.

"We still have to be very careful," Selene continued. "But yes I think I have some tricks that will help." She turned to face Aedan and put her hands on his shoulders. "First I am going to cast a small illusion spell on Aedan so that he isn't as recognizable." She started to mutter a few words and then instantly stopped. She reached back into her pocket and pulled out another concealing spell and handed it to him. "On second thought, you should probably take another one of these before I start."

Aedan popped it into his mouth soundlessly and Selene put her hands back on his shoulders.

Selene's mouth started moving and Arleth felt certain she was chanting something, but even though Arleth was sitting right beside her, she couldn't hear what the woman was saying. She didn't need to hear to know what was happening though. She watched in awe as

Aedan's body started to glow a bright blue. And remarkably, right before her eyes, Arleth watched as Aedan's nose grew longer and wider; his eye colour changed from purple to brown; he shrunk in height *and* he was wearing the same clothes that one of Absalom's soliders would wear.

Selene took her hands away from his shoulders and the blue light faded instantly. She looked him up and down, appraising her work. "What do you think?" She turned to Zeeshan and Arleth. "Does he look like a soldier?"

Arleth and Zeeshan just stared at him open-mouthed. They were too suprised to say anything.

Selene let out a quiet giggle "I guess that is a yes then?" She smiled at them.

"Oh my goodness yes," Arleth said. "How? What? Does he actually look different now?"

"Oh no, no," Selene said with a smile. "Aedan hasn't changed at all."

"EH?" Arleth and Zeeshan said together.

"An illusion spell, like what I cast on Aedan, is just that: an illusion. It just changes the perception of others. Aedan is still the same, but when other people - like us - look at him, we see a different man in front of us."

"Wow that is incredible!" Said Zeeshan. "He isn't even recognizable."

"I am glad you think that way," Said Selene slowly. "Because I would also like to perform the same spell on you."

Zeeshan turned his head sharply to face her, his dinner-plate sized eyes, somehow even larger.

"I know I am asking a lot of you," She said to the Talwyag gently. "You have *just* had a terrible experience with magic, and I can't begin to imagine all the things you are feeling right now. But if you let me do this, I know that it will help us to escape." She put her hand on his furry arm, "But I fully understand if you don't want me to."

Zeeshan stayed quiet for a moment, thinking.

"You know, I don't think I mind." he said relatively calmly. "It didn't seem to hurt Aedan."

Aedan shook his head "Completely painless."

"Would I look like a solider too?" He asked Selene.

"No, I was thinking a Greken would be better. In the off chance that we still raise some suspicions, a Greken would be more likely to make someone not ask any questions and leave us alone. And.." She fished around for a nice way to say it. "It is easier for me to make as little modification as possible, and since you are already a similiar size..." She left the sentence unfinished.

"I understand." Zeeshan said "I just want to get back home. Please do what you must."

"Thank you," Selene said gratefully. "Here take this first please." She handed Zeeshan the last concealing spell. He popped it in his mouth without argument.

Just like she had done with Aedan, Selene put her hands on Zeeshan's shoulders and started to mutter under her breath.

If Arleth had been in shock with Aedan's transformation, she didn't even know how to describe her reaction to Zeeshan's. Through the blue glow, she watched as his white fur disappeared to be replaced with serpentine scales. His body sprouted a long snake head, his eyes shrunk and changed from green to yellow. And Arleth could make out tentacles hovering in the air, attached to his back. If she hadn't known, there would have been no way she would have realized he wasn't a real Greken.

"How do you feel?" Arleth asked her new friend.

"Different." Zeeshan said, "I guess? More different?"

Arleth silently chastized herself. What a ridiculously stupid question to ask him. Of course he feels different. He was just turned from a Talywag, into whatever he is now. And before he was even used to his body at all, he was magicked into a Greken.

"Sorry Zeeshan, that was a stupid question."

"No, Arleth it's ok. I just don't know how I feel. I guess... fuzzy?"

"Fuzzy?" Arleth said.

"It's like the edges of your body are tingly." Aedan interrupted. "Really weird actually." He lifted up his arm and waved it in front of him. "Really *Really* weird."

Selene shook her head at him. "Ok Mr weird, do you think you can keep it together so we can leave?" She smiled at him teasingly.

"Yes Ma'am!" Aedan looked at Arleth and Zeeshan and winked.

"Ok jokes aside," Selene said seriously, her smile gone. "Zeeshan, Aedan, you two are both good right? Neither of you are in pain or feel anything other than tingling or fuzziness?"

Both of them shook their heads.

"Ok great. Zeeshan, you are going to have to lead us. It would make the most sense for a Greken to be at the front of this group. Arleth and I look like servants, and Aedan obviously looks like a soldier. I don't think anyone will bother us. With Absalom's entire army and servants being enchanted, they shouldn't question us, unless we look like the escaping enemy. So let's walk as calmly as we can, and pretend that we belong here. Also, Zeeshan, even though I want you to walk in front. Make sure you stay as close to me as you can. I know there are protection charms all over the place and I don't want you to trip one by accident."

Selene looked at each one of them in turn. "Is everyone clear on what we need to do?"

When it was Arleth's turn, she gulped audibly but nodded. She was ready. Scared, but ready. Selene seemed satisfied. She grunted to herself and then without another word, she extinguished the ball of light and they were off, with Zeeshan leading the way.

* * *

A few hours later, Absalom and Rogan stood in Absalom's bed chamber looking out the window across the Iridian plains. It was dark, but even still they could make out 4 figures, 3 small and one rather large, bulky one just beginning to enter the mountains.

Rogan was pleased, although trying to hide it.

Absalom was pissed.

To Rogan, everything had worked out perfectly. He had wasted just enough time in the dungeons, pretending to check his 'traps' and to follow Selene and Aedan's path to ensure that they had enough time to escape. Because the truth was, he didn't especially want to capture Aedan, Selene and Arleth; at least not like this.

It wasn't any fun.

He had hatched his own plan – and it wouldn't kill just those three, but Aedan's *entire* stronghold as well. But in order for it to work, they had to actually get back to their stronghold.

It had taken him years to figure out how to create this particular piece of magic – his Ranin Bud. They had never been able to get inside Aedan's mountain base because of Selene's protection spells. In fact they had never even come close to finding where it was located

– Selene's magic was that impenetrable. So a few years ago, Rogan had decided to change tactics – instead of trying to find a way to break Selene's spells, he had worked on creating an object that would implant itself inside a host. It would be magically invisible to Selene's spells and it would therefore get inside her barriers and into the stronghold, being carried unbeknownst by the person it had implanted in. Once inside, it would detach itself from the person, multiply and grow to maturity. 14 days later, hundreds of bloodthirsty Ranin would be inside Aedan's mountain camp, destroying everyone and everything in sight.

And now he had finally finished it. Even better, it was currently implanted inside Aedan Amara.

Rogan was finding it hard to contain his excitement.

Absalom, however, didn't know about the Ranin Bud yet and was slightly more than annoyed that the four of them had gotten away.

"If you had just managed to kill the damn girl 7 years ago, and not been fooled by that sorceress, none of this would have happened. Arleth would not now be with Aedan. We would not be at the disadvantage we are now." Absalom screamed at Rogan, his spit flying onto Rogan's face.

Rogan casually wiped Absalom's saliva off of his cheek, as he thought back to that day on Tocarra seven years ago.

He had chased Arleth and a blonde girl into a storage room. He had killed the blonde girl quickly with a light spear and was just about to do the same to Arleth when Neve caught him in a web. He had been flown across the room and had landed in a heap against the far door. Neve and him had battled viciously for a long time before they had both passed out from exhaustion and magical overuse. When he had woken up, Neve was just coming to as well. She was slumped against the wall with Arleth crouched beside her. With his last shred of energy, Rogan had cast two spears of light and had sent them soaring across the room to land spectacularly, one through the heart of Arleth and one cleanly decapitating Neve. He had watched the last of Arleth's laboured breaths from across the room and then had drifted off into a peaceful sleep.

At least that was what he had thought happened. To be honest, what he still *remembered*. Even though he now knew it hadn't happened quite like that at all.

A few weeks ago, after years of working at it, Absalom had managed to figure out how to read the Erum. The original goal was to be able to follow Aedan. It would be impossible for him to ambush and raid Absalom's troops if he could see what the man was planning as he was doing it. But they had quickly realized the Erum wasn't just writing the story of one Amara, it was following the life of the still very much alive Arleth.

Apparently Neve hadn't been as close to exhaustion as Rogan had thought she had been. When he had been unconscious, she had helped Arleth to escape the orphanage and used an illusion spell to trick him into thinking he had killed her.

"You weren't so upset a couple of weeks ago to learn she was alive. I remember you distinctly saying something about how it was fortunate Neve had tricked me like that. How having Arleth's powers would bring about the end of Aedan's miserable little life that much sooner." Rogan countered.

"Well I didn't expect you to just let her slip out of your grasp." Absalom shot back.

Rogan had to smile to himself, *how* he *let her slip out of his grasp?* Absalom was always so delusional when he was angry, and he was never quite as angry as when his revenge seemed to be in peril. Normally Rogan would have been a bit annoyed by this offhand comment from Absalom, but right now he was in too good a mood. He let Absalom continue yelling at him for a few more minutes before he said quietly "Well it doesn't matter anyways. I planted a Ranin Bud on Aedan so it is even better that he got away."

Absalom paused, the insult he was about to hurl at his sorcerer silenced on his tongue. The corners of his mouth curled up in the hint of a smile. And then into a full out grin, followed by a laugh. "How were you able to plant it on him?"

"I left it in the dungeon cell we placed him in. It was lying in the corner, as visible and as large as a grain of dust. Then as he sat obliviously in the cell, undoubtedly planning his own escape, it would have rolled its way over to him and burrowed under his skin. When we went back to the dungeon a little while ago, I could sense the remnants of its magic still in the air. It has successfully implanted into Aedan."

"Well isn't that wonderful," Absalom replied his anger vanished without a trace, as if it had never been there. He had been pacing through the chamber during his bout of yelling and now he returned back to the window to stand beside Rogan. Through the darkness he could just barely make out the four of them, slightly darker shadows against an almost as dark background. He watched as they ventured deeper into the mountains and then disappeared from sight completely. It wouldn't be long now before Aedan had returned to his stronghold.

Absalom turned away from the window to look at his sorcerer, the smile still on his lips, "We will have to get planning then. We only have two weeks to coordinate the destruction of our beloved Aedan."

Chapter 21

"Oomph!" Arleth exclaimed as she stumbled ungracefully into Selene's back.

Selene had been guiding them through the mountains to the stronghold and in the dark, Arleth hadn't noticed when Selene had abruptly stopped in front of her.

"Oh sorry," Selene said distractedly as she put a hand behind her to steady Arleth.

With Selene's help, Arleth managed to steady herself on the uneven rocks. Curious though, she stretched to her right as far as she safely could on the narrow mountain pass in order to see what had made Selene stop so abruptly in the first place. But for her troubles, all she could see was much of the same; the mountain pass they were on seemed to continue for at least a mile before it disappeared into the darkness. Confused, Arleth began to ask why they had stopped, but was quickly silenced by a hand over her mouth.

"Sshhh," Aedan whispered gently into Arleth's ear as he came up closer behind her. Shortly after reaching the mountains, the illusion spell had worn off for both him and Zeeshan. So Aedan, once again looked like himself.

"Look," he said removing his hand from her mouth.

Doing as she was told, Arleth stopped trying to look past Selene, and instead focused on her. Selene, deep in concentration, had turned slightly to her left and in the darkness, Arleth could just make out the subtle movements of her lips. As she watched, Selene began to speak louder and she raised her arms in front of her.

"What is she doing?" Arleth whispered back to Aedan.

A faint blue light began to pulse from Selene's outstretched hands.

"She's opening the front door."

"Huh?" Arleth was still confused.

"We are right outside the entrance of our mountain home. Selene is re-working her protection spells so that we can get in."

They were right outside? Arleth thought in surprise. She looked around her again. The four of them were on a narrow, uneven rocky path that spiraled its way through the mountains. Ahead of her, past Selene, there was still nothing but more path and more mountains. To her right, the cliff dropped off hundreds of feet below and to her left there was nothing but a sheer rock face.

But to the left was where Selene was focusing.

Arleth squinted in the darkness trying to find some indent or groove on the solid rock wall; anything at all really that looked even remotely close to a door.

"The fact that you can't see a door," Aedan whispered to her, as if reading her mind, "The fact that this spot looks exactly like every other spot in the mountains, means that Selene's secrecy spells are working. She has woven incredibly powerful magic all around the entrance to our stronghold. It is designed to hide its location from anyone that happens to pass by. You can see for yourself how effective it is."

Arleth nodded in awe, looking around her for the third time, but this time with a newfound appreciation for her surroundings.

"In all the years we have been here," Aedan continued with more than a hint of pride in his voice, "Absalom, Rogan, their soldiers, any creatures, nothing they can conjure up, no spells Rogan can create have managed to even come close to finding where our stronghold is, let alone getting inside. Selene's magic is that strong."

"Wow!" Zeeshan said behind Aedan as he too took in the unchanging scenery. "That is incredible! If I was here by myself, I would have just kept on walking not even realizing I had passed anything at all."

Aedan nodded, "Yes, and that is exactly what Absalom and Rogan's followers do as well; those that even get this far that is."

"Okay," Selene said, interrupting their admiration of her work, "I'm ready. I had altered the spells a bit when Aedan and I left   so that in case something happened to me, Aedan would still be able to find his way back and so that our camp would still be protected."

Aedan looked over at her in surprise; he hadn't seen her doing this when they had left; and he hadn't suspected how unsure she had been that their plan would work.

Selene carefully avoided looking at him as she continued, "But everything is back to normal now, so let's go." She smiled and beckoned Arleth to come over to her. Arleth obeyed, and Aedan followed her with Zeeshan coming up behind him.

"Everyone needs to be touching me in order to get safely through the barrier," Selene instructed holding out her arms to the three of them. "Please, Arleth, Zeeshan take my hands."

They did as they were bidden and Aedan wrapped his arm around Selene's waist. He leaned close to her and whispered in her ear, "You weren't sure we were going to make it huh?"

"I always like to be prepared, you know that," Selene responded. "Remember, if Absalom had found the Alondrane I was actually in, I wouldn't be here now."

Aedan winced, he didn't want to be reminded of that, "But you were so confident in reassuring me when I was worried if the plan would work."

"Of course I was silly, I couldn't have us *both* scared out of our minds." Selene moved her head slightly back from his so that he could see her winking at him.

A few inches from her face, Aedan looked into her eyes, "You are wonderful you know that right?" He leaned over and kissed her on the mouth.

Arleth and Zeeshan, who had been watching their exchange up to this point, although not being able to hear what was said, averted their eyes and smiled at each other.

"Ok is everyone ready?" Selene said, "Zeeshan, Arleth you will feel coldness as you pass through the barrier and a slight tingling. It shouldn't be very unpleasant and it will only last a few seconds.

She tightened her grip on Arleth and Zeeshan's hands and felt Aedan's hands resting on her shoulders. She started to take a step forward and then stopped.

"Aedan, we aren't telling Val we were anything but 100% certain of our plan."

"Of course not," Aedan said seriously. "I do not have a death wish."

Selene nodded, "Good."

She paused for a few more seconds and then led them forward through the invisible barrier.

Even though she had been warned, Arleth still wasn't prepared for the rush of cold that flooded through her. She closed her eyes against the cold and gasped audibly in shock; she could feel the goosebumps form instantly on her exposed skin. It was as though her entire body had been plunged into a pool of ice. Involuntarily, the muscles in Arleth's legs began to constrict against the cold, and if it wasn't for Selene's hand pulling her along, she wasn't so sure her legs would have carried her forward. Teeth chattering, she allowed herself to be led forward blindly by Selene's steady hand. After a few seconds though, she braced against the cold and squinted one eye open.

What she saw, took her breath away.

When Arleth was still a young child at the orphanage, Neve had taken her aside one day at recess to show her a massive spider web that had been spun between two oak trees in the centre of the courtyard. Arleth had been fascinated, tracing each strand with her eyes, marvelling at the sheer size of it. When the sun came out from behind the clouds, the strands still wet with morning dew had shone brilliantly in the light; shimmering with a reflected radiance.

Arleth remembered this now as she looked around her. She was quite literally inside what looked like a massive spider web. Brilliant blue fibers were extended in all directions from Selene's wrists, reaching up to the sky and around to surround the four of them in a massive net-like web that floated with them as they walked. Although it was way past nightfall, the fibers were shimmering as though they were bathed in full sunlight. With her free hand, Arleth cautiously reached out to touch one of the strands that hovered just in front of her face. When the point of her finger touched it, the fiber bounced slightly from the impact and then dissipated, only to be reformed again as soon as she removed her hand.

So this was what it was like to be literally inside magic?

Mesmerized, Arleth followed the web down to her feet. She watched with delight as the strands around her legs continually evaporated and reformed as she walked through them.

Then all of a sudden, the strands all disappeared. Arleth looked up in surprise and found that she was inside a huge cavern. Selene gently let go of Arleth's hand. Arleth turned around to look behind her and was met with a solid rock wall.

"We are here," Selene said, shaking out her hands, "Welcome to our home."

Arleth had turned back around at the sound of Selene's voice and now walked up a few paces to stand beside Zeeshan. The two of them stood together in silence, taking in their first glimpse of the mountain stronghold.

They were standing at the entrance of a huge natural cavern. It had to have been at least 15 metres high and as far back as Arleth could see; there was no end in sight. Although it should have been pitch dark, Arleth realized that the walls were glowing faintly which bathed the entire cave in a dusk-like light. Rows and rows of neatly ordered tents took up the majority of the space on the ground. Towering trees and gardens (grown through magic Arleth assumed) interspersed these tents, giving the impression of a small permanent city instead of a war-time hideout.

Since it was late at night, only a handful of people were outside of their tents. Some were sitting and talking in small groups; one rather rambunctious group was playing some sort of game with coloured stones; and there were a few couples walking hand in hand through the gardens.

But none as yet, had noticed the entrance of the four newcomers. That is, aside from the two guards that had been talking with Selene and Aedan since they had first arrived. As Arleth watched this exchange, Aedan tilted his head in her direction and smiled. Both guards eyes' opened in surprise and simultaneously turned to look at her. Their faces lit up into huge smiles and they turned back around to face Aedan and Selene. One of them said something to Aedan and clasped his left shoulder; Aedan smiled and returned the gesture.

This discourse might have continued, but Selene, who had been looking over the shoulder of the shorter guard, let out a loud laugh which she immediately tried to stifle with a hand over her mouth. Aedan looked over at her in surprise and then, following her gaze also broke into laughter, although he didn't try to hide it.

"Your hap-hazard birdbrained plan actually worked! It actually friggen worked!" Val Odane yelled as he all but flew over to them. The guard Aedan had been talking with had a split second to move out of the way before Val cannonballed into his friend. Aedan laughed and put his arm around him. Selene, who had a front row seat to this action, was almost doubled over in laughter.

"Oh no you don't," Val said, reaching out to her with his free arm and pulled her into what was now a group hug.

"So I guess you were worried about us, eh Val?" Aedan said with a smile, pulling away after a few moments.

"Worried?!?" Val spluttered, "How could I *not* be. How could *you* not have been....?"

Selene looked over at Aedan and he gave her a knowing wink. They both knew what was coming.

"...Going in there without a solid plan. 'I'll just walk right up to Iridian castle,' Aedan says. 'Let the grekens take me, Absalom will be expecting me, don't worry Val it will be fine.' *But what if it wasn't fine?* And then putting Selene into an Alondrane and just *hoping, HOPING,* that Absalom wouldn't find the real one. And *then* assuming this plan all worked magically, banking on the fact that he would put you in the only type of dungeon cell that you would even be able to use the Alondrane in. And don't even get me started on the likelihood of actually finding Arleth without being recaptured and managing to somehow get back out of the castle."

Val broke off, looking at his two friends expectantly. Selene and Aedan exchanged a glance, "Nope, we weren't worried," Aedan said shaking his head nonchalantly.

"Gah!" Val gave an exasperated sigh, "You guys...just...ahh!"

Selene smiled innocently at Val. He was a hard man, tough and fearless in battle. Rational to a fault. He would take on the craziest, most dangerous missions himself without a second thought, but when it came to her or Aedan he became as overprotective as a mother hen. It always made her and Aedan laugh – it was so at odds with the rest of his personality. Val didn't see it of course; he just found the pair of them exasperating.

"But anyways," Aedan said, getting back to business, "We were successful," he muttered under his breath "*As we knew we would be.*" Aedan gave his friend a winning smile.

Val just glared back.

"Which means we have Arleth," Aedan continued, looking over in the direction of his younger sister. "Umm.... Arleth?"

At the first sight of Val, Arleth had almost involuntarily retreated backwards a few steps. Now she was practically hiding behind Zeeshan. At the sound of Aedan calling her name, she poked her head out from behind Zeeshan's back. Cautiously, she took a step to her right so half of her body was visible along with her head.

Aedan looked at her puzzled for a few moments and then realization dawned in his eyes. He let out a loud laugh, and turned to Val, "What have you done to my little sister?"

"What do you mean, what have I done?" Val protested. He looked over at Arleth who was still half hidden and was staring at him with bright, fearful eyes. "Oh," he said flatly, "That."

Aedan laughed even harder.

"I saw her. A greken attacked me. I killed it. She ran. I followed after her," Val said matter of factly.

"Uh huh..." Aedan said when he paused to draw breath. "Are you sure that is all that happened?"

Selene shook her head at the two of them and came over to stand in front of Arleth.

"Arleth, you have no need to be afraid of Val. I know the first time you saw him was on Tocarra. He was following you and you had no idea who this strange man was. And I'm sure Absalom gave you some kind of explanation that would have made perfect sense and portrayed himself as the hero."

Arleth thought about Absalom's explanation of the Black Thorn assassin group. It *had* seemed perfectly reasonable, although she now knew from Neve's brother that there was no such thing.

"But Val is one of our oldest and closest friends. We sent him to Tocarra in order to bring you back with him, before Absalom could get to you. Unfortunately he wasn't able to do this, and so you were left thinking that he was the villain, while Absalom portrayed himself as your saviour." Selene practically spat out those last few words, not because she blamed Arleth. Not in the least. It was perfectly reasonable that she would trust the 'King of Oherra' over a vagabond she had no idea about. Just on the reputation of his name alone, not to mention how manipulative and charismatic the traitor was when he wanted to be. No, she said those words so vehemently because she hated Absalom with a pure unadulterated fire.

Arleth however, was thinking at that moment that she was somewhat of an idiot. Neve's brother had told her there was no such thing as the Black Thorn, and she had believed him, but she hadn't questioned who it *was* that had chased her. To be fair, that had been an overwhelming day, with the splitting women in the courtyard, being questioned by Absalom and then of course all the information that Neve's brother told her. But she still thought that it should have prompted at least a flicker of a question in her mind.

In addition to that however, Arleth now felt quite foolish at being afraid of Val. "Well he did chase me across the desert and through town while holding up his dagger," she said, trying to explain herself into some dignity.

Aedan burst into laughter again, "You ran at her for miles with your dagger, and you don't know why she would be afraid of you?"

"I was running, I had my dagger, I couldn't very well *not* run with it." Val said defensively.

Aedan was about to make another jab at his friend, when a child's scream echoed through the cave. Aedan and Val turned instantly to face the source of the cry, instinctively crouched in a defensive position, weapons already drawn.

Unbeknownst to them, while they had been talking, a sizeable group of people had formed. They had come out of their tents, most of them likely drawn by Val's initial outburst upon finding his friends still alive. At the front of this group was a small boy of about four. His short blonde hair was dishevelled and his pale, freckled face was splotched with red. Tears poured down his face as he screamed and pointed a chubby arm in front of him. His mother was trying desperately to quiet him down, but she was having no luck. Other children, drawn by the sound started pushing their way through their parents' legs to see what was going on. One by one, they each caught a glimpse of Zeeshan and added their tears and screams to that of the first boy. In little over a minute, the situation had erupted into complete chaos. Parents were running over to their children, trying to calm them down, while they themselves looked with barely disguised fear at the unknown creature in front of them.

Selene opened her mouth to try and calm the situation, but she was not fast enough.

"WHAT IS WRONG WITH ALL OF YOU?" Roared Zeeshan, "I'M NOT A FREAK SHOW!" He advanced a few paces towards the crowd menacingly, raising one huge paw, claws outstretched.

The children instantly stopped crying, they were staring, open-mouthed, frozen in terror at the creature advancing on them. The adults however, reacted quickly. Both the men and women pushed themselves in front of the children and brandished weapons Arleth hadn't even seen them carrying. The two guards that had been talking to Aedan and Selene moments before; now rushed in front of them, weapons drawn in an effort to form a protective barrier around their leader.

Zeeshan however, only took a few paces before he stopped in shock and slumped down heavily on the ground. He burst into tears and buried his head in his paws. Selene rushed over to him, motioning for everyone to put away their weapons, which they did reluctantly and only after a few minutes had passed.

Selene crouched in front of Zeeshan and touched his paws, trying to get him to move them away from his face.

"Why.. What... Why has this happened to me?" Zeeshan said miserably, in between sobs. At Selene's touch, he had reluctantly moved his paws away from his face, but he was still looking down at his lap. He was utterly ashamed. "I'm a Talywag, I don't have outbursts, I don't roar, I don't, I don't..." he raised one paw in front of his face "I don't have paws, and claws and fur." He burst into uncontrollable crying. Selene rubbed his arm sympathetically, the pain she felt for him evident in her eyes. When his tears had quieted down a bit, Selene put her hand under his chin and raised his head up to face hers. She wiped his tears away with her hands and smiled gently at him.

She desperately wanted to tell the child in front of her that everything would be ok, that he wouldn't get this kind of reaction everywhere he went from now on in his life. But she knew she couldn't lie to him like that. He wouldn't believe her anyways. Instead she said "Zeeshan, remember how I said I could teach you how to control the snow bear anger in you? So that you would hardly even know it was there?"

Zeeshan nodded at her, the faint glimmer of hope appeared in his tear-filled eyes.

"Well," Selene said, "How about we start those lessons right now?"

Zeeshan looked at her nodded. "Yes please." He said quietly.

Selene smiled, "Alright then, come on."

Zeeshan slowly stood up and Selene took a hold of one of his huge paws in her hand and led him away. As they passed Val, he looked at Zeeshan and then at Selene with a "Tell me about *that* later" look. Selene nodded discretely back at him. She planned on taking him to the combat training grounds which were at the far end of the cavern, past all of the tents. This would give them the space and hopefully the privacy that they needed. Unfortunately, the crowd was so large that it spread across the entire width of the cavern, and so

Selene was forced to lead Zeeshan through them in order to get there. As they walked through, people gave them a wide berth and watched Zeeshan warily as they walked past. Selene rubbed his paw soothingly, but Zeeshan was too ashamed to do anything more than look at his feet resolutely as he walked.

Aedan watched the pair walk away. It was only when they had gone far enough that they were out of earshot, and the crowd was beginning to reform and relax again, that he attempted to explain what had just happened. They deserved to know what new army Rogan was creating; after all, many of them would end up finding themselves face to face with one on a battlefield or in a skirmish. And likely in the very near future.

"Please don't be frightened by what you just saw. That 'creature' is a seven year old child named Zeeshan. A few days ago he was a Talywag."

There was a collective murmur from the crowd as they took in this information.

"He was captured while he was playing in the Frasht Forest and taken back to Iridian. Rogan performed experiments on him in order to fuse his body with that of a snow bear. We believe that he is creating a new army of snow bear-Talywag combined creatures. Zeeshan was one of his first tries. He has been through a lot of pain and suffering over the last few days. But he is just a child."

"If Rogan has experimented on him, how do we know he is not going to turn on us?" A man near the front of the crowd asked. A number of others voiced their agreement.

"Ya, how do we know he won't attack us?"

"He looked dangerous to me."

"Me too!"

"We know what Rogan's magic does to people. It takes their souls, there is nothing left of them. We have fought armies of our former friends and neighbours who no longer remembered us. How can we trust this creature?"

Aedan answered this last question.

"These are very reasonable concerns. We have all seen the horrible effects of Rogan's magic enough times to last us many lifetimes. However, this particular experiment done on Zeeshan was not successful. His physical body may look like a complete fusion between a snow bear and a Talywag, but something went wrong. He still has his personality and his mind. You saw his reaction to his outburst." Aedan looked around at the crowd trying to gage their acceptance. "He was ashamed. He is just a child and has gone through so much in the past couple of days. Imagine what it was like for him to not only have his entire life (and his body) thrown upside down almost overnight. But to then have that thrown in his face the moment he walked in here. That would be enough for anyone to get upset." Aedan met the eyes of the adults standing closest to him. He was relieved to see that many of them were nodding in agreement. "And he is only seven years old!"

Aedan thought it was best not to mention that Zeeshan was still very much at war with his snow bear anger. He trusted Selene to help him control it. At the moment, he didn't want another reason for Zeeshan to be even more alienated then he already was.

"Trust me," Aedan said. "If I or Selene had thought, even if there was a slight chance that Zeeshan was fully transformed, we would have killed him on the spot."

Arleth turned to stare at Aedan so fast that she got a bit dizzy. *Was he telling the truth? In that moment when he and Selene had been staring at Zeeshan in the dungeon, were they actually contemplating whether to let him live or kill him?"*

"I wouldn't bring an enemy into the midst of our camp."

This seemed to convince everyone. There was a general murmur of agreement and a succession of nodding heads.

Aedan took this as a success and continued on before anyone could change their mind.

"I am sure you have all heard by now that my sister, Arleth, wasn't killed in Absalom's attack 17 years ago, and is in fact very much alive."

The lack of surprise shown by the crowd in front of him convinced Aedan that this was old news. He hadn't made any type of public announcement when he had learned Arleth was still alive. But he had of course discussed it with his inner circle - Selene, Val, Bain, Winn and Graydon. They had spent hours discussing how best to bring her to them, both before and after Absalom had captured her. Aedan hadn't discussed any of these plans with his army officers, but he had given them the general sense of what was going on. He knew from here, it would get passed on to the rest of the army, their families and in enough time, to the entire stronghold.

And it seemed he had been right.

"Well," Aedan continued without further preamble, "Here she is, Arleth Amara." He turned towards his sister, gesturing in her direction.

The crowd turned as one unit, seeing Arleth now for the first time. There was a second of silence as the throng took in the teenager in front of them and then it erupted into a buzz of excitement.

Above the general hum of noise, Arleth could make out bits and pieces of conversation.

"Oh my, she is as beautiful as her mother was," said one elderly lady holding a sleeping baby in her arms.

"Yes she is," her companion agreed, "But look she has the Amaran eyes like her brother."

"Oh very right she does," the first agreed.

Aedan walked over to Arleth, an apologetic smile on his face, "I'm sorry Arleth, but these are your people now too. Let's go talk to them shall we? I'm afraid there isn't really a better way to ease you into it. And if you don't talk to them now, they won't leave you alone all night." He said this last bit with a wink, grabbing her hand before she had time to object and all but dragging her into the mass of people.

For the better part of an hour, Arleth was introduced to hundreds of men, women and children, learning so many names that she could never hope to remember even half of them. They complimented her, asked her questions, told her their stories and Arleth for her part smiled, blushed and offered thanks, complimented in turn, answered their questions as best she could and asked a few of her own. Aedan stood by her the whole time, jumping in when she needed it and helping to divert some of the more personal questions he didn't feel Arleth should have to answer but felt she probably would, not knowing any better.

Arleth felt completely out of her league – she hadn't spoken to so many people in her entire life. And now they were all being thrown at her in 60 short minutes. Not to mention that they were all treating her like Arleth *Amara*, a person she hadn't come to terms with being and certainly didn't even know *how* to be yet. And so at the end, she was completely exhausted.

Aedan, seeing his sister's fatigue, held up his hands to the multitude of people still waiting to speak with Arleth. "Sorry everyone, I know you are all anxious to meet Arleth, but that is enough for one night. She has had a very long and tiring day and I'm sure she would like to get some sleep. There will be plenty of time tomorrow to introduce yourselves and get to know her."

Arleth looked up at Aedan with a tired and grateful smile.

A few grumbles emerged from the crowd, but they, although slowly and reluctantly, listened to Aedan and started to move away. Ten minutes later the crowd had dispersed.

"Sorry to do that to you Arleth, I know that couldn't have been easy. But you did remarkably well for your first time."

Arleth was about to comment on how she didn't feel that she had done anything even close to being remarkable, but she was interrupted by a man's voice.

"Aedan! You are back!" A tall man in his late twenties was making his way towards them, against the retreating crowd. Just behind him was a younger man who Arleth thought looked to be about her own age. On first glance, it was easy to tell that they were brothers. Both were tall and thin with short dark brown hair, dark features and tanned skin. The older man had a short beard and a mustache, while the younger one was clean-shaven. Other than that, they were the spitting image of each other.

"Winn. Graydon," Aedan said with a huge smile as he clasped each man's arm in turn as they approached him.

"You don't know how glad I am to see you alive." Winn said.

Graydon nodded, "We were all worried about your plan; more than we had cared to admit."

"Haven't I heard that before," Aedan said with a grin rolling his eyes at the two brothers.

"Val." Winn and Graydon said at the same time.

Aedan nodded.

The two brothers shared a knowing glance, "Well I'm sure Val has covered it then."

Aedan held his hands together in front of him as if he was praying, looking at the two brothers pleadingly; a smile tugging at the corners of his mouth.

"Definitely," Graydon agreed. He too was trying not to laugh.

Aedan let out an exaggerated sigh of relief and dropped his hands back to his sides.

"So, Aedan." Winn said, instantly getting serious. "We saw Selene on the training grounds a little while ago, that's how we knew you were back. She told us what had....happened." Winn raised his eyebrows at Aedan in an expression meant to indicate Zeeshan.

Aedan picked up on it. "Ya, it wasn't the best news we had heard either. We will need to take action quickly, let Bain and Val know that we will meet first thing tomorrow morning after breakfast. We have a lot to discuss."

"Sure thing boss," Winn said with a wink, his good spirits returning. "So.... you aren't going to introduce us?" Winn turned to look at Arleth who had been silently observing this exchange up until now.

"I had rather hoped to avoid it..." Aedan said jokingly. "But if I must." Turning to Arleth, "Please let me introduce Winn and Graydon Firwood. They are the lords of Jaya and two of my oldest friends. Winn", Aedan gestured to the older man, "I have been friends with since we were both young children, and Graydon," He indicated the younger man, "I have known since he was born."

"He also forgot that we are ridiculously handsome, and insanely clever," Winn said stepping forward and enveloping Arleth in a bear hug.

Arleth burst into laughter but it was drowned out by Winn's chest in her face.

Winn smiled and pulled away from Arleth. "See she agrees. I like her already, she has good sense."

Aedan just rolled his eyes good humouredly.

Graydon, younger and not as suave as his brother, also gave Arleth a hug. But his was more awkward and as he pulled away from her he had to turn his head to hide his blush.

"So Arleth," Winn said, "How overwhelmed are you right now?"

Arleth smiled at him, "Unmeasurably! A day ago I thought I was just another ordinary servant, and now..."

Winn nodded sympathetically, "I'm sure you are. It's not every day someone is told that they are an Amara and inherit an entire stronghold of followers."

Arleth shook her head in agreement, "No it most certainly isn't."

Winn opened his mouth to respond when Graydon blurted out, "So are you on our side or what? Did you believe the lies that Absalom told you?"

Winn turned to his brother, his jaw dropping open, "Graydon!"

"What? We are all thinking it." He replied indignantly.

"Okay then," Aedan said cutting in smoothly. "Arleth has had a busy day, it is quite time she got some sleep." He grabbed Arleth hand and led her away from the two men.

"It was nice to meet you both," Arleth called behind her.

"Likewise Arleth," Winn said. Graydon remained silent.

Behind Arleth and Aedan's back, Winn shoved his brother' shoulder, "What was that about?!"

"We are all wondering it," Graydon repeated defensively.

"Of course we are. But there is a time and a place brother." And then more gently, with a smile on his face. "I know she is a beautiful girl, but sheesh man, control yourself."

"What! No!" Graydon responded too quickly, his face turning a bright shade of red.

Winn just smiled and kept silent.

Up ahead, Arleth turned to her brother as she walked beside him. "Why did Graydon say that?" She asked.

Arleth turned to his sister, "Graydon is young and can be hot-headed at times. He tends to say things he doesn't mean without thinking. I wouldn't give it any thought."

The thing was, Graydon *was* right. They all were thinking just how much influence Absalom had exerted on her already. She seemed to believe what Aedan had told her, but she had spent a number of days with Absalom, and who knows what he had told her or what he had Rogan do to her. He would need to find out soon, but it would have to be much more subtle than Graydon's approach and it certainly wasn't a conversation to have tonight.

So he changed the topic.

"So Arleth, I'm sure you are exhausted and would love to go to sleep, but would you like to have a bath first?"

"Oh my goodness yes," Arleth said enthusiastically. Relaxing in a bath right now sounded like a perfect idea.

Aedan laughed, "Well good because we are right outside the women's bathing tent."

"Bathing tent!?" Arleth exclaimed.

Aedan nodded, and pointed towards a huge tent directly in front of them. "Men and women each have their own area to bathe. The men's bath tent is over there," he pointed to a second huge tent right beside this one.

"How do you have a bathing tent in a cave?" Arleth asked incredulously.

"Ha!" Aedan said, "With magic." He winked at her. 'If you look up there," he said, pointing to a black coloured pipe that was coming out from the back of the tent. "The mountains we are in right now are called the Iridian mountains. They are the tallest mountains on Oherra and many of their peaks are snow covered all year round. Using magic, Selene burrowed a hole from here all the way through the mountain to the top and we put that pipe up through it. The pipe is enchanted so that at the top, it melts the snow. The water is then carried in the pipe all the way down through the mountain. At the bottom, right before it enters the pool there is a second enchantment that multiplies the water droplets by 10,000 and heats them up. The result is a huge pool of steaming water."

Arleth was amazed, "That is incredible."

"It certainly is. Selene has done quite a bit of work around here to make this much more than just a cave. Thanks to her, it is more like a small city than a hideout."

Arleth nodded in appreciation.

"Well Arleth, I am in desperate need of a bath. So I am going to go in, I'll meet you out here after and show you which tent is yours to sleep in." Without another word, he turned and disappeared into the tent he had indicated was the men's bathing tent.

Arleth followed suit, entering the women's bath tent. Inside, covering almost the entire surface area was an enormous pool that was dug right into the cave floor. At the far end, Arleth could see the water flowing into the pool from the black pipe that Aedan had described. Steam was rising from the water and where it mixed with the cooler air, a mist formed.

Arleth was completely alone, she imagined that during the day it would be busy, but right now she was glad for the lack of prying eyes. She untied her sash, slipped off her dress and stepped into the pool. She followed the stone steps into the centre of the pool and swam over to the edge. There was a ledge against the side and when Arleth sat down on it, the water came up to her shoulders. Arleth closed her eyes, letting the warm water soothe her tired muscles. She leaned her back against the stone edge of the pool and stretched out her feet in front of her. *This was perfect.*

* * *

In the tent beside her, Aedan was similarly exulting in the soothing waters. He too closed his eyes, letting the stress of the day wash away.

He heard soft footsteps behind him and turned to see the beautiful form of Selene coming towards him.

"Care for some company," She asked him, dropping her robe on the ground.

"Always," Aedan smiled at her, admiring her naked body.

She slipped into the warm water with barely a splash and swam towards him. Aedan put his arm around her and kissed her forehead. They got so few of these moments, he wanted to exult in it forever, but he had to ask, "Why did you lie to Arleth about why Aban killed his wife and daughter?"

"We are trying to get her to trust us, I didn't really want to tell her the truth. At least not yet. It's not really our-side friendly."

Aedan nodded he hadn't even thought about that. "That's a good point."

"I'm suprised you told her about her birthright already. The poor girl just had her whole world turned upside down in a few hours."

"Yes I know." Aedan said with a sigh. "She asked why Absalom would want her, I didn't really want to lie to her about that. Plus it's common knowledge, *I thought it was common knowledge anyways*, that the female Amaran's have magic. I thought she would have already known that."

Selene nodded, "That's fair." She twirled the water in lazy circles with her finger. "At least you didn't tell her that it would kill her."

"No. That we will leave for another day."

Selene and Aedan lay in the water in silence for a few moments thinking about the successes of the day. And everything that lay ahead of them.

Suddenly Selene broke away from Aedan's arm and turned to face him in the water. She looked at him coyly and smiled. "So I put up some charms at the bath entrance when I came in."

"What kind of charms," Aedan said returning the smile. He pulled her towards him again.

"You know the kind where we won't be disturbed for a while." She put her hand on his chest and slowly slid it down until it disappeared under the water.

* * *

As Selene and Aedan enjoyed their privacy, the Ranin bud detached itself from Aedan's leg and floated upwards unseen to the surface of the water. From there it floated unhurriedly to the nearest edge and rolled itself up and out of the pool. Once out of the pool, it rolled across the floor and exited the tent. Almost immediately, it started to divide, becoming two then four, then six... for the next 5 minutes the bud split, until thousands of tiny buds were lying on the ground outside the tent. As if on cue, as soon as the last division had occurred, a set of six legs sprouted out of each newly created bud. One of the buds emitted an inaudible hum and the entire army scampered away in all different directions, spreading out across the entire length of the cave. They attached themselves to whatever surface they were against – cave wall, ground, tree etc. – there they would wait and grow to their full size, completely invisible until their growth was done and they were ready to launch their attack.

Back in the pool, Aedan sighed in contentment, blissfully unaware of the destruction that had just been set in motion.

Chapter 22

Arleth couldn't sleep.

After her bath, Aedan had shown her to the tent where she would sleep. She had been surprised to learn that each family had their own tent and that this one was now hers alone. But her surprise was fleeting - as soon as Aedan had wished her goodnight and left, Arleth had fallen asleep.

She had woken up minutes later and hadn't been able to fall back asleep.

There was too much on her mind.

Arleth gave a sigh of resignation, pushed back her blankets, and sat up. She wasn't about to fall back asleep any time soon and she was growing restless just staring at the ceiling of the tent. Getting to her feet, she walked the few paces to the door of her tent and lifted the flap. The light coming from the cave walls had dimmed, so it was now only possible to make out shadows in the dark. In the distance, Arleth could hear the faint shuffling of feet as the guards did their rounds. Other than that, there was complete silence. It had to have been well past midnight and everyone was sound asleep in their tents.

Arleth left her tent, closing the flap silently behind her. She walked aimlessly down the rows of tents, letting her feet lead the way as her mind tried to comprehend how thoroughly her life had changed in the last week. A mere seven days ago, she had been a slave on Tocarra, a life she had known since she was 10 years old. Although she had wished for a better life, a future, even dreamed of adventure, deep down she had known that she would always be a slave. Her daydreams were just that, dreams - a way to escape the terrible life she had. But that had all changed in a heartbeat. First, she had met King Absalom, which had in itself seemed like a dream come true. But then in less time than she had to even pause to think, she had been chased by who she thought was an assassin, and had been all but rushed off to Oherra. Spending the rest of her life on Oherra as a servant to the king was surprising enough. She had never expected to travel to another world, let alone to Oherra, to meet the king, or to actually spend the rest of her life in Iridian castle. She had been overwhelmed and overjoyed *then* by this sudden turn in her life.

But now?

Now she was much, *much* more than a servant. She had learned who her true family was, and it was none other than the most important family in the universe. She had gone to bed last night as a servant to the king. She had gone to bed tonight as Arleth Amara, sister to Aedan Amara, princess of Oherra. Not to mention all that she had learned about Absalom and Rogan, Rogan's experiments, the rebellion..... And she was supposed to have magic! One woman had even kissed her hand, calling her the "saviour" of the Oherran people.

Saviour

She was 17 years old and had known she was an Amara for all of half a day.

All of a sudden, Arleth felt extremely light-headed. She sat down heavily on a nearby bench and put her head in her hands. She stayed that way for a few minutes, letting the dizziness wash over her. *Calm down Arleth* she told herself, as she struggled to control her breathing. *Just calm down.*

Her mind thus occupied, she didn't hear the footsteps until their owner was practically on top of her.

"Can't sleep either?" Val asked gently, walking up to her.

Arleth flinched slightly in surprise, but quickly recovered and gave Val a small smile. She shook her head "Nope. I guess you couldn't either."

Val shook his head in response. "Mind if I sit here?" He waved his arm to indicate the spot beside her on the bench.

"Go ahead."

Val sat down, rested his elbows on his knees, and his head on his hands. He stared ahead of him in silence, pointedly not looking at Arleth. Although Arleth hadn't seen him until the last moment, he had seen her collapse onto the bench, the nauseous look on her face, and her efforts to control her breathing. He was far from a mind reader, but that combined with her insomnia, told him that she had a lot on her mind and it likely was reeling from all that she had been told today. He would give her the time she needed in silence.

Arleth for her part didn't know that Val's silence and averted attention was on purpose, but she was grateful for it. After a few more minutes, her breathing had returned to normal and her head no longer felt like it weighed 1,000 pounds.

Val cleared his throat, "I'm not very good at this sort of thing," he began, turning on the bench to face her. "But I wanted to apologize for scaring you on Tocarra."

Arleth stared at him for a moment and then burst out laughing. Maybe it was a measure of how stressed she was, of how much was on her mind, but she found Val's comment ridiculously funny. He had said it so seriously, and based on everything she had gone through just today, being upset that she had been chased wasn't even on her radar. She laughed even harder, unable to control herself. Tears started to roll down her face.

Arleth's laughter proved infectious and Val smiled despite himself.

"It's totally fine," Arleth said when her laughter had finally died down. "You didn't have much of a choice and I started running away first. You couldn't really have just yelled at me 'Hey Arleth you are an Amara, I'm taking you back to Oherra with me to be reunited with your brother.'"

"True, I just wanted to make sure there were no hard feelings."

Arleth laughed again, but much less this time, "Definitely not! Sadly being chased by a so-called assassin, doesn't rate so high on my list of surprising things to have happened in the last week of my life."

Val nodded in sympathy, "Yes I suppose you are right."

"So Val, how did you get your scar?" the-ever-curious-and-after her-laughing-fit-much-calmer, Arleth asked.

Val paused a moment before he answered. "It was 10 years ago now. Just after Absalom's Northern annihilation," he paused to look at Arleth. She nodded in understanding; she remembered what Aedan and Selene had told her earlier today in the dungeons.

Val continued, "After that is when we believe Rogan started doing his enchantments – turning his enemies (our friends) into his mindless slaves. He might have started before this, but it was just after that time that we started coming across them in the field of battle."

Arleth nodded, "Yes Selene told me a bit about that, she said it was horrific. Fighting against people you once knew."

"Horrific doesn't even begin to cover it. Each of us still come across familiar faces in Absalom's army almost every week, and it still hurts us to have to fight them. But after so many years we have become hardened to it. But then.... we were about your age, and we had no experience with this. None of us wanted to fight against people we knew. We didn't want to believe that there was no longer anything left in them of who they once were. We couldn't accept that there was nothing we could do to turn them back into our allies." Val drifted off, lost in his own painful memories.

Arleth remained silent trying to imagine how terrible it would have been for them. She wouldn't have minded if she had to fight Bella or Kiran, in fact she might have even enjoyed it. But if she had to fight anyone she had known in the orphanage... any of her friends, Flora.. Neve? Arleth couldn't imagine what sort of courage was needed, what sort of hardened resolve to know you had to kill someone that had once been your friend. She didn't think she could have killed Flora, even if Flora had been enchanted and was trying to kill her.

"And that is how I got my scar," Val continued, returning to the present and interrupting Arleth's thoughts. "One day soon after the annihilation, we came across one of Absalom's soldiers by himself in the Frasht Forest. He was not very much older than us, still basically a child like we were. And I recognized him. His name was Stanley and he was from Kresh – one of the northern cities that Absalom had destroyed. His father had been a high ranking officer in their army and before Absalom's usurpation; he had been part of an official envoy sent to Iridian Castle. Stanley had come with his father and it had been Aedan and my job to entertain him while the adults talked. We had all been carefree children then, and we played and laughed together for hours. And then here I was years later, seeing that same boy again. Our whole world had changed, but I didn't want to believe it. In my mind I still saw Stanley as the smiling boy we had played with all those years before. I dropped my weapons and walked over to him. Foolishly, I thought that I could make him remember me and that he wouldn't hurt me. I didn't want to believe that *he* was 'gone.' As soon as I stepped within swinging distance of him, he unsheathed his knife and with one fluid motion," Val swiped downward across his face along his scar, "Did this to me. If Aedan hadn't been there to aim an arrow at Stanley's heart, he likely would have killed me on the spot. As it was, I almost died from blood loss before Aedan was able to take me to Selene to be healed. It is a constant reminder to all three of us that we can't let our emotions get in the way of killing our enemies."

"I can't imagine what that must have been like," Arleth said gently. "I don't know if I could have killed people I once knew." In her mind's eye, she visualized the story Val had told her. Except instead of Stanley holding the knife, it was Flora, and it was Arleth's face the blade was rapidly approaching. Arleth shuddered.

"Unfortunately you get used to it," Val replied.

Arleth was more than doubtful.

"It's not something I'm proud of, don't get me wrong. But it's amazing what you can learn to tolerate and even accept when you have no other option. Look at you for example. You were a slave back on Tocarra were you not?"

Arleth nodded hesitantly, not sure where he was going with this.

"Well I'm sure you didn't like being a slave, but you had no other option so you learned to tolerate the conditions and accept your life. Am I wrong?"

"No, you are right."

"Exactly, so this is the same kind of thing. We don't like what we have been forced to do, but we have no other choice so we have learned to accept it."

Arleth nodded, his explanation actually made a lot of sense to her.

But Val wasn't done, it was now his turn to be curious, "So Arleth, how exactly did you become a slave on Toccara. When we learned that you were alive, we figured that someone we had thought had died in the attack had escaped and taken you with them. But I can't imagine they would have just given you over to slave traders."

"Oh no, no", Arleth replied. "Neve rescued me from the castle the night of the attack and she brought me to an orphanage." Arleth continued on, telling Val the same story she had told to Selene, Aedan and Zeeshan earlier that day. He interrupted her a few times to ask questions, and just like Aedan and Selene, Val too, was surprised to learn that Absalom had tried to kill her when she was 10.

"And then I was chased by a scary man with a dagger halfway across the desert." She looked over at Val expectantly.

"Wait! What?" Val said "I thought that...." he trailed off as he saw Arleth trying to hold back a laugh.

"Hmph, you really are an Amara," he said with as much annoyance as he could muster. "Your brother would be so proud."

Arleth smiled. But with the mention that she was an Amara, the events of the past 24 hours came flooding back to her. All of her fears and doubts resurfaced.

"I can't believe I let Absalom fool me so easily," she said quietly, more to herself than to Val.

"What do you mean?" Just how much influence Absalom had on her was something that all of them were trying to figure out. Val wasn't going to let this opportunity pass.

"Well, I believed his explanation of you as being an assassin from the Black Thorn trying to kill him. I accepted that even though I was pretty sure you had called me by name in the alley in Sonohan. But not only that. Not for one minute, even with all the strange things I saw at the castle, did I think that he was anything other than the rightful heir. I never once suspected that he had evil intentions towards me or that his kindness to me was all an act. If it wasn't for Neve's brother who gave me that key to the dungeon and made me see for myself, made me see the experiments, Zeeshan, his dread mage, I don't know..." She trailed off. "How could I have been so blind, so stupid?"

"I wouldn't be so hard on yourself Arleth," Val said. "The title of the King of Oherra holds a lot of prestige. Shit, the history of our universe is based on the fact that the person holding the Crystal Throne is supposed to protect all the worlds from evil. You met him for the first time, with this impression in mind. You had no reason to expect that he was anything different than what he was pretending to be to you."

"I guess you are right," Arleth said. "But still, I noticed things were odd – none of the servants ever laughed, smiled or even talked to each other; I saw a girl in the courtyard whose back was completely coming apart at her spine. And I had conversations with him one on one. I was even inside his private quarters. How could I not have picked up on his true personality?"

"Absalom is a great actor. You aren't the only person he has fooled. Your own mother and father for example; they never suspected he would be capable of attacking the castle. Even after he had usurped the throne, and despite the excellent relations your father had with the other worlds, Absalom still managed to convince the leaders of our three neighbouring worlds – Senan, Rizod and Lothe - that he was justified in seizing control. Absalom's charm is one of his greatest advantages. If anything, it is remarkable that you didn't fall further under his spell. It must have pissed him off to no end." Val chuckled to himself at this last part.

"I don't feel remarkable. I am only 17, I've been a slave for almost half my life. I've never had to lead anyone, make any tough decisions, heck, I've only lived on this planet for a week. And I'm now expected to help lead a rebellion. I couldn't even see through a man I had many conversations with, when the evidence was all but slapping me in the face. What kind of a leader am I going to be? I think I'm going to let you all down." Arleth was surprised that she had voiced all her concerns to Val, a man she barely knew. Perhaps it was the darkness, the late hour, or simply that she wanted a confidante, but she was glad she had gotten it all out.

Val sighed, "It is a lot of responsibility for someone so young. I can understand how you must be feeling. Aedan, Selene and I were younger than you when we had the fate of Oherra thrust on us. When Absalom attacked, I was 12, Aedan and Selene were 10. My father Bain took us into the mountains and started training us from day one on how to lead a rebellion and take back Iridian. One day we were carefree children, the next we were the sole survivors, Selene and Aedan had lost their parents and we were expected to lead an army. Aedan became the King of Oherra overnight and Selene was suddenly the only living sorceress. At 10, she was the only person that had even the slightest chance of standing up to a dread mage."

"And my magic," Arleth said. "In 17 years I have never felt a magical bone in my body. What if I don't have it, what if you are all wrong?"

Val smiled at Arleth, "That is almost exactly what Selene said all those years ago when she realized the burden placed on her."

"Selene didn't know she had magic either?"

"No, she knew she did. Her mother was your father's sorceress, she is an Ayan – magical ability runs in her blood. But at 10, she had never once tried to use her ability; she had no idea even where to begin."

"But then how did she learn?"

"There is a woman named Samara Sunai. She lives by herself on Edika, and there she holds all the magical books and secrets of this world. Samara is ageless; she has been alive since before the Great War two thousand years ago. She is and always will be neutral to our affairs, but since the Great War, each female Amaran has gone to her to be trained on how to use her magic. Usually, normal sorceresses are trained by their mothers or other relatives, but in Selene's case there was no one else. She spent 2 years in Edika with Samara being trained on her gift. When she came back, she was a full blown sorceress, more than proficient in her ability."

"So I will go to Samara too?"

"I imagine so. I don't know anything about magic, and all I know about Samara I just told you. You will have to ask Selene. But don't worry, you definitely have magic, and you are not expected to be able to know how to use it until you have been taught."

Arleth made a mental note to ask Selene tomorrow about Samara and her training there. But for the time being she was more at ease. If even Selene didn't think she had magic, and now she was a match for a dread mage, there was hope for Arleth yet.

"And Arleth," Val added. "I am not going to lie and say that this is going to be easy. All three of us had to grow up fast and it certainly wasn't easy. But I believe that you are a lot stronger than you give yourself credit for. You lost everyone you knew when you were 10, just like us. But we at least had each other and my father to help us out. You were by yourself and then you spent the next seven years of your life as a slave in brutal conditions. I don't think there is very much that you won't be able to handle."

Val smiled at Arleth and stood up. "I'm going to go off to bed now, we have a busy day ahead of us."

Arleth stood up too and put her arms around Val. Awkwardly he returned her hug. "Thanks Val," She said into his chest. "I feel a lot better now."

And she did. As she walked back to her tent she thought about what Val had told her. He was right; she might be new to Oherra, still struggling to come to terms with the fact that she was an Amara and the responsibilities that entailed. But she *had* been through a lot already in her life and she had come through it all. She supposed she was pretty strong, it wasn't going to be easy, but she could do this.

When she got back to her tent she fell asleep as soon as her head hit her pillow. And this time she stayed asleep until morning.

* * *

He ran, his breaths coming in ragged gasps. His lungs ached, the icy air felt like a dagger plunging into his throat. But he kept on running; he could feel the snow bear directly behind him. He could almost feel the creature breathing down his neck.

Where was his father?

He had gotten him into this mess, he was the reason he was exiled to the Ice Plains. Where was he?

14 year old Absalom kept running, looking desperately for something to hide behind, maybe something he could use as a weapon. Nothing but miles of flat, open ice met his frantic searching.

He wasn't going to make it.

He was going to die out here, all alone, mauled to death by a snow bear.

Terrified, he turned his head to look behind him. The snow bear, red eyes intent on its prey was steadily advancing.

In a blind panic, Absalom turned back around, and when he did, his feet lost their traction on the ice. He fell heavily onto his bottom, skidding across the ice a few metres before coming to a stop.

He only had a moment to look up before the snow bear was on top of him. He screamed even as a huge taloned paw swiped viciously towards his face.

Absalom sat up in bed, he was breathing heavily and his shirt was drenched from sweat. That nightmare had haunted him most nights as a teenager, but he hadn't had it in a long time. His failures of the past few days must have brought it on.

Completely awake now, he got out of bed and walked over to the window. He looked out across the plains. Through the darkness, he could just make out the rows of tents and campfire pits. He commanded a formidable army. Absalom smiled, an army that to a man would die for him. He caught movement between the tents, and watched as one of the guards walked down the row and then upon reaching the end, turned to scan the mountain range.

The mountains.

Absalom's smile fell away in a heartbeat. Somewhere in those damn mountains, Aedan was sleeping soundly. He hated Aedan, he hated the Amaras, and he hated what they had done to him and his family.

Unbidden, his mind returned to that dark corridor in Iridan Castle where he had first heard his mother's screams.

He hadn't been allowed into the room when his mother was giving birth, but he was curious and excited for a baby sister so he had waited outside. At first he had heard her screams of labour. Painful, bloodcurdling cries that had seemed to go on forever. Absalom remembered how hard it was for him to hear, but he wanted to be there the moment his sister was born. He paced up and down the corridor, with his hands over his ears. And then, when he could bear it no longer, her screams had stopped. There was silence for a moment and then a baby cried. Absalom smiled, his sister was born. His pacing had taken him to the far end of the hall. Smiling, he hurried back so he could see her. He had taken only a few steps when he heard his father yelling and his mother's weak responses. He hesitated; he didn't want to walk in on them having an argument. He already wasn't supposed to be here, but he figured their joy at the baby would mean he wouldn't get punished. But if they were arguing? He didn't want to get in trouble. But his mother's screams made up his mind.

"Aban! Don't." Her screams suddenly turned into hysterical crying.

Absalom hurried to the door and pushed it open. He was just in time to see his father slam the sword into his mother's chest. His mother's tear-streaked face turned to look at her son in the doorway in that last instant, her mouth opened in an "O" of shock.

Absalom had screamed then and had rushed into the room. His father turned to him, trying to shield him from his mother's body, but it was too late. He rushed over to his mother and buried his head in her chest. With her last bit of strength, she put a weak hand on her son's head, "I love you Absalom," she said, "Don't ever forget it."

"I love you too mom," he sobbed into her chest. "Please don't die."

But she was already dead, her mouth frozen in a smile meant for her son. It was then, when Absalom looked up into the dead face of his mother, that he noticed the bloody body of his baby sister lying beside her.

His sorrow turned to rage in a flash. He rounded on his father, "What have you done?"

His father, not knowing how to respond to his son and in his own rage, didn't answer. Instead he took one last look at his dead wife and baby daughter and ran out of the room.

"Answer me you coward," Absalom screamed after him. But there was nothing but silence in response. He turned back to his mother and gently closed her eyes. "I will avenge you," he whispered into his mother's ear. He stood up and turned to the midwife who was cowering, wide eyed and white-faced in the corner.

"Take care of them," he all but growled at her as he raced out of the room after his father. When he had caught up to him, his father was being restrained by the king's guards. He was yelling, cursing and spitting at the king who was standing in front of him. To Absalom, he looked like a rabid dog. In that instant he lost what little feeling was left for his father. He was utterly embarrassed that this man was related to him, he hated him more than he could even begin to explain. He would never again look on his father with respect; he just wanted to see him dead.

But that hadn't happened. No, the virtuous king had decided it was best to exile them both. They were both outlaws; any city that allowed them to stay would be considered traitors. Absalom had hated the king for his decision, but the man he blamed for his fate was his father. He hated him more than anyone else on the planet.

For the ten years they lived on the Ice Plains, not a day went by that he didn't wish his father was dead. When he went to bed night after night starving, frozen to the bone, he blamed his father. When his skin turned red and raw from the wind, he blamed his father. When he fell through the ice and became so sick they had to beg help off of the Dursk warriors, he blamed his father. But the Ice Plains were a harsh environment, no matter how much Absalom wanted to kill his father, he was smart enough to know that the only way he would survive was if his father did too.

So he bided his time, keeping himself warm with thoughts of his revenge, until finally the day came when he didn't need his father anymore. It had been 10 years since they had first entered the Ice Plains. Unbeknownst to his father, he had established a sort of uneasy alliance with the Dursk who had healed him when he was a child. Absalom had grown from a boy, into a hard man, strengthened by the harsh climate and the constant danger. The Dursk, a warrior clan, respected this in him. The chief also had hopes that Absalom would marry his daughter, a fact that Absalom was not shy to play up to his advantage.

With the Dursk his allies, he no longer had any reason to keep his father alive. He remembered the pure joy he had felt when he had plunged the dagger through his father's heart. With his dying breaths, though, Aban had told his son the true reason he had killed his wife and baby.

That was the moment that Absalom should have been liberated. His revenge fulfilled. But he was far from satisfied. His father's revelation had taken the joy out of his death. His father was a coward and he deserved death and Absalom was happy to deliver it to him.

But his revenge was not over. With his father dead, all of his anger towards him transferred to the king.

It was at that moment, hovering over the body of his father, bloody knife in his hand, that he knew he would do whatever it took to become king of Oherra. He would kill the king and avenge the death of his mother and sister. And he would ruin the Amaran name so thoroughly that no one would ever respect their line again.

Absalom slammed his hand against the window. He hated how he had been forced to beg to the king. How he had made himself seem weak. It didn't matter that it was all an act, a carefully contrived plan to enact his revenge, it still galled him that he had been forced to subjugate himself before that man.

Absalom heard footsteps behind him and turned quickly around. Rogan was just entering his bed chamber and was making his way towards him.

Did the man never knock?

"Ah you are awake, good." The dread mage rasped at him.

And if I wasn't, what were you going to do? Wake me up? Absalom thought angrily.

"I have started the torture of the kitchen servants. It has proven to be quite pleasing..."

Absalom barely listened as Rogan explained in detail the torture of each servant.

Why Rogan had the need to come to his bed chambers in the middle of the night, to give him these details was beyond him. The dread mage loved death and torture, but really couldn't it have waited until the morning?

"....And the Ranin Bud...." Rogan droned on.

"Wait! What about the Ranin Bud?" Absalom interrupted, this was actually something he was interested in.

"As I was saying," Rogan said, "The Ranin bud was activated a couple of hours ago, I sensed it. It seems to have gone off perfectly according to plan."

"Well that is good news," Absalom smiled.

He turned away from Rogan as his sorcerer continued on describing his torture methods. He gazed back out the window.

A lot had changed since he was that 14 year old running from the snow bear. He was no longer that scared boy. He was no longer the young man that had been forced to beg before the king. Absalom looked out at the mountains, a smile growing on his face.

Sleep soundly Aedan dear; your death is fast approaching.

Chapter 23

"I don't think we have to worry about Absalom having any influence over Arleth," Val said.

"Why not?" Graydon interjected.

The two of them were sitting in a circle with Aedan, Selene, Winn and Bain. They were in Aedan and Selene's tent, catching each other up on what each had missed over the last few days. Breakfast was laid out on the floor in the middle, but they had hardly touched it.

"I spoke with her last night. She voiced her concerns to me that she had let Absalom fool her so easily. She was quite mad at herself and her lack of judgement. It was quite obvious to me that although she trusted him before, she is not questioning what we have told her in the slightest. She recognizes Absalom for the usurping bastard that he is."

"That's good," Aedan replied. That was one less thing he needed to worry about.

"How do you know she was telling the truth?" Graydon asked.

Val shot Graydon a look of incredulity. "Why would she lie?"

"How am I supposed to know? But how can you be so sure she isn't?"

"Because I know what I heard and saw," Val said, a hard edge coming into his voice. "Are you suggesting that I don't know what I'm talking about?"

"Graydon you are right to be concerned," Aedan cut in smoothly, trying to avoid an argument.

Val looked at Aedan in shock.

"However," Aedan continued, holding Val's gaze. "Don't forget that both Selene and I spent an entire afternoon with her." He turned to look at Graydon. "I had come to much the same conclusion as Val from those few hours. Since she is my sister though, I thought my judgement might be at risk. So it is comforting to have a second opinion." He looked back at Val and smiled, "And your judgment has always proven accurate in the past. Even still though, just because Arleth herself believes us and believes herself to be in control of her emotions and thoughts, it doesn't mean that Rogan didn't do something to her without her even knowing. She was in Iridian castle for a few days, there is no telling what could have been done to her without her knowledge."

There were nods of agreement from around the circle.

"And that is why Aedan and I have decided that I will cast some spells on her to figure that out," Selene cut in. She and Aedan had discussed this late last night before they fell asleep. They had agreed that it would stay between them; Arleth likely wouldn't take kindly to the idea that Selene was prying around in her head with magic. But this was too important for them to risk her saying no if they asked her. So they had agreed that only the two of them would know. Now however, she had no choice but to tell them. Aedan had opened up the door, and the questions were inevitably going to follow anyways.

"This information is not to leave this circle," Selene cautioned. "We are not going to tell Arleth what we are doing. One, we don't want to worry her, and two, regardless if she agrees or not, I have to do this, so it is better if we don't ask at all." Her conscience didn't like this very much, but she knew that she had no choice. It was not only for their sakes, but also for Arleth's. If something *had* been done to her, there was likely still time to reverse it, at least she hoped so anyways.

"Don't worry, we understand," Winn said, looking around at the confirming nods from his friends.

"Yes," Bain agreed, "This secret is safe with us."

Selene smiled, "Good, I knew it would be."

"So what about that..." Val paused searching for the right word, and not finding it settled on "*creature* that you brought with you from Iridian?"

"His name is Zeeshan." Selene corrected

"Sure, Zeeshan. What is he? And what was that outburst all about?"

As one, Winn, Graydon and Bain turned expectantly to look at Aedan. Along with Arleth's appearance, the commotion caused by the 'weird creature' had been top news last night. None of them had actually witnessed it, but they had heard enough from those who had, to be more than curious.

"First of all, his name is *Zeeshan,* not 'it' or 'weird creature' and he is only a child, Aedan looked sternly around at his friends, "I expect him to be referred to as such. He was born a Talywag," his face softened "but what he is now, I'm not so sure. Zeeshan heard

Rogan call his friend an Imari after the *experiment* was completed. So perhaps that is what he calls them."

Aedan continued to tell them the whole story of how Arleth found him in the dungeon, the experiments done on him, what Zeeshan had told them about his friend Thom, and then finished with the outburst in the stronghold.

"So Rogan *is* doing experimental combinations again?" Winn asked.

"That is what it looks like," Selene replied.

"So Tobin was right."

Aedan nodded. He opened his mouth, hesitated, closed it again and then with a resigned sigh "Tobin is dead; he was murdered by Rogan shortly before I got to the castle."

Winn nodded, "We had assumed as much"

"Absalom knew I was chasing Arleth on Tocarra," Val said, "We knew it was only a matter of time before he realized there was still a spy in his midst."

Aedan nodded sadly. All of his spies knew that they would likely be caught and tortured to death; at least that had been the track record so far. But it didn't hurt him any less each time a new one was discovered. "I guess we will have to sort out the maps and cross off all the secret passageways that Tobin had been taught. And of course find someone to replace him," He said this last bit reluctantly.

"Winn and I actually took care of that when you were in Iridian yesterday," Val said. "I tore up the maps that we had given to Tobin and created a fresh set with all new passages."

"And when I asked around, a number of my men wanted to be Tobin's replacement." Winn added. "I have narrowed it down to the three best candidates. Maybe today, you will have time to talk with them and choose one?" He looked at Aedan questioningly.

"Yes, later today."

"Good, I will let them know." Winn got up to go find his men, but his brother's question stopped him in his tracks.

"Rogan, isn't going to stop with just two Talywag creations. He is likely creating an army. And if he is, that means that the Talywags are no longer safe."

"You are quite right Graydon," Selene said. "It definitely seems like Rogan plans to create a new army." She turned to Aedan, letting him describe the plan that they had discussed together in private.

"The Talywags are definitely in danger." Aedan began. "By now Absalom will know that Zeeshan is missing. He will have to assume we know what was done to him and have guessed what he plans for the Talywags. That means he will have to hit Occa hard and fast. He will know he has to beat us there."

"So we don't let him get there first," Graydon interjected.

"Exactly! Winn, Graydon, I want you to take half of your soldiers and defend Occa. Build up their defences, fight for them when the attack comes, but mostly try and convince them to come back to the stronghold with you. Even if you defend against Absalom once, we know he's not going to give up, and you can't stay in Occa forever."

Winn and Graydon nodded, "We will leave for Occa tonight. That will give us time to gather our men, and get supplies."

"Right, and that way we will be travelling through Frasht Forest in the daylight." Graydon added.

"Val and I are going to be coming with you. We will help you convince the Talywags to come back with us. Oh and Zeeshan too of course, we will be taking him back home. He will likely be of help to us in convincing the Talywags of the danger they are in. But no matter what happens, Val and I are only going to stay a few days at the most. We will head east to Bronton to see if we can convince Lord Kalshek to join our side. His father recently passed away, which ironically is good news for us as Kalshek was always more favourable to our cause."

"And he commands a formidable army," Val commented.

"That he does."

"Excellent," Val said, slamming his fist into his palm. "I'm ready."

Aedan smiled at his friend's eagerness. "And Selene will be taking Arleth to Edika to learn from Samara."

"And I will probably stay with her throughout her training." Selene added.

Aedan nodded, "Bain, you will be in charge here when we are gone. Hopefully it won't be for very long and we will be bringing both the Talywags and Kalshek's men back with us."

"Damn right we will!" Graydon said, catching Val's enthusiasm.

Winn smiled and punched his brother good-naturedly in the shoulder. "The Talywags will come with us, all thanks to me of course."

He stood up just in time to miss his brother's retaliatory slap.

"Well," Winn said laughing, "I am going to go tell those three men that you will meet with them later. Graydon, I'll catch up with you later to organize the Jayans we will take with us to Occa."

He walked out of the tent to the laughter of the group. He assumed, correctly, that Graydon was making a face at him behind his back.

* * *

Arleth opened her eyes and groaned. Her head was pounding and even the dim light in her tent was causing her to squint in pain. She closed her eyes and instantly her head swam dizzingly and she felt nauseous. Quickly she re-opened them and turned over on her side, rolling herself into a ball and using her hands to shield her face from the light.

In this position she felt slightly less like dying......*slightly*. Arleth groaned again and massaged her temple.

Why did she feel like this? Last night she had felt perfectly fine, it didn't make any sense.

Something vague and blurry tugged at the corners of her mind, struggling to come to consciousness. She had been having a dream, she knew, but the outlines of it she couldn't quite remember. *It had been dark and damp, and with the confidence that comes in dreams, Arleth felt that she knew this place. And there had been screaming, so much screaming....*

"Uh oh," Arleth breathed as her stomach lurched sickeningly, returning her to the present. "Oh no no no." *Please don't..* The feeling in her stomach moved upwards, edging along her esophagus towards her throat. Frantically she searched around her small tent for something that would serve as a bucket.

It now threatened to escape the confines of her throat.

With no other option, Arleth made a mad dash for her tent flap, pushed it aside and promptly threw up all over the cave floor just outside her tent.

She had a few seconds to breathe, before round one was followed by a vicious round two.

And that was how Winn found her; crouched on the cave floor at the entrance to her tent on all fours, one arm holding back her hair, the other supporting her, with a marvellous puddle of puke in front of her.

"Not doing so well Arleth?" Winn asked gently, coming over to stand near her. He crouched down in front of her on the far side of the puddle at what he hoped was non-firing distance.

Arleth rocked back so she was crouching on her back legs and looked at him, her face turning red as she took in the puddle in front of her and Winn carefully avoiding it. She could only imagine what she must look like.

"No," Arleth responded quietly, not meeting his eyes.

Winn laughed good naturedly, "Don't worry Arleth, everyone gets sick at some point, it's nothing to be embarrassed about."

That was all well and good, Arleth thought, *but that didn't take away the fact that she felt like crap right now, the noxious odour that was emanating from her puke puddle, or to her horror, the fact that the puddle was spreading - and towards* him *of course.*

Smoothly, still in his crouch, Winn took a step sideways and backwards to avoid the growing puddle. He looked at her still very red and miserable looking face and tried again.

"You know Arleth, when I was about your age, and Graydon was still a child, we went with Aedan to Erto, one of the southern cities. We were trying to convince Erto's stubborn Lord Gorn to join our cause. It was all pointless of course but we had to go through the protocols so Gorn held a feast for us and our men. Aedan had been to the south before, but this was the first time for Graydon and myself and we didn't know what to expect so we ate everything that was put in front of us. We were used to eating leaves, berries and whatever animals we were able to kill; so the food in front of us seemed like it was out of a dream. We didn't listen to Aedan's, warnings not to eat too much, not to eat the yusa meat or the piron eggs because our stomachs wouldn't be able to handle it. No we ate everything and then some. Well, we made it almost through the feast before my brother and I started throwing up. And throwing up in spectacular fashion I might add; almost everyone at the table got a bit of the action. We threw up on Aedan, on each other, all over the food, on a few of Gorn's servants, and of course on Lord Gorn himself."

Despite herself, Arleth looked up at him and started laughing, the blush faded slightly from her cheeks.

Winn smiled at her, "Needless to say, we were promptly excused from the feast and were all kicked out of his castle."

"Did that really happen?" Arleth asked, still laughing a bit.

"It sure did," Winn said, "To this day, Graydon and I have never gone back to Erto, and every once in a while, when the two of us get very witty and Aedan has nothing to defend himself with, he will use some vomit-related nickname or joke."

Arleth laughed again and Winn laughed with her.

"So you feeling better?" Winn reached over the puddle to offer Arleth a hand, "Come, I'll take you to get some breakfast, some bread should settle your stomach."

Arleth nodded and took his hand, letting him lift her to her feet, "That sounds good."

A few minutes later, they were back at the tent where Winn had come from.

With flourish, he lifted back the tent flap and poked his head inside, "You miss me

"No," his brother answered immediately.

"You speak with your men already?" Aedan asked.

"Nope, never got there," Winn said, stepping back a bit to half coax, half push Arleth into the tent. "I found someone on the way."

"Oh hi Arleth!" Selene said with a smile, moving over a bit and gesturing towards the spot beside her, "Come sit here and get some food."

Arleth did as she was told, seating herself between Selene and Aedan. As soon as she was seated, Selene grabbed Arleth a plate and started filling it with a bit of everything that was laid out before them.

"Arleth isn't feeling very well this morning," Winn said, raising an eyebrow at Selene as she lifted a heaping spoonful of stewed apples onto Arleth's plate. She paused, spoon poised in mid-air. Winn put his hand to his stomach and made a sick face.

"Ahh," Selene said. She emptied the spoon back into the pot and looked critically at the plate she had made for Arleth.

Graydon, who had been watching this exchange, made a disgusted face, "Arleth, you threw up?"

Arleth's blushed and made a half-nod.

"Gross!"

"Ya, because you have never thrown up before?" Selene countered, handing a plate with a piece of white bread and an apple biscuit on it to Arleth.

"Pfffhhht," Graydon sputtered in reply.

"I seem to remember a certain young man projectile vomiting all over an entire dinner party. What was he called? Hmmm its coming back to me now, those pretty serving girls were yelling it at him as he ran out of the hall... Oh right! *Grossdon*."

Graydon's face turned bright red and his mouth opened and closed silently. Winn for his part, smiled and winked at Arleth. "Alright, I'm off, for good this time. Catch up with you later Graydon."

Graydon continued to glare at his brother as he left the tent.

Arleth smiled despite herself and tried unsuccessfully to hide it by taking a bite of the bread.

Graydon glared at her too.

"Children," Bain said shaking his head. "You three were just the same, you know. Always poking fun at each other."

"So not much has changed then? Aedan laughed.

"No I suppose not. Slapping you upside the head was sometimes the only way to get you to listen."

"We remember," Val said unhappily.

Selene laughed, "You two certainly were troublemakers."

"Hey now!" Aedan and Val both chimed in at the same time. "You weren't innocent either!"

"Arleth," Selene cut in, cleanly changing the topic, "I don't think you have met Bain yet."

Aedan and Val glared at her as she smiled sweetly back at them.

Arleth, her face full of biscuit, shook her head.

"Nice to meet you officially Arleth," Bain said extending his hand out towards her. Arleth shook it and smiled at him.

"Bain is Val's father," Selene explained. "And after both Aedan and my families were murdered in the attack, he became our father too."

"Yep. He raised all three of us, taught us how to fight, scavenge, and survive on our own." Aedan grew serious "All joking aside, this man is the reason we are even alive today to be able to reclaim the Amara birthright. He showed us what it took to be leaders."

"And these pip squeaks didn't make it easy let me tell you," Bain said good naturedly.

Arleth laughed. She had only met these people a day ago but she already felt as comfortable with them as she had in 10 years with her friends from the orphanage. And although the orphanage was the first home she could remember, she somehow felt more at home sitting in this tent in the middle of a cave with the five of them (even Graydon), than she had ever felt there.

Aedan's voice interrupted her thoughts, "So Arleth, you seem to be feeling a bit better."

"Hmm? Oh, ya! I'm pretty good right now. I don't feel like throwing up anymore."

"That's good. It was likely just your body adjusting to all the stress and change of the last week."

Arleth, her head down, concentrating on snagging a runaway apricot missed the look Aedan gave Selene. Selene nodded at him in understanding - she would dig more into the cause of Arleth's sickness later.

Arleth snatched up the apricot and looked back up at Aedan. "Maybe, ya."

"Ok well, since you are feeling better, would you like a tour of our stronghold? See what we have been up to for the past 10 years?"

"Sure!"

"Great, are you done eating?"

Arleth contemplated, grabbed another apricot and a slab of cheese, "Yup. I'll take these with me."

Aedan smiled, "Ok let's go."

Chapter 24

Once outside the tent, Arleth paused to look around. She hadn't been paying attention to much except her own embarrassment when Winn had brought her here and so she was surprised to see that they were standing at the very back of the cave. Last night when she had first seen the stronghold, she had been astounded by how large the cave actually was and how far back it stretched. But now, when she was literally a few feet away from the rock wall, she was blown away by how large the cave really was. She felt dwarfed by the sheer magnitude of it.

"It's pretty amazing isn't it?"

"It's... breathtaking! I can't even see the top, it just keeps going."

Aedan followed his sister's eyes up the wall, taking it all in again. Ten years ago when he had first made this cave his home, he had much the same reaction Arleth was having now. He smiled remembering how excited and scared he had been.

"The walls... are glowing?"

Aedan nodded. "Selene's work. But the whole wall isn't glowing exactly. You are probably too close to see it from here, but Selene has actually created a concentrated sphere of light which moves across the cave, mimicking the pattern of the sun outside. It is morning now so the sun is low on the wall on this side so to you it looks like the whole wall is lit up.

"So when the sun sets outside, the light disappears here and the cave goes black?"

"The light here sets too. Selene creates some magnificent sunsets sometimes if she's feeling particularly inspired. And since she controls it, she's not bound to the normal colours. On my birthday last year the sunset was a wonderful green, blue and yellow."

"That's incredible!"

"Living in a cave isn't really an ideal situation so we try our best to make it seem as normal as possible. Matching the daylight outside and having sunrises and sunsets is certainly a huge help.... But come," Aedan put his arm around Arleth's shoulders, "there are a lot more things for you to see."

As they walked, they passed rows upon rows of tents. Although, Arleth thought, *rows* was not the best way to describe them. Spread out all around her were clusters of tents; some had just 2 or 3, while others had as many as 10 or 15 together in a group. The tents themselves were as varied as their organization. Some were square, some triangular some domed, one that Arleth saw was even shaped like a tower and stood upright and towered over its neighbours. And the colours! It would be safe to say that all the colours Arleth had seen in her life were reflected in the tents surrounding her.

Alreth gasped in surprise and let out a giggle. Just coming into view was a large bright purple tent. It had two large eyes painted on the front, complete with long curling eyelashes. The door was outlined to look like lips and sprouting out from each side were strips of cloth that were meant to be wings.

"That tent looks like a giant purple bug!" Arleth laughed.

"That it does." The smile disappeared from Aedan's face. "Absalom's Northern Annihilation created many orphans. With their parents dead and their cities destroyed, they had nowhere to go so we took them all with us. Once here, they formed their own little families, grouping together with other children from their village. When we decided that everyone could design their homes however they wanted, that included these children. They had lost everything so we didn't care how bizarre their requests were; they told Selene what they wanted and she helped them create it. This isn't the only tent like this, there are a number of them scattered around."

"So, these tents are people's homes?" Arleth couldn't imagine spending her life in a home that looked like a giant bug. Even a younger, more childish version of herself wouldn't have wanted something like that.

"Yes, each family or, if they don't have a family, each person, has their own tent."

"I see. So then... where is everyone?" Aside from a few children chasing each other a little ahead of them, there was no one in sight.

"All men and women over the age of 12 spend the day in support of the war effort. Most train in the use of different weapons, battle techniques and strength and cardio training. Those that are too old, too weak, or don't have a predisposition for fighting help out in the kitchens or bath houses; with producing or mending clothes; or forging and fixing weapons in the armoury. We are very much a city at war. We try to make it as normal as possible for everyone, which is why we have a residential area, where we are now, which is separate from the army district As well, everyone is allowed to sleep together with their families at night. But first and foremost, our first priority is waging war."

Arleth looked up at a tree growing out of the cave floor that by all rights had no business being there. "And for what it's worth, I think you have done a really good job. I mean it's easy to forget we aren't actually outside."

"Selene is certainly a miracle worker. She has even created gardens complete with fountains, flowers, benches..."

"Wow! Really?"

"Hmm mmm." Aedan answered distractedly, a movement to his right had caught his attention.

Arleth turned to look at Aedan, "So how do the gardens grow ins...." he was already 5 feet away from her, rushing off in the direction of the noise he had heard. "...ide a cave." She finished.

She waited a couple of seconds to see if he would remember he had left her.

He didn't so much as break stride.

"Um ok, I'll just follow you then," she muttered to herself.

She caught up with him beside what looked to her to be a huge stone cylinder. He was deep in conversation with a group of 5 boys.

"How many water skins do you have?"

"Here we only have 500," answered the boys standing closest to him. He pointed at a towering stack standing precariously beside him.

"That won't be nearly enough. We need at least 4,000 filled and ready to distribute by tonight. We leave just after sunset." A shadow fell on Aedan's shoulder " Oh! Arleth, right." He looked slightly embarrassed. "Sorry I got distracted."

"It's alright," Arleth said to his already turning back.

"John," Aedan said pointing to the boy who had answered his question, "Go to the storage tents see how many you can find there. Then go talk with Beth Namion. Tell her to stop all clothing production and instead focus all her manpower on sewing water skins. We need 3,500 more by the end of the day."

"Ok I'm on it," The boy hurried off.

Aedan looked at a tall red-headed boy. "I need you to go find Selene and tell her what I have just told you. She will be extremely busy but ask her to visit Beth to see if she needs any magical help to speed things along."

"Done," he too rushed off.

"You three, I need you to continue to fill all of these water skins. When you have finished all of the ones here, go and get the new ones that are being made and fill those too. We need all 4,000 filled."

When Aedan had been giving directions, Arleth had been investigating the stone cylinder, which she now knew to be a huge basin filled with water. The water seemed to come from a long spout that poured into the top of the basin. It's source, Arleth didn't know but the spout stretched all the way up the side of the cave wall. It originated too high up for Arleth to see the top, but if she had to guess she would have said it extended all the way to the top and outside of the cave. Back at Bella's estate, water had been collected in a similar manner from rainwater. She imagined this worked in a similar way, but she would bet that the quantity of water it produced was helped significantly by magic. Extending outwards at 45 degree angles from the basin at regular intervals were long tubes. Each tube had a hatch at the end that could be lifted up or closed. This would be how the water was retrieved. Lifting the hatch would allow the water to flow out, closing it would stop the water. Arleth watched the first boy fill his water skin and was gratified to see that her theory had been correct.

"So, 4,000 water skins need to be filled by sundown... Are we going somewhere?" Arleth asked her brother.

"Yes we are going to Occa." He stood watching the boys fill the water skins for a few moments, before he turned to walk away, motioning for Arleth to follow him. When they were a good distance from the boys, he continued "What Absalom did to Zeeshan is horrible, not just to him, but because it means that Occa itself is no longer safe. He won't be appeased with creating just one creature, he will want to create an army." Aedan told her everything he had discussed in his tent a few hours earlier.

"So I won't be going to Occa with you then?"

"No you will be leaving at the same time as us. But you and Selene will be going to Edika. You need to begin your training with Samara."

Arleth didn't know how she felt about this. On the one hand she was excited to learn about her gift and to discover the kinds of things she could do. But at the same time she felt almost as if she was being left out.

Arleth voiced these thoughts to him.

"You are right Arleth, these are your people too and you have every right to want to help them. And by all means you should be and will be leading many battles both with me and by yourself. But right now the most important thing for you to do is to learn how to use your gift. If you can awaken your power, there is no telling what you will be capable of."

That made sense, Arleth thought. It wasn't like she was much help to anyone the way she was now. And altruism aside, Aedan's *there is no telling what you will be capable of*, was incredibly appealing.

"No, you are right. My most useful place is in Edika, training with Samara."

Aedan stopped walking and turned to give his sister a hug. "Thanks for understanding. I know this is a lot all at once. I've had almost two decades to get used to being a leader and realizing that means making choices for the better good; you've had only a day."

Arleth hugged him back "I am learning."

He squeezed her shoulder, "And you are doing great."

They continued walking. As they did, the distinction Aedan had mentioned between the residential and military sections became clear. The trees and colourful, disorganized tents were replaced with stark barracks, stone buildings and training grounds. Not only that, but the farther they walked into the military district, the more and more people they saw.

And the more and more people saw *them*.

It started with just a few coming over to ask Aedan a question -- what units to bring to Occa and how to organize them all for the journey, updates on how many weapons were in the armoury -- or for those that didn't see her last night, to speak with Arleth. But soon they were each surrounded by a swarm of people vying for their attention.

With practiced ease, Aedan fended off his circle with a few words of advice to each and soon the mass around him cleared. Arleth however, was struggling.

"Where were you this whole time, on Oherra somewhere?" A burly red haired man with a beard asked.

"No, Toc -

"Who was hiding you?" An older man burst in

"I was on Tocarra, no one was hid -"

"Someone must have saved you? Do you remember?" A third man interupted.

"What no I was a *baby*!"

"Oh but you are quite beautiful aren't you?" A woman with a long blonde pony tail cupped Arleth's cheek and turned her around to face her.

"So like her mother, don't you think?" The two women on either side of her nodded,

"Oh yes, very much."

"Same violet eyes."

"Errrr," Arleth blushed. She looked up to avoid the examination of the three women and over their heads she saw the top of what looked to be Winn's head. She stood on tip toe to get a better look. *Yes it was Winn. He was talking to Aedan. Aedan who had no crowd around him! How* did *he do that so fast?*

"What are you looking at dear? The blonde haired woman asked turning around behind her to look in the direction Arleth had been.

"What? Oh nothing, no." Arleth dropped back down to flat feet and with an inner sign of resignation re-faced her mob.

A strong hand latched itself onto Arleth's shoulder and started pulling her to her left. The crowd parted slightly and the hand materialized into Winn. Aedan was right behind him.

"Sorry everyone, Arleth has to come with us right now. We have a lot to do in a short amount of time. You will get the chance to get to know her better later."

The people around her gave a collective groan but slowly dispersed. When the last person left, Arleth turned to her two saviours "Thank you!"

They both laughed at her.

Arleth made a face. They laughed even harder.

"Oh don't look like that Arleth," Aedan said when he paused for breath. "Dealing with a crowd like that isn't easy."

"But you dealt with yours in five seconds!"

"Practice."

"Ya, but."

"That's all it is, just practice. I was just like you in the beginning."

"No, he was worse!" Winn chipped in.

"Ok," Aedan smirked at his friend, "I was worse."

Winn nodded contentedly, "Good. And besides Arleth, you are quite famous. You arriving is the most interesting thing that has happened here in a long time."

Aedan nodded in agreement. "But sorry Arleth, I will have to leave you - Winn and I have a lot to do before we leave."

Arleth looked around worriedly.

"Don't worry your admirer's have left," Winn grinned.

"Do you know how to get back to your tent?" Aedan asked.

"Yes I believe so."

"Ok great, see you later."

Arleth watched their backs for a while as they walked away. She had no intention of returning to her tent any time soon. There was way too much to explore here. The only thing she had to be careful of was to make sure she didn't get swarmed by another huge crowd of curious Oherrans. She was NOT interested in having that experience again.

Arleth started walking again, in the direction that her and Aedan had been going before they had been interrupted. She crept along hesitantly at first, her head a constant swivel looking for people that would jump out at her. But after a few minutes when no one approached her, Arleth relaxed and resumed a steady pace.

She had reached an area that appeared to be a practice grounds of some sort. To her right a line of men and women were shooting bows and arrows into targets. The archers had impeccable accuracy; in the shots she saw, not a single one missed the centre of the target. To her left, two men were locked in a sword fight while a group of their colleagues looked on. An older man with black hair greying at the temples was yelling out both instructions and insults to the two fighters. Arleth watched from where she was until one of the men pinned the other down and held his sword at the other's throat. A whistle blew, the fallen man got up and the two swordsmen retreated to the watching group to be replaced by two new fighters. She kept on going.

She passed row upon row of training grounds until she came to one that was at the very back a little removed from the rest of them. Sitting on it, with his huge paws covering his ears was Zeeshan.

"What are you doing?" Arleth asked him, coming to sit cross-legged in front of him.

"Oh hi Arleth. I'm practicing."

"Practicing what?"

"How to control my anger."

"Ahh"

"Selene came and found me earlier this morning and asked me if I wanted to continue my lessons. She brought me out here to avoid any - *interruptions*." Zeeshan slumped over and buried his face in his paws.

"Aww, Zeehsan! Don't worry." Arleth rubbed his arm gently. "People will get used to you, you just frightened them because you are something new that they haven't seen before." Zeeshan didn't look convinced. "And besides," she continued smiling at him, "Selene seems incredibly capable and if she says she can teach you to control your anger, then I'm willing to bet she can." Zeeshan raised his head to look at her. "And that will help people to relax around you right?"

"Ya I suppose so."

"Not suppose so! Yes it will... So tell me about Selene's training."

Zeeshan explained for the better part of 10 minutes. Arleth asked questions and reacted enthusiastically when she was supposed to. And by the end, his dejection had been replaced with hope.

Arleth began to ask Zeeshan a question, but was distracted by a flicker behind his head. She stared in shock for a few seconds, "Is that *snow?!?*"

Zeeshan turned to look. "Oh ya! It's really neat huh?"

"Why is there snow?"

"I asked Selene the same question when she was here. Apparently each training ground goes through all of the different weather patterns that soldiers might get outside - rain, strong winds, blinding sun, extreme heat or cold, and of course snow. If they practice in all possible conditions, when they encounter them outside, they will be ready. It's brilliant really!"

"Wow, ya that *is* brilliant!" Arleth could see how training inside a cave would leave someone very unprepared if they had to fight a battle in rain for example. But clearly her brother had thought of this.

"Your brother is quite smart!" Zeeshan said as though he was reading her thoughts. "He could be a Talywag. We are known as the smartest race you know."

Arleth smiled despite herself. "I know Zeeshan, you have told me."

"Right, of course. Well you will see for yourself anyways when you come to Occa."

Before Arleth could tell him that she wasn't going to be going to Occa with the rest of them, she suddenly got a bone-chilling blast of cold air. Her exposed skin immediately broke out in goosebumps. "I tttthink ttthiiiss ttttraining ground is gggoing through some extreme ccccold right now," Arleth chattered.

"Oh is it?" Zeeshan looked at her goosebumps and chattering teeth. "I don't feel anything."

"Ok, wwwell I can't stay hhheere. I'm gggoing to go."

She got up, turned to go and then hesitated. She didn't know if she would get the chance to see him again before he left for Occa. And after that... who knew. She turned back and threw herself at him, wrapping her arms as far around him as she could - which really only reached halfway along his side. Surprised, he let out a rough laugh and then wrapped his arms gently around her.

"Bye Zeeshan," She said into the thick fur of his chest.

"Bye..." Zeeshan was bewildered by her sudden rush of emotion.

"I'm glad we could save you."

Arleth pulled herself away, smiled at Zeeshan once more and hurried off out of the cold.

Zeeshan shook his head at her retreating figure, a huge smile on his face, "And I'm the one that's emotionally unstable."

* * *

"Do you like this one?" Selene asked the child sitting in her lap.

"Ya it's pretty."

Selene adjusted herself so she was sitting more comfortably on the grass and held out the glowing circle of light so the child could see it better.

"Are you sure?"

"Well... umm.. can it be pink?"

"Of course it can." Selene cupped her hand over the light in her hand and blew on it. Blowing on it was completely unnecessary for the magic to work but Lucy loved this part. She smiled delightedly and added her own "puff" of air to Selene's hands. "Perfect."

Selene opened her hands, the sphere now glowed a bright pink.

"Yay!" Lucy clapped her hands. "Pretty."

As the child stared in fascination, Selene made pulling motions on one side of the sphere. The girl copied her, miming Selene's actions in the air. Slowly a thread of pink light started growing out of the side of the sphere.

"Oooohhh" Lucy squealed.

Selene laughed and continued her pulling motion but stopped abruptly. "Lucy you have to help me, I can't do this alone!"

"Oh right!"

Selene, with Lucy mimicking her, continued until the strand of pink was about a foot long.

"Ok let's see if this is good."

Used to the drill, Lucy pulled up her hair and Selene wrapped the strand around her neck. She leaned over the child to make sure the pendant was hanging properly on her chest. Satisfied, she grabbed the pendant and the end of the strand in one hand and squeezed it shut. A faint glow pulsed in her closed fist and then went dark.

There was a rustling in the grass behind her. Selene dropped the pendant on instinct and turned her head to see who was behind her.

"Oh Arleth, it's you."

"Thanks Selene!" Lucy bounded out of her lap and turned to face the newcomer. "Do you like my necklace? Selene made it for me."

"It's very nice," Arleth responded. "Is pink your favourite colour?"

"For today. I also have a purple one. Purple was my favourite colour yesterday.

"Oh I see," Arleth smiled. "My favourite colour is green."

"I have a green one too! Green was my favourite colour last week. Ok, gonna show my friends!" Lucy raced away.

Arleth sat down on the grass beside Selene. "She has a lot of favourite colours."

Selene laughed, "She sure does. Keeps me busy."

"Is she your... daughter?"

"Oh gosh no! Aedan and I are not ready for kids yet. The whole waging war thing kind of gets in the way."

"Ok phew, so I'm not also an Aunt."

"No! When you are you will be prepared trust me. Aedan and I want to be married before we have kids and we don't want to get married until the war is over."

"But...uh... might you not get pregnant by accident? You can't exactly plan these things..."

"You can when you have magic." Selene winked at her. "Your brother probably won't want us to have had this conversation, but ask Samara about it. She taught me."

Arleth blushed "I don't think I will need to know that any time soon."

Selene reached over and grabbed her hand, "Good your brother will let me live long enough to see our wedding after all."

Both of them laughed.

"Selene?"

"hmm"

"If Rogan did something to me, magically, would you be able to tell?"

"Why did Rogan use some kind of magic on you?"

"Yes, but I'm not sure if it's bad or not....Absalom had wanted to question me about the Black Thorn assassin group."

Selene looked at her with confusion, "The what?"

"It was a thing he made up so that he could bring me to Oherra with him. Val attacked his Grekens and Absalom told me that he was a member of the Black Thorn and I was the only one that had seen one of their faces so he needed me to go back with him to Oherra so that he could question me."

"Ahh ok, continue."

"Anyways, Absalom told Rogan to question me using magic because apparently it gave the clearest evidence. I might be forgetting something, but with magic it wouldn't matter, they could still see it. But well now I'm worried, because, well, there is no Black Thorn so he wasn't trying to see what I had witnessed. So *why* did he use magic on me? What was he trying to find out - *or do to* me. And the whole thing with Zeeshan.... I don't want something like that to happen to me."

"It is right of you to be concerned. But don't worry, I can find out what he really did." Selene was glad that Arleth was smart enough to have come to this conclusion on her own. She hadn't liked the idea of probing around in Arleth's brain without her knowing. It was too close to Rogan's style for her comfort.

"And fix it?"

"Yes and fix it," Selene lied.

Arleth let out a sigh of relief.

Selene wasn't entirely sure if she *could* fix anything that Rogan may have done to her. But she sure as heck would try. There was no use worrying Arleth until she had inspected her to see what, if any, damage there was.

"Come sit in front of me, please."

Arleth shuffled over.

" No facing me."

Arleth turned around and crossed her legs."

"Closer."

She slid as close to Selene as she could, until their knees were just a hair's length away from touching.

"Ok great. I am going to need you to relax as best you can. I am going to place my hands on each of your temples. As the magic runs through your head you will feel slight bursts of heat - that is normal, it's just the magical energy at work. But if it hurts let me know right away ok? It shouldn't ever cause pain."

Arleth nodded. "I'm ready."

Selene placed her hands gently on either side of Arleth's head and closed her eyes. She let a few exploratory strands flow through Arleth's brain.

"Does that feel ok Arleth?"

"Ya, it's certainly weird, but not unpleasant."

"Good."

Selene increased the strands a bit, changing their chemistry so they would seek out any imprint that Rogan left. She had dealt with his magic enough that she could recognize his stain. Each sorcerer or sorceress left a characteristic mark, a magical signature on anything that they touched. Rogan's signature was a nasty stain - a rot.

And there it was! She latched onto his imprint and crafted her strands around it, unravelling it so she could determine what it had done. She continued for a few minutes, unravelling it and reading its pattern, probing deeper into Arleth's brain a few times to follow its trail. When she was satisfied, she squeezed her strands around the rot Rogan had left until it whiffed out. She pulled her own strands back into her hands and removed them from Arleth's temples.

"So?"

"It's good news Arleth."

Arleth let out the breath she didn't realize she had been holding.

"The magic that Rogan used on you was not harmful. He was in essence trying to read your thoughts. He used magic that would trace whatever you were thinking of at the time, to all its points of origin. So for example if you were thinking of me, and I cast that spell on you, it would allow me to access every single instance in your brain where you and I ever interacted, you ever saw me, or you ever even thought of me."

"This is good news?" Arleth felt extremely violated.

"Yes it is. It's not pleasant by any means that he was searching around in your brain like that, but he didn't do any harm. He left nothing in there that would manifest later, he didn't try to change anything, it was all just exploratory."

"Manifest later?!?"

Selene nodded, "Rogan has done it before. He will leave a small web of magic in someone's brain. It's virtually undetectable. The person will appear completely normal for days, maybe even weeks. And then the piece he left will mature and wreak havoc on the person."

Arleth was almost too afraid to ask, but her curiosity got the better of her, "Wreak havoc how?"

"In any number of ways really. But the latest one before I learned how to recognize it and correct it... Are you sure you wanted to know?"

"Yes," Arleth responded with more confidence than she felt.

"Well... he walked into a group of people and.... exploded. Killed himself and 4 other people."

Arleth felt like she might be sick.

"And you are sure, there is nothing like that in my brain?"

"Positive."

"Wow, I guess that is good news then. Compared to *exploding*."

Selene grimaced, "Unfortunately yes, the fact that a lunatic *only* poked around in your brain is good news."

Arleth sat in silence for a while contemplating what Selene had just told her. She realized she had been incredibly lucky to have spent as long as she did with Rogan and Absalom and come out unscathed. She was getting the distinct impression that not too many people could say the same.

Selene sat in silence beside Arleth, letting her have her time to process. She couldn't imagine how hard learning all of this at once must be for Arleth. She had grown up in a world with magic, had lived all of the things for years that Arleth was getting bombarded with all now in the space of a few days. At her age, Selene didn't know how she would have handled it, certainly not as well as Arleth was. Heck, she wasn't sure she would handle it any better now. Not for the first time, she marvelled at the girl's strength.

"Are you feeling better now? Not feeling nauseous anymore?" Selene asked, breaking the silence.

"Yes, I'm back to normal now. It went away shortly after I started eating breakfast."

"That's good to hear. Arleth do you find that you get sick, feel nauseous I mean, often?"

"I hadn't really thought about it, but I guess, maybe? I *have* noticed it more in the last few days though."

Selene didn't seem surprised. In fact it seemed like she had been expecting that answer.

"Why?" Arleth asked.

"It's based on your magic. Your powers work differently than mine. For you, the basis of your power is empathy. This means you can influence other living things, and do much more than I could ever hope to. But it also means that until you learn to control your powers, you will empathize with other living things.... to the point of nausea."

"I don't get it."

"Since your magic works through empathy, you will feel other's pain and sickness as your own. The everyday stuff, like a child gets sick, or a woman gives birth you won't feel. But the big stuff, battles, war, torture, will affect you. The closer you are in proximity to the suffering the worse it is for you. Also, the closer you are emotionally to the person or people affected, the worse it will be. This is one of the reasons you need to go to Samara so quickly, quicker than I had to. If you don't learn to control this side of your power, your nausea will keep getting worse and worse, eventually, if you are never taught to control it, it will kill you."

Arleth's mouth opened in shock, "So if I had never come to Oherra, never been able to meet Samara and learn to control my power, I would have become so sick that I would have died? A power, I didn't even know I had, would have killed me?"

"No, not necessarily."

"But you just said..."

"On Tocarra, you were unlikely to face the same magnitude of pain and suffering that you are here. Every day on Oherra, there are battles, raids, skirmishes, ambushes you name it. On top of that, every day, Rogan kills more people, enchants them, tortures them just for the fun of it. In a world like this, you are in much more danger if you don't learn how to control your power."

"I guess that's why Aedan was so insistent on me not going to Occa, he wanted me to get to Samara as soon as possible."

"That could be, yes."

"But why wouldn't he just tell me that?"

"He probably didn't want to worry you."

"You told me."

"Yes, but I understand magic a lot better than your brother, and I have an ulterior motive."

That gave Arleth pause, "You do?"

"Yes, I know the plan is for us to leave for Samara tonight when everyone else leaves for Occa. But the more I have been thinking about it, the more I think I should go to Occa. Talywags are a stubborn, timid race - I don't think they will have much luck convincing them to come back with them here. Or at least not before Absalom attacks. I want to put up magical barriers, protection spells, that sort of thing."

"So what does that have to do with telling me about the problem with my powers?"

"Because you are more important. If you were still sick and in pain, you would need to go to Samara right away. But you aren't. And since I'm making the decision to delay your training, I wanted to give you all the facts first."

"I would like to go to Occa..."

"I thought you might. It will only be a two day delay. We will go with them to Occa, stay a day so I have time to set up my magic and then we will leave for Edika."

"But I am scared about getting sick..."

"Understandable. But honestly I don't think you are in danger right now."

"How come?"

"Your biggest threat comes from Absalom and Rogan and I'm willing to bet they are focused right now on waging war on the Talywags. They will have to prepare just like we do, so it should buy you a couple of days at least. If the war does happen, you will be safely with Samara by then."

Arleth thought about it for a few minutes. She *did* want to go to Occa. And what Selene was telling her made sense. Two days wouldn't delay her training by very long and that way the Talywags would be more protected too since Selene would have time to help them.

"Ok, I want to go to Occa."

"Excellent."

Arleth's heart sank, "But what about Aedan?" He had been so set on her going to Edika right away.

"Don't worry about him. I can be very convincing."

Arleth gave her a blank look.

"Wait right here, I'll go talk to him now. Be back in a few."

Arleth didn't know how successful Selene would be, but she hoped for the best. She pulled on a blade of grass and waited.

* * *

Twenty minutes later, Selene returned.

"You'd better get some sleep Arleth, we are leaving for Occa in a few hours."

Chapter 25

A gentle shaking of her shoulder woke Arleth out of her dream.

"Huh... what?" Arleth said blearily.

"Wake up Arleth. We are leaving shortly." Selene handed her a soft bundle.

"What's this?" In the darkness Arleth couldn't make out what it was.

"It's some warmer clothes for you - pants, a cloak, boots."

Arleth rubbed the sleep from her eyes and took the bundle from Selene. "Thank you."

"No problem." Selene got up and started to walk out of the tent. "Put them on, I'll be waiting out here for you." She lifted the flap and disappeared outside.

A few moments later, Arleth came out of the tent, yawning.

"Why did we have to leave in the middle of the night again?" Arleth asked as Selene and her started walking.

"Absalom has scouts everywhere. We don't want to be attacked when we leave Iridian, and preferably, we don't even want to be seen. There is a lot of open ground between us and Frasht Forest and with 4,000 of us making the journey - we need the cover of darkness."

"Ah, right," Arleth yawned again.

"Come on," Selene laughed, pushing her gently along. "We need to move faster."

By the time they reached the cave entrance, most of the soldiers had already left. The few hundred who remained were standing in a group off to the side. Graydon and Winn were giving them instructions, most of which Arleth couldn't hear, but she did pick out "rear-guard" and "watch for threats from behind." Zeeshan stood by himself, energetically hopping from one foot to the next. It was clear he couldn't wait to get going. Near him, Aedan was deep in conversation with Bain, who was nodding fervently to whatever his leader was telling him.

Aedan looked up when he heard them approach, "You are just in time ladies. If we leave now, we will be right behind Val and the first group." He whispered one last thing to Bain as the women approached, then smiled and clasped the man's forearm. "I know I'm leaving our stronghold in good hands."

Bain grasped Aedan's forearm in return. "Be safe out there Aedan," Bain replied. "Absalom hasn't made a move this aggressive in a while, and now that he knows we have Arleth....I don't need to remind you, he's planning something big."

Aedan forced out a laugh he didn't feel, "We aren't 12 year old kids any more Bain." It was meant to sound like a joking rebuke, but it came out hollow. Aedan was just as tense as Bain was.

And Bain knew it too, "Just be careful." He made a move to walk away, but Selene grabbed his wrist and pulled him towards her.

"You aren't getting away that easy old man," she said, wrapping her arms around him. "You be careful too." Before he could reply, she reached into the pocket of her cloak and pulled out a small brown cloth bag and dropped it in Bain's palm. "This is for you."

He undid the drawstring and looked inside. He nodded, retied the drawstring and put it into an inside pocket on his cloak.

"In case you need it, or in case we need to tell you something urgent." Selene instructed.

Bain nodded again. "Hopefully neither of us will have need of it, but thank you." He gave one final, meaningful glance at Aedan and a quick smile and a nod in Arleth's direction and walked away.

Aedan stared at Bain's retreating figure for a few moments and then without further ado, "Ok let's go."

* * *

Fifteen minutes later, Arleth found herself in a single file line, slowly making her way down the treacherous passes of the Iridian mountains. Directly in front of her Graydon seemed to be navigating the steep declines with ease. For what seemed like the hundredth time he stopped, turned, sighed in over-exaggerated displeasure and all but stamped his foot waiting for her to catch up. When she finally reached him, he whispered angrily "Hurry up, I don't know why you are taking so long. If I didn't keep turning around you would be left behind." He sighed again and turned back around.

What a jerk, Arleth thought. She highly doubted Zeeshan, and the hundreds of men behind him would allow her to get left behind, even if Graydon stopped his 'generosity'. But she kept this to herself. Even if she had wanted to tell him, he was already 10 steps away from her and rapidly increasing the distance.

Crap, she thought, is the guy a mountain goat? She did her best to hurry after him, tripped and would have fallen if not for the supporting paw of Zeeshan directly behind her.

"Go slowly," Zeeshan grumbled into her ear, "It's better to go slow and stay alive than rush down the mountain like a damn fool."

With his help, she regained her balance and continued down the pass, more carefully this time.

Selene had given them all patches of light that they stuck to their hands so they could see better in the dark. But even with both hands held out in front of her, Arleth couldn't see very much. In an earlier altercation with Graydon, she had complained that if she could see better, maybe she could have gone faster. Graydon had called her an idiot and told her *obviously* the light couldn't be that bright because they were trying to *hide*, not tell all of Oherra *exactly* where they were.

So Arleth continued on as best she could. To her left was a sheer drop, and to her right was the cliff face. She moved as far to the right as she could and held her hand out so that she could feel her way along the side. Her left hand was held out in front of her so that she could vaguely see where her feet were stepping. The pass was littered everywhere with chunks of fallen rock. Even if she had been able to see clearly, in broad daylight, she would have still had to move slowly to choose where to step.

She sighed, put her head down and tried to forget the fact that if she tripped and fell to her left, there was nothing to stop her from going over the side of the cliff. And it was a *very* far way down.

* * *

Two excruciating hours later, an exhausted and very frazzled Arleth finally stepped onto solid ground. She had never been so thankful for grass in her entire life. She looked down almost lovingly, her hand held out in front of her so she could better see the blades of grass on the ground. Arleth started to bend over to run her fingers through it, when a rush of movement behind her jolted her back up again.

"WHOA, WATCHA DOING?"

Arleth turned around and her nose brushed against the fur of Zeeshan's chest.

"I almost ran you over" Zeeshan said, taking a step backwards. "Why did you stop so suddenly?"

Arleth felt the heat come to her cheeks. For the first time in the last two hours, she was thankful for the dark so Zeeshan couldn't see her blush. *I bent to pick up grass, because it seems like the best thing in the world right now.... Ya that's a good reason.*

"It's so dark, and I don't know where we are. I was trying to see what was ahead of me" she held both arms out in front of her, illustrating how little of the ground ahead of her was lit up by Selene's patch of light. "I was trying to.... catch my bearings..." she trailed off.

"Oh right, I forgot that you weren't born here. You have no idea where we are do you?"

Arleth let out a sigh of relief. He had bought her terrible excuse. And she realized he was right, she really did have no idea where they were. She knew they were leaving the stronghold (which they had done) and going to Occa, which was in a forest, Frasht forest to be exact. But beyond that she knew next to nothing of where they were, what kind of terrain they would have to go through, what animals or plants or people they might encounter, heck she realized she didn't even know in which direction they were travelling.

"Ok well," Zeeshan said as he moved up to walk beside her. "I will start with Iridian castle then. Let's say Iridian castle is here," He held his left fist out in front of him. It was illuminated just enough by the patch of light on his wrist that Arleth could see it. "The Iridian mountains circle all around the castle." He made a circular motion with his right hand around his left fist. "The stronghold we were in, was in these mountains. I don't know exactly where, but let's say it's here." He pointed to a spot to the right of his left fist which was still illustrating Iridian castle. "We just travelled down the mountain," He trailed a path in the air in front of him and now we are here. To the right or east of the stronghold. Right now we are walking across the plains which stretch all the way east to the Frasht Forest. Hey Arleth hold out your hand."

She held out her left hand.

"No, the other one."

Zeeshan pointed to her now extended right hand, "This is Occa." He motioned an area all around her hand, " And this is Frasht Forest."

"So we are heading east, crossing the plains, until we get to Frasht Forest and then Occa is inside the forest."

"Yes exactly."

Arleth nodded. She was relieved that they had flat land to walk on for the foreseeable future.

"The plains are pretty boring, but it's dark anyways so who cares. The Frasht forest is more interesting, scary, but better than the plains. More to look at. I think we will probably be going through the forest tomorrow when it's light so you will be able to see. But the best thing in the forest is definitely Occa." The pride in his voice was evident.

Arleth smiled at him in the dark, "You love your home, don't you?" She couldn't remember ever loving her home, or even considering anything really home. Certainly not at Bella's. And in the orphanage she was happy, but it had never really felt like home.

"Of course I do! I can't wait to see my mom and my dad. I can't wait to introduce you to them."

Arleth laughed at his excitement.

"Will you shut up!" Graydon whispered angrily at them. "Zeeshan you are talking loud enough to wake the dead."

"He's just excited to be going home." Arleth said

"Excited? That's nice, how excited will you be when Absalom and Rogan set up an ambush for us?"

Arleth and Zeeshan stared at him

"Stupid children," Graydon muttered under his breath

"WHO YOU CALLING STUPID?" Zeeshan roared, taking a menacing step towards Graydon.

"SSSSH, SHUT UP," Graydon yelled back at him.

Zeeshan took another step towards Graydon, "NO YOU SHUT UP, YOU LITTLE PIP-SQUEAK." He took a swipe at Graydon's head, which he just managed to avoid. "I AM BIG ENOUGH TO BREAK YOU IN TWO."

"YOU WANT TO FIGHT?" Graydon yelled back, balling his hands into fists. "BRING IT ON."

A blur of white appeared, and Selene forced her way between them. She put one hand on Zeeshan's waist and one hand on Graydon's chest, forcing them apart.

"What the hell are you doing?" She said angrily, but quietly. "We need to be quiet. We don't want Absalom to know where we are going. We need the element of surprise... which is probably ruined now."

Even in the dark, the force of her glare at the two of them was burning.

Zeeshan dropped his arms and looked down ashamedly.

"I was trying to tell them just that, but they weren't listening."

Selene riveted her head towards Graydon, "You," She punctuated this by pointing a finger into his chest, "Were being just as loud as they were."

"But.."

"And fighting! You are on the same side for God's sake, grow up."

Graydon smirked.

"Both of you." She grabbed Graydon's arm. "You walk up with me, and all three of you, I want no talking beyond a whisper for the rest of the night."

She strode off, half dragging Graydon with her.

* * *

A few silent hours later, they reached the edge of Frasht Forest and the column halted. Arleth and Zeeshan joined the others in setting up camp for the night.

"What is happening?" Arleth whispered to a nearby soldier, "Why are we stopping?"

"It is not safe to go into Frasht Forest at night."

AHHHHHOOOOOOO, a loud howl broke through the night. It was followed by a feral scream and then abruptly silence as the creature's life was snuffed out.

Arleth shivered despite the heat.

"All manner of creatures come out at night." The soldier continued. "Most you don't want to cross paths with."

"What was that?" Arleth whispered back.

"Sounded like a Vrog. Deadly creatures, sleep in caves during the day. Come out at night to hunt. Anyways, I reckon we only have a few hours to get some sleep before daybreak and we have to start moving again. I'm going to catch some sleep, I suggest you do the same." The man disappeared into the darkness.

"That sounds like a good idea," Zeeshan said. "Come I've set up our bed rolls."

Arleth took one last look into the abyss of the forest, before turning away to follow Zeeshan.

* * *

A loud knock on the door, violently shook Absalom out of his reverie. It was four in the morning, but he was still awake. Good thing for whoever was on the other side of the door, that's for sure.

"Come in."

The door creaked open and a familiar face stepped in. Absalom didn't know the man's name, didn't care actually. But he recognized him as one of the scouts he had deployed earlier that day to monitor any movement around the mountains.

"Sorry, it's late." The man stammered. "But you said to inform you of any important news as soon as it happened."

"Yes," Absalom said impatiently. "Well what is it?"

"Aedan, and a few thousand of his soldiers are heading across the Dari plains, in the direction of Frasht Forest."

Absalom sat up in his chair, instantly more alert. "A few thousand are you sure?"

"Yes, very."

"Interesting. Who else was with him? Selene? Any of his commanders?"

"Selene for sure. I don't know about the commanders," the man stammered again. "But I did see Arleth and some big white bear-looking creature. They were arguing with a young man, so loud I could have heard them from miles away."

Absalom didn' t care if they were all arguing, he had the information he needed. He stared at the man in annoyance "Bye!"

The man bowed and all but ran out the door, closing it behind him.

This was very interesting, Absalom thought. Heading towards Frasht Forest... clearly they were going to Occa. And he was bringing a sizeable portion of his force with him. A risky move, leaving his stronghold with only a skeleton guard.

He would have to bring more soldiers now when he attacked Occa, but no matter. He now had the chance to take out Aedan,

Selene, Arleth and most of their force. Much better than he was hoping for.

And he still had the Ranin Bud set in their stronghold. With any luck any survivors from his annihilation at Occa would just make it back in time, to be killed by the Bud. But if not, it was still good; less soldiers left in the stronghold meant, his Bud was more likely to succeed. Most of the soldiers would be gone, leaving old men and women and children. And without a sorceress... they would be all but defenceless.

Absalom smiled in pure glee.

"What a remarkably stupid move Aedan Amara." He said out loud. "I just hope you live long enough to truly realize the mistake you have made."

Chapter 26

Selene yawned and rolled over on her stomach. Groggily she reached out her arm, expecting it to land on Aedan's chest, and felt nothing but the fabric of the bed roll. She patted around, more fabric. Where was Aedan? She opened her eyes, blinking against the sunlight and looked at Aedan's empty bed roll beside her. With a sigh she rolled back over and sat up, rubbing the sleep out of her eyes.

Was there ever going to be a time in her life when she could sleep comfortably, *in a bed*, for longer than a few hours?

She kneeded her lower back with her fingers and looked around for Aedan. He was sitting a few paces away on a fallen log. He was hunched over the Erum, clearly deep in thought. One hand rested on his forehead and even from here she could see that he was biting his lower lip in concentration. Selene shook her head with a smile and went over to sit beside him.

Aedan looked up when he saw her and smiled.

"Morning hun," He kissed her.

"Reading the Erum?" It was more a statement than question.

"Mhmm, look what I found." He pushed the open book over to her so that it rested on both of their laps. "This is the part that Arleth told us about, when she last saw Neve." He pointed near the top of the page. "Neve fought Rogan while Arleth was in a storage closet, then when Rogan was unconscious, Neve forced Arleth to run away, while she stayed behind. We know this part already from Arleth. But read here, what happened when Arleth left." He pointed lower down on the page.

Selene looked at the page Aedan had indicated and saw meaningless symbols. "Aedan I can't read it, remember. Not an Amara."

"Oh right. Sorry."

Aedan read aloud,

> "Neve watched Arleth leave and then turned back to Rogan. He was stirring and she knew he would become conscious at any moment. Neve knew that Arleth's only chance of survival was if the dread mage thought that she was dead. So without

> hesitation, Neve cast an illusion charm on herself. A few seconds later, Neve no longer looked like herself, in her place stood the image of Arleth Amara. Quickly, she stumbled into the storage closet where the real Arleth had been hiding and waited for Rogan to become conscious. A few minutes later, the door of the storage closet flew open and Rogan entered. He smiled and a spear of green light formed in his hand. Neve screamed as he jammed it through her heart, killing her instantly."

"Well, that explains why Rogan didn't continue searching for Arleth."

"It sure does," Aedan replied. "Absalom must have read this passage a few weeks ago and that was how he knew Arleth was still alive."

"It's a very good thing we got back the Erum, who knows what else Absalom might have been able to find out."

Aedan nodded in agreement. "But I wonder why the Erum recorded that passage at all, it followed Neve *as well* as Arleth until Neve died. It was almost as if the Erum got confused by Neve's illusion charm."

"Hmmm, or perhaps it was on purpose?" Selene thought out loud.

"What do you mean?"

"Well the Erum is only supposed to follow the lives of the Amara's right?"

"Yes."

"What if it was designed that any attempt to mimic one of the Amara's would be recorded as well."

"So Neve's illusion charm."

"Exactly. I can only think of two reasons why someone would want to cast an illusion charm on themselves to make them look like an Amara. One to protect them, or two to cause them harm or impersonate them. Either of which, I'm sure, you or Arleth would want to know about."

"Ya, actually that makes a lot of sense. Kind of a built-in way to help protect us. That's pretty genius."

"It is. Except in this case it worked against you."

Aedan nodded, "True. Oh, there was something else I wanted to show you too." He flipped the book ahead a bunch of pages. "Arleth hasn't had a very easy life. Here listen to this, it's from when she was 12. She was a slave to a woman named Bella."

> "For the second morning in a row, Arleth woke up in the cage. She was shivering from the cold and her empty stomach grumbled - she realized she hadn't eaten anything in two days. Her legs ached from being cramped up. She tried to stretch them as much as she could in the confines of her cage. As she did, she noticed that the dark purple bruises had faded overnight to a dull hue."

"It's all like that - seven years of *that*. She was treated like an animal, *worse than an animal*."

"Wow," Selene shook her head sadly, "That is awful. She endured that for seven years?"

"Ya. Her life after the orphanage is just page after page of the same thing."

"Wow," Selene said again. "It does explain a lot about her personality though."

"That's for sure. How brave and mature she is for one."

"And how Absalom didn't have as much an effect on her as we expected he would - she has learned to be guarded and to rely on herself."

Aedan nodded.

"You know we can't let on that we know this about her. She doesn't seem like the kind of person that would want to share this part of her life. At least not yet anyways."

"Yes I know," Aedan replied. "And speaking of which," he gestured with his head. "She seems to be awake." A distance away Arleth stood up and stretched. Yawning she caught sight of Selene and Aedan watching her. She smiled and waved at them.

"Let's go get breakfast," Aedan said to Selene as he waved back. He closed the Erum with a snap and put it under his arm.

"Breakfast it is." Selene agreed, taking Aedan's hand as he headed over to his sister.

* * *

"Arrumph" Arleth swore as the branch snapped back and hit her in the face.

"Huh? Oh sorry Arleth" Zeeshan said, turning to look behind him. "I didn't realize the branch would be so swingy."

"Arrumph." Arleth put a hand up to her forehead, it felt warm and sticky. She brought it back down, it was red.. blood.

Zeeshan smiled sheepishly at her and held up his paws, "oops?"

"Let's keep it moving." A voice called out from close behind them. "We don't want to be in these woods when it gets dark.

"Sorry," Zeeshan mumbled. He turned back around and continued walking.

Arleth wiped the blood off on her tunic, and still bristling, followed Zeeshan.

Arleth estimated that they had been walking through Frasht forest for about three hours. Normally she would have been overjoyed by such a journey, but not today. When she had woken up, she had been fine, but almost as soon as they had entered the forest, Arleth had been hit with a huge wave of nausea which still hadn't abated. With each step, she fought the simultaneous urge to vomit and pass out. And now, thanks to Zeeshan, her head also throbbed. Even better, a swarm of insects, seemingly attracted to the blood had taken up residence buzzing around her head and no amount of arm waving would dislodge them.

The next branch, Zeeshan held carefully for her and smiled at her hopefully.

Arleth just glared at him.

They continued trudging along until a little while later, the entire column halted and the order was whispered down the line, to be quiet. From her vantage point, Arleth could see nothing out of the ordinary and despite her throbbing head, she craned her neck to see why they had stopped. Her effort yielded no results and so she was forced to wait impatiently until they started moving again, this time in dead silence.

After a few minutes, the trees in front of Arleth thinned and she stepped out into a clearing. The sudden difference in terrain was staggering - in one stride, she had stepped out of a forest, into a barren wasteland. Ahead of her stretched a long tunnel-shaped clearing. The foliage and rich soil of the forest was replaced with dry, cracked clay. Aside from the column, making its way through, there was no movement. Nothing here lived. On either side, separating the wasteland from the rest of the forest were rows of caves, stacked one on top of the other. As she continued walking, she heard a faint humming. At first she thought she was imagining it, but as she went farther into the wasteland, it became louder and louder.

But where was it coming from?

The ground was completely flat, she could see all the way through to where it, just as abruptly, turned back into forest. There were no plants, no animals, just dry, dead earth.

The caves, she thought with horror. *There must be something in the caves.* She looked to her left scanning the rows of caves that she could see. They all looked deserted.

CRUNCH!

Arleth looked down to see what she had stepped on.

It was a bone.

The ground was littered with them. She didn't know how she hadn't seen it before. All the ones she could see were completely stripped of flesh and ranged in size. The one she had stepped on looked remarkably like a human arm bone and there were indents in it that looked like bite marks. But that was a small bone compared to some of the others, although some were the size of small twigs, many more were twice the size of her leg. She didn't like to think how big something would have to be to eat and kill something with bones that big - *or how small she was in comparison.*

Up ahead, there was a commotion in the column. All heads turned to the right and a few pointed excitedly. Arleth turned to see what they were looking at, and had to put both hands over her mouth to stifle a scream. Directly to her right, a huge hairy arm was draped lazily out of a cave. A piece of bloody flesh was dangling from its massive claws - remnants of a prior meal. The arm was swaying up and down slightly, almost in time to the humming.

The creature is sleeping, Arleth thought with relief. *It's snoring.*
The force of its snoring, finally caused the flesh to become dislodged and it drifted lazily down to land at Arleth's feet. She recoiled instantly and would have fallen had a firm hand not steadied her.

"It's ok Arleth, they are all asleep," Selene whispered in Arleth's ear.

"All!?!" Arleth whispered back.

"Vrog, these caves are full of them. Don't worry they are nocturnal. They are the main reason we waited to cross Frasht forest until the day."

Arleth remembered the screams coming from the forest last night. What was left of the creature that had made them, had just floated to her feet. Her nausea re-asserted itself with full force and she gagged.

Selene put her hand on Arleth's back and for the first time, took in the gash on her forehead and her blood-shot eyes.

"You aren't ok are you?" Selene whispered.

Arleth just shook her head.

"When we get away from the caves, we will stop and I'll help you."

Arleth forced a smile.

* * *

"We really need to get you to Samara." Selene muttered as she bandaged up Arleth's head. They were back in the forest, a safe distance from the caves and the column had halted for a quick lunch break. At Selene's insistence, Arleth had described her morning of nausea and dizziness. "I can numb the side effects for a bit, but that is the best I can do. We will sleep in Occa tonight, but first thing in the morning, I am taking you to Edika."

Arleth nodded. "You can numb the side effects?"

Selene secured the bandage and nodded. She put her hands on either side of Arleth's head, over her temples and closed her eyes. Almost immediately Arleth's nausea and dizziness went away.

"There, how's that?"

"I'm good as new, thank you!"

"I'm glad you feel better, but no you aren't. I can take away the pain for a bit, but it's going to keep getting worse and worse until Samara teaches you how to control your gift."

"ARLETH! did you see the Vrog?" Zeeshan bounded over. "We are all taught as children to be careful of them and stay inside at night, but I have never actually seen one! They are even bigger than I am now!"

"I know! Did you see the size of its claw?"

"And all the bones?"

"You know that is why we Talywags build our homes in the trees, the Vrog don't know how to climb."

"You live in trees? Cool!"

"Ya we do, you will be so surprised when we get there."

"Thanks Selene!" Arleth called over her shoulder as her and Zeeshan ran off.

Selene sighed.

"You are doing the right thing." Aedan said, coming up behind her.

"Am I though? What if taking her to Occa is one day too long? What if I can't get her to Samara in time?"

"If you leave tomorrow morning, you are only losing half a day. I'm sure the Talywag council will let you take a couple of horses. You will make much better time on horseback than if you left from Iridian yesterday on foot."

"Yes I suppose so."

"Cheer up, you will forget all about it in a few hours when we are arguing with the Talywags."

Selene groaned. "Don't remind me."

Chapter 27

Zeeshan hadn't been exaggerating, Occa was unlike anything Arleth had ever seen before.

For starters, the entire city was built in the trees.

And not just any trees, these trees were by far the largest and tallest that Arleth had ever laid eyes on. In fact, even right in front of her, she almost didn't believe they existed. If Arleth spread out her arms to either side of her, it would easily take at least 10 of her to encircle the base of one of these trees. And the tops were lost to her sight - they stretched farther than she could see from the ground. Arleth knew next to nothing about plants or nature, she had always preferred history or cultural studies back at the orphanage. But she was willing to bet that these trees were thousands of years old. Just looking at the sheer magnitude of them took her breath away.

And that was just the trees.

Built into the lowest branches (about 10 metres off the ground) to the very highest branches that Arleth could see were hundreds of platforms, buildings and bridges.

"As I said before," explained Zeeshan "Occa is built into the trees to protect us from the Vrog. They can't climb trees you see. Every night they come out of their caves and a few of them circle at the bottom here, but they can never reach us."

"I'm sure that pisses them off," Winn said cheerfully as he and Graydon passed by.

"It sure does," Zeeshan smiled.

"Too bad hiding in trees won't save them from Absalom's armies," Graydon muttered when he and his brother were still in earshot.

Arleth looked over at Zeeshan, expecting an angry response, but he seemed not to have heard.

"So if the Vrog can't get up, how do you get up.. or down?" She asked.

"Do you see that rectangular box over there?" Zeeshan pointed at a spot on one of the lowest platforms.

"Right there, at the edge of that platform?"

"Yup, that's an upper."

Arleth stared at him blankly, "A what?"

"An upper." He said it matter of factly, as if it was the most obvious statement in the world.

"Ok, and what is an upper?"

Zeeshan finally noticed her blank stare, "Oh you don't know what an upper is? Really? Hmmm. Ok, well, do you see the ropes that are attached to each corner of it?"

Arleth looked more closely, "Yes."

"They are attached at the top to a crank, which you can't see from here. Someone at the top turns it and the rectangular box travels down the rope to the bottom. To go up, you simply turn the crank in the opposite direction."

"And people sit in the box?"

"Exactly. We pull them all up at night so that the Vrogs can't break them or somehow use them. But during the day it is how we get down to the ground. We have them higher up too, to get from different platform levels. Those are always functional regardless of what time it is. Oh look, the one we were looking at is being lowered to the ground now."

Arleth watched in fascination as the rectangular box was lowered along the ropes to the ground.

"Do they never break?"

"Occasionally a rope gets worn out and frays a bit and it gets replaced. Or the crank get stuck and needs to be replaced."

"No I mean, when people are in them?" Arleth was a little hesitant to ride up so high in a box supported by nothing but ropes.

"Oh, no it has never happened. Certain talywags are specifically responsible for upper safety and maintenance. They report and fix any problems before an issue arises. Also there are weight and number limitations on how many can fit in an upper at one time."

"Oh really, so how many can fi..."

"DAAAAAADDDD!" Zeeshan cut her off with his roar. He ran full speed at the door to the upper that had just opened. A pale green creature stepped out, followed by the messenger that had been sent to find him. The creature was quite short, about shoulder height Arleth guessed and very slender. It had a rather disproportionately large head with two bulging brown eyes the size of plates. To Arleth, the creature, which she assumed was a Talywag, looked quite awkward, as if it would tip over on its head at any moment.

The Talywag took one look at the creature flying at him, uttered a high-pitched scream and ran back into the upper, practically pushing the messenger out of his way.

"Shit!" Aedan raced past Arleth after Zeeshan.

Arleth, not wanting to miss anything followed after him at full speed.

When Arleth and Aedan reached them, Zeeshan was banging on the bars of the upper calling for his dad to come out. The talywag was cowering in the corner as far away from Zeeshan as he could be.

"Whhaaaattt issss iittttt?" The Talywag stammered.

Aedan winced at his choice of words. "Zeeshan," he put his hand gently on the child's arm, "Zeeshan, stop for a second."

"Zeeeessshhhannn?" the Talywag said in confusion.

"High Councilman Crean, this is your son."

The Councilman screamed.

Zeeshan, realizing for the first time that his own dad didn't recognize him and was in fact terrified of him, collapsed on the ground and burst into tears.

Arleth and Aedan looked at each other and without a word, Arleth turned to Zeeshan, and went over to him. Arleth walked over to her friend and climbed into his lap. His whole body shook with the force of his sobs. Arleth desperately wanted to say something, anything that would make Zeeshan feel better, but she had no idea what that would be. Instead she just wrapped her arms around him as best she could and hugged him silently.

After a few minutes, Zeeshan's sobs subsided slightly and Arleth felt a tap on her shoulder. She turned around to see Aedan, with Zeeshan's dad close behind. Aedan tilted his head as a signal and Arleth, picking up on it climbed off Zeeshan. Aedan took his sister's hand and the two of them walked a little distance off to give Zeeshan and his father some privacy.

The Talywag climbed into his son's lap, the same way Arleth had and reached up to wipe the tears from his eyes.

"I can't imagine how hard that is for both of them," Aedan said to Arleth as they could see father and son begin to talk to each other.

"Is Zeeshan's dad going to accept him?"

"Yes of course. He loves his son, I just had to calm him down enough to realize his son really was the huge creature he sees now, not the small 7 year old Talywag he thought went missing a week ago."

"That's good," Arleth was relieved.

Selene came up behind them. "I hate to break up their reunion, but we have a lot to discuss and I think we should get started."

"True, you are right."

The three of them walked over to Zeeshan and his father. "High Councilman Crean, I hate to interrupt, but we have a lot we need to discuss. I suggest you call a council immediately."

The Talywag looked at his king and nodded. "I will have the council ready in an hour and half."

The Talywag held his son's paw in his much smaller hand and together the two of them made their way to the upper. Aedan and Selene, with Arleth following close behind walked away to organize their army's ascent into Occa.

* * *

"You can't possibly expect us to abandon Occa at the drop of a hat, and what, live in a *cave*?"

Selene, Aedan and Zeeshan were sitting in the high council meeting with Zeeshan's father and the other six members. It had started later than planned, due mostly in part to the extra hour it had taken to calm down the council and explain who and what Zeeshan was and why he was no longer a Talywag. And when the council had finally started, it hadn't gotten much better. In fact, so far it was going pretty much exactly as well as Selene had expected.

Terribly

"You will not be safe in Occa," Aedan repeated for the third time. "Absalom has made it clear he is targeting Talywags. You yourself said that a number of children have gone missing."

"That is nothing new," councilman Duhn continued. "Talywag children go missing occasionally, they go exploring, or aren't back before it gets dark and they get eaten."

"Fine, but not this time. Isn't Zeeshan proof that Absalom is specifically using Talywags. Now that he has created a successful creature, do you think he will stop with just one? No of course not."

"And he knows that Zeeshan is with us," Selene continued. "He knows we know. He will strike hard and fast."

"So what if he does?" Zeeshan's father countered. "We have been safe in Occa for generations."

Aedan struggled to control his anger. How stubborn could someone be? "Safe by hiding in trees, from mindless Vrog."

"It has been successful for hundreds of years," councilman Yurin interjected.

"Yes and against the Vrog, it likely always will be." Aedan agreed, "However, Absalom's armies are not the Vrog. They are not mindless, they will not be deterred by mere trees. They will use magic and fire and weapons. None of which the Talywags can defend against. You are utterly defenceless. Not to mention, the creatures Absalom is making - Talywags and snow bear hybrids - *snow bears climb trees*."

"Bah," Duhn retorted, "So what? Our own children wouldn't hurt us, regardless if they are part snow bear."

The stupidity of that comment stunned Aedan and Selene speechless for a moment.

"Right Zeeshan? You have been...*combined*... but you wouldn't try and kill us right?"

"No, but.."

"See, problem solved." Duhn sat back and crossed his arms, satisfied with his logic.

"But," Zeeshan continued. "My combination wasn't fully successful. My friend Thom... his was. When it was done, he didn't recognize me anymore. He was.. gone.... a puppet. I have no doubt he would have killed me had Rogan ordered it." He shivered at the memory.

"You cannot be certain."

"I can, " Selene countered. "We have had enough experience with Rogan's experiments to know that the person left over is no longer themselves. They are just a mindless husk left to do Rogan or Absalom's will as they command. Zeeshan was very lucky that his experiment was a failure, it only affected his physical appearance, not his mind."

The council burst into an uproar.

"Calm down, calm down." High Councilman Crean yelled, trying to take back control of the council. "Let's say that everything you are saying is correct."

"It's not," councilman Duhn and Yurin said in unison.

"Assuming it is," Crean continued, glaring at them. "Why do we need to leave Occa? Can't we just stay here? You brought part of your army, can't you defend off Absalom's attack?"

Aedan sighed.

"We may be able to defend Absalom's attack, *if* we are able to build up your defences, *if* there is time. But Occa is not easily defended, plus we don't know how many Absalom will get to attack us. On top of that, even if we are able to push back Absalom's attack, we can't stay to help you defend against him in the future. He will keep coming back until he gets what he wants."

"Come with us and we can defend you in our stronghold. So far Absalom hasn't even been able to find where it is." Selene added.

The seven council members looked at each other.

"Give us ten minutes to discuss and we will let you know what we decide."

"Sure," Aedan said, not having any other choice.

The Talywags stood up and left the room.

"This is frustrating," Zeeshan growled.

"It sure is," Selene agreed. "For such a smart race, they are passive to the point of stupidity. It just boggles my mind."

"How can they possibly expect that sitting and hiding in trees will protect them from Absalom's army?" Aedan seethed.

Zeeshan and Selene just shook their heads.

* * *

Almost 45 minutes later, the council returned.

"We have reached a decision," Zeeshan's father announced. "We will stay in Occa. It is our home, we have been safe here for hundreds of years, we will continue to be so. We will however, except your help in building fortifications and defence for when the attack comes."

"And what will you do when we are gone and Absalom attacks again?" Aedan queried.

"We will repel them again," Crean said unworriedly.

"You are an idiot." Zeeshan roared at him. "You are all idiots." He stormed from the room.

Aedan wanted to do the exact same thing, but he restrained himself. "Fine, Winn and Graydon will lead the defence of Occa with their army. Selene, Arleth, Val and I need to leave immediately so we will begin fortifications tonight."

"Tonight? Nonsense. You are the true king after all," Crean said. "It would not be proper for you to visit and us not to throw a party. Not proper at all."

"We really don't have time for a party." Selene said.

"No arguments, the preparations are already underway. You can begin tomorrow morning. Absalom won't attack at night and contend with the Vrog."

And with that the seven Talywags left on mass as if to ensure no further arguments ensued.

Aedan and Selene were left in the council chamber alone.

"Ridiculous," Aedan shook his head.

"I'll go put up some detection spells before this stupid party. I won't have time to do much else, but at least we will know if an attack is coming."

"Good idea, and I'll ensure a guard is posted."

"Crean probably is right that Absalom won't attack tonight, even he would hesitate to cross Frasht Forest at night, but that doesn't mean he won't come first thing in the morning."

"Yup," Selene agreed "It doesn't mean that at all."

As they left the council chamber, Val was waiting for them outside. He looked at their angry faces, "So how did it go?"

Aedan rolled his eyes, "We are having a party."

"Oh how splendid, I love parties."

Chapter 28

"They are all idiots." Zeeshan complained to Arleth, explaining to her what had happened in the council meeting. "I used to think we were the smartest race, now I don't think so."

Arleth frowned in sympathy.

"I mean, how could they do NOTHING?"

"I dunno."

Zeeshan slumped heavily onto the bed and it groaned under his weight, "They saw what Rogan did to me... I don't get it."

There was a knock on the door and Selene's head popped in, "Can I come in?"

Arleth nodded.

Selene walked in, resplendent in a knee length pale yellow dress. She was holding something blue in her arms.

"I didn't imagine you wanted to wear your dusty travelling clothes to the party?" Selene asked, giving Arleth the once over.

"Oh, no?" Arleth looked down at her clothes and blushed. "No, I guess not."

"I found this for you." She unrolled the blue bundle in her arms and held it out to Arleth.

She looked at the blue dress the woman was holding out to her and smiled. "Thank you Selene!"

"It's Talwag so likely much too short for you, but try it on and I can adjust it for you."

Arleth took the dress from Selene and hugged her, "I've never had a dress to wear to a party before, it's beautiful." She turned and skipped away towards the adjoining room to change.

Selene laughed, at least there was one person who was looking forward to the party.

"You sure you don't want to come to the party," Selene turned to ask Zeeshan.

"No!" he slammed his paws down on the bed with enthusiasm. The bed make a dangerous creaking noise and Zeeshan quickly folded is arms up, "I'm sick of Talywags right now."

So was Selene to be honest, "But they are your people, don't you want to see your friends again?"

"No!" It looked like Zeeshan was pouting, "I see how everyone looks at me, like some kind of freak. Even my own dad ran away from me."

Selene came over to sit beside him and put her hand on his arm.

"It might take a while, Zeeshan, I'm not going to lie to you. But they are still your people and they will accept you, just like your dad did. He was only startled because he had never seen you like that before."

"I know, it's not only my dad... the entire council... I'm scared to even see my mom... I just, I want to avoid it for now."

Selene couldn't blame him.

"And besides, I'm already angry right now at the stupid council, I don't want to make things even worse by having an outburst."

"You are much wiser than your 7 years Zeeshan." Selene said, patting him on the arm.

Zeeshan sighed.

"It will get easier, Zeeshan, I guarantee it," Selene said with a conviction she didn't feel.

Zeeshan just put his head in his hands, Selene sighed sadly and rubbed his back.

"OK what do you think?" Zeeshan and Selene looked up as Arleth bounded into the room.

"Arleth! I can see your underwear!" Zeeshan said, covering his face with his paw.

"Oh ya," Arleth looked down un-phased, "It's a bit short. But Selene you can help me with that right?"

"I sure can. It fits nicely everywhere else though which is good."
Selene put her hands on the hem at the front of Arleth's dress and pulled. A stream of light flowed from Selene's hands onto the dress and as Arleth watched, the dress extended slowly until it was knee length. Selene turned Arleth around and did the same to the back.

"Perfect," Selene said stepping back to admire her work. "Looks like it was that long to begin with. Zeeshan, it's safe to look now."

Zeeshan peered through a crack in his fingers, and then assessing that Selene was telling the truth, removed his hand altogether.

"Arleth you look beautiful."

"I do?" Arleth blushed.

"You sure do," Selene agreed. "Let me just fix up your hair."

From out of nowhere, a hair brush materialized and Selene handed it to Arleth.

Arleth took it and brushed her hair. "You sure you don't want to come to the party Zeeshan?"

"No, it's ok. I've told you why I want to stay."

Arleth nodded, her smile fading, "I know, I'm sorry."

"And besides," Zeeshan continued, wanting his friend's smile to return, "You are too beautiful, you would put me to shame."

Arleth laughed despite herself, "You are silly."

* * *

"It has been a long time since the rightful ruler of Oherra has held power in Iridian," High Councilman Crean began. "But at least today we are finally able to welcome the mighty Aedan Amara to Occa."

There was a loud roar of applause. Aedan raised his mug and smiled in acknowledgement.

"But Aedan is not all we have," Crean continued when the cheering died down. "Travelling with him is his once-presumed dead, sister Arleth." Pointing at her, "Who we can see is very much alive and radiant."

"He has quite the flare for the dramatic, doesn't he?" Graydon whispered over to his brother.

"I dunno the excessive drool might season the food."

Graydon smiled and rolled his eyes.

"..And the ever beautiful Selene," Crean continued.

"This is such a waste of time," Graydon whispered back, *"We need to be setting up defences, preparing for war, not listen to flattery at a banquet."*

"See that is where we are different brother. If we are guaranteed certain death defending a people that don't want the help, I at least want to go out with a fancy name. Crean seems good at that...Winn the Magnificent, Winn the Handsome..."

"Winn the Annoying," Graydon whispered back, rolling his eyes yet again.

"Winn the conqueror of women's hearts," he continued unphased.

"And lastly, Winn and Graydon, brothers and Aedan's trusted friends," Crean finished.

Graydon looked over at this brother and put his hand over his mouth to control his laughter.

Winn's eyes were open in shock.

"Not quite the dropper of women's underpants just yet, brother," Graydon nudged his brother, enjoying himself immensely.

"ONLY. trusted. friends?!" Winn mouthed.

"And now let the feast begin," Crean announced as the banquet doors behind him flew open and dozens of talywags came out, laden with platters

"Hey cheer up," Graydon poked his brother "The food is here. You may not die with a fancy name, but at least with a full stomach."

* * *

"And whatf isf thess?" Arleth asked, her mouth full.

Aedan ripped himself off a piece of the pastry Arleth had taken and took a bite. "Hmm maybe orange custard?" Aedan said chewing slowly.

"WOrangh Whatft?" Arleth asked, shoving another huge piece in her mouth.

"Orange Custard."

"Ahh." Arleth swallowed with a gulp. "I like orange custard." She wiped cream from her face with the back of her hand.

"I can see that," Aedan replied, bemused.

"You also liked the rabbit soup, the yuntafruit salad.." Selene started.

"The candied yams," Aedan continued

"The fillet of Tros," Selene added

"The poached Olope eggs."

"And of course, the fresh gho cheese *was just to die for*," Aedan and Selene said in unison, laughing.

Arleth blushed, "Well the food is delicious and I'm just being a good guest.. eating everything."

"A lot of everything," Aedan interjected with a huge smile.

"Naturally," Arleth nodded putting another huge chunk of orange custard pastry in her mouth.

"I hope you are enjoying yourselves," High Councilman Crean approached the trio.

Arleth nodded as politely as she could with her mouth stuffed full.

"We are," Aedan agreed. "You have shown us the utmost hospitality." He hesitated not sure if he should continue or not, "But it still doesn't solve the problem of your safety. It would have been much more prudent if we had spent this time preparing for Absalom's armies."

Crean looked annoyed by this, but tried to hide it. "Selene, Aedan, you two come with me, I want to show you something."

Selene and Aedan rose from the table and looked back at Arleth.

"You two go, I'm fine here" A young talywag wearing a flowery yellow dress came up to the table carrying a new plate of desserts. Arleth took one from the child with a smile, "Make that *very* fine here."

The two of them shook their head at her in amusement and turned to follow the Talywag. He led them across the room, away from the massive dining tables they had been sitting at, across the dance floor where a few brave talywags were just beginning to venture onto and out to a huge balcony. Crean walked over to the railing and gestured for them to follow.

"Look down, what do you see?" He implored at his guests.

Aedan and Selene peered over the railing. From the light of the banquet behind them, they could just make out a throng of dark shapes milling around below them. But they didn't need to see them clearly to know what they were.

"Vrog." Selene said

"Yes, Vrog." Crean asserted. "Every night it is the same. As soon as the sun goes down, dozens of them flock to the base of our city and growl up at us." Almost as if on cue, one of the beasts let out an eerie howl, followed by a second and a third.

"They come every night, they are angry and hungry. They are frustrated they can't get to us in the trees. Children even like to throw things at them and tease them. But they have never been able to attack us, not even close. Not once, in hundreds of years."

Aedan sighed. "I am not arguing that High Councilman. The Vrog are a terrifying species. Because of them, travellers only go through the Frast Forest when they absolutely have no other choice, and even then only during the day, with the utmost caution. Yet the Talywags have discovered a way to live right among them in safety for, as you said, hundreds of years."

"Exactly," Crean said beaming in pride.

"But Absalom's army is not like the Vrog. They are not mindless beasts, unable to adapt to be able to climb a tree." Aedan paused here, he was at a loss. What more could he say that he hadn't already said?

"You remember the Northern Annihilation?" Selene jumped in, trying a different tactic. "Of course you do. Everyone who was alive then remembers it. It was terrible. Absalom wiped out five entire cities in a few weeks. *A few weeks*. And he destroyed some of Oherra's best defensive cities, home to the world's elite military forces. And he did this at the beginning of his power. Before Rogan became as powerful as he is now, before the Grekens, before this new snow bear- Talywag combination. And before who knows what else he has created since then. If he can wipe out 5 cities who fight back with full armies, how can you expect to defend yourself against him when the Talywag don't know how to fight, your city is unprotected and Absalom's strength has increased immeasurably?"

But Crean was unmoved. "Who's to say Absalom is even going to attack us? You seem so certain, but he has left us alone since he usurped the throne. The Northern Annihilation that you mention, he could have easily destroyed us then, as you say it would be easy," he added distainfully," along with the other cities. We are the closest city to the five he destroyed as you know. But he didn't. He didn't care about us then, he won't care about us now."

Aedan threw up his hands in desperation. "How can you be so blind?" He yelled. "Have you not seen what happened to your son? You must realize that the number of Talywags 'gone missing' has far exceeded what is normal."

"If Absalom comes, we will defeat him." The High Councilman retorted. "We will have part of the Jayan army led by Winn and Graydon, so our city will no longer be *defenceless*. If they come we will repel them. And if they don't, which I'm willing to bet on, then I guess we will be better able to defeat the Vrog who are clearly such a threat." He pointed down to the milling mass below and laughed derisively.

Aedan stared in shock for a few minutes, unable to believe what he was hearing. "For a smart race you Talywags can be pretty stubbornly stupid, you know that?"

"I will not stand here and be spoken to like this in my own city. If you weren't who you are, I wouldn't have stood here this long. But you are Aedan Amara and so the council agreed to entertain your *ideas*. But as I said I will not take this abuse. Good night Aedan, I hope you enjoy the rest of Talywag hospitality." He turned on his heel and stormed off, back into the banquet.

Aedan and Selene stared after him in silence. Selene took hold of Aedan's arm and rubbed it gently.

"How can they be so ignorant, so stubborn, so..." Aedan sputtered. "I almost want to leave them to their own defences and let them deal with the consequences."

"You don't mean that," Selene said.

"No I don't, of course I don't. We have to help them regardless of how little they want us too. But I can't help thinking how many of our soldiers we are risking for a useless cause, for a people that don't appreciate it. If anything happens to Winn or Graydon.." Aedan left the rest unsaid.

"I know," Selene said as soothingly as she could. She was as frustrated as Aedan was, but trying to not show it.

"So what did you say to our host to piss him off so much?" Val said, coming out onto the balcony. Winn and Graydon were close behind him. " He stormed in to the banquet like a child that had been scolded."

Aedan sighed. "He was arguing with me again for the merits of staying and doing nothing."

"Ahh."

"The council apparently doesn't even think there is a threat of attack," Aedan continued.

"Oh fun, that should make our jobs easier," Winn replied sarcastically. "Train an army of non-fighters in perhaps only one day for a battle they don't believe will happen."

"Less than one day, we still have to set up defences, " Graydon added.

"I'm sorry," Aedan said. "This isn't fair to you two, or your army. You will likely lose a lot of men in this, because the Talywag are too stubborn to listen to reason."

Winn got serious instantly. "It's alright Aedan," He clapped him on the shoulder. "We have no choice but to defend the Talywags and we are honoured to do so. Just because the council is stubborn and set in their ways, it doesn't mean that the entire city deserves to be destroyed. When the battle starts we will do the best we can for as long as we can. When it becomes apparent what the outcome will be, and if it's not in our favour we will get out as many Talywags and people to safety as we can."

"Including yourselves."

"Including ourselves. Speaking of that Selene, since Occa is kind of in the trees and all, I may need your magical assistance in creating an escape route."

"I already have some ideas."

"Perfect."

Aedan put his hand on both Winn and Graydon's shoulders. "Val and I will be leaving here at first light, as soon as the Vrog are gone, so I probably won't get another chance to say this. I don't want to waste another minute here, and I certainly don't relish the thought of meeting with the High Councilman again."

"I thoroughly second that." Val agreed.

"Winn, Graydon, I know I am asking a lot of you and your men and I know you do it gladly. But please keep your safety in mind. This is just one battle in the war and we need both of you for the long road ahead. Not to mention both of you are like brothers to me and I don't want to lose either of you."

"Don't worry, we are a hardy bunch," Winn said trying to lighten the mood a bit.

"We won't let you down," Graydon agreed, clasping Aedan's forearm.

"I know you won't."

A burst of laughter erupted from inside the banquet hall, cutting the tension in the group outside. They all turned to look. Arleth was on the dance floor. She and a group of Talywag children had their arms linked together and were spinning around in circles, laughing and giggling the whole time.

"That is why we fight," Winn said softly. "So those children can have a future, regardless of what their parents believe."

* * *

Halfway across Oherra, Absalom couldn't sleep. He stood at the window in his bed chamber, gazing to the East.

Torch light reflected off the window causing him to look down at the plains below where his armies were assembling. From his height it looked like the entire plain was alive, a writhing mass of shadows.

Ten thousand men.

Add in the four dozen Imari he hoped to have created before they set off, and a handful of Greken, *Enjoy your last night Occa*, he thought, a smile forming on his lips.

Chapter 29

It was still pitch black outside when Aedan woke from a restless sleep. He had tossed and turned all night, his mind racing with a million thoughts. He regretted how angry he had let himself become at Crean, he kept going over and over in his head what he said to him, wishing he could take it back and at the same time wishing he could have been stronger in convincing the Talywags to leave Occa. He hated leaving two of his best friends to defend Occa in what he couldn't help thinking was sure to be a slaughter. Should he have forced them all to leave, made them leave by brute strength?

He worried about Arleth and if Samara would be able to help her. Was she even ready to use her gift? Or would it destroy her?

He tried to think of a strategy for when him and Val reached Kalshek, but there were too many intangibles.

And on top of all that, every time he was close to drifting off, his body jolted awake in shock at the thought that it was almost dawn and he should be leaving.

"What time is it?" Selene said, stirring in the bed beside him. She half sat up and peered at the window at the foot of the bed, "It still seems like the middle of the night."

"It is, I just couldn't sleep."

"Neither could I, too many things on my mind."

"Tell me about it."

Selene rolled over to face Aedan, although she couldn't make out more than a shadow of him in the darkness. "Do you ever wonder what it would be like to not be us, and to lead a normal life."

"Or how different things would be if my parents were still alive?"

"Exactly."

"Every day."

"Me too."

Aedan reached for Selene in the darkness and pulled her into his arms. "Don't worry, when this is all over, I will make good on that promise to marry you. And we can go about seeing how boring and normal we can be."

Selene laughed, "Boring sounds wonderful."

They lay in each other's arms for a while, until there was a faint knock at the door.

"Are you two awake? I heard talking."

"Come in Val, we are awake."

They could hear the doorknob turning and then abruptly it stopped. "Um is it safe?"

Selene laughed, "Yes Val, come on in." She disentangled herself from Aedan and sat up.

The door opened, and a wash of light from the hall seeped in. Val entered, already fully clothed for the trip, with his travel bag on his back.

"You couldn't sleep either?" Aedan asked.

"No, I've bloody been up for hours."

Aedan and Selene murmured in agreement. Aedan sat up and swung his legs over the side of the bed, his stomach grumbled loudly. "I don't suppose you have any food in that pack of yours?"

"Ahh, no."

"Alright, give us a few minutes and we will go see what food we can find."

Val stepped back out of the bedroom into the hall, closing the door behind him.

Ten minutes later, Selene and Aedan appeared, both were fully dressed and Aedan was carrying his travel bag. Occa wasn't used to receiving important travellers - or travellers at all - and since they were run by a council, no one residence was big enough to hold them all. So Arleth, Aedan, Val, Selene, Winn and Graydon had spent the night in Occa's only hotel, aptly aimed *The Inn*. The six of them had taken up the entire 5 rooms it contained. Their army had been forced to find space where they could with individual Talwag families, and a large number of them had pulled out their bed rolls and slept on the floor of the banquet hall once last night's party had ended.

Aside from the three of them, *The Inn* was dead quiet as they made their way softly down the hall.

"The other three must still be sleeping," Aedan whispered. Selene and Val nodded.

They made their way to the *The Inn's* kitchen and Selene created a light ball so they could see what they were doing. "You said bye to

Arleth last night, right?" She asked Aedan as he started opening cupboards.

"Yes, she seemed quite relieved I wasn't going to wake her up at the crack of dawn to say my goodbyes then."

"Ok well that's good then."

There was a bang as Val slammed a cupboard closed.

"There's nothing in here. In any of these. They must really NEVER get visitors."

"Shh, we don't want to wake all of Occa," Aedan admonished softly. "But you are right." He closed the cupboard he had just opened, "There is nothing in here."

"They must have some food in the banquet hall kitchens. If not anything in storage, at least left-overs from last night."

Selene and Val nodded in agreement and the three of them made their way across Occa to the banquet hall. Aside from their own soldiers they had posted the night before to keep guard, they didn't pass a single soul. The city was silent except for the constant low level growl of the Vrog far below.

"The Talywags feel way too safe here," Val said, "It's kind of incredible that the entire city completely shuts down at night. Completely. And they have no defences. Zero."

"Preaching to the choir, Val." Aedan said.

Val sighed, "I know."

When they reached the banquet hall kitchens, they found a storage room that was stocked with dried meat, fruit and cheese. Aedan and Val opened up their packs and stuffed in as much as they could fit. What they couldn't fit they ate as breakfast.

"Much better," Aedan said, satisfied.

"Definitely." Val agreed. "Let's go see what our hairy friends are doing, see if we can leave soon."

Aedan nodded in agreement, and the two of them made their way across the hall to the same balcony where last night Aedan and Crean had exchanged words. They tiptoed around the outside of the room to avoid stepping on their sleeping soldiers, nodding acknowledgments to those that were already awake.

They found Selene already out on the balcony looking off into the trees. "The Vrog are still here." Selene said, turning as she heard them approach.

Aedan came to stand beside her and looked down at the Vrog and then off at the forest. "It should be getting light soon. I guess all we can do is wait."

45 impatient minutes later, the rising sun just cleared the top of shortest trees in Frasht Forest. As soon as the first beam of light reached them, as if they were controlled by an invisible master, the Vrog as one stopped growling. They turned around as a unit and in a trance, started slowly making their way back towards the forest, their arms hanging limply at their sides.

"Wow," Selene breathed in awe, "Talk about a biological clock."

"Talk about creepy." Val said.

"Ya that too," Selene agreed.

"Well I guess we are safe to leave now." Aedan chimed in.

Val walked over to Selene and gave her a hug, "Good luck Selene, be safe."

"You too, Val." She replied squeezing him tight.

After a few seconds Val pulled away, "I'll go back inside, talk to the soldiers a bit, give you guys some privacy." He turned and walked away.

Selene reached into her pocket and produced a worn brown cloth bag, which she handed over to Aedan. He took it quizzically and reached inside. His hand grasped onto the round, smooth object inside and realization suddenly dawned on him. "It's a communication ball."

"Yes. It's not a particularly strong one. I made a few of them last night, but I had to use most of my strength to erect the protection shield around Occa. Still though it should last for a few uses, assuming you only use it for a few minutes at a time, so only use it when you absolutely need to. You will have one, I will be giving Winn and Graydon one and I have one for Arleth and myself. It's already created to communicate with each of the other two. You just need to say one of our names and it will open up communication. If someone is trying to reach you on yours, it will light up, and hum. It will keep getting louder and louder until you answer it."

"Answer it the same way as always?"

"Yes."

"Ok." Aedan drew the drawstrings on the bag closed again and put it into his breast pocket. "I'm sure this will come in handy. At the very least I will let you know how my discussions with Kalshek go."

"And when you do, I'll tell you about how Arleth is fairing with Selene.

She reached out and grabbed Aedan's hands, bringing them together against her chest. "Good luck my dear. I have faith that you will convince him to join with us."

Aedan smiled and bent down to kiss her forehead. "Good luck to you as well." He took his hands out from hers and wrapped her in a hug, pulling her close. "Make sure you get out of Occa as soon as you can. Not only for Arleth, I don't want either of you stuck in this city when the battle begins."

"Don't worry. We will be out of here by noon."

"Perfect."

The two of them were silent for a few minutes, wrapped in each others' arms enjoying the last few minutes they would have with each other for the foreseeable future.

After a while, Aedan sighed and pulled away. "I really should be going." He kissed her. "I love you Selene."

"I love you too."

He kissed her one more time and then, fighting every urge to stay a bit longer, he turned and walked away.

Selene watched his retreating back and then when he was out of sight, she turned and walked back to the railing. She looked out across the clearing at the forest. All the Vrog were already out of sight. It was approaching mid-morning and was fully light now. She knew she should be going, but she lingered a bit longer. This was the calm before the storm, the last few minutes she had to herself. Despite everything, the morning was beautiful, she took in as much as she could, to feed her memory for when she needed it. The sunlight, on the trees in the distance, the clear blue sky without a trace of cloud, the faint smells of bread just beginning to bake...

"Lost in thought?"

Selene turned and came face to face with Winn and Graydon.

"Yes, I was."

"Val and Aedan have already left, I'm assuming?" Winn asked.

"Ya, a little while ago."

Graydon nodded. "Did you guys raid all the food at *The Inn*?"

Selene smiled, "No we couldn't find any either, that's why we came here. The kitchen is full of food."

"Oh we know, we have already been there." Winn said with a grin, a slice of cheese materializing out of nowhere. He popped it in his mouth. "And we took some with us, clearly."

"Do you guys know if Arleth was awake when you left?"

"Actually yes, she knocked on my door this morning," Graydon said.

"Oh?" Selene said

Graydon promptly blushed. "Err, not like that, she wanted to tell me something."

"Go on." Selene smiled and stole a glance at Winn. He was shaking his head, as if trying to tell her something.

"She wanted to say goodbye to Zeeshan before she left, so she said she was going to his house. And asked if you could meet her there when it was time to leave."

"Ahh," Selene said. Kind of disappointed. She looked over at Winn, he was giving her a *see I tried to tell you* kind of look.

"What are you two doing?" Graydon asked, noticing their back and forth looks for the first time. "What is happening?"

"Don't worry about it." Winn said

"And yes Graydon. I will gladly meet Arleth at Zeeshan's house."

"Good. That is what I told her you would say."

"Ok well time is a wasting," Winn said getting serious. "The three of us need to talk some battle strategy."

"We shouldn't do it here. Some place more private," Selene said.

"We could go back to *The Inn,* it's now deserted," Graydon offered.

"Good idea little brother."

* * *

"I built a rudimentary shield over Occa last night before the banquet." Selene was sitting cross-legged on the end of Winn's bed back at *The Inn*. Winn and Graydon were sitting at the opposite end of the bed, facing her, with their backs against the wall. "Shield's take an enormous amount of power and time, especially to hold up to the sort of onslaught we expect Absalom will hit us with. A normal protective shield like the one I built around our stronghold, is built a little each day for many months. That particular one I built to be self-sustaining. Each day I poured my strength into it, building on what was already there until after a few months, the shield was able to self-sustain. It is almost like a living organism, it will heal itself if physically or magically damaged. I even built it to take nutrients from the air so it will keep growing stronger and stronger gradually over time. It would take months of sustained, constant attack to bring it down, and that's if it was left alone, with no one (me) to keep pouring magic into it."

"Wow that's pretty incredible," Graydon said in awe.

"Thanks," Selene said. "But that being said. I can't do the same here. I don't have months to pour more and more of my strength into it, and the shield won't have time to develop to be self-sustaining before it is attacked."

"Naturally, so you are doing the best you can. We understand Selene." Winn lifted his knees up to his body. "So what are we working with?"

"Well as I mentioned, I started the shield last night. The way it is currently it will last for about one hour of constant attack."

"Describe constant attack, please." Winn queried.

"A continual onslaught of non-magical weapons, such as arrows, spears etc. This also includes any physical attacks by the Imari, Grekens, soldiers or any other creature Absalom may have. However, if there is any sort of magical attack, the one hour would lessen considerably, according to how powerful the spell that was used."

"Ok that makes sense. but.."

"But," Selene interrupted Winn, holding up one finger at him to hold on."I will be pouring a lot more strength into it today. I have already created everything I wanted to, so I will be able to spare a large amount of energy to use in it. After we are done here, I plan on doing exactly this. The shield should then be able to last about four hours of onslaught, with the same reduction if magic is used against it."

"That is a much better number to work with." Winn nodded in approval.

"And I created this." Selene reached into the right breast pocket of her tunic and pulled out a small object, which she offered to Winn.

"What is it?" The object was a dull black rectangular slab, about half the size of Winn's hand. In the middle was a green cross.

"It is the best I could do to offer a patch, when the shield starts to fail. You will notice it start to fail when a few objects will begin to get through; for example one out of every 10 arrows will come though.

That sort of thing. When that happens, the shield will completely fail within minutes. Press the green cross and it will buy you a bit more time, minutes only. But hopefully enough to help. I hope you have some plans" Selene urged hopefully. "Four hours of duration is based on a constant barrage. Any type of defence you are able to muster that would prevent the shield from having to work, would of course increase how long it lasts."

Graydon and Winn looked at each other and smiled. "We have some plans."

For the next thirty minutes, Graydon and Winn outlined their defences to Selene. She listened, approved for the most part and added some of her own improvements. By the end, they were all fairly satisfied with what they had come up with.

"Oh I almost forgot," Selene said. "I also have a communication ball for you two. Aedan and Val have one as well, as will Arleth and I." She gave them the same synopsis she had given Aedan a little earlier.

Winn reached out to take it from her. "Thanks Sele... Ahh, Oh!"

Graydon slapped his hand away. "I don't think so brother, you got the last toy. This one is mine." He took it from Selene and put it in his pocket.

"Pfft," Winn humpfed, "You had better not lose it."

"Like I would."

Selene looked back and forth at the brothers and shook her head with a smile. "If you two children would like to say good bye to Arleth before we leave." Selene paused as Graydon punched his brother playfully in the shoulder. "I am heading there now," she continued rolling her eyes.

Winn punched his brother back "We will come."

* * *

Zeeshan roared with laughter as Arleth tottered around the room. Her cheeks were bulged out as far as possible and she held her arms out at her sides. "I am Bella, I am the most beautiful person in the universe. If only I could see my toes." She looked down and craned her neck, frowning. "I know they are there somewhere." Arleth continued her comical tottering for a few more minutes as Zeeshan howled with laughter. Suddenly she stopped, smiled at Zeeshan and dropped onto the floor at Zeeshan's feet. "And that is Bella."

The two of them were in Zeeshan's bedroom back at his house. When it was built, it was a suitably sized room for a Talywag child, now however, Zeeshan was much too large for it. As he had learned last night, he didn't fit in his room with his bed, so it had been removed, along with all of his furniture. A pile of blankets with a heap of pillows sufficed as his makeshift bed for now. Even still, Zeeshan, sitting on his "bed" just about touched the ceiling and with his legs outstretched, touched the far wall.

Crean approached the closed door of his son's room and lifted his fist to knock. Zeeshan's laughter erupted from within and Crean smiled and hesitated, holding his fist back from the door. It was good to hear his son laugh. Zeeshan was still his son, but he was no longer the innocent 7 year old that had disappeared in Frast forest not so long ago. Not only the physical changes, which Crean was still trying to wrap his head around, but emotionally his son had matured exponentially. He knew his son was going to have a long, hard road ahead of him and he hoped he would be strong enough to help him through it. Zeeshan's laughter eased up, and Crean knocked. "I have snacks."

He shook his head to clear it, forced a smiled on his face and, holding the wooden tray in one hand, pushed the door open with the other. Crean put the tray down on Zeeshan's right leg, closed the door behind him and squeezed himself down into the tiny space left between his son and the door. Crean looked at his son's head crammed against the ceiling and his legs taking up most of the room and forced back a sigh. "I talked to the builder's guild this morning like I promised. Apparently they are busy with the Yonish's house right now. But as soon as they are done, they tell me a few weeks, they have assured me there next contract will be to expand our house to give you a bedroom that is suitable for you."

"Ok thanks Dad."

"Are you sure you don't want to move into the living room for now, you would have more room."

"No, this is my room!"

Arleth, sensing that this was an argument that they had earlier and reading that Zeeshan was starting to get heated, changed the topic. "Ooo what kind of fruit is this?" She asked Crean pointing to a red coloured object in the tray. Crean looked to her and then back at Zeeshan and slumped his shoulder's resignedly. He put a smile on his face, "Oh that is a taquir fruit. Quite sweet."

Arleth took one and bit into it, juice dribbled down her chin and she grabbed a cloth from the tray to wipe it. "That *is* good."

For the next while they sat together and ate. In between bites, they engaged in trivial small talk. None of them wanting to venture into any of the serious issues that lay just beneath the surface.

A soft knock came from the door. Bonnie, Crean's housekeeper popped her head in. "Sorry to disturb you, but you have guests."

"Oh it must be Selene," Arleth said, half getting up.

"Selene, yes. I recognize her from last night. There are also those two brothers with her, I forget their names."

"Winn and Graydon?" Arleth asked.

"Yes, that seems right."

"Send them in," Crean said. "Oh and wait, take this." He handed Bonnie the empty tray.

"Right away." Bonnie took the tray and disappeared from sight. Crean climbed over his son's legs to the far side of the room, to make space for the newcomers. There was no space to sit, so he stood at the far side of the room, wedged against the wall. No sooner had he done that, then the door opened and Selene's head popped in.

"Good morning." She said as she slid her way into the room, squeezing herself against the wall and Zeeshan.

Winn and Graydon quickly assessed the situation and stood side by side in the door way, "Morning," they said in unison.

"Good morning," Crean replied to the trio. He looked at Selene and looked down. "Selene I would like to apologize to you and Aedan, I'm assuming he has left already." Crean looked to Selene who nodded in agreement. "Well next time you speak to him, if you could pass on my regrets. I didn't treat you or Aedan fairly last night. You have travelled all this way, returned my son to me and are trying to protect us from an evil you think is imminent and I did nothing but spit on your efforts."

"There is no need for that, Crean." Selene said. "Tempers got heated on both sides, things were said that were regrettable."

"I sincerely apologize for my outburst." Crean continued. "I still don't believe we are in danger but I will cooperate with you as you see fit. It is only fair."

Arleth looked at Zeeshan across the room with a *What the heck happened last night* look. Zeeshan merely shrugged, as confused as she was.

"Thank you for that Crean, it is very noble of you. I also apologize on behalf of myself and Aedan for how we handled the situation." She paused for a few seconds. "But now that we have your cooperation, perhaps you will assist Winn and Graydon in their preparations."

"Yes, certainly."

"Great." Winn said. "Would you be able to organize the adult Talywag in 2 hours time? Tell them to meet us on the ground in front of the main upper we came up on yesterday. We will hand out weapons and organize defence."

"I can't guarantee that all the Talywags will be willing to fight, but I will do the best I can." Crean turned to Arleth and shuffled his way across the room towards her. "Arleth, my dear. It was very nice to meet you." He held her hands in his. "Thank you for being such a good friend to my son. I know you will do the Amara name proud."

Arleth blushed, "Thank you sir. I am glad I got to meet you as well."

Crean smiled and crawled across his son to reach Selene. "Good luck Selene, and please remember to pass on my message to Aedan."

"I will," Selene said softly. "Please take care of yourself."

Graydon and Winn moved back out of the door to allow Crean to pass. "I will see you two in two hours," the Talywag said.

Winn nodded at him and Crean walked bristly down the hall and out of his sight.

"Arleth, it's time for us to go as well." Selene said

Arleth nodded and crawled her way over to the door. She reached Winn first and gave him a big hug "Bye Winn. Be safe."

Winn hugged her back "I will Arleth, don't you worry. Just focus on your training. Next time I see you, you will be a powerful sorceress."

For the second time, Arleth blushed. "I don't know about that.."

"I do." Winn squeezed her again and released her.

Arleth turned to Graydon. "Bye Graydon." Hesitantly she reached her arms out to give him a hug and then dropped them. Graydon shuffled awkwardly and then pulled Arleth into a bear hug. "Bye Arleth, good luck."

Surprised, Arleth hugged him back. "Good luck to you too."

"Winn," Zeeshan called out to him. "Would you be able to train me with the rest of the Talywags? I know I am only a child. But I'm part snow bear now and, well that will probably count for something."

Winn smiled at him, "Of course you can train with the rest of the Talywags. And you are right, the snow bear in you will likely make you quite a skilled fighter, even though you have never fought before."

"Oh I hope so." And then with true snow bear menace, "I want Absalom and his shitty armies to pay for what they did to me"

"Then you shall. We will meet you in two hours with the rest of the Talywags." And with that Winn and Graydon turned and left the room.

Selene turned to Zeeshan "Goodbye Zeeshan. Remember all that I have taught you about controlling your anger?"

Zeeshan nodded.

"Forget it for the next few days. You will need all your snow bear instincts for the battle. Unleash all your fury when the fighting starts."

"I don't think that will be a problem. When I even think of Absalom, I can feel it boiling under the surface."

Selene nodded, "understandable."

"Thank you for all your help Selene, and safe journey."

"I will leave you two to say goodbye in private, I will be waiting down the hall Arleth."

"Bye again Zeeshan," she said as she left the room.

Arleth, with tears already forming in her eyes, crawled across the room to sit in Zeeshan's lap.

Over an hour later, after a long and tearful goodbye and struggling to convince their skittish horses to get in the upper and not freak out during the ride down; Selene and Arleth were finally on their way to Edika.

* * *

"Where the hell is everybody?" Zeeshan stormed. "Where are all the Talywags?"

Winn and Graydon just looked at each other: they had the same question.

2 hours had come and gone since Winn had asked Zeeshan's father to gather the adult Talywags and still not a *single* Talywag (other than Zeeshan) had shown up.

Winn looked out at his army of Jayan soldiers, who were growing ever more impatient, and tried to think of something to say to the boy.

"I'm so dissapointed in them." Zeeshan said quietly, shaking his head.

"Don't be too hard on them," Winn said. "Talywags are a timid race, you know that. Smart as all hell, but fighters, they are not." He was just as dissapointed in the Talywags as Zeeshan was, if not more, but it wouldn't help to show his true feelings now. Zeeshan needed him to keep his spirits up and so did his men. He looked at his army again. His men were risking their lives, all be it willingly, to defend a city that clearly had no interest in helping itself. He certainly didn't need to add to the morale killling.

As if reading his thoughts, "But you and your men are risking your lives to save us," Zeeshan continued."Us Talywags could at least have the decency to *show up*."

A creaking sound behind Winn saved him from having to answer. He turned around,"Ah there you go Zeeshan, some Talywags have come after all."

The main upper had just reached the ground and a dozen Talywags stepped hesitantly out. At the top of the platform were another 20 or so Talywags waiting for the upper to return so they could descend as well. So in total, *32* Talywags.

When Zeeshan turned to look at the Talywags headed their way, Graydon shot Winn a "Is that seriously it?" look behind his back. Winn responded with a shrug and what he hoped was a "I guess its better than nothing look."

"Dad!" Zeeshan said proudly. "You came."

Winn looked over at high councilman Crean in barely disguised suprise. He was one of the last people he had expected to show up, based on his outburst last night. "High Councilman Crean, it is really good to see you here."

Crean walked over to his son and laid his arm on Zeeshan's huge paw. "I wasn't going to come, but I thought if my son was brave enough to be here, than so was I. There is no harm in learning a bit of weaponry I suppose."

It was hardly the confident answer he wished the leaders of Occa would have, but at least it was something. It had gotten him here, which was more than could be said for the other councilmen or most of the adult Talywag population.

"We are glad to have you." Winn said extending a hand to Crean. The councilman shook his hand firmly and gave a brief smile.

By this point, the rest of the Talywags had reached the ground and the group of them were standing hesitantly behind Crean, a bit apart from the Jayan soliders. Winn surveyed them; all were tall and musclar - by Talywag standards - meaning they were about the size and build of a 10 year old human. Some were openly fearful, some were trying their best to put on a brave face, but to a man, it was clear just by looking at them, that none had ever picked up a weapon before. Winn and Graydon hadn't expected anything less. They knew that the defence would come down to them and their men. However they had hoped for a bit more Talywag support - 10 arrows badly fired have a better chance of hitting a target than 1. Winn fought back a sigh.

"Alright," he boomed, "Let's get started."

Chapter 30

Aedan snapped the twig in half and threw the pieces on the ground. They hit the top of the small pile he had created and he watched as they ricocheted down to land at the bottom. He sighed and picked up another twig.

"If you are that bored, I'm sure there is something else you could be doing," Val said dryly. Just before dusk, they had set up camp at the northeast edge of Frasht Forest. Since then, Val had caught a pair of small hares for their dinner, chopped some branches for firewood, gathered kindling and he was now starting a fire. Aedan on the other hand, had plopped down on the ground and set about breaking every twig in his vicinity. "Like skinning these hares," Val continued, throwing the hares at his friend. They landed on the twig pile crushing it.

"What!? Oh. Sorry," Aedan said picking up the hare in his lap. "I was thinking." In his other hand, he grabbed the hare from the middle of the broken twig pile and got to his feet. "I can't stop worrying about Occa."

"Winn and Graydon are very resourceful. I've seen them succeed many times in situations that were almost as daunting."

"Exactly, Aedan said, "*Almost* as daunting." He grabbed his knife from his pack and sat down across the budding fire from Val to skin the hares.

"They're in a damned spot, that's for sure," Val agreed. "But what choice did you have? You couldn't leave Occa undefended. The Talywags can't defend themselves. The only chance they *have* is with the Jayan army. Selene had to take Arleth to Edika. We both know you have to be the one to go to Kalshek, anyone other than an Amara would be disrespectful." Val paused for a second looking into his friend's eyes. "Winn and Graydon have to do this on their own."

Aedan sighed. "You're right, I know."

"Of course I am."

The two fell silent. After a few minutes, Val got up and added another log to the fire. Aedan stared into the flames, his mind lost in thought. His practiced hands continued to skin the hares with deft strokes. Suddenly he smiled. "Do you remember when the travelling *magician* 'Harold the Magnificent' came to Iridian when we were all young children and Winn was visting with his father?"

Val laughed, "Winn couldn't have been much more than three, it was before Graydon was born. He was so enamoured with the man that he made us call him 'Winn the Magnificent.'"

"He wore that blanked wrapped around his shoulders like a cape for weeks."

"Oh and he had that stick that he insisted was his magic wand." Val added.

Aedan laughed. "And he performed 'magic tricks' for us."

"That lasted for weeks. And then he saw Selene's mother perform real magic and it broke his poor little heart."

"I wonder if he remembers that?" Aedan asked. He gave Val an impish grin "We will need to be sure to remind him the next time we see him."

"Oh for sure."

Aedan laughed again at the thought and handed the skinned hares back to Val. Val skewered each one with a sturdy stick he had chiseled into a point and handed one back to Aedan. "It was always such fun when Winn, and later Graydon came to visit the castle with their father." Val said as he settled back down beside the fire to roast his hare.

Aedan nodded holding his skewered hare above the fire beside Val's to cook.

"Remember when they came in the winter one year, and Winn was convinced that he could skate along the outside open pathways."

"Despite not knowing how to skate, or in fact even having skates." Aedan cut in. "Didn't he convince one of the kitchen maids to make him some?".

Val shook his head laughing, "Make is a strong word. He convinved her to give him some kitchen knives which he then strapped to his boots."

"Oh *right*!" Aedan watched a drop of fat drip off his hare and fall into the fire with a sizzle. "I still remember his face as he tumbled head over heels down the pathway... many *many* times." He laughed at the memory.

"I sure learned a lot of swear words that day," Val chuckled.

"From him," Aedan agreed "And from the man he fell on when he tumbled off the pathway."

Val let out a big belly laugh, "It sure was a good thing he had the sense to try on the *lowest* platform."

Aedan grunted, "No kidding."

"I would say our dinners are almost ready," Val said abruptly changing the topic. He held his hare up to his face for closer inspection and nodded approvingly. "Yep I would say maybe 10 more minutes and they should be done."

The two friends continued cooking their dinner and trading stories back and forth about Winn and Graydon's childhood exploits. They continued long after the hares had been eaten, the skewers consumed by the fire and the fire itself reduced to embers. Although neither wanted to admit it out loud, they both felt like next time they would be sharing stories of their friends it would be as a eulogy. And so they continued talking long past the point of exhaustion, desperate to recall every fond memory they had.

* * *

When Aedan and Val were just sitting down to roast their hares, on the other side of Frasht Forest, Arleth and Selene were just about to reach the southernmost edge.

Selene had hoped to have left the forest hours ago and be much closer to Samara in Edika by now. But they had made very slow going.

Arleth's nausea from the day before had come back with full force after they had been riding for less than an hour. They had to stop many times so Arleth could dismount and throw up. Eventually they had given up riding the horses altogether. Selene had hoped that without the constant bumping up and down in the saddle, Arleth may feel a bit better. She had been right, and after a while Arleth's nausea lessened enough so that they could ride the horses again *slowly*.

A lot of time had been lost and Selene was worried. She looked over at Arleth who was sitting on a boulder and carefully nibbling a loaf of bread they had brought with them from Occa.

Arleth's nausea was getting worse.

Arleth looked up from her food, "Selene," she said hesitantly. "I saw *things* this time."

"What do you mean?"

"Back in the forest when I was throwing up. Whenever I would get an especially strong bout of nausea, I would see flashes. A giant white paw, talons, terrified eyes as large as dinner plates. And the noises..." Arleth put her hands over her ears and closed her eyes as if to shield herself from the memory. "Screams, so many screams. And then...the most terrifying laughter I have ever heard."

Selene had walked over to her when she had been talking. She now sat down on the boulder by her side and wrapped her up in her arms.

"Was I seeing... *real* things?"

Selene nodded "I am afraid you probably were." She didn't want to scare Arleth any more than necessary, but she also didnt want to sugar coat it either. "It sounds like you may have saw flashes of Rogan's enchantments."

Arleth thought back to the white paws and talons. "He is making more creatures like Zeeshan." She said it matter of factly.

"Yes," Selene hesitated, unsure whether to continue. "I would say probably a lot, based on how sick you felt this afternoon." She looked over to Arleth to gauge her reaction.

Arleth just nodded, she had already suspected this. "What is going to happen to me when the battle starts?"

Selene' s heart sunk. She had been dreading this question. She turned to face Arleth and looked into her eyes. "I don't want to lie to you Arleth."

Arleth nodded.

"You will know when the battle begins. You have visited Occa, and you have met and developed friendships with people still there: namely Zeeshan, Winn and Graydon. Your mind has a connection there so your empathic powers will be heightened. Before any weapons are fired, or anybody is killed you will be able to feel the growing threat to Occa. I am not sure how this will manifest, but I do know as the battle begins and then worsens, you will get sicker and sicker. If the battle continues for any length of time, your mind will eventually seek to protect itself and you will fall into a coma."

Arleth gave a sudden intake of breath, "Will I come out of this coma?"

"The truth?"

"Yes," Arleth said quietly, not sure she actually wanted to hear it.

"Ok." Selene continued "First, let me say that if we are safely in Edika when the battle starts, Samara will take control the first moment you feel anything and she will protect you from feeling anything further. So this next part is only if the battle starts before we get there. If you fall into a coma and we get to Samara's in time, she will still be able to help you. If we don't.."

"I die." Arleth finished for her.

"But that isn't going to happen." Selene tried to reassure her. "Samara is very powerful and she has been helping Amaran women with their gift for thousands of years. You would have to be in a coma for a *long* time for Samara to not be able to help you."

Selene wasn't too sure about this last part, but she wasn't going to take away this bit of hope. "Besides," she continued. "We will get to Edika in time, before the battle starts, so this won't be an issue." She tried to force a smile onto her face, but only partly succeeded.

Arleth saw the gesture and gave a small smile herself. She appreciated the intent. "Thank you." She said to the older woman.

Selene let Arleth sit in silence for a while to process her thoughts.

After a while, "You should really try and eat some more of that bread," she pointed at the barely eaten loaf Arleth was still holding. "And some cheese too. Regardless what happens, you will need your strength for what comes next."

Arleth nodded and did what she was told.

While she was eating, Selene walked around her and the two horses in a big circle, waving her arms and muttering under her breath.

"What are you doing?" Arleth asked her.

"I'm setting up some invisible barriers. Anyone or anything walking by us will feel the sudden need to turn in a different direction, away from our camp. I am also setting up a few surprises in case we have any magic-wielding guests. Absalom and Rogan and their army shouldn't be anywhere near this side of Frasht Forest, but I don't want to take that chance."

Arleth nodded in agreement through a mouthful of cheese.

"We will rest here a few hours. Try and get some sleep if you can. I will wake you up a few hours after midnight and we will continue our journey overnight. I want to be at Samara's by sunrise."

Arleth was quite happy to travel through the night if it meant she reached the safety of Edika sooner. She was going to voice this thought to Selene, but she could tell that the woman was deep in thought so she stayed silent.

Selene was so focused, that she didn't even hear Arleth get up from the boulder and lie down in her bed roll. It wasn't until Arleth's deep breathing broke into her train of thought that she realized Arleth was asleep.

Good she thought. *Tomorrow will be better for her if she is less exhausted from today.* Selene, still sitting on the boulder, pulled her knees up into her chest. She knew she wasn't going to get any sleep tonight - her mind was too heavy with worry.

Chapter 31

Steve shuffled back and forth on his feet nervously. Something didn't seem right, but he couldn't quite put his finger on it. For the third time in as many minutes, he squinted his eyes to look through the binoculars.

Still nothing. He couldn't see any shadows moving down in the forest below, no signs that an army was approaching. All seemed peaceful.

So why was he so on edge?

He ran his fingers along the edge of his bow, taking comfort from its familiar weight and feel. As he did, the quiver of arrows on his back jostled him ever so slightly.

Footsteps sounded behind him and Steve turned to look at who was approaching.

"Ah Gary! Is it midnight already?"

"It is."

"Wonderful." Steve picked up his bow and gave Gary a pat on the shoulder. "I haven't seen anything, all seems quiet."

"MMM" Gary mumbled by way of acknowledgment before turning away and assuming his post. Steve watched the man stare out at the forest for a few seconds and then turned away himself. He had a long day and was more than ready to catch some rest before it was his turn to stand watch again... or until the battle started.

Steve started to walk towards the town square which himself and a hundred or so fellow Jayans were using as a makeshift barracks. It was eerily quiet.

The calm before the storm.

"My mind is just playing tricks on me," Steve whispered to himself. "It's been a long day."

Steve continued walking, and then he stopped with a start, "Oh fuck!" He blurted. He knew what had been bothering him "It's *too* quiet, where in the hell are the Vrog?"

In an instant, Steve was running back to the post he had just left. "Gary!" He yelled as he approached.

Gary turned. Hearing the panic in Steve's voice, he already had his bow poised and strung, ready to fend off whatever was the source of the alarm.

"DO YOU SEE ANY VROGS?" Steve yelled at him.

"No..." Gary said slowly, confusion etched on his face. And then, realization dawned, replaced almost instantly with horror. "NO," he yelled turning around to look back into the forest. "There are no vrogs!" Even in the darkness, Steve could see how pale his friend's face had become.

"You stay here, sound the alarm." Gary said, already turning away, "I'll go find Winn and Graydon. Tell them the battle is starting."

Without waiting for a reply, Steve sprinted back towards the town square yelling, "WAKE UP, WAKE UP. THE BATTLE IS STARTING!"

A loud horn sounded from behind him. Gary had rung the alarm.

As Steve ran, he continued yelling. He ran through a residential street, and banged as loudly as he could on each door. He didn't have time to wait to see if anyone was actually waking up, but he hoped the general cacophony he was making would do the trick. By the time he had reached the town square, most of the Jayans were either awake or quickly waking up.

"The Vrogs never came," Steve yelled as he raced past. "The battle is starting."

Steve reached the Inn where he knew Winn and Graydon were staying. Before he could rush inside, the door flung open and Winn appeared, Graydon right behind him. They were fully dressed in their battle gear, weapons drawn, eyes alert.

"Is Absalom here?" Winn asked Steve, assuming correctly he was the sentry that had raised the alarm.

"Not yet, but there are no vrogs."

"Shit," Graydon said pushing past Winn. "Rogan must have done something to them."

Winn nodded, "The battle is starting."

Graydon smacked his forehead with the palm of his hand "How could we be so stupid as to think Absalom would wait until morning to avoid the Vrogs? Rogan is a *dread mage*. Of COURSE he would do something to them."

"It was a stupid mistake," Winn agreed. "But luckily not a fatal one." He put his hand on Steve's shoulder and squeezed. "You said that Absalom wasn't here yet right?"

"No, it was all quiet when I left."

"Good," Winn said "So we still have a bit of time. Graydon, go wake up highcouncilman Crean and Zeeshan. Get them to wake everyone in Occa. Even if they aren't going to fight. We don't want anyone hiding in their houses if we have to make a quick escape."

Graydon raced off to find the Talywags.

"And you," Winn turned to Steve, "Come with me." Winn sprinted to the town square, Steve right behind him.

By the time they had reached the square, Winn was pleased to see that all of the Jayans were awake and alert. Hundreds more were pouring in by the minute.

"Absalom's army is on it's way," he addressed the group. "We don't know how much time we have before they arrive. But we do know that when they come, Absalom will throw everything he has at us. In all likelihood Rogan will be with him."

He looked at the faces of his men, and was gratified to see their confident, determined expressions hadn't faltered.

"I won't lie to you, it is going to be a tough, hard battle. Not like the quick ambushes and skirmishes we have fought for so long. No matter what happens, we will keep up hope, fight hard and show those bastards what a TRUE JAYAN IS MADE OF!"

"JAYA!!!!!!!!!!!" yelled his army in unison, stomping their feet. Winn yelled with them and lifted his arm, "LET'S GET EM!" The Jayans roared again and raced to take up their posts, Winn in the lead.

In a few minutes they had reached the platform where Gary was still keeping watch. "Nothing yet." Gary said, handing Winn his binoculars and stepping back so he could take his place.

"Good." Winn said. He held up the binoculars and looked through. All he saw were trees and darkness. There didn't *appear* to be anything there yet. "We need some light," Winn said almost to himself.

"Light?" Zeeshan's voice came from right behind him. "I can get that for you." Taking full advantage of his new snowbear qualities, Zeehsan started climbing the nearest tree, heading to the higher platforms.

"Nothing yet I'm assuming," Graydon asked, coming to stand beside his brother.

Winn handed him the binoculars. "Not that I can tell, but it's too dark to be sure."

Graydon held up the binoculars to see for himself and immediately lowered them, "Yup."

Crean came beside them "We have a spotlight at the very top of the city." He pointed upwards to where his son was deftly climbing a second tree. "Its right up there." Zeeshan leapt off the tree and landed on the uppermost platform.

A blinding light hit Graydon in the face. "ACK," he cried, shielding his eyes. "Don't point it at us!"

There was a faint creaking noise and the ray of light slowly turned, pointing into the forest below them.

"That's better." Graydon handed the binoculars back to Gary and peered out into the forest.

As soon as he did, he saw movement among the trees, and a row of soliders emerged.

Winn saw it too, "Archers take your positions."

Instantly there was a shuffling and the archers organized themselves into three rows, facing outwards toward the advancing army. The first row picked up their bows and strung them, holding them poised, waiting for the command to fire.

"Where do you want us?" Crean said.

"And me," Zeeshan added, dropping back down onto the platform behind them with a thud.

"For now, go stand behind the last row of archers." He wanted them protected in case the shield didn't hold up as well as it should.

The Talywags hurried to do what they had been asked.

"There are at least fifty of those *Zeeshan-things*," Graydon said with horror, his eyes peeled on the advancing troops. "Rogan has somehow made *way* more of them than we had expected."

"And a bunch of Grekens."

"At least five thousand soldiers" Graydon added

"And they keep coming...."

"And there. Our two best friends," Graydon pointed at the two familiar figures who had appeared out of the trees.

Winn nodded "Yup, both Absalom *and* Rogan."

"I guess overkill gets lost when you are a total asshole huh?" Graydon chirped.

Winn let out a little smile, "Totally lost."

The first row of advancing soldiers looked like they were now within the archers range.

"ARCHERS READY. FIRE!" Winn called

A hail of arrows shot out into the sky and landed on the advancing army. Screams sounded as the first wave of arrows hit their targets. Soliders stumbled and fell down, to be instantly replaced with their comrades advancing from behind them.

"FIRE!" Winn called again. More screams, as hundreds more men fell down, fatally wounded.

The advancing army didn't falter, if anything the blood seemed to spur on the snow bear creatures. Winn watched in disgust as they tore through their own army to make it to the front of the pack.

"FIRE!"

This time the arrows hit mostly the Imari and did little damage. Serving more to irritate them than anything. One in particular let out a loud guttural roar. With one paw he ripped an arrow out of his arm, broke it in two and threw it on the ground. In anger, he swiped at the body of the man dying beside him. The man let out a bloodcurdling scream as the creature lifted him up with one large paw and hurtled him 10 feet into the air in the direction of Occa. The man landed with a crunch that was audible from where Winn and Graydon were standing and his screaming abruptly stopped.

"Well he seems pleasant." Graydon said dryly. "Absalom sure keeps some fine company."

"They should be coming on Selene's traps soon." Winn said quietly to his brother.

As if on cue, there was an explosion, and a brilliant band of purple light shot out in a line across the first rows of Absalom's army. The Imari caught in it were ripped apart, their limbs flying in all directions. The humans that had been caught in it... there were white puddles on the ground where they had stood seconds before.

* * *

Miles away, Arleth shot awake with a scream.

Selene instantly sprung to action. *The battle was starting already?* As Arleth continued to scream and hold her head, Selene grabbed their packs, all but threw Arleth onto a horse and climbed onto the second one herself.

"So much death." Arleth moaned looking at Selene with bloodshot eyes. "I see piles of bodies, I see.. AHHHHHHHH" She screamed again, and began to foam at the mouth.

Selene's heart raced in terror. *How was the battle already this bad? At this rate, was Arleth going to make it?*

"Make it stop, make it stop," Arleth moaned holding her head and rocking forward on her horse.

Selene reached forward to steady Arleth. "As much as I want to, I can't make it stop. We have to get to Samara's. NOW! Are you able to hold on to ride?"

Arleth made a barely perceptable nod.

"Good," Selene said and spurred the horses into a gallop.

* * *

A second explosion of purple light illuminated the forest as Absalom's army reached the second of Selene's traps. Absalom roared in anger at his sorceror "DO SOMETHING."

He didn't care if his soliders died, he had thousands more just behind him, and thousands more back at Iridian.

But he was embarassed.

They hadn't even reached Occa yet and already his troops were getting decimated.

Rogan sighed, *As if he was going to do nothing*. Almost lazily, a web of green light shot out from his hand, probing the area infront of the army for more of Selene's traps. It pulsed slightly and Rogan closed his outstretched hand into a fist.

"There." He said to Absalom as the last of Selene's traps exploded into purple light, way ahead of the army, causing no damage. "They are all gone."

Absalom huffed.

* * *

"Well there goes that", Graydon said as Rogan exploded the last of the traps harmlessly.

"Let's hope Selene's shield holds." Winn added, fighting every urge not to cross his fingers.

"FIRE AT WILL." Winn called to his archers. "If you have a good shot at a Greken or snow bear thing, use one of your special arrows."

"RIGHT" the Jayans responded in unison, never pausing thier enslaught.

Selene had created a few thousand charmed arrows before she had left yesterday. They had the weight and feel of a normal arrow so the archers would be able to fire them with ease. However these arrows glowed ever so slightly so the archers could recognize them easily. Upon hitting its mark, they would explode much like the traps had done, setting the target on fire. If they didn't hit flesh, they would just fizzle and become useless. Each archer had been given a few to use in close quarters against one of Absalom's creatures.

Absalom's army continued advancing. The soldiers, maintaining a steady quick march, while the Imari raced ahead, eager for blood. The latter quickly reached the base of the trees supporting Occa and started a rapid climb, all but drooling with anticipation at the prey in front of them.

Winn peered over the edge of the platform and saw the top of a massive white head. As though it could sense it was being watched, it looked up at Winn, barred its teeth and let out a loud roar. It was close enough that Winn could see the drool fly from its mouth and the pieces of what looked like human flesh stuck in its teeth.

Winn stepped back, calmly drew his dagger and waited.

A half second later, a monstrous white shape lunged up from the tree trunk. Winn could see the glint from its extended claws as it raised its arms. The look of triumph was unmistakable. It let out a final roar and lunged full force at Winn.

THUD

The creature hit Selene's invisible shield like a ton of bricks. It had barely a second to register shock before Winn's dagger stabbed into his heart. The creature clutched at his chest, as thick red blood oozed out of the wound. Impossibly fast, Winn stabbed the creature three more times to the chest and once in the throat. It let out a frothy gurgling as it staggered a step backwards. Winn put his boot on the dying creature's chest and kicked as hard as he could. It staggered a few more steps and fell backwards off the platform.

"So the shield works," Graydon said as he watched the creature land on the ground with a crash.

"For how long is the question," Winn responded. "We need to avoid as much direct strain on it as possible."

A flash of purple light exploded to his right and Winn turned to look. Another creature had reached the platform, further down and was currently screaming in pain as it tried ineffectively to bat the scorching purple fire off its fur. The archer who had made the shot took half a step back as the creature tried a final lunge. It hit the shield, lost its balance and fell off the platform much like its predecessor had.

"The shield is holding." Winn called to his men. "Take out your daggers, your axes, use the special arrows, whatever weapon you have. Kill as many as you can. They can't harm you right now."

Winn turned behind him, "Crean," he called.

The Talywag appeared hesitantly from behind a row of archers, he looked even greener than usual. "Uhh yes," he faltered.

"The shield is holding," Winn repeated. "The Talywags will be safe for now, we need their help. We need to keep as much pressure off the shield as we can. Get all the Talywags that came out yesterday and any more that want to help. Gather the oil buckets we created yesterday. Zeeshan, help him, it will be faster."

Zeeshan and Crean raced off to do what he had asked. Zeeshan, eager to help; his father just happy to be momentarily away from the carnage and realities of war.

* * *

Lydia hummed to herself, trying to drown out the screams from outside.

It didn't help.

At first, they had sounded far away and she had been able to cover them up with her voice. But for a while now, they were much louder, *closer*, and constant. They varied in pitch, or intensity but were terrifying all the same.

An explosion interupted her thoughts. Instictively, she covered her ears. *The screams were always the worst after an explosion.*

"LA LA LA LA LA," She sang loudly, rocking back and forth.

"What was that?" Qualo asked, walking into the banquet hall, his arms full of boxes.

"Oh nothing, just talking to myself," Lydia said quickly, removing her hands from her ears.

Qualo put the boxes down beside her. She looked at his harrowed eyes. He looked just as bad as she felt. It was good to know she wasn't the only one.

"What have we got." Lydia asked, indicating the pile of boxes on the floor in front of her.

"By my count; 8 boxes of bread, 17 boxes of juntafruit, apples, berries and potatoes, and 10 boxes of dried meat."

"Not nearly enough."

"No," Qualo agreed. "Winn was very firm, we need to be able to feed all of Occa and the Jayans for 3 days at bare minimum."

Lydia stepped back as 6 more boxes were added onto the pile.

"3 bread... and 3 cheese." Twins Mark and Abby said as they dropped their cargo and turned to walk back to the kitchen for another load.

"We need lots of water too." Lydia said to Qualo. A bloodcurtling scream pierced the night.

Lydia and Qualo looked at each other in undisguised horror

"And I think we need to hurry."

Qualo nodded, his mouth dry.

The scream abruptly cut off, replaced by a deafening explosion.

This time Lydia didn't care who saw her. She resumed her humming, covered her ears and raced back to the kitchen after Qualo.

* * *

One more left. Graydon held the glowing yellow orb in his hand. He peered over the edge, waiting for the right moment. At the base of the closest tree one of the snow bear creatures was starting to climb. It was quickly pulled down by a second creature, trying to get to the top before him. Graydon cocked his arm back to throw. A third creature, taking advantage of the other two grappling for position, started to make its way up the tree. *Perfect.* Graydon let loose and threw the orb. It landed in the middle of all three. It exploded upon impact, throwing all three snow bear creatures into the air, to land on the ground in a jumble of severed body parts.

"Was that your last one too?" Winn peered over the edge with Graydon.

"Yes. I wanted to use them before they breached the shield. They are hella powerful - I didn't want to break a hole in Occa."

Winn nodded "Same."

There was a shuffling down the ranks as Crean and Zeeshan returned with the Talwags. Winn was happy to see far more Talywags with him than had come out yesterday.

Hesitantly, they made their way and were led to the front of the archers line. There were so many Talywags that only about every 5th one had a pot of oil, the rest carried whatever weapon they had found - kitchen knives, axes, even bricks.

"It was a smart plan to save the bows and arrows for the Jayans." Graydon said to his brother.

Winn nodded again, "Yes this should work much better." After two hours of target practice yesterday, and not one Talywag having hit a single target, Winn had decided to try a different strategy.

A sizzling sounded beside him as a Talywag set their oil pot on fire with a fire-starter. Winn turned to help her lift it and together they dumped it out over the side. The ensuing screams said it had hit its mark.

"Take that you bastard! And that!" Zeeshan had pushed his way to the edge and was launching bricks down into the army. Graydon looked at the pile of bricks sitting beside Zeeshan and raised his eyebrows "Did he take a whole house?"

"Who cares" Winn said with a slight smile. "He's ridiculously good at it."

"You want one too? Take that you miserable shit stain." Zeeshan hurled a brick into the mass. It hit a soldier right on the forehead with such force that he fell over, instantly dead.

Before the man had even fallen over, Zeeshan was already cocking his arm to throw another one.

"Wow" Graydon mouthed.

A brilliant flash of green suddenly illuminated the shield in front of them. It spread out along the entire length, as far as Graydon could see, causing the very air to pulsate. There was a sickly sweet smell in the air.

Rogan

Graydon followed the source of the light and sure enough, at the edge of the forest, sitting on a Greken was Rogan with his arms outstretched towards Occa. A steady spear of light was flowing from his hands, across the battlefield, to the shield.

The shield wouldn't last long now

Graydon looked up and down the line of his men. The Jayans were still firing arrows as if nothing had happened and killing anything that popped up onto the platform.

The Talywags on the other hand, looked terrified. He turned to his brother, "We should start having the Talywags retreat."

Winn agreed. "Crean," he called behind him.

Upon returning, the highcouncilman had been cowering a few steps behind Winn, so when he heard his name he popped his head out.

"With Rogan attacking it now, the shield won't last long. We need to retreat to safety."

Crean, no longer disillusioned that Occa could hold and vividly seeing what being at war actually meant, just stared at Winn, his face slowly losing colour.

"Gather all the Talywags, here and those still in the city. Go to *every* house, knock on *every* door. Make sure *everyone* follows you. Take them to the banquet hall. Do it as fast as you can, we don't know how much time we have."

Crean stammered, "Uh.. Uh.. Ok." He wiped his sweaty palms on his pants and with a deep breath, tried to regain his composure. "Talywags, come with me. We need to rouse the city and get to safety."

On hearing the word safety, the Talywags were more than happy to oblige. They all but pushed the bigger Jayans out of the way as they rushed away from the front lines and back towards the centre of their city.

Winn turned his head sharply as a flash of white appeared. Another snowbear creature had crested the platform and was rushing at him. He lowered his body into a crouch and held up his dagger, ready to impale the creature. At the moment it was going to hit the shield, Winn stepped forward to stab it in the neck.

And had to take a quick step back as a massive paw swiped *through* the shield, missing him by mere millimeters. Winn recovered quickly, re-balanced himself and drew his sword. The creature, emboldened by his minor triumph, opened its gigantic maw and roared at Winn.

Winn took the split second, this afforded him and with a ferocious swing, he chopped off the creature's head. It's roar still echoed in the air even as it's head rolled off the platform and over the side.

CRASH!

Winn instantly turned toward the sound, the dead Imari's blood flying of his raised sword.

A Greken had somehow made it onto the platform and had slashed a massive hole in it with its axe. The soldiers that had been unlucky enough to have been standing there, screamed as they plummeted to the ground. The Greken, now standing firmly on the platform, swung its axe in a massive semi-circle around it. Standing as close together as they had been, the Jayans never stood a chance. They screamed as the Greken's axe cleaved them in two. Their blood erupted onto the Greken's chest and face. It paused for a second, snaked out its tongue and licked the blood off its cheek with a blood-chilling smile. The Jayans that were remaining around it, dropped into defensive positions, weapons raised. One of the soldiers threw his axe. It was a great throw, landing directly at the Greken's head. But the skill of the shot made little difference. It bounced off the Greken's scales to fall harmlessly to the ground.

The Greken hissed, wrapped its tentacles around the soldier's waist and lifted him into the air. The man, desperate to save his life, drew his dagger and tried unsuccesfully to cut the tentacles from around his body. He managed to chop a piece into one of them before he was hurled off the platform, 10 feet into the air. He screamed as he fell to the ground, landing with a sickening crunch.

Before Winn could get there, a flash of white whizzed past him. Zeeshan flung himself onto the Greken's back. He wrapped one massive arm around the creature's neck. The Greken roared in frustration as it tried to shake Zeeshan off. Zeeshan tightened his grip and clawed at the Greken's face with his free hand. Rivers of red appeared on the Greken's face as Zeeshan broke the skin.

The Greken hissed. It turned around violently, shaking it's body as forcefully as it could, trying to dislodge Zeeshan. It lifted one tentacle into the air and with a whoosh of air, whipped it back towards its body, to land with a crack on Zeehsan's back. Zeeshan grunted but didn't let go. The Greken tried again. This time a ribbon of red appeared on Zeeshan's back, but he still didn't let go. Zeeshan lifted his head slightly and watched in horror as the Greken lifted 4 tentacles ino the air. They interlaced each other, forming one large tentacle. Zeeshan winced in anticipation as they came crashing onto his back. He let out a scream and let go, falling off the Greken's back.

The Greken hissed in satisfaction and turned around, its large half-moon axe already drawn. Zeeshan, lying in a heap on the platform didn't even see the giant axe crashing towards his body.

* * *

Arleth screamed, "Zeeshan!!! NOOOO" Her eyes rolled back in her head and her hands lost their grip on the reins.

"Whooaa" Selene yelled, stopping her horse in mid gallop. She jumped off and ran to Arleth. The girl wobbled in the saddle and started to lean sideways. "Insapen," She yelled, arms outstretched. Flashes of light flew from the sorceress' hands and shot out towards Arleth. They formed into a net, reaching her just in time to catch her before she hit the ground.

Selene reached her side and kneeled down beside her. Arleth's eyes were white, her eyeballs rolled back in her head.

"Arleth, Arleth, ARLETH." Selene called, slapping Arleth's cheek with her hand.

There was no response.

Arleth was in a coma.

Selene bent Arleth's knees up to her chest and, putting one arm under them and one arm under her head, she lifted her up with a grunt. She stumbled backwards a few steps, getting used to the girl's weight.

This wasn't going to work.

She gently dropped Arleth's legs back to the ground and wrapped her arms around the girl's waist. She half carried, half dragged her back to her horse. With great effort, Selene managed to sling Arleth into the saddle and she climbed up behind her. She reshuffled Arleth's legs so they straddled the horse. Arleth's head fell limply forward, bouncing slightly on her chest. Selene grabbed the reins with one hand, and put her arm around Arleth's waist with the other, pushing the girl's body back into her own. Arleth's head flopped back to rest at a more normal angle against Selene's chest.

They were still a few hours away from Edika, "Please hold on, Arleth," Selene whispered in her ear. "I will get you to safety."

With a brief thought for the horse she was leaving behind, she spurred her mount into a gallop and rushed off to Edika.

Praying that Arleth had enough time.

* * *

The axe dropped beside Zeeshan with a giant clang. And then behind him, a massive crash as the body of the Greken hit the platform. Painfully, Zeeshan turned to look. With a grunt, Winn removed his sword from the base of the Greken's neck. He wiped it's bloody edge on the Greken's body and walked over to Zeeshan.

"Are you ok?"

Zeeshan moaned in reply "Yes, I think so." His back was on fire and he could feel that it was wet with blood. He struggled to stand up, Winn offering as much help as he could. His body felt bruised and battered, but it didn't seem like anything had been broken.

Graydon rushed over, helping his brother with Zeeshan.

"I think its time we used the artefact," he said.

Winn reached into his inside breast pocket and handed a small silver key to Graydon. "Here take this. Open it up. Take Zeeshan with you. I will follow you soon."

Graydon closed it in his palm. He put a hand on Zeeshan's arm to steady him and started to lead him away. He stopped, hesitated, and turned back around.

"Be careful brother," he said. "I'm not ready to lead Jaya by myself."

"Don't worry I will follow."

Graydon nodded, took one last look at his brother and turned away.

"What in the holy hell is that?"

Winn turned sharply to see what his soldier was talking about. His mouth dropped open in horror.

Rogan, still powering his spear of light with one arm, had switched tactics and was now lifting up soldiers from his army with the other. He was currently floating 10 soldiers in the air, pushing them towards Occa. They hit the failing shield with a slight thud. Most were stopped and were cut down instantly by the Jayans, but some managed to hit a part of the shield that was weakened and got through. The Jayans still cut them down. But the result seemed to encourage Rogan.

No sooner had the last soldier been cut down, than 20 more were already in the air being floated towards Occa.

Rogan didn't care how many men died. He was going to break through with brute force.

Winn choked back his disgust and ran to the front to help his men fight the next onslaught.

They withheld the first 20, and the next 20, and the next 20. But more and more of the soldiers were getting through with each pass. He didn't want to risk his men unecessarily but he needed to give Graydon enough time to use the artefact and open the passageway. And enough time for the Talywags to all get in, with the food and supplies he hoped had been gathered.

He lifted up his bow and shot an arrow at the soldier that was floating in front of him. The man died in mid air, but propelled by Rogan's magic he was carried forward to fall face down at Winn's feet.

This is disgusting, Winn thought. *I have to end it.*

He reached back into his breast pocked and pulled out the device Selene had given him. He put his thumb on the green cross in the middle and pressed. Selene had said it should re-power the shield for 10 minutes.

Let's hope that is enough time Winn thought.

"To me everyone!" he called. "Retreat to the banquet hall!"

There was a clatter of boots and clang of metal as his army re-sheathed their weapons and turned away from the battle. Winn stayed where he was for a few moments, watching his army run ahead of him.

He looked out over Absalom's army. "You may have won this battle." He said quietly to himself, "But we *will* win the war."

He turned and raced after his army.

* * *

"Everyone get inside!" He yelled at the horde of frightened Talwyags who were staring at him with large tearful eyes. The artefact had worked seemlessly and there was now a large cavernous door shimmering in mid air in the banquet hall. All the supplies had been loaded inside, but the Talywags were proving a different matter.

"In there? It's so dark."

Graydon sighed in exasperation, *were they serious!?*

"It's a passageway, we will be safe in there."

"But how will we see?"

"I used an artefact, once we are inside we will call to the Garrupi, they will light it for us."

The Talywags looked unconvinced.

A horrendous crash sounded and Graydon stumbled for balance as the ground shifted under his feet. He could hear ringing in his ears. The Talywags screamed. A few passed out.

"The shield has broken," Graydon yelled at them. "Absalom's army will be inside Occa in a matter of moments. GET IN NOW!"

He all but grabbed the Talywag closest to him and half threw, half pushed im into the opening.

Zeeshan followed behind "COME ON," He growled at them.

Whether it was Graydon's words, or the Zeeshan's terrifying form, the Talywags were finally convinced and they rushed into the opening.

* * *

Miles away, on the edge of Frasht Forest, Aedan woke with a start. He had dreamt of an explosion, it had been impossibly loud.

"It came from Occa," Val said to him. He was sitting up in his bed roll beside Aedan.

So it hadn't been a dream

"A noise that loud...."

"I know." Said Val. "It didn't come from our side."

Aedan stood up in a hurry, Val close behind him. It was still dark, Aedan put it at somewhere just before dawn.

"Let's get going." Aedan said quickly folding up his bed roll and shoving it into his pack. "I can't sit here doing nothing."

Val humphed in agreement.

With heavy hearts, the pair started walking.

* * *

Winn and his men had just reached the town square when he heard the shield breaking. He looked over his shoulder has he ran, half-expecting to see a Greken breathing down his neck. But there was nothing. They should still have a few minutes before enough of Absalom's army made it up.

He faced forward again. *I really hope all the Talywags and supplies are already in the passageway and they are just waiting for us.* Even if that was the case though, he knew it would be tight. There were thousands of Jayan soldiers running ahead of him.

He turned a corner and the banquet hall came into view. At least no one was outside. That was a good sign, *he hoped.* The first of his men reached the doors and raced inside.

Graydon had the good sense to open the passageway at the back of the banquet hall. This meant that it only took a few minutes for enough Jayans to enter the passageway for all of the remaining soldiers to be able to fit inside the banquet hall.

Winn, still at the doors, turned to look behind him.

And none too soon.

Three snow bear creatures, heads to the ground, sniffing out their prey, had just come into view. They looked up at the same time, spotted him and let out a roar. Spittle flying from their open mouths, they charged. Winn retreated. He couldn't afford to get into hand to hand combat with three of them at the same time. He rushed into the banquet hall and slammed the doors behind him. A few of his soliders, seeing what was happening rushed to bar the door.

CRASH!

The creatures hit the door, causing the hinges to rattle.

Winn looked behind him, there were still a few hundred Jayans left to enter the passageway.

The door won't hold for long.

He heard scratching and banging as the animals tried to claw their way through.

100 Jayans left

There was another crash and the wood splintered slightly. Winn could see tufts of white fur through the crack.

The door wouldn't survive another attack.

50 Jayans left

"Come on," Graydon called to him "You won't be able to hold the door yourself."

Winn looked back at his brother. The last of the Jayans were entering the passageway.

From outside the door, Winn heard a booming voice

"MOVE"

It was Rogan!

Winn jumped away from the door as it exploded in a giant flash of green light, splinters of wood flying everywhere. He dodged the pieces as he raced back to the passageway. An arrow whistled by his head.

A few more steps and he was there.

Graydon's head appeared in the passageway. "Hurry," He yelled at his brother desperately, looking at something behind his shoulder, eyes wide with horror. "Rogan is lifting his arms, he's going to cast a spell."

Winn sprinted the last few steps and lunged into the passageway. He turned around just in time to see Rogan's angry face before the passageway door closed and he was engulfed in darkness.

Chapter 32

"How long has she been in a coma for?" Samara asked, opening Arleth's eyelid gently with her finger.

"About two hours, if not more," Selene replied, biting her lip with worry.

Selene had reached Edika a few minutes ago and Samara, as if sensing that they were coming had ran out to meet them. Together the two women had brought Arleth's comatose body inside and lain her down in a spare bedroom. The two women were now huddled over Arleth's body on opposite sides of the thin bed.

"Not good," Samara said to herself, "Not good at all." She looked up at Selene. "Arleth is in a lot of trouble."

Selene gasped and collapsed onto the side of the bed.

"I can't help her from out here." Samara continued, "I need to go inside her head. It's an exhausting process, here wait one sec." Samara rushed out of the bedroom and disappeared down the hall.

Selene put her head in her hands and looked down at Arleth. "I'm so sorry, I should have gotten you here faster." She put her hand on top of Arleth's and rubbed the girl's cold fingers. She hoped that wherever Arleth was in there, she could hear her.

"I need you to make me this." Samara rushed back into the room and thrust a paper into Selene's hands. "I am going to be completely spent when I return. I will likely have to use all my energy to rescue her. When I come out I will need this," she gestured at the paper in Selene's hands. "You may have to help me drink it."

Selene nodded, "I will make it right away." She climbed off the bed.

"Thank you," Samara said, her head down focused on Arleth. She put her hands on the girl's stomach and a bright light appeared between her fingertips. Selene watched from the door as Samara's whole body became engulfed in light. Slowly the light shifted upwards towards Samara's head. The woman's head glowed brighter and brighter until it was almost unbearable. With a loud pop, Samara's consciousness flew out of her body. It coalesced into a humanoid form which hovered for a brief moment in the air above Arleth's head, before diving into her open mouth. Samara's body, now just an empty shell, slumped over, her head coming to rest on Arleth's stomach.

Samara opened her eyes and looked around. She was standing in a barren, gray, wasteland. A wasteland deep in the throws of a torrential storm. Samara put an arm up to brace herself against the pelting rain. As she did, there was a deafening boom of thunder and a crack of lightening. A huge gust of wind whipped her hair across her face, stinging her cheek from the impact.

Samara pulled her drenched hair away from her face and squinted through the rain.

Where was Arleth?

Another peal of thunder sounded, followed instantly by a brilliant flash of lightening. In the momentary flash of light, Samara thought she saw that the clouds were getting darker and darker ahead of her. She knew that the worst part of the storm was where she would find Arleth. Straight ahead seemed like a good bet.

Arms out in front of her, crossed over her body to protect herself from the rain and wind, Samara started to push her way forward. It was slow going; for every 5 steps she took forward, a huge gust of wind would push her 2 steps back.

She had only been walking for a few minutes and she was already exhausted. She shivered as another gust of wind pushed her backward. Her clothes were completely soaked through, her boots made splooshing sounds as she walked. Samara looked up to see how much headway she had made.

Not much.

She needed to go faster.

She crouched down into a sprinter's squat and with a deep intake of breath, burst forward with all her strength. Bent over, body as close to the ground as she could go and still remain upright, Samara sprinted. She gave up trying to shield her body from the rain, and pumped her arms to gain more speed. The rain pelted her cheeks turning them red and raw. She bit her lip, bracing from the pain and kept going.

Arleth needed her.

She sprinted as long and as hard as she could. Her breath started coming in ragged gasps, but she still tried. With one last final heave, she collapsed on the ground. She pushed herself flat on the ground so that the wind wouldn't push back her hard fought gains.

Struggling, she forced her head up to see where she was. She was really close to the darkest of the storm clouds now. And now, as close as she was, she could see that they weren't clouds at all. They were three giant, dark grey, pulsating bubbles in the air. Samara could make out forms swirling around in them. She saw a flash of red and then a man's head popped out, eyes opened in terror before a giant white paw grabbed the man's face and pulled him back in. A spray of red shot out and landed in a puddle on the ground.

Arleth's visions!

Gathering what little strength she had left, Samara forced herself up onto her hands and knees. Her arms wobbled and her legs felt like jelly. A sword slashed it's way out of the bubble and Samara followed the path with her eyes. When she did, she noticed a girl's body lying face down on the ground underneath the largest bubble.

Arleth!

With a burst of adrenaline, Samara half crawled, half slithered her way over to her. She put her arms under Arleth's body and flipped her over onto her back. Arleth's eyes were open but her eyeballs were rolled back in her head. There was a stream of blood coming from her nose. Samara put her head to Arleth's chest and let out a sigh of relief. She was still breathing - faintly. She was clearly struggling to take each breath, but the fact that Arleth still had energy to struggle gave Samara hope.

Samara forced herself to stand. She stepped over Arleth with one leg, straddling the girl's torso. The nearest bubble was so low to the ground that standing as she was, her head was almost touching the bottom. She could see a flurry of images; many of them involving blood and dismembered body parts.

If this was the enslaught Arleth was dealing with, no wonder the poor girl was in the state she was in.

Samara reached her arms up and put her palms flat on the surface of the bubble. It felt cold and squishy to the touch.

"Leave her alone!" She shouted. A spasm of light shot out of her hands into the bubble.

Instantly the images stopped spinning around inside. They swam their way towards Samara, as if curious to see what the disturbance was. A large yellow eye pressed itself against the bubble and looked out at her.

With a fierce blow, Samara punched through the bubble, directly connecting with the eye. There was a loud roar and the eye disappeared.

"Get out of her head!" Samara shouted again, sending another flash of light into the bubble. The bubble pulsated, wobbled and condensed slightly.

A giant taloned paw shot out of the bubble and grabbed Samara's arm. She was lifted into the air as the owner tried to drag her into the bubble. The yellow eye she had just punched stared at her from inside with undisguised bloodlust.

Samara reached up with her free arm and put her hand on the beast's paw. "Ignito," She yelled. The paw started smoking but the beast didn't let go. "IGNITO!" She yelled again. This time it burst into flames. There was a howl of pain and she was dropped to the ground. Samara fell heavily onto her knees beside Arleth. She barely noticed the pain as she leapt back up, arms outstretched once more.

No sooner had her skin touched the surface of the bubble then the creature grabbed her again. This time it grabbed both of her wrists, enclosing them in its talons. The arm that she had burned was still smoking and smelled like charred meat, but the creature didn't seem to care. Once again she was lifted off her feet.

With her wrists clasped tight in its talons, Samara was only able to move her hand slightly. She tried to stretch out her fingers as much as possible in what she hoped was the direction of the beast's head. A spear of light shot from her fingers into the bubble. There was a roar of pain and the creature dropped her again.

This time Samara was ready and she landed on her feet in a crouch. Quick as a flash she formed another spear of light and waited. A massive furry head erupted from the bubble, inches from Samara. She had absolutely no idea what it was. It was vaguely reminiscent of a snow bear but it had massive yellow eyes that took up close to half of its face. The other half was all mouth, a mouth wide open and reaching for Samara with razor sharp teeth. She ducked down to get underneath the head and with every ounce of energy she had left, she rammed the spear of light upwards into the creature's throat. She pushed it up as hard as she could, penetrating fur and bone. The beast made a gurgling sound in its throat and blood started to pour out of its still open mouth. With a loud grunt, Samara shoved one last time. The creature's noises stopped and it slouched over, dead. Samara leapt out of its path, as it dropped out of the bubble to fall heavily on the ground in a heap.

Samara took a few deep breaths. When her breathing had returned somewhat to normal, she drew in for one final burst.

"LEAVE HER ALONE!" she shouted. She shot every last bit of energy she had into the bubble and collapsed on the ground beside Arleth. From her back, she looked up at the bubble on top of her.

Please let that be enough, she thought.

At first nothing happened, the bubble still pulsated a few feet above Samara's head. And then, miraculously it started to shrink. A burst of lightening shot out, striking both of the other, smaller bubbles. They glowed a bright white and then too, started to shrink.

Samara let out her breath. She had done it. Arleth's mind was clearing.

But had she been in time?

She rolled onto her side to look at the girl beside her.

Arleth's chest was falling in regular deep breaths, and her eyes were firmly closed. There was a faint smile on her lips.

With a sigh, Samara rolled back over onto her back.

Arleth was going to be fine.

The bubbles had all but disappeared by now, floating up into the sky harmlessly. The dark storm clouds faded away and the sun shone through. There was a rainbow starting to form in the distance.

Samara lay on her back, letting the rays of the sun warm her face. She took a deep breath and reached for Arleth's hand. She closed her fingers around the girl's and held on tight. As much as she wanted to lie here and feel the sun, they had to get back. She squeezed Arleth's hand and the two of them started to glow.

All of a sudden Samara's body jerked backwards off of Arleth's stomach. Selene, who had been watching nervously from the end of the bed almost fell off in surprise. As it was, she had to put a second hand around the cup she was holding to steady it.

Samara let out a low groan and slouched against the wall.

Selene rushed over and crouched down in front of the other woman. She could tell Samara was in no shape to take the drink herself. Selene put her hand under the woman's chin and lifted her head. Samara stared at her weakly. There were dark circles around her eyes as though she hadn't slept in weeks. Selene gently pushed the woman's mouth open and poured some of the liquid in. Samara swallowed slowly and Selene poured a bit more.

They continued like this for a few minutes, until Samara held up her hand. "Thank you Selene." She said tiredly. "I can continue from here." She took the cup from Selene and cradled it in her lap. She rested her head back against the wall.

"Arleth will be ok."

"Oh thank God," Selene said.

"She is no longer in a coma, but she will be asleep for a few days. Her mind and body have gone through an ordeal. She will need to regain her strength before she wakes."

Selene looked over at Arleth sleeping in the bed. Now that she was looking at her again, she could see that the girl's colour had returned and her breathing was deep and even.

"I am also going to sleep. Can you please help me to my room."

"Of course," Selene helped pull the woman up off the floor, and with an arm around her waist she helped the woman walk down the hall to her bedroom. When they got there, Samara put the drink down on the nightstand and crawled under the covers. "Do you remember where the other rooms are?" She asked Selene, half asleep already.

"Yes." Selene said, "I'm sure I can find one." The woman was already fast asleep. Selene tiptoed out of the room. She didn't go searching for a bed immediately. Instead she returned to Arleth's room and sat down on the end of the bed for a few moments. She watched the girl's even breathing. With each breath Arleth took, Selene felt a bit of her stress melt away. She was overjoyed that Samara had been able to save Arleth, but she knew there was still a long road ahead for her. She had been saved this time, but she still had no idea how to use her powers, or how to stop such an onslaught from happening again. Selene saw a faint smile appear on Arleth's lips. Selene hoped the girl was strong enough to face what was to come.

Printed in Great Britain
by Amazon